Praise for *Age of Myth*

"*Age of Myth* is a win on all fronts. . . . Sullivan has crafted yet another entertaining tale filled with action, adventure, humor and heart."
—*Fantasy Faction*

"With hints of Jim Butcher's Codex Alera and Brandon Sanderson's Mistborn, the visceral and traitorous nature of George R. R. Martin . . . This is a world I'll be happy to go back to again and again."
—*Fanbase Press*

"Newcomers to Michael J. Sullivan's work will find this to be a perfect place to jump on board, and if you're already a fan, there's absolutely no excuse—you must read this book!"
—*The BiblioSanctum*

BY MICHAEL J. SULLIVAN

THE LEGENDS OF THE FIRST EMPIRE
Age of Myth • *Age of Swords* • *Age of War*
Forthcoming:
Age of Legends • *Age of Wonder*
Age of Empire

THE RIYRIA REVELATIONS
Theft of Swords
(contains *The Crown Conspiracy* and *Avempartha*)
Rise of Empire
(contains *Nyphron Rising* and *The Emerald Storm*)
Heir of Novron (contains *Wintertide* and *Percepliquis*)

THE RIYRIA CHRONICLES
The Crown Tower
The Rose and the Thorn
The Death of Dulgath

STANDALONE NOVEL
Hollow World

ANTHOLOGIES
Unfettered: The Jester (Fantasy: The Riyria Chronicles)
Blackguards: Professional Integrity
(Fantasy: The Riyria Chronicles)
Unbound: The Game (Fantasy: Contemporary)
Unfettered II: Little Wren and the Big Forest
(Fantasy: The Legends of the First Empire)
The End: Visions of the Apocalypse: Burning Alexandria
(Dystopian Science Fiction)
Triumph over Tragedy: Traditions
(Fantasy: Tales from Elan)
The Fantasy Faction Anthology: Autumn Mists
(Fantasy: Contemporary)
Help Fund My Robot Army: Be Careful What You Wish For
(Fantasy)

Age
OF
Myth

Age
OF
Myth

BOOK ONE OF
The Legends of the First Empire

MICHAEL J. SULLIVAN

DEL REY • NEW YORK

Age of Myth is a work of fiction. Names, places, and incidents either
are products of the author's imagination or are used fictitiously.
Any resemblance to actual events, locales, or persons,
living or dead, is entirely coincidental.

2017 Del Rey Mass Market Edition

Copyright © 2016 by Michael J. Sullivan
Map copyright © 2016 by David Lindroth, Inc.
Excerpt from *Age of Swords* by Michael J. Sullivan
copyright © 2017 by Michael J. Sullivan

Published in the United States by
Del Rey, an imprint of Random House, a division of
Penguin Random House LLC, New York.

DEL REY and the HOUSE colophon are registered
trademarks of Penguin Random House LLC.

Originally published in hardcover in the United States by
Del Rey, an imprint of Random House, a division of
Penguin Random House LLC, in 2016.

This book contains an excerpt from the forthcoming book
Age of Swords by Michael J. Sullivan. This excerpt has been set
for this edition only and may not reflect the final
content of the forthcoming edition.

ISBN 978-1-101-96535-1
Ebook ISBN 978-1-101-96534-4

Printed in the United States of America

randomhousebooks.com

8 9 7

Del Rey mass market edition: February 2017

*To all the readers who've enjoyed my stories
and have shared them with loved ones.
My success is largely due to your generous support,
and I thank you for making my dream a reality.*

Contents

Author's Note   xi

Map   xv

Chapter 1: *Of Gods and Men*   1

Chapter 2: *The Mystic*   17

Chapter 3: *The God Killer*   28

Chapter 4: *The New Chieftain*   48

Chapter 5: *Before the Door*   57

Chapter 6: *Rumors*   72

Chapter 7: *The Black Tree*   89

Chapter 8: *Asking the Oak*   101

Chapter 9: *Tight Places*   120

Chapter 10: *The Galantians*   138

Chapter 11: *The Tutor*   161

Chapter 12: *Gods Among Us*   173

Chapter 13: *The Bones*   198

Chapter 14: *Into the West*   203

Chapter 15: *The Lost One*   219

Chapter 16: *Miralyith*   234

Chapter 17: *The Boulder*   250

Chapter 18: *Healing the Injured*   267

Chapter 19: *Waiting on the Moon*   280

Chapter 20: *The Prince*   299

Chapter 21: *The Full Moon*   310

Chapter 22: *Curse of the Brown Bear*   320

Chapter 23: *The Cave*   336

Chapter 24: *Demons in the Forest*   344

Chapter 25: *Trapped*   355

Chapter 26: *Beneath the Falls*   367

Chapter 27: *When Gods Collide*   379

Chapter 28: *The First Chair*   400

Glossary of Terms and Names   415

Acknowledgments   427

Sneak Peek: *Age of Swords*   431

Author's Note

Welcome to The Legends of the First Empire, my latest fantasy series. If you haven't read any of my previous work, have no fear. This is a new series, and no knowledge of either The Riyria Chronicles or The Riyria Revelations is necessary to fully enjoy this tale. Also, reading this book won't expose you to spoilers, so there are no concerns on that front. This series is meant to be a separate entryway into the world of Elan, and if you want to read more—well, there are nine books (told in six volumes) waiting for you.

For those who have read the Riyria books, I should mention that this series is set three thousand years before the events in those novels. You might think you know how the First Empire was formed, or at least have some general ideas about the events. But, having read my books, you probably realize that things aren't always as they seem. The accounts I've revealed through Riyria haven't been entirely accurate. After all, history is written by the victors. In this series, I can set the record straight, and you'll know the truth in myths and the lies of legends.

For those unfamiliar with my process, I write sagas in an unusual way. I finish the entire series before publishing the first novel, and these books continue that tradition. Why is this important? Well, there are several reasons. First, it allows me to weave threads throughout the entire narrative. Minor references that seem initially unimportant will usually provide some interesting insights upon re-reading. This is possible because I'm able to spread out details across the entire story line.

Second, writing this way assures me (and my readers) that the books are working toward an ultimate conclusion. Too often, series wander off track, and it's questionable if the author will be able to rein in everything when all is said and done. I'm honored by the praise The Riyria Revelations' conclusion has received. The series' satisfying ending was mostly due to my ability to make tweaks, add characters, or provide foundation support in earlier books when an interesting idea came to me as I wrote a later one. Plus, there is no fear about me being hit by a bus or meeting some other unfortunate end, leaving you hanging and wondering how the full story works out.

Third, writing all the books in advance allows me to tell the story unburdened by the constraints of publishing contracts or business concerns. In fact, when I started this series I had intended a trilogy. But as the plot emerged, it grew into four and then five and then six books. Had I signed a contract with just one book completed, I might have been forced to make some difficult decisions to fit the narrative into a box that was determined by the deal brokered. Without that restriction, I was able to tell the story in the way that makes the most sense for the narrative as a whole.

Fourth, writing the entire series relieves me from deadline pressures. I'll admit that I hate trying to create on the clock. The muse doesn't always cooperate on demand, and I really enjoy being able to write the books without the company of a ticking time bomb. Without constraints, I'll produce the best work possible because a book is finished when I say it is finished rather than when the clock runs out.

Last, but certainly not least, you are guaranteed to get the books in a timely manner. Too often readers are frustrated by constantly wondering when (or if) the next book of a series will appear. Having all the books written eliminates that concern. Sure, there could be publishing concerns regarding when to release a particular title, but my job has been completed, and I can move on to the next project.

One final thing I should note—for any aspiring authors out there   this isn't how I recommend approaching your own writing. There are many good reasons why most series aren't produced this way. I'm an outlier by using this method, and while it produces the highest-quality product for me, it could result in years and years of wasted effort when employed by others.

Well, that's more than enough preamble. I just wanted to give a little peek behind the process to help set expectations. Now turn the page, tap the screen, or adjust the volume—a new adventure awaits.

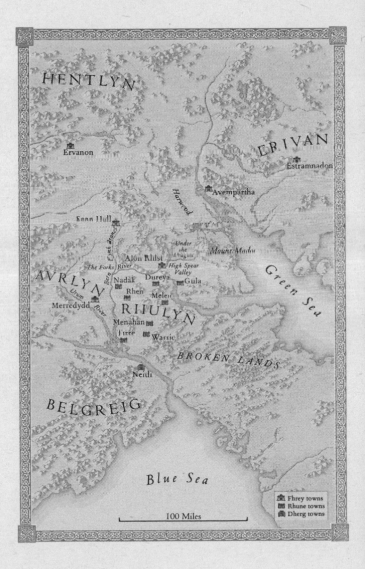

Age
OF
Myth

CHAPTER ONE

Of Gods and Men

In the days of darkness before the war, men were called Rhunes. We lived in Rhuneland or Rhulyn as it was once known. We had little to eat and much to fear. What we feared most were the gods across the Bern River, where we were not allowed. Most people believe our conflict with the Fhrey started at the Battle of Grandford, but it actually began on a day in early spring when two men crossed the river.

— THE BOOK OF BRIN

Raithe's first impulse was to pray. Curse, cry, scream, pray—people did such things in their last minutes of life. But praying struck Raithe as absurd given that his problem was the angry god twenty feet away. Gods weren't known for their tolerance, and this one appeared on the verge of striking them both dead. Neither Raithe nor his father had noticed the god approach. The waters of the nearby converging rivers made enough noise to mask an army's passage. Raithe would have preferred an army.

Dressed in shimmering clothes, the god sat on a horse and was accompanied by two servants on foot. They were men, but dressed in the same remarkable clothing. All three silent, watching.

"Hey?" Raithe called to his father.

Herkimer knelt beside a deer, opening its stomach with his knife. Earlier, Raithe had landed a spear in the stag's side, and he and his father had spent most of the morning chasing it. Herkimer had stripped off his wool leigh mor as well as his shirt because opening a deer's belly was a bloody business. "What?" He looked up.

Raithe jerked his head toward the god, and his father's sight tracked to the three figures. The old man's eyes widened, and the color left his face.

I knew this was a bad idea, Raithe thought.

His father had seemed so confident, so sure that cross-ing the forbidden river would solve their problems. But he'd mentioned his certainty enough times to make Raithe wonder. Now the old man looked as if he'd for-gotten how to breathe. Herkimer wiped his knife on the deer's side before slipping it into his belt and getting up.

"Ah . . ." Raithe's father began. Herkimer looked at the half-gutted deer, then back at the god. "It's . . . okay."

This was the total sum of his father's wisdom, his grand defense for their high crime of trespassing on di-vine land. Raithe wasn't sure if slaughtering one of the deities' deer was also an offense but assumed it didn't help their situation. And although Herkimer said it was *okay,* his face told a different story. Raithe's stomach sank. He had no idea what he'd expected his father to say, but something more than that.

Not surprisingly, the god wasn't appeased, and the three continued to stare in growing irritation.

They were on a tiny point of open meadowland where the Bern and North Branch rivers met. A pine forest, thick and rich, grew a short distance up the slope be-hind them. Down at the point where the rivers converged lay a stony beach. Beneath a snow-gray blanket of sky, the river's roar was the only sound. Just minutes earlier Raithe had seen the tiny field as a paradise. That was then.

Raithe took a slow breath and reminded himself that he didn't have experience with gods or their expressions. He'd never observed a god up close, never seen beech-leaf-shaped ears, eyes blue as the sky, or hair that spilled like molten gold. Such smooth skin and white teeth were beyond reason. This was a being born not of the earth but of air and light. His robes billowed in the breeze and shimmered in the sun, proclaiming an otherworldly glory. The harsh, judgmental glare was exactly the ex-pression Raithe expected from an immortal being.

The horse was an even bigger surprise. Raithe's father had told him about such animals, but until then Raithe hadn't believed. His old man had a habit of embellishing the truth, and for more than twenty years Raithe had heard the tales. After a few drinks, his father would tell everyone how he'd killed five men with a single swing or fought the North Wind to a standstill. The older Herkimer got, the larger the stories grew. But this four-hooved tall tale was looking back at Raithe with large glossy eyes, and when the horse shook its head, he wondered if the mounts of gods understood speech.

"No, really, it's okay," Raithe's father told them again, maybe thinking they hadn't heard his previous genius. "I'm allowed here." He took a step forward and pointed to the medal hanging from a strip of hide amid the dirt and pine needles stuck to the sweat on his chest. Half naked, sunbaked, and covered in blood up to his elbows, his father appeared the embodiment of a mad barbarian. Raithe wouldn't have believed him, either.

"See this?" his father went on. The burnished metal clutched by thick ruddy fingers reflected the midday sun. "I fought for your people against the Gula-Rhunes in the High Spear Valley. I did well. A Fhrey commander gave me this. Said I earned a reward."

"Dureyan clan," the taller servant told the god, his tone somewhere between disappointment and disgust. He wore a rich-looking silver torc around his neck—both servants did. The jewelry must be a mark of their station.

The gangly man lacked a beard but sported a long nose, sharp cheeks, and small clever eyes. He reminded Raithe of a weasel or a fox, and he wasn't fond of either. Raithe was also repulsed by how the man stood: stooped, eyes low, hands clasped. Abused dogs exhibited more self-esteem.

What kind of men travel with a god?

"That's right. I'm Herkimer, son of Hiemdal, and this is my son Raithe."

"You've broken the law," the servant stated. The nasal tone even sounded the way a weasel might talk.

"No, no. It's not like that. Not at all."

The lines on his father's face deepened, and his lips stretched tighter. He stopped walking forward but held the medal out like a talisman, his eyes hopeful. "This proves what I'm saying, that I earned a reward. See, I sort of figured we"—he gestured toward Raithe—"my son and I could live on this little point." He waved at the meadow. "We don't need much. Hardly anything, really. You see, on our side of the river, back in Dureya, the dirt's no good. We can't grow anything, and there's nothing to hunt."

The pleading in his father's voice was something Raithe hadn't heard before and didn't like.

"You're not allowed here." This time it was the other servant, the balding one. Like the tall weasel-faced fellow, he lacked a proper beard, as if growing one were a thing that needed to be taught. The lack of hair exposed in fine detail a decidedly sour expression.

"But you don't understand. I *fought* for your people. I *bled* for your people. I *lost three sons* fighting for your kind. And I was promised a reward." Herkimer held out the medal again, but the god didn't look at it. He stared past them, focusing on some distant, irrelevant point.

Herkimer let go of the medal. "If this spot is a problem, we'll move. My son actually liked another place west of here. We'd be farther away from you. Would that be better?"

Although the god still didn't look at them, he appeared even more annoyed. Finally he spoke. "You will obey."

An average voice. Raithe was disappointed. He had expected thunder.

The god then addressed his servants in the divine language. Raithe's father had taught him some of their tongue. He wasn't fluent but knew enough to understand the god didn't want them to have weapons on this side of the river. A moment later the tall servant relayed the message in Rhunic. "Only Fhrey are permitted to possess weapons west of the Bern. Cast yours into the river."

Herkimer glanced at their gear piled near a stump and in a resigned voice told Raithe, "Get your spear and do as they say."

"And the sword off your back," the tall servant said.

Herkimer looked shocked and glanced over his shoulder as if he'd forgotten the weapon was there. Then he faced the god and spoke directly to him in the Fhrey language. "*This is my family blade. I cannot throw it away.*"

The god sneered, showing teeth.

"It's a sword," the servant insisted.

Herkimer hesitated only a moment. "Okay, okay, fine. We'll go back across the river, right now. C'mon, Raithe."

The god made an unhappy sound.

"After you give up the sword," the servant said.

Herkimer glared. "This copper has been in my family for generations."

"It's a weapon. Toss it down."

Herkimer looked at his son, a sidelong glance.

Although he might not have been a good father—wasn't as far as Raithe was concerned—Herkimer had instilled one thing in all his sons: pride. Self-respect came from the ability to defend oneself. Such things gave a man dignity. In all of Dureya, in their entire clan, his father was the only man to wield a sword—a *metal* blade. Wrought from beaten copper, its marred, dull sheen was the color of a summer sunset, and legend held that the short-bladed heirloom had been mined and fashioned by a genuine Dherg smith. In comparison with the god's sword, whose hilt was intricately etched and encrusted with gems, the copper blade was pathetic. Still, Herkimer's weapon defined him; enemy clans knew him as Coppersword—a feared and respected title. His father could never give up that blade.

The roar of the river was cut by the cry of a hawk soaring above. Birds were known to be the embodiment of omens, and Raithe didn't take the soaring wail as a positive sign. In its eerie echo, his father faced the god. "I can't give you this sword."

Raithe couldn't help but smile. Herkimer, son of Hiemdal, of Clan Dureya wouldn't bend so far, not even for a god.

The smaller servant took the horse's lead as the god dismounted.

Raithe watched—impossible not to. The way the god moved was mesmerizing, so graceful, fluid, and poised. Despite the impressive movement, the god wasn't physically imposing. He wasn't tall, broad, or muscled. Raithe and his father had built strong shoulders and arms by wielding spear and shield throughout their lives. The god, on the other hand, appeared delicate, as if he had lived bedridden and spoon-fed. If the Fhrey were a man, Raithe wouldn't have been afraid. Given the disparity between them in weight and height, he'd avoid a fight, even if challenged. To engage in such an unfair match would be cruel, and he wasn't cruel. His brothers had received Raithe's share of that particular trait.

"You don't understand." Herkimer tried once more to explain. "This sword has been handed down from father to son—"

The god rushed forward and punched Raithe's father in the stomach, doubling him over. Then the Fhrey stole the copper sword, a dull scrape sounding as the weapon came free of its sheath. While Herkimer was catching his breath, the god examined the weapon with revulsion. Shaking his head, the god turned his back on Herkimer to show the tall servant the pitiable blade. Instead of joining the god's ridicule of the weapon, the servant cringed. Raithe saw the future through the weasel man's expression, for he was the first to notice Herkimer's reaction.

Raithe's father drew the skinning knife from his belt and lunged.

This time the god didn't disappoint. With astounding speed, he whirled and drove the copper blade into Raithe's father's chest. Herkimer's forward momentum did the work of running the sword deep. The fight ended the moment it began. His father gasped and fell, the sword still in his chest.

Raithe didn't think. If he had paused even for an instant, he might have reconsidered, but there was more of his father in him than he wanted to believe. The sword being the only weapon within reach, he pulled the copper from his father's body. With all his might, Raithe swung at the god's neck. He fully expected the blade to cut clean through, but the copper sliced only air as the divine being dodged. The god drew his own weapon as Raithe swung again. The two swords met. A dull *ping* sounded, and the weight in Raithe's hands vanished along with most of the blade. When he finished his swing, only the hilt of his family's heritage remained; the rest flew through the air and landed in a tuft of young pines.

The god stared at him with a disgusted smirk, then spoke in the divine language. *"Not worth dying for, was it?"*

Then the god raised his blade once more as Raithe shuffled backward.

Too slow! Too slow!

His retreat was futile. Raithe was dead. Years of combat training told him so. In that instant before understanding became reality, he had the chance to regret his entire life.

I've done nothing, he thought as his muscles tightened for the expected burst of pain.

It never came.

Raithe had lost track of the servants—so had the god. Neither of the combatants expected, nor saw, the tall weasel-faced man slam his master in the back of the head with a river rock the size and shape of a round loaf of bread. Raithe realized what had happened only after the god collapsed, revealing the servant and his stone.

"Run," the rock bearer said. "With any luck, his head will hurt too much for him to chase us when he wakes."

"What have you done!" the other servant shouted, his eyes wide as he backed up, pulling the god's horse away.

"Calm down," the one holding the rock told the other servant.

Raithe looked at his father, lying on his back. Herkimer's eyes were still open, as if watching clouds. Raithe had cursed his father many times over the years. The man neglected his family, pitted his sons against one another, and had been away when Raithe's mother and sister died. In some ways—many ways—Raithe hated his father, but at that moment what he saw was a man who had taught his sons to fight and not give in. Herkimer had done the best with what he had, and what he had was a life trapped on barren soil because the gods made capricious demands. Raithe's father never stole, cheated, or held his tongue when something needed to be said. He was a hard man, a cold man, but one who had the courage to stand up for himself and what was right. What Raithe saw on the ground at his feet was the last of his dead family.

He felt the broken sword in his hands.

"No!" the servant holding the horse cried out as Raithe drove the remainder of the jagged copper blade through the god's throat.

Both servants had fled, the smaller one on the horse and the other chasing on foot. Now the one who had wielded the rock returned. Covered in sweat and shaking his head, he trotted back to the meadow. "Meryl's gone," he said. "He isn't the best rider, but he doesn't have to be. The horse knows the way back to Alon Rhist." He stopped after noticing Raithe. "What are you doing?"

Raithe was standing over the body of the god. He'd picked up the Fhrey's sword and was pressing the tip against the god's throat. "Waiting. How long does it usually take?"

"How long does what take?"

"For him to get up."

"He's dead. Dead people don't generally *get up,*" the servant said.

Reluctant to take his eyes off the god, Raithe ventured only the briefest glance at the servant, who was bent and struggling to catch his breath. "What are you talking about?"

"What are *you* talking about?"

"I want to know how long we have before he rises. If I cut off his head, will he stay down longer?"

The servant rolled his eyes. "He's not getting up! You killed him."

"My Tetlin ass! That's a god. Gods don't die. They're immortal."

"Really not so much," the servant said, and to Raithe's shock he kicked the god's body, which barely moved. He kicked it again, and the head rocked to one side, sand sticking to its cheek. "See? Dead. Get it? Not immortal. Not a god, just a Fhrey. They die. There's a difference between long-lived and immortal. Immortal means you can't die . . . even if you want to. Fact is, the Fhrey are a lot more similar to Rhunes than we'd like to think."

"We're nothing alike. Look at him." Raithe pointed at the fallen Fhrey.

"Oh, yes," the servant replied. "He's so different. He has only one head, walks on two feet, and has two hands and ten fingers. You're right. Nothing like us at all."

The servant looked down at the body and sighed. "His name was Shegon. An incredibly talented harp player, a cheat at cards, and a *brideeth eyn mer*—which is to say . . ." The servant paused. "No, there is no other way to say it. He wasn't well liked, and now he's dead."

Raithe looked over suspiciously.

Is he lying? Trying to put me off guard?

"You're wrong," Raithe said with full conviction. "Have you ever seen a dead Fhrey? I haven't. My father hasn't. No one I've ever known has. And they don't age."

"They do, just very slowly."

Raithe shook his head. "No, they don't. My father mentioned a time when he was a boy, and he met a

Fhrey named Neason. Forty-five years later, they met again, but Neason looked exactly the same."

"Of course he did. I just told you they age slowly. Fhrey can live for thousands of years. A bumblebee lives for only a few months. To a bumblebee, you appear immortal."

Raithe wasn't fully convinced, but it would explain the blood. He hadn't expected any. In retrospect, he shouldn't have attacked the Fhrey at all. His father had taught him not to start a fight he couldn't win, and fighting an immortal god fell squarely into that category. But then again it was his father who had started the whole thing.

Sure is a lot of blood.

An ugly pool had formed underneath the god, staining the grass and his glistening robes. His neck still had the gash, a nasty, jagged tear like a second mouth. Raithe had expected the wound to miraculously heal or simply vanish. When the god rose, Raithe would have the advantage. He was strong and could best most men in Dureya, which meant he could best most men. Even his father thought twice about making his son too angry.

Raithe stared down at the Fhrey, whose eyes were open and rolled up. The gash in his throat was wider now. A god—a real god—would never permit kicks from a servant. "Okay, maybe they aren't immortal." He relaxed and took a step back.

"My name is Malcolm," the servant said. "Yours is Raithe?"

"Uh-huh," Raithe said. With one last glare at the Fhrey's corpse, Raithe tucked the jeweled weapon into his belt and then lifted his father's body.

"Now what are you doing?" Malcolm asked.

"Can't bury him down here. These rivers are bound to flood this plain."

"*Bury* him? When word gets back to Alon Rhist, the Fhrey will . . ." He looked sick. "We need to leave."

"So go."

Raithe carried his father to a small hill in the meadow

and gently lowered him to the ground. As a final resting place, it wasn't much but would have to do. Turning around, he found the god's ex-servant staring in disbelief. "What?"

Malcolm started to laugh, then stopped, confused. "You don't understand. Glyn is a fast horse and has the stamina of a wolf. Meryl will reach Alon Rhist by nightfall. He'll tell the Instarya everything to save himself. They'll come after us. We need to get moving."

"Go ahead," Raithe said, taking Herkimer's medal and putting it on. Then he closed his father's eyes. He couldn't remember having touched the old man's face before.

"You need to go, too."

"After I bury my father."

"The Rhune is dead."

Raithe cringed at the word. "He was a *man*."

"Rhune—man—same thing."

"Not to me—and not to him." Raithe strode down to the riverbank, littered with thousands of rocks of various sizes. The problem wasn't finding proper stones but deciding which ones to choose.

Malcolm planted his hands on his hips, glaring with an expression somewhere between astonishment and anger. "It'll take hours! You're wasting time."

Raithe crouched and picked up a rock. The top had been baked warm by the sun; the bottom was damp, cool, and covered in wet sand. "He deserves a proper burial and would have done the same for me." Raithe found it ironic given that his father had rarely shown him any kindness. But it was true; Herkimer would have faced death to see his son properly buried. "Besides, do you have any idea what can happen to the spirit of an unburied body?"

The man stared back, bewildered.

"They return as manes to haunt you for not showing the proper respect. And manes can be vicious." Raithe hoisted another large sand-colored rock and walked up the slope. "My father could be a real cul when he was alive. I don't need him stalking me for the rest of my life."

"But—"

"But what?" Raithe set the rocks down near his father's shoulders. He'd do the outline before starting the pile. "He's not your father. I don't expect you to stay."

"That's not the point."

"What *is* the point?"

The servant hesitated, and Raithe took the opportunity to return to the bank and search for more rocks.

"I need your help," the man finally said.

Raithe picked up a large stone and carried it up the bank, clutched against his stomach. "With what?"

"You know how to . . . well, you know . . . live . . . out here, I mean." The servant looked at the deer carcass, which had gathered a host of flies. "You can hunt, cook, and find shelter, right? You know what berries to eat, which animals you can pet and which to run away from."

"You don't pet any animals."

"See? Good example of how little I know about this sort of thing. Alone, I'd be dead in a day or two. Frozen stiff, buried in a landslide, or gored by some antlered beast."

Raithe set the stone and returned down the slope, clapping his hands together to clean off the sand. "Makes sense."

"Of course it makes sense. I'm a sensible fellow. And if you were sensible, we'd go. Now."

Raithe lifted another rock. "If you're bent on sticking with me and in such a hurry, you might consider helping."

The man looked at the riverbank's rounded stones and sighed. "Do we have to use such big ones?"

"Big ones for the bottom, smaller ones on top."

"Sounds like you've done this before."

"People die often where I come from, and we have a lot of rocks." Raithe wiped his brow with his forearm, pushing back a mat of dark hair. He'd rolled the woolen sleeves of his undertunic up. The spring days were still chilly, but the work made him sweat. He considered taking off his leigh mor and leather but decided against it. Burying his father should be an unpleasant task, and a good son should feel something at such a time. If *uncomfortable* was the best he could manage, Raithe would settle for that.

Malcolm carried over a pair of rocks and set them down, letting Raithe place them. He paused to rub his hands clean.

"Okay, Malcolm," Raithe said, "you need to pick bigger ones or we'll be here forever."

Malcolm scowled but returned to the bank, gathered two good-sized stones, and carried them under his arms like melons. He walked unsteadily in sandals. Thin, with a simple strap, they were ill suited to the landscape. Raithe's clothes were shoddy—sewn scraps of wool with leather accents that he'd cured himself—but at least they were durable.

Raithe searched for and found a small smooth stone.

"I thought you wanted bigger rocks?" Malcolm asked.

"This isn't for the pile." Raithe opened his father's right hand and exchanged the rock for the skinning knife. "He'll need it to get to Rel or Alysin if he's worthy—Nifrel if he's not."

"Oh, right."

After outlining the body, Raithe piled the stones from the feet upward. Then he retrieved his father's leigh mor, which still lay next to the deer's carcass, and laid it over Herkimer's face. A quick search in the little patch of pines produced the other end of the copper sword. Raithe considered leaving the weapon but worried about grave robbers. His father had died for the shattered blade; it deserved to be cared for.

Raithe glanced at the Fhrey once more. "You're certain he won't get up?"

Malcolm looked over from where he was lifting a rock. "Positive. Shegon *is* dead."

Together they hoisted a dozen more rocks onto the

growing pile before Raithe asked, "Why were you with him?"

Malcolm pointed to the torc around his neck as if it explained everything. Raithe was puzzled until he noticed the necklace was a complete circle. The ring of metal wasn't a torc, not jewelry at all—it was a collar.

Not a servant—a slave.

The sun was low in the sky when they dropped the last rocks to complete the mound. Malcolm washed in the river while Raithe sang his mourning song. Then he slung his father's broken blade over his shoulder, adjusted the Fhrey's sword in his belt, and gathered his things and those of his father. They didn't have much: a wooden shield, a bag containing a good hammer stone, a rabbit pelt Raithe planned to make into a pouch as soon as it cured, the last of the cheese, the single blanket they had shared, a stone hand ax, his father's knife, and Raithe's spear.

"Where to?" Malcolm asked. His face and hair were covered in sweat, and the man had nothing, not even a sharpened stick to defend himself.

"Here, sling this blanket over your shoulder. Tie it tight, and take my spear."

"I don't know how to use a spear."

"It's not complicated. Just point and stick."

Raithe looked around. Going home didn't make sense. That was back east, closer to Alon Rhist. Besides, his family was gone. The clan would still welcome him, but it was impossible to build a life in Dureya. Another option would be to push farther west into the untamed wilderness of Avrlyn. To do so they'd need to get past a series of Fhrey outposts along the western rivers. Like Alon Rhist, the strongholds were built to keep men out. Herkimer had warned Raithe about the fortifications of Merredydd and Seon Hall, but his father never explained exactly where those were. By himself, Raithe could likely avoid walking into one, but he wouldn't have much of a life alone in the wilderness. Taking Malcolm wouldn't help. By the look and sound of the ex-slave, he wouldn't survive a year in the wild.

"We'll cross back into Rhulyn but go south." He pointed over the river at the dramatic rising hillside covered with evergreens. "That's the Crescent Forest, runs for miles in all directions. Not the safest place, but it'll provide cover—help hide us." He glanced up at the sky. "Still early in the season, but there should be some food to forage and game to hunt."

"What do you mean by *not the safest place*?"

"Well, I've not been there myself, but I've heard things."

"What sorts of things?"

Raithe tightened his belt and the strap holding the copper to his back before offering a shrug. "Oh, you know, tabors, raow, leshies. Stuff like that."

Malcolm continued to stare. "Vicious animals?"

"Oh, yeah—those, too, I suppose."

"Those . . . *too*?"

"Sure, bound to be in a forest that size."

"Oh," Malcolm said, looking apprehensive as his eyes followed a branch floating past them at a quick pace. "How will we get across?"

"You can swim, right?"

Malcolm looked stunned. "That's a thousand feet from bank to bank."

"It has a nice current, too. Depending on how well you swim, we'll probably reach the far side several miles south of here. But that's good. It'll make us harder to track."

"Impossible, I'd imagine," Malcolm said, grimacing, his sight chained to the river.

The ex-slave of the Fhrey looked terrified, and Raithe understood why. He'd felt the same way when Herkimer had forced him across.

"Ready?" Raithe asked.

Malcolm pursed his lips; the skin of his hands was white as he clutched the spear. "You realize this water is cold—comes down as snowmelt from Mount Mador."

"Not only that," Raithe added, "but since we're going to be hunted, we won't be able to make a fire when we get out."

The slender man with the pointed nose and narrow eyes forced a tight smile. "Lovely. Thanks for the reminder."

"You up for this?" Raithe asked as he led the way into the icy water.

"I'll admit it's not my typical day." The sound of his words rose in octaves as he waded into the river.

"What was your typical day like?" Raithe gritted his teeth as the water reached knee depth. The current churned around his legs and pushed, forcing him to dig his feet into the riverbed.

"Mostly I poured wine."

Raithe chuckled. "Yeah—this will be different."

A moment later, the river pulled both of them off their feet.

CHAPTER TWO

The Mystic

Dahl Rhen was a grassy hill nestled alongside the Crescent Forest where a log lodge and several hundred mud-and-thatch roundhouses were protected by a wood-and-earthwork wall. Looking back, I realize it was a crude, tiny place where chickens and pigs roamed free, but it was also where the chieftain of Clan Rhen lived and ruled. And it was my home.

—THE BOOK OF BRIN

Persephone knew everyone on the dahl, making strangers stand out, and the girl at the gate was stranger than most. Small, young, and slender, the visitor was boyish with short unevenly hacked hair. Persephone couldn't tell if the sun had darkened her face or if it was merely dirty, but it was decorated with elaborate tattoos: delicate curling thorns that swirled along cheeks, bracketing her eyes and mouth. The designs lent her a mysterious quality. Framing her face, they provided an expression both permanently quizzical and intensely serious. She wore a dirty cape of ruddy wool, a leather-and-fur vest, a skirt of cured hide, and an odd belt. Persephone wasn't certain, but she thought the belt was made of animals' teeth. Curled up at the girl's side lay a white wolf. Its keen blue eyes darted, watching the movements of everyone who walked toward them. Few did.

The newcomer stood outside the dahl's gate next to Cobb, who'd come down from his perch on the wall and held his spear as menacingly as he could, which was to say not at all. The man's usual job was feeding the pigs and keeping them out of the communal garden, a task previously held by eight-year-old Thea Wedon and one at which Cobb often failed. Most men took turns keeping watch on the wall above the gate. That morning it was Cobb, and, as with the pigs, he was having trouble.

"We have a visitor, ma'am," Cobb told her, pointing at the girl with his spear. He nodded toward the ram's horn tethered around his neck and grinned as if blowing it had been an achievement worthy of praise. Persephone had to admit he'd done a better job watching the gate than the pigs. "She says she's a mystic and wants to speak to the chieftain."

The girl couldn't be much more than twelve, and although she did look like she'd spent most of her life in the wilderness, she was too young to be a mystic.

"I'm Persephone, Lady of the Lodge." She waited for any sign of understanding. When none came, she added, "I'm Chieftain Reglan's wife. My husband is away on a hunt, but you can talk to me."

The girl nodded but said nothing more. She stood there, biting her lower lip and shifting her sight with every dropped hoe, shout, or hammer fall.

On closer inspection, Persephone decided the girl was more malnourished than thin, and *filthy* didn't begin to describe her. Pine needles and leaves littered her hair, and dirt caked her legs. She had bruises on her arms, scrapes on her knees, and it *was* dirt rather than the sun's tan on her face.

"May I help you?"

"What's he hunting?" the girl asked.

"Excuse me?"

"The chieftain."

Persephone hesitated. She'd been doing well that day by not letting herself think too much, banishing the horrible event to a dark corner that she'd revisit only once her husband returned. But the question had shone a bright light, and Persephone struggled to maintain her composure.

"None of your business." Cobb came alive, taking a genuinely menacing step forward. The threat wasn't in the spear, which at that moment hung slack and forgotten at his side, but rather in his voice, which was heartfelt and angry.

"A bear," Persephone said. She took a breath and straightened her back. "A terrible bear called The Brown."

The girl nodded with a frown.

"You know it?" Persephone asked.

"Oh, yes, Grin the Brown is famous in the forest, ma'am. And not well liked."

"*Grin* the Brown?"

"That's what we call her on account of how she sneers at everyone and everything. I've even seen her sneer at the sun, and who doesn't like the sun?"

"That bear killed my son," Persephone said, the words coming out more easily than she'd expected. This was the first time she'd said them, and somehow she thought they would refuse to pass her lips.

"Killed Minna's family, too," the girl said, looking at the wolf. "Found her in the Crescent, just like Tura found me. I took Minna in, clearly we're sisters, and you can't turn away family. Tura thought so, too."

"You know Tura?"

"She raised me."

All at once the tooth belt, the facial markings, and even the weathered ash staff made sense. Persephone remembered Tura's bony hands holding just such a staff. "So Tura sent you to us?"

The girl shook her head. "Tura is dead. I set fire to her myself."

"You did what?"

"Was her wish, ma'am. Didn't like the idea of worms. I think she wanted to fly. Who wouldn't?"

Persephone stared at the girl for a moment, then said, "*I see,*" even though she didn't. Persephone had no clue what any of that meant, then realized it didn't matter.

"What's your name?"

"Suri," the girl said.

"Okay, Suri." Persephone looked at the wolf. "I'd like

to invite you in, but we have chickens and pigs inside the dahl, so—Minna, is it?—can't come in."

"Minna won't hurt them," Suri said, sounding insulted and a dash angry. Tattoo tendrils around her eyes curled tight.

"Wolves eat chickens and pigs."

The girl smirked and folded her arms roughly over her chest. "They eat people, too, but you don't see her gnawing on your leg, do you?"

Persephone looked at the wolf, which lay curled up, innocent as a shepherd's dog. "Does seem pretty tame. What do you think, Cobb?"

The ineffective pig wrangler turned mediocre gate guard shrugged.

"All right, but keep an eye on her. If she attacks anything, there's a good chance someone will put a spear through her."

Persephone led the way inside the gate.

As she did, Suri whispered, "Not a very welcoming place is it, Minna? Wonder how they'd like it if we put a spear in their sides when they come to the forest and hunt *our* animals."

Spring was dragging its feet, leaving a colorless world of matted grass, leafless trees, and gray skies, but the people of Dahl Rhen weren't waiting. Everyone was more than tired of the long winter, and with the first mild day of the year, the inhabitants of the dahl were out working. The Killian boys, wellsprings of pent-up energy even in midsummer, were up on the sagging cone-shaped roof of their family's home. They were tying in new sheaves of thatch to replace the ones winter had ripped away. Bergin the Brewer was splitting wood and feeding the fire under boiling vats of sap he'd gathered. Others were prepping the communal garden, which at that time of year was nothing more than a miserable patch of bare mud where last autumn's stubble remained like sun-bleached bones.

Cobb returned to his perch on the wall, and Persephone led Suri up the gravel path to the large lodge in the center of the dahl. The almost forgotten song of birds was back, and Persephone spotted yellow and blue wildflowers on the sunny side of the well. Winter was over, according to the stars, birds, and flowers, but snow remained in the shady places. Persephone pulled her mourning shawl tight. Spring was being selective that year. It hadn't come for everyone.

Persephone paused in the open common before the lodge's steps and bowed to the stone statue of the goddess Mari. Suri watched with curious interest, then followed. The big doors to the lodge stood open, casting sunshine into the Hall of Reglan, which had been a smoky wooden cave since autumn. Illuminated by fire light in the dark of winter, the twelve pillars holding up the roof always appeared golden, but in harsh sunlight they were revealed as old and weathered. The bright light exposed more reality than just the pillars; discarded shoes, a cloak hanging from the antlers of a deer's head, and a ram's-horn goblet in the corner where Oswald had thrown it at Sackett months before. The raised wooden floor surrounding the smoldering fire pit was coated with dirt and ash. Sunlight had a way of showing the realities that shadows born of firelight hid.

The eternal fire burned low in the central pit, and Habet, whose job was to keep it stoked, was missing. Persephone added a split of wood, and the room brightened a little. Crossing to the pair of chairs near the far wall—the only chairs in the room—Persephone sat in the one on the right.

Suri had stopped at the door. She peered at the rafters of the peaked roof, where shields of past chieftains hung along with trophy heads of stags, wolves, and bears. She grimaced, then looked across the room toward Persephone, eyeing the floor as if it were a deep lake and she unable to swim. Then, with effort, the girl and the wolf entered.

"How old are you, Suri?" Persephone asked as the girl made her way across the hall.

"Don't know—maybe fourteen." The girl spoke absently, her attention still on the rafters.

"Maybe?"

"That's my best guess. Might be more. Might be less."

"You don't know?"

"Depends on how long I spent with the crimbals. Tura was fairly certain I'm a malkin."

"A—a what? A *malkin*?"

Suri nodded. "When a crimbal steals—you know what a crimbal is, ma'am?"

Persephone shook her head.

Suri sucked in a breath, glancing at the wolf beside her as if the two shared a secret, then explained. "Well, a crimbal is a creature of the forest. They don't actually live there, just come and go, you see? They're common in the Crescent, lots of doorways because of all the trees. They dwell in Nog, a place deep underground where they have grand halls and banquets. They dance and make merry in ways you can only imagine. Anyway, when a crimbal steals a baby, they—"

"They steal babies?"

"Oh, Grand Mother of All, yes. All the time. No one knows why. Just a thing with them, I suppose. Anyway, when they steal one, they take it back to Nog, where who knows what happens. On rare occasions, one sneaks out. They're called malkins and aren't quite right again because anyone spending time in Nog is forever changed. Now, usually a malkin is older, like ten or twelve, but somehow I managed to get out before my first year. That's when Tura found me."

"How did you get out before you could walk?"

Suri, who by then had completed the bulk of her journey, looked at Persephone as if she'd said the craziest thing. "How should I know, ma'am? I was just a baby."

Persephone arched her brows and nodded. "I see," she said, but what she actually saw was how even an innocuous question such as *How old are you?* wasn't a simple matter for a girl with a belt of teeth and a pet wolf. Best to keep matters simple. "All right, Suri, what is it you need?"

"Need, ma'am?" the girl asked.

"Why are you here?"

"Oh—I came to tell the chieftain we're going to die." The girl said it quickly and with the same casual indifference as if she were announcing that the sun sets in the evening.

Persephone narrowed her eyes. "Excuse me? What did you say? Who's going to die?"

"All of us."

"All of whom?"

"Us." The girl looked puzzled, but this time Persephone wasn't certain if it was the tattoos or not.

"You and I?"

Suri sighed. "Yes—you, me, the funny man with the horn at the gate, everyone."

"Everyone in Dahl Rhen?"

The girl sighed again. "Not just Dahl Rhen—everywhere."

Persephone laughed. "Are you saying all living things are going to die? Because that's not exactly news."

Suri looked to Minna, a pleading in her eyes as if the wolf might help explain. "Not *all* living things, just *people*—people like you and me."

"You mean Rhunes? All the *Rhunes* are going to die?"

Suri shrugged. "I suppose."

"I think perhaps you should back up. Start with when and how this will happen."

"Don't know how . . . soon, though. Should start before high summer, I suspect. Definitely before winter." She paused, thought, and then nodded. "Yes, definitely before the snows come, and by this time next year we'll be in the worst of it. That will be the edge of the knife, the peak of the storm."

"So it's a storm that's coming?"

The girl blinked, furrowed her brow, scowled, and shook her head. "Not an *actual* storm, just a bad thing, although . . ." She shrugged. "It could be a storm, I suppose."

"And you have no idea what is going to cause this or why such a terrible thing will happen?"

"No—not at all," the mystic said as if such things held no importance.

Persephone leaned back in her chair and studied the girl. She was a sad case, an orphan alone and scared. "Why are you *really* here, Suri? Are you hungry? Lonely now that Tura is dead?"

Suri looked confused.

"It's okay. I'll ask someone to find you a place to sleep. Get you some bread, too. Would you like some bread?"

The mystic thought a moment. "Bread would be nice."

"And would you like to live here? Here on the dahl?"

Suri's eyes grew wide, and she took a fearful step back, glancing once more at the rafters. Her head shook. "No, ma'am. I could *never* live here. I only came because Tura told me it's what I should do if I ever discovered such a thing. '*Go to the hill in the big field at the crux of the forest and ask to speak to the chieftain.*' That's what she said. Not that there's anything to do about it right now. Need to talk to the trees. They could tell us more, but they're still asleep."

Persephone sighed. This wasn't like talking to Tura, who'd had her own eccentricities.

I can leave this for Reglan. Maybe he can make sense of her.

"Well, thank you." Persephone stood and offered the girl a smile. "I'll see that you get the bread I mentioned, and you can take this up with my husband when he returns. If you'd like, you can wait in here." Seeing the girl take another step backward, Persephone added, "Or out on the steps if you prefer."

Suri nodded, pivoted, and walked away, the wolf following at her heels.

So thin.

Persephone was certain the prophecy was a ruse.

Clever, but the girl had overdone it. She should have kept it simple, like predicting a poor harvest, approaching fevers, or a drought. She was just young and hadn't thought things through. With Tura dead, she didn't have a hope of surviving alone in the forest.

"Suri?" Persephone stopped her. "I wouldn't tell anyone else about what you told me. You know, about the deaths."

The girl turned around, a hand resting against the nearest of the three winter pillars. "Why?"

"Because they won't understand. They'll think you're lying."

"I'm not."

Persephone sighed. *Stubborn, too.*

Suri took a few more steps toward the door, then paused and turned back once more. "I'm not Tura, but I know something awful is coming. Our only hope is to heed what counsel the trees can tell. Watch for the leaves, ma'am, watch for the leaves."

Just then, Cobb's horn sounded again.

By the time Persephone passed through the doorway, she knew something terrible had happened. Mattocks and hoes lay abandoned in the garden. The Killian brothers had come down off their roof, and people scurried to the gate or fell to their knees, weeping. Those with tear-filled eyes spread their pain to the bewildered around them. The whispered words were followed by shock and a shaking of heads. Then they, too, cried.

As if she were seeing rain cross a field, Persephone braced for the approaching tempest. She'd weathered many storms. For twenty years, she'd helped her husband guide their people. She'd faced the Long Winter and the Great Famine that followed. She'd lost her first son at birth, the second to sickness, and recently the only one who had grown to adulthood. Mahn had been a fine young man whom the gods inexplicably had failed to protect. Whatever came through the gate, she would endure it like all the other events. She had to. If not for her sake, then for her people.

At the gate, both wooden doors had been pushed open, but the view was obscured by people clustered on the pathway. Several had climbed the ladders and lined the ramparts, pointing over the wall. Persephone reached the lodge steps at the same instant the crowd finally parted to reveal the mystery.

The hunting party had returned.

Eight men had left. Six had come back. One on a shield.

They carried Reglan through the gate—two men on each side, Konniger walking in front. The sleeve of his shirt had been torn away and wrapped around his head, one side stained red. Adler, who always had keen eyes, returned with only one of the two he'd left with. Hegner had a bloody stump where his right hand had been.

Persephone didn't move beyond the steps. The downpour had reached her, and there was no need to go farther.

What struck her the most acutely wasn't the shock of her husband's death but that the scene was so familiar. Persephone wondered if she were losing her mind, reliving the events of three days before when they had brought her son back. He, too, had been on a hunting trip and carried home. She remembered standing in the exact same spot at the exact same time of day.

But it's not the same.

With Mahn, her husband had stood by her side. He'd held her hand, and his strength had kept her standing. Anger had radiated off him, his fingers squeezing too hard. Reglan had left the next day to seek vengeance.

The bearers approached the steps. Grim faces looked to their feet. Only one dared look at her. The crowd folded behind the procession.

"We return to you your husband," Konniger said. "Reglan of the House of Mont, chieftain of Dahl Rhen, has fallen in battle this day."

With his words, the crowd quieted. Above Persephone,

the lodge banners snapped in the wind. She was supposed to acknowledge this the way her husband had accepted the death of Mahn—of their boy. Reglan had done so with dignity and understanding while silently crushing her hand in his. Persephone didn't have a hand to squeeze and lacked all understanding. Instead, she asked, "And what of the bear?"

Taken by surprise, Konniger didn't answer right away. He took a moment and dragged a bloodstained hand down the wounded side of his face. "It's not a bear. The thing we hunted is a demon. Men cannot kill such a thing."

CHAPTER THREE

The God Killer

He was called the God Killer, and we first heard about him from the traders traveling the northern routes. His legend grew, but no one believed, not in the beginning. Except me.

—THE BOOK OF BRIN

Raithe enjoyed a good campfire. Something comforting about the dancing light, the smell of smoke, and the way his face and chest were hot but his backside cold. He sensed a profound meaning in this duality as well as in the enigma of flickering flames. The fire spirit spoke in spitting sparks and shifts of choking smoke, but the meaning of each remained a mystery. Everything in nature was that way. All of it spoke to him—to everyone— in a language few could understand. What secrets, what wisdom, and what horrors might he learn if only he knew what it all meant.

"One of the few spirits I get along with," Raithe said, tossing another branch on the flames.

"What is?" Malcolm asked. The ex-slave turned fugitive compatriot was seated beside Raithe, both windward to avoid the smoke. He was busy removing the blanket from around his neck. The material was thin enough to tie in a knot, and when they traveled, he wore it like a sash.

"The fire," Raithe said, grabbing another branch from the pile they had gathered. He snapped it in half and tossed the pieces into the flames.

"You think fires are spirits?"

Raithe raised a brow. "What? You think it's a demon?" He'd heard it before, most notably from a neighbor who'd left his cook fire unattended while taking a piss in the river. When the man returned, his dung house was burning. "Could be," Raithe considered. "It has a nasty temper when loose, but I honestly don't think a demon would come so easily when summoned. Certainly not by the likes of me."

Malcolm stared at him, something he did often. The light of the fire cast his eyes in shadow. Raithe wasn't one for conversation, and Malcolm's blank stares after such comments didn't provide much incentive. The Fhrey slave must have lived a sheltered life. Everything Raithe told him came as a surprise.

"My father always said fires were only dangerous if they got bored," Raithe pressed on. "Left alone, they get frustrated and resort to evil. Best way to keep a fire happy is by letting it lick food and hear stories."

Malcolm continued to watch him, blinking this time, his mouth partially open.

He's tired, Raithe decided. *Cold, miserable, and, most of all, scared.* All understandable given their situation; even Raithe struggled to keep a positive outlook. *I would have never guessed a forest could be stingier than the rocky plains of Dureya.*

This was their eighth night in the Crescent Forest, and the world of giant trees still hadn't welcomed them. The wood offered few paths, forced them through thorny brambles, and denied them all but the most meager subsistence. That day they had feasted on six black beetles the size of his thumbnail, seven larvae they found under peeling bark, sap leaking out of a broad-leaf tree, and a bunch of pinecones, which they'd had to roast to get at the nuts. At a clear stream, Raithe had tried to spear fish while Malcolm attempted to grab them, but after several frustrating hours, they gave up. This would be another hungry night.

In the dark of the canopy-induced premature night, the two sat side by side in a tiny clearing carpeted in brown needles. They watched the fire and listened to the wind and creaking trees. The massive evergreens swayed, their tops sweeping the sky and denying any glimpse of stars. Raithe could have oriented himself if he could have seen them. Trapped under the canopy, he was blind and convinced they'd been walking in circles.

"The evening meal is being served in Alon Rhist," Malcolm said in a wistful tone as he shook out the blanket and wrapped it around himself. "Venison probably—slow-roasted so it's tender. There'd be cheese, too, and some poultry like partridge or quail, certainly fresh bread, pudding—oh, and wine, of course. Bet they're eating right now. Evening meals were wonderful." He looked like a man recalling a lost love. "Are you familiar with the concept? That's when you eat something in the evening." He sighed in remembrance. "I used to partake of that particular ritual all the time when I was a slave, but thank the gods I'm free now."

It was Raithe's turn to stare at Malcolm.

"Sorry. I'm just hungry."

Raithe continued to glare.

"What?"

"Did he beat you?" Raithe asked.

"Who? Shegon?"

Raithe nodded. "Because if he did, I could see why."

Malcolm frowned. "No, he didn't beat me. The Fhrey treat their slaves well. Certainly better than you."

"You're not my slave."

"And I thank all that is sacred for that." Malcolm waved at a pair of tiny black bugs that had gathered in front of his face. Insects were coming out with the warmer weather, which wasn't all that warm yet.

"If the Fhrey were so great, why'd you bash ole Shegon on the head?" Raithe asked, realizing he ought to have inquired sooner, but the death of his father, concern over being hunted, and their constant search for food had pushed out other thoughts.

Malcolm plucked up a brown pine needle, of which there were millions. Rubbing it between his fingers, he shrugged. "Even a well-treated slave prefers to control his own destiny. I saw a way out and took it. Everything would have been fine if you hadn't lost your mind. Shegon would have been angry, but not enough to bother chasing after us—he wasn't that ambitious—but now that he's dead, revenge will be a matter of honor." He paused, looked over, and asked, "What about you? Why'd you do it?"

"Kill him?"

Malcolm nodded.

"I don't know. Shouldn't have. When he killed my father, I didn't think. I just acted. Just like Herkimer would have. Funny thing is, I never wanted to be like him. Didn't want to go off and fight in the wars. Had no desire to seek fame and glory. That was his ambition . . . his and my brothers'. I would be happy living a simple life with a wife and a few children. And yet all the years my father spent teaching me to fight just kinda kicked in. You know what I mean?" He looked at Malcolm and realized he didn't. Not the blank stare this time but no recognition. A Dureyan would have understood, but Malcolm had spent too much time with the Fhrey and barely seemed human.

"I have no excuse other than to say I did it for him. Sons are supposed to do that, aren't they? Avenge their fathers. That's how things are done in Dureya, at least."

"Not a nice place, I gather, this Dureya."

"Barren rock and dirt mostly. Lots of thin brittle grass, too. Wonderful if you're a goat."

"And the people?"

"Mean."

"You're not mean."

Raithe raised a brow. "You don't know me or my people. Clan Dureya is famous for growing offensive bastards who'd rather drink than work, fight than talk, and are the source of all evil in the world."

"If you were as nasty as you suggest, you probably would have killed Meryl and me, taken the horse, and not bothered to bury your father."

Raithe threw up his hands. "I'm odd. A disappointment to my clan. The son of Coppersword who never went to war. In Dureya, everyone fights. The Fhrey call for warriors, and up go the hands. It's how we eat, because we aren't goats. And you know you're living the high life when you envy goats." Raithe frowned, threw a stick into the fire, and sighed. "My father just wanted some decent land. Crossing the river was the first sensible thing he'd ever done."

"Your father was being unreasonable. Dragged you to where you aren't allowed—the Rhune chieftains all signed treaties assuring you'd keep to your own lands."

"Shegon was unreasonable, too. Telling us to leave is one thing, but you can't ask a man to throw away a sword. Swords might be common in Alon Rhist, but they're rare on this side of the rivers."

"That wasn't unreasonable. A treaty violation is one thing, but doing so with weapons is an act of war. You and your father would have been killed on sight had an Instarya patrol found you. But Shegon was from the Asendwayr tribe, and he was giving you a way out. Still, leaving you with the sword would have been irresponsible. If you lingered or doubled back and the Instarya found you, they would view your armed presence as an invasion—a scouting party perhaps. The Instarya would have marched on Rhulyn. What Shegon did wasn't unreasonable; it was an act of kindness."

Raithe hadn't known any of that. He wished he still didn't.

"It's not all your fault," Malcolm added in a softer tone. "Shegon could have explained things better, but the Fhrey aren't in the habit of reasoning with those they consider only slightly above animals."

"Wouldn't have mattered. The sword was my father's pride, his honor. It's who he was. Handing it over would have been the same as placing his head on a chopping block. Worse, he'd have been giving up his soul."

"And now his great blade is yours."

"Such as it is." Raithe drew the broken copper out of

the scabbard and looked at the severed edge. "Shegon's blade cut through it like I was holding a stick, and this was the best weapon in our clan. It's been handed down from father to son for generations. Legend holds it was crafted for my great-great-grandfather by a Dherg in return for saving his life." Raithe slipped the shattered sword back into its sheath. Then he bit his lip and took a breath. "I haven't thanked you."

"Don't bother. I did you no favor," Malcolm assured.

"I would have died if you hadn't."

Malcolm raised his head to peer curiously at Raithe. "You're still going to die. You're just going to spend some time beforehand with a hungry stomach and sore legs. But on the bright side, you'll be remembered. One doesn't kill a god and go unnoticed."

Clap!

Out in the dark, beyond the ring of the firelight, a loud wood-on-wood strike ripped through the night. Not a snapping branch, although that would have been disturbing as well. They had heard those sounds before, animals of unknown size roaming in the night. The sounds of the forest made it hard to sleep. But this wasn't that. Not a crack, this was a slap, an odd hollow sound, and both of them got to their feet. Together they peered into the gloom as Raithe put more wood on the fire.

"What was that?" Malcolm whispered.

"Dunno," Raithe whispered back. "Could be anything."

"How about some examples?"

"I suppose the worst thing would be a raow."

"Worst thing? Why did you have to start with the worst thing? Why not assume it was a dead tree falling on another?"

"Relax. I don't think it's a raow. We'd have seen human bones by now, and we'd also be dead."

"Oh, well, thanks for the reassurance. So what else might it be?"

Raithe looked across at him and smiled. "A falling tree?"

Malcolm smirked. "Seriously, though . . ."

Raithe looked around at the moss-covered rocks and then at the trees. "Leshie?"

"And what is a leshie?"

"Woodland spirit. They're probably covering our path so we won't know which way to go in the morning. They're mischievous but not generally dangerous to grown men."

Malcolm stepped back as the heat of the fire grew with the added wood. Part skeptical, part hopeful, the two locked eyes with each other.

Raithe nodded. "I've seen them before during a spring wood gathering. They're these little lights that float above the grass."

"Those are fireflies."

"Sure, some are, but the brightest lights are leshies, whose favorite sport is luring children away from home. Sometimes to a fast-flowing river or deep lake where they drown."

"Don't you have any happy stories?" Malcolm grimaced. "You're depressing the fire spirit."

Raithe shrugged and tossed another stick in the flames. "I'm from Dureya; it's what we have."

Malcolm peered back over the top of the flames at the dark of the woods beyond, then shook his head. "I don't think it's leshies."

For a person who had been certain of his own death without Raithe, Malcolm was decidedly resistant to his guide's wisdom. "I'm not so sure. I think they've been confounding us," Raithe said, "hiding the obvious trails, keeping us lost in this blasted forest."

Malcolm opened his mouth to speak just as another clap rent the air. This time it creaked first, a yawning wrench and then the slap. More than that, Raithe heard faint laughter and distant singing.

The two men stared at each other, shocked.

"I smell food," Malcolm said.

Raithe was nodding. He did, too, something savory. The breeze had shifted, sending smoke in their direction but also the smell of cooked meat. "You might be right about it not being leshies. Could be crimbals instead. They're known to have great feasts and parties."

"Parties?" Malcolm got to his feet. "Maybe we should—"

"No, don't!" Raithe grabbed Malcolm's arm.

"But . . . *food*. You remember *food*, right? I mean *real* food?"

"That's how they lure you. Doorways in the trees lead to their homeland, a magical place called Nog. Once there, they'll lay you down in feather beds and play music while treating you to roasted boar, deer, beef, and lamb covered in cream and sweetened with honey—all you can eat."

Malcolm was licking his lips.

"Then they fill you with ale, wine, mead, and pies."

"Really? Pies? What kind?"

"Doesn't matter what kind, because you can't get out. Once you go in, once you eat their food, you're trapped forever in Nog."

Malcolm blinked. "So?"

"What do you mean *so*?"

"Is the food good?"

"I've heard it's supposed to be incredible."

"And the beds are soft and warm?"

Raithe nodded.

"So what you're saying is that we can stay here"— Malcolm gestured around them—"and starve in this horrific forest, or we could live the rest of our lives in a wonderland of abundance, music, and mirth. Sounds awful; let's go."

Raithe tried to think of a rebuttal. Framed that way, he was hard-pressed.

"Also"—Malcolm held up a finger—"what are the odds of the Fhrey finding us in this magical land of Nog?"

Raithe found it was his turn to stare blankly. Then he

looked into the dark of the trees in the direction of the laughter and song. "Help me put the fire out."

They scattered the sticks and stomped the flames to glowing coals, and then Raithe led the way into the trees beyond. With each step, the sounds grew louder. Voices, and at times a dog's bark, drifted on the night air. The world grew lighter as stars emerged from the thinning canopy. Raithe realized they had been on the edge of the forest. Together, the two climbed out into a field where a well-trodden road snaked beneath a half-moon. In the distance, firelight shone out of a wooden building's windows.

"Is *that* the land of Nog?" Malcolm asked.

"No," Raithe replied. "It's a roadhouse, a way station for travelers."

"We're travelers," Malcolm said with bubbling, hope-filled glee. "Do you think they'll give us food?"

Raithe shrugged. "Only one way to find out."

Raithe hated being stared at; all too often it marked the prelude to a fight. He also didn't care much for strangers; they set him on edge. Little wonder, then, that he wasn't pleased as he and Malcolm sat in a room surrounded by a dozen unfamiliar faces staring at them as they ate. Nothing had been said, at least nothing loud enough to hear. The whispers had started near a large wooden bowl where a pair of women dished out lamb stew, speaking softly to each man. After receiving a portion, the one getting his meal looked over. Sometimes they glanced at Malcolm, but mostly they stared at Raithe—as if he wore a pig for a hat. When the men returned to their places, they continued to stare, whispering among themselves.

"What do you think they're saying?" Raithe asked, nudging Malcolm in the ribs.

The former slave didn't raise his face from his bowl. "That you're a fine-looking man, followed by a debate

as to which of their sisters should be given in marriage."
He shrugged. "How should I know?"

"I think they're planning to cut our throats."

"I like my guess better." Malcolm finished the statement by wiping the bottom of the bowl with his finger and sucking it. "Maybe after my story we can get seconds."

"I didn't think you were hungry. You've taken forever to finish the little taste they gave us."

"I wanted to make it last in case it's all we get," Malcolm said, licking his bowl. "In general Rhune society, is it bad manners to suck on a bowl?"

"In general Rhune society, there's no such thing as manners, but I wouldn't refer to anyone as a *Rhune*. That's a Fhrey word, and we don't like it much, at least not in Dureya. Down here it might be different. They're more accustomed to doing what they're told. And as for the story you promised—you don't plan on telling them the truth, do you?"

"Of course not. I'm hungry, not a fool, and *that* story won't feed us. We'll get tossed out by those still awake."

"Well, just don't say anything that anyone would take offense at."

"Have a little faith."

Malcolm began sucking on the rim of the bowl.

Such an odd man, Raithe thought. Not because of Malcolm's affection for the bowl—that was the most normal thing he'd done. He was strange because of everything else. The former slave didn't have a beard and wore his hair short and combed. He sat too straight, cleaned his hands and face each morning and before every meal, complained about the stains on his clothes, spoke with a weird kind of elegance, and used a host of words that Raithe didn't recognize.

"Are you a good storyteller?"

"Ell ee," Malcolm replied with the bowl still in his mouth.

"What?"

Malcolm stopped sucking. "We'll see."

The roundhouse occupied most of the area within the palisade. There were pens to house animals and a shed for supplies, but the bulk of the road station was taken up by the hall they sat in. In Dureya, the hut's walls would have been made of clay and the cone-shaped roof fashioned from bundles of grass. This one was nicer, built of solid wood with a sturdy shake roof that probably wouldn't blow off with every strong wind. The space was large and there was plenty of room around an open fire pit—a pit that burned wood instead of dried dung.

"What's your names?" a man inquired, one of the older ones who'd finished his meal and was stretching his legs.

Maybe he was pushed into addressing them. More likely he was a leader or wanted to be seen as such. When he spoke, the whispers stopped, and everyone looked their way.

"What's yours?" Raithe asked, a sharpness in his voice.

"No need to be that way—just curious is all. A man can be curious, can't he?" He looked over his shoulder for support. Soft and squat, he was the sort who needed reassurance. "We know everyone else here. Seen each other on the road for years. That's Kane over there"—he pointed—"son of Hale, who passed on his route five years ago. He's done well with it, too. Over there is Hemp of Clan Menahan, a respected wool trader. I'm Justen of Dahl Rhen. Everyone knows me, but none of us have seen either of you before. So who are you?"

"But you already know our names," Raithe said. "The man at the gate asked and spread the word about us. I see you whispering, but I'm not hiding anything. Just trying to get by. We got lost in the forest. Seeing smoke and smelling food, we hoped to find some hospitality; that's all. Not here to make any trouble or push anyone around. Go ahead. Ask what you want. I'll answer."

"No reason to be so touchy. We're only traders." The

man looked around again, and many heads in the hall bobbed over their bowls. A few grumbled affirmative replies. All stared hard at Raithe, as if they expected him to perform magic. "See, we're trying to survive, same as you. My oxen drag logs up and down the trail between Dahl Rhen and Nadak, sometimes over to Menahan—they need wood out that way. I'm not the sort to look for trouble, either." Justen held up his hands and turned around. "You can see I don't have nothing. We leave our spears outside the hall—makes it friendlier, you know? An unspoken rule. But you're sitting here with copper on your back. Ain't no call for weapons."

"It's broken."

"Is that so?" He looked around at the other men, most of whom were putting down their bowls or turning in their seats. Eyes shifted and necks strained.

"The pattern of your leigh mor and the bedding you're sitting on . . . Is that the design of Clan Dureya?"

"That's right. What of it?" Raithe had expected this. "Go ahead, say it. You got something stuck in your teeth, some plague you want to blame on me? Go on and ask what you *really* want to know."

The man's face tightened. "All right. There's a rumor that a god was slain."

Of all things, Raithe hadn't expected *that*.

"Gods are immortal," he replied, pleased with how clever his response was. He picked up his empty bowl and pretended he was still eating.

"We thought so, too."

Raithe ran his finger around the inside of the empty bowl the way Malcolm had. "A rumor, then, some guy boasting."

Faces in the hall looked at one another.

"Weren't no man who said it. Word is the Fhrey themselves came down from Alon Rhist. They're looking for a Rhune who killed one of their own. They say it was a man from Dureya who used a copper sword. Not many of those around. Funny you have one. Also said the weapon broke in the fight. Apparently, it happened a week ago on the other side of the Bern." The man looked hard at Raithe. "Where *exactly* are you coming from?"

"Of course, of course. Makes sense, doesn't it?" Raithe was nodding. "Menahan is known for wool and pretty daughters. Everyone knows the best poets and musicians come from Melen. Nadak provides the finest furs, but what is Dureya known for? Causing trouble, right? That's what you're thinking. If a loaf of bread goes missing, a brawl starts, or an unwed daughter ends up with child, Dureyans are to blame. And when the gods come looking for a troublemaker, who's it gonna be?"

"Then how did your blade break? And come to think of it, that's a pretty specific detail, isn't it? Kinda strange that was mentioned and now you're here. You know what I think? I reckon a god was killed, and it was you who done it," Justen said.

He was standing as firmly as he could, making a fine show, but Raithe could knock him down easily enough. Justen should have known that, too. Fighting was the other thing the men of Dureya were known for. Living on rocks and stone made hard men, and Dureyan boys learned to swing early. That was the way of it—the only way for them at least.

"You're right!" Malcolm shouted as he stood up. All eyes shifted, including Raithe's. "He was the one who killed Shegon of the Asendwayr."

Raithe wanted to throttle the skinny, weasel-faced man, but it was out there now. The question was what to do about it. Raithe was never one for lying. That was what others did, not Dureyans. "Yeah, I did it."

"Why?" Justen asked.

"He killed my father. Right in front of me, with my father's blade. This one here." Raithe patted the scabbard still strapped to his back.

"But how is that possible?" a younger man asked. He sat bundled on a blanket, part of it over his shoulders like a woman's shawl. He might have been Kane, son of

Hale, but Raithe didn't have a head for faces and names. "They can't die."

Now you say that? Where was your tongue a minute ago, Kane? Raithe thought, but all he said was, "Apparently, they can."

"But *how* did you do it?" This time it was Justen again.

"I took the sword from my father's body and swung as hard as I could. The Fhrey had a weapon that sliced right through it. Cut it clean in half. I was dead. I knew it, and the Fhrey knew it. That's when—"

"That's when Raithe, son of Herkimer, the hero of Dureya, did something amazing," Malcolm interrupted. The thin man moved to the center of the roundhouse. He crouched slightly, fanning his fingers. He spoke in a loud, clear voice that carried across the hall and demanded attention. "You see, Shegon was a master of the hunt. All members of the Asendwayr are. I should know. I lived with him in Alon Rhist." He pointed to the metal collar around his neck. "His slave and personal valet. He was the worst possible sort of Fhrey, a cul if ever there was one. I've seen him and his kind raid Rhu—ah, *our*—villages and capture women. They don't rape them. Oh, no! Fhrey won't defile themselves with our women. Do you know what they do with them?"

"What?" several men in the hall asked together.

"They feed them to their hounds, because their beasts like soft meat."

Gasps and grumbles escaped lips.

"But as I said, Shegon was the worst of all. He and his band of butchers traveled the lands beyond the Bern, a pack of bloodthirsty wolves. I once saw him test a blade's sharpness by cutting off a child's hand. Severed it with two hacks. Unsatisfied, he commanded his smith to sharpen the blade further, then tried it once more. The child's other hand came free with a single slice. Shegon was a fiend—a vile monster—and a Fhrey, which meant he was arrogant. His overconfidence proved to be his undoing. Shegon saw no threat in Raithe or any man. A

Rhune—that's what they call us, and that's all they see—couldn't possibly inflict any harm. But never before had a Rhune fought back. No one had the courage, and none possessed the skill. The Fhrey have ruled the world for eons. They vanquished the Dherg, routed the giants, and chased the goblins into the sea. They have no equal, no fear of any living thing—until now."

Malcolm paused and scanned the room, and seeing he had everyone's attention, he continued. "So casual, so callous, was Shegon's attack that Raithe dodged it with a skillful leap. Shegon, who was so certain of an easy victory, stood in shock when Raithe slipped through his grasp. *How dare he!* I saw that thought painted on his face. *How dare Raithe not die!* In that moment of disbelief, Raithe acted brilliantly. For what Shegon couldn't know was that this was no ordinary Rhune before him. Raithe is a master of combat the likes of which this world has yet to see. The metal of his blade had broken, but the mettle of the man rang true. Using only the broken hilt of his sword, Raithe slashed at the villain's exposed wrist. So unaccustomed to pain, so shocked and dismayed, Shegon dropped his sword. Before it hit the ground, Raithe, son of Herkimer, caught it and stabbed upward, driving the blade home—right through the monster's throat!"

Every mouth in the hall hung agape, and each man leaned forward to hear better.

"Shegon—vile lord of the Fhrey—fell dead before Raithe. So shocked were the dozen other Fhrey—murderers and oppressors of men—that they ran in fear. As they took flight, he shouted after them that mankind would no longer bow to false gods!"

Malcolm straightened the folds of his stained and torn robes. "It was then that the great Raithe of Clan Dureya took the time to cleave my bonds of servitude. *Come with me!* he said. *Come with me and breathe the air of freedom.* We journeyed together through the terrible Crescent Forest, but I traveled unafraid, for Raithe the God Killer was by my side. Not even when leshies confounded our path, leaving us lost for days and nearing starvation, did I despair. You see, the spirits of the forest delighted in having so great a champion as the God Killer within its eaves. They confused us to keep him within their realm. After many days, he knew he wouldn't escape unless he could outwit the forest. Raithe cleverly posed a riddle. *Four brothers visit this wood,* he said. *The first is greeted with great joy; the second is beloved; the third always brings sad tidings; and the last is feared. They visit each year, but never together. What are their names?* While the forest was trying to solve the riddle, Raithe and I made our escape and only now emerged, starved and exhausted. And that is how we came to sit with you this night in this honored hall."

Malcolm returned to their blanket and gestured in Raithe's direction. "Before you— before all of you—sits a hero of the clans, a man who refused to die when a bloodthirsty Fhrey demanded a Rhune's life on a whim. Here is a hero who for one brief, wondrous moment struck a blow for the dignity and freedom of us all. Raithe, son of Herkimer, of Clan Dureya!"

He took his seat while the men in the hall clapped their bowls against the tables, drumming their approval. Justen raised a hand to stop them. "Hold on. Hold on. Wouldn't a man who killed a god and broke his blade take the god's sword as his own?"

Before Raithe could think, Malcolm threw back the blanket and revealed Shegon's golden-hilted sword, its blade and jewels gleaming in the firelight. "Indeed he would!"

The hall erupted in drumming once more.

"Are you crazy?" Raithe whispered.

"They liked the story."

"But it's not true."

"Really? I remember it *exactly* that way."

"But—"

A big man with a shaved head and a curly black beard stood up. He was taller than Raithe, and there were few people who fit that description. He wasn't merely tall. He looked as solid as an ox.

"Bollocks," he said, thrusting his chin out and pointing a finger at both of them. "So you have a pretty sword. So what? What does that prove? You don't look like a god killer to me. I'm Donny of Nadak, and you look like a pair of liars hoping for a free meal."

His words silenced the room, an uneasy void interrupted only by the pop and hiss of the fire.

Raithe looked over at Malcolm and whispered, "See. *This* is the problem with your plan. There's *always* going to be a Donny."

"'Course, you could prove it," Donny said. "The way I figure, a man capable of killing a god ought to be able to best little old me. What do you say, Raithe of Dureya? Think you could manage that?"

"Can you beat him?" Malcolm whispered.

Raithe looked at Donny and shrugged. "Looks a lot like my older brother Hegel."

"Can you do it without killing him?"

"Well, that makes it a lot harder," Raithe replied.

"Killing him won't get us more food."

"What did they do to you in Alon Rhist, feed you every day?"

"One of the many bad habits I've picked up."

"Well, little man?" Donny taunted. "I'm calling you a liar."

"You also called me little. I'm still trying to figure out which offends me the most."

Donny walked to the back of the roundhouse, where the remains of the lamb lay. He picked up a butcher knife.

"He's got a knife now," Raithe told Malcolm.

The ex-slave patted his belly and smiled.

Raithe removed the broken sword and gave it to Malcolm to go along with Shegon's blade. "Better hang on to these or I might be tempted."

The big man stepped away from the lamb and laughed

when he saw Raithe disarming. "I'm still using this knife."

"Figured you would," Raithe said.

"And I'm going to gut you."

"Maybe."

Raithe took off his leigh mor, leaving him in his buckskin. Growing up with three older, sadistic brothers, all of whom had been trained by a father who'd learned fighting from the Fhrey, had taught Raithe a few things. The first was that he could take a beating. The second was how much opponents underestimated a smaller man, especially when he was unarmed. His brothers often made that mistake.

Donny raised the knife, and Raithe saw the smile he had hoped would appear. His oldest brother, Heim, had made that same face—once.

Raithe expected Donny to move in slowly with his blade held high, perhaps holding his free hand outstretched to block anything Raithe might try. That was how Heim had fought, but Herkimer had trained his sons, and the old man didn't care how much damage they inflicted on one another. Didan had lost a finger once because Herkimer wanted to prove a point about losing concentration. Fact was, they all had learned to fight the Dureyan way—for survival.

Donny wasn't Dureyan.

The big man charged like a bull, flailing the knife above his head and screaming. Raithe could hardly believe it. This was the type of move an old woman with a broom might use to scare rabbits from the vegetable garden.

Raithe waited until the last moment, then stepped aside, leaving a knee behind. Donny didn't even try to swing. Maybe he'd planned to stab Raithe after knocking him down. Unfortunately for Donny, Raithe's knee landed squarely in the man's stomach. A whoosh of air came out, and Donny collapsed in a ball. Raithe stomped on the hand holding the knife, breaking at least one finger and persuading Donny to let go. A kick to the face left the big man whimpering.

"Are we done?" Raithe asked.

Donny had both hands over his face, sobbing.

"I asked, are we done?"

Donny howled but managed to nod.

"Okay, then, here—let me see." Raithe bent over the ox and pried the big man's hands away.

Blood ran from Donny's nose, which was skewed to one side.

"You're all right. You only broke your nose," Raithe lied. The last two fingers on Donny's right hand were unnaturally twisted, but Raithe didn't see any point bringing that up. Donny probably wasn't feeling them . . . not yet. His whole hand was probably numb.

Raithe got on his knees next to Donny. "I can fix your nose, but you have to trust me."

Donny looked nervous. "We're done fighting, right?"

Raithe nodded. "Didn't want to in the first place, remember? Now relax. I know how to do this. Done it to myself once—but don't try this yourself without lying down first or you might have to do it twice."

Raithe gently placed his fingers on the fractured bridge. "I won't lie to you. This will—"

Raithe snapped Donny's nose back in place with a practiced wrench. His father had taught them the importance of distraction, and one of the best ways was to act in midsentence, assuming the opponent was willing to talk. But it was his sister, Kaylin, who had applied the technique for medical purposes when she pulled out one of Raithe's baby teeth.

Donny screamed, then cringed in the dirt. He lay panting, as his uninjured fingers gingerly explored what his eyes couldn't see.

"All better," Raithe declared. "Well, it will be after you go through the black-eyed-raccoon stage, but you'll keep your handsome profile."

Several of the men approached, led by Justen. "Hingus!" he shouted to the proprietor. "Bring as much food as these two can eat and take it from my balance. It's not every day a man gets to dine with a hero."

"Bring mead," a man in a red cap said. "I'll give you another bundle of wool."

The young man with a blanket over his shoulders declared, "I'll give another pot of honey to have Raithe and his servant share the best spot near the fire with me."

Malcolm offered Raithe a wide smile.

Raithe nodded and replied, "You *are* a good storyteller."

CHAPTER FOUR

The New Chieftain

Strict laws governed the succession of power within the clan, traditions passed down through the generations by the Keeper of Ways. Nearly all involved men fighting, and it was the strongest among us who ruled.

— THE BOOK OF BRIN

Persephone winced and pulled, but the ring refused to come off. Little wonder, given that Reglan had slipped it on her finger twenty years before, when she was seventeen and he forty-one. She hadn't removed it since.

Twenty years.

It didn't seem so long ago, yet Persephone felt as if they'd always been together. The day he'd put the ring on, it had been too large. She'd wrapped string around the little silver band to hold it snug. The ring was a sacred relic handed down since the time of Gath, and she was terrified she'd lose it. She never did. The need for the string had disappeared during her first pregnancy. Staring at her hand, she realized how much she had changed over the years.

We changed each other.

"I'll get some chicken fat." Sarah moved toward the door.

"Hang on," Persephone said, stopping her. She wet her finger in her mouth. Then, with a firm grasp and clenched teeth, she painfully wrenched the metal band over her knuckle.

"Ow," Sarah said with a sympathetic grimace. "That

looked painful." Her wise, motherly tone spoke about more than the pain of a finger.

With a curious sort of mental hiccup, Persephone remembered that Sarah had been there when the ring was placed on her hand. Most marriages were informal and gradually built over time. The only public declaration came when a couple began sharing the same roof or a child was born. But Persephone had married a chieftain, which required a formal ceremony, and Sarah, her closest friend, had stood beside her. The ring and the torc were the badges of the Second Chair's office. But in Persephone's mind, the silver band had always been the symbol of Reglan's love.

Persephone nodded and tried not to cry. She'd done enough of that already, and her eyes and nose throbbed from rubbing.

After the death of her husband and with no son to inherit his father's position, Persephone was expected to leave the lodge to make way for the new chieftain and his family. More than a hundred years had passed since a chieftain's wife had failed in her most important responsibility: bearing a child who lived to assume the First Chair. Maeve, the Keeper of Ways, had been consulted, and she decreed that Konniger, Reglan's Shield, would assume the position. There might be challengers, so the matter wasn't *officially* settled. But no matter who prevailed, Persephone's fate would be the same; she had nowhere to go.

Sarah had been there for her twenty years before, and she once again stood by Persephone's side, offering a place to live. From the outside, all roundhouses were as identical as the materials and land allowed. On the inside, Sarah's was by far the most welcoming. Filled with animal-hide rugs, baskets, a spinning wheel, a sophisticated loom, and a huge bed covered in furs, it offered a comforting respite. An open-hearth fire in the center of the floor kept the space warm. Without a chimney, a thick layer of smoke hovered at the peak of the cone-shaped thatched roof. Its slow escape dried herbs and cured meat and fish hanging from the rafters.

Part of the coziness came from the piles of wool, thread, yarn, and the stacks of folded cloth that provided softness. But what made this roundhouse special were the walls—or wall—as roundhouses had only one. The interior was plastered in daub, and designs of great beauty had been painted by Sarah's daughter, Brin. Some were as simple as charcoal outlines of little hands; others were circles and swirls of yellow and orange paint. A few were complex illustrations of people and events. Even the logs framing the entryway, not to mention the door itself, displayed celestial swirls and stars. The circular wall of Sarah's home was a marvel of artistic wonder.

"I can't believe I forgot to take it off." Persephone held out the ring. "Would you mind returning this to the lodge?"

Sarah took it and nodded, offering pitying eyes. Persephone didn't want to be pitied. She'd always seen her role as an example to her people and found herself ill suited to the role of woeful widow.

"No, wait." Persephone stopped her. "I should be the one to give it to Tressa. It will look like I disapprove if I don't."

"Might not be Tressa," Sarah said. She walked to the door and peered out. "Holliman has challenged Konniger. They're getting ready to fight now."

"Holliman?" Persephone said, confused. "Are you serious?"

Persephone joined her friend at the door. The front of Sarah's home faced the little grassy patch of open space before the lodge steps, which the dahl's residents used for outdoor gatherings. Between the burning braziers in front of the stone statue of Mari, the two men checked the straps on their wooden shields, each armed with an ax.

"It's not like he doesn't stand *any* chance." Sarah held the door open as the two looked out.

"Holliman is only a huntsman," Persephone said. "Konniger has been Reglan's Shield for years."

"He's big."

"Konniger is bigger."

"Not by much. And there's more to combat than size. There's speed and—"

"Experience?" Persephone stared at Sarah as she let the door close. "I guess it's good that the matchup is so one-sided, Konniger won't have to kill Holliman. He'll yield quickly. We can't afford to lose such a talented hunter."

The door jerked open, and Sarah's daughter entered. "Sorry I'm late."

Brin was tall for her age, most of the height in her legs, and in many ways she was a ganglier version of her mother. Sarah possessed a tiny nose and an easy smile, and although not particularly beautiful, she'd always been remarkably cute. Both braided their hair, or more likely Sarah braided both, the obvious choice in style given that Sarah was the dahl's most talented weaver.

The girl flopped on the bed and sighed heavily.

"Something wrong?" Sarah asked.

"It's Maeve. She's crazy and being stupid."

"Brin!" her mother scolded.

"I mean, I don't know how she expects me to learn everything down to the emphasis on words and the order of lists of names."

"Maeve is an extremely talented and capable Keeper."

"But she's old," Brin said.

"So am I. So is Seph, and I can assure you we aren't crazy."

"Okay, but if you're old, *she's ancient,* and definitely losing her mind." Brin bounced up to a sitting position and crossed her legs. "It's insane to think a person can remember *that* much detail. Who cares if Hagen comes after Doden in the list of men slain at the Battle of Glenmoor?"

"I know it must be difficult keeping everything straight," Sarah told her. "But you shouldn't blame your failures on others. You won't be Keeper that way. You need to pay better attention."

"But . . ." Brin frowned and folded her arms.

"Your mother is right," Persephone said. "Being a Keeper isn't only about remembering the stories; it's an important responsibility. It's crucial that you know the customs and laws. I realize you find details such as when to plant which crops boring, but those are the kinds of things that determine whether everyone lives or dies. That's why Keepers are so revered."

"I know, but . . ." Brin looked hurt and turned away.

Persephone sighed. "Brin, I'm sorry. I'm just . . . listen, you'll make a fine Keeper, but you're still young. You're only fifteen and have plenty of time to learn. You need to listen to Maeve, do as she says, and don't argue. If she gets frustrated, she'll pick someone else."

"Which wouldn't be so awful," Sarah said. "You could get back to learning the loom."

"Mother, please!" Brin rolled her eyes, then got up and reached for the empty water gourd.

"Well, you were the one pointing out how old I am. I'm going to need someone to take over when I'm too feeble."

"I didn't say you are old. I said Maeve is old—then I clarified that she is ancient. You were the one who brought up your age."

"Pretty good memory," Persephone said.

Brin flashed her a mischievous grin.

"You're supposed to be on my side, Seph," Sarah told her, then turned to her daughter. "Your grandmother, Brinhilda, taught me her secrets to making Rhen cloth, and—"

"And you hated it," Brin said. "You despised how Dad's mother forced you to work at it for hours at a time."

"Of course I did. I was a stubborn young lady like you, but I did it. I learned, and it's a good thing, too. Otherwise, you and half the dahl would be standing here naked, and what would we do with the wool your father shears?"

"Being a Keeper is important, as well. Persephone just said so, and she's the Second Cha—" Brin stopped herself and covered her mouth, looking as if she'd accidentally stepped on a newborn chick.

"It's okay," Persephone told her. She rubbed the empty place where the ring used to be. "We all have changes to get used to."

The clangs of battle erupted outside as the fight commenced. A curse was followed by a grunt. Then came the gasp of spectators followed by cheers, boos, and the thud of ax on shield. Brin rushed toward the door, but her mother caught her by the wrist. "You don't need to see."

"I'm getting water. You need water, right?"

"Brin . . ." Sarah spoke the name dressed in a heavy coat of disappointment.

"But I—"

More grunts could be heard and the sound of shuffling feet, then a crack was followed by a scream. Another collective gasp was heard, but this time there wasn't a cheer.

The fight for chieftain had ended, and another battle began—this one waged by a team of women trying to save a man's life.

"Move!" Padera shouted.

The little woman was the first to react. With a round head, full bosom, and ample hips, she looked much like a skirted snowman as she bustled forward, shoving aside men twice her size. Ancient when Persephone was born, Padera was the oldest living member of Clan Rhen. She'd been a farmer's wife and had successfully raised six children and countless cows, pigs, chickens, and goats. Padera also regularly won the fall harvest contest for biggest vegetables and best pies. There wasn't anyone more respected on the dahl.

The ring of onlookers broke on Padera's approach,

giving Persephone a clear view of the common where the two men had fought. The sight made her gasp. From the knee down, Holliman's leg was covered in blood. Glistening with sweat, Konniger backed away, his ax dangling from loose fingers, the sharpened stone edge dark and dripping. He stared at Holliman with an expression Persephone struggled to place. If anything, Konniger looked guilty.

Holliman rose up on elbows that he jabbed into the grass. Arching his back and wailing in pain, he dragged his body to . . . well, to nowhere Persephone could discern. She didn't think Holliman knew, either. He probably didn't realize that he was moving or that he was pumping a stream of blood, which soaked a wide swath of spring grass in a thick coat of brilliant red.

"Hold him down!" Padera called out. "And get me a rope!"

At her command, several people grabbed Holliman's arms, pinning him, while others ran off in search of twine.

Roan, who had been in the ring of spectators, rushed to Padera's side and stripped off Holliman's thin rawhide belt. She held it out to Padera.

"Around the thigh, girl." The old woman held up the bleeding leg. "Loop it above the knee."

Roan executed the instructions as if she'd been asked to tie closed a bag of apples. Padera's indifference in the face of so much carnage was understandable. The old woman regularly set bones, even those that had broken through skin. She also sewed up deep wounds and delivered breech babies from both women and livestock. But Roan taking the initiative, and with such stoicism, was surprising. The young woman, who until recently had been the slave of Iver the Carver, was normally timid as a field mouse. She rarely spoke and was seldom seen outside the carver's home, which she had inherited upon his death. But there she was, acting with precision and clarity, undaunted by Holliman's screams, and either unconcerned or unaware that her dress was soaking up blood.

Each woman took an end of the rawhide strap and then pulled it tight. The fountain of blood slowed to a stream.

"Get a stick!" Padera growled.

Straining with both hands on the leather, Roan focused on Sarah's daughter. "Brin! Get the hammer from my bag."

Brin squeezed through the crowd, rushed to Roan's side, and pulled open the satchel. Out of it the girl drew a small hammer.

"Here, child. Lay the handle where the straps cross," Padera ordered.

Brin hesitated, looking at the blood and cringing with Holliman's screams.

"Do it!" Padera shouted.

Persephone pushed forward and took the hammer. She placed it where indicated. Padera and Roan crossed the straps, wrapping it.

"Twist," Padera ordered.

With weak, shaking hands, Persephone managed to find the strength to tighten the belt. The stream of blood subsided to a trickle, then a drip.

"Hold it there," Padera commanded, then pointed in the direction of Mari's statue. "Fetch down a brazier."

The closest man removed his shirt and wrapped his hands. He placed the pan on the ground near the women. Padera snuffed out the fire, leaving the smoldering wood.

Holliman's struggles were subsiding even before the hot poker used to stir coals was pressed to his leg. He let out a violent scream, then went limp. The smell was horrific, and Persephone held one hand under her nose while the other remained clamped tightly to Roan's hammer.

Around them, faces clustered, peering over shoulders. Those who spoke did so in worried whispers.

Holliman was one of the dahl's best hunters. The deer he killed in winter were often the difference between life and death. He had no children, and his wife had been lost to a fever three winters back. He hadn't taken another. Too heartbroken it was said. Although not someone Persephone would pick as chieftain, he was a good man.

Konniger leaned against the well, waiting and still holding his bloody ax. Persephone wouldn't have chosen him, either. He didn't impress her as being wise or the sort to inspire others. He was a warrior, a shield, an ax.

Padera, who was wrapping the blackened flesh of Holliman's knee, paused. She stared at his face as if the unconscious man had asked a question. Putting aside the wounded leg, she reached over and laid a hand to the side of the man's neck. As she did, the furrows on her craggy face deepened. The urgency the old woman had radiated died along with Holliman. She untied the leg and returned Roan's hammer. Then the old woman walked to the well to clean up.

"Congratulations," Padera told Konniger. "You're the new chieftain."

CHAPTER FIVE

Before the Door

Delicate, radiant, beautiful, in our eyes she was every inch a god, and she scared us to death.
— THE BOOK OF BRIN

While every other Fhrey in Erivan celebrated, Arion stood alone in a darkened tomb. She put a hand on the marble urn that held Fane Fenelyus's ashes. The vessel was eight feet tall, wider at the top, tapered near the bottom, and polished to a smooth luster.

Just outside, crowds filled Florella Plaza, all the avenues, and even the palace. A thousand bonfires blazed, commemorating the start of Fane Lothian's reign.

Less than a month and they've already forgotten you.

Arion rested her head against the urn. The stone was cold, so very cold. "I worry about what's to come and could use your counsel." She paused, straining to hear any faint sound.

Fenelyus had been the first to wield the Art and founded the Miralyith tribe. In her time, she'd single-handedly defeated entire armies, built the great tower of Avempartha, and become the fifth fane, leader of all Fhrey.

Is it so unreasonable to hope she can speak to me from the other side? Why not? The old lady did everything else.

But if Fenelyus had replied, Arion couldn't have heard

over the whoops, cheers, and laughter of the city's celebration.

The tomb of the old fane was dark; Arion hadn't bothered to light the braziers. Instead, she left the door open to admit the moonlight, and along with it came the noise. Somewhere a group was singing "Awake the Spring Dawn," but their rendition was so bad that winter was certain to return. The clamor ruined her mood. The very idea that anyone could be happy after Fenelyus's passing made her angry. Death wasn't something Arion was used to. None of them were.

Why am I the only one here? The only one who seems to care?

Arion tried to block out the shouts and the singing and focused on the urn. She wasn't going to hear any messages that night, but that wasn't really why she was there. Arion just wanted to say goodbye, again. "I'm going to teach Mawyndulë as you asked. Lothian has decided to allow it. But will that be enough? After all you did, after all you gave me, taught me, will anything ever be enough? I just wanted to—"

Outside, cries of celebration became shrieks of terror.

She rushed out to find a flooded Florella Plaza, the entire square had turned into a lake. From the steps of Fenelyus's tomb, Arion could have dived from the porch of the sepulcher and not hit bottom. Streamers and banners, splintered boards that once had been part of a stage, and other debris bobbed and spun on the surface. People thrashed and gasped for air. Those who could swim, screamed; those who couldn't weren't able to.

Arion flung out her arms and with one loud clap exploded the water. Like stomping in a puddle, the lake burst in a spray that flew in all directions. She did this three more times before the stone was visible again. What had been a marketplace recently decorated for the coronation was now a disaster of shattered shops and horrified people spitting water and holding on to poles or one another.

A gaggle of soggy youth picked themselves up, laughing. Arion marched toward them. "Who's responsible?"

Eyes shifted to the tall one in a powder-blue robe with a smirk on his face.

His name was Aiden, a graduate from the Estramnadon Academy of the Art less than a decade ago. Arion had taught him advanced chords. A bright kid. Looking at their faces, she remembered having taught all of them. Some of the younger ones were still in school.

Aiden held up his hands in defense. "Hey, we all agreed there was absolutely no better use for water on a night like this than a living sculpture of Fane Lothian. Am I right?" He grinned at his fellow conspirators. A few smiled and sniggered. "Certainly no sense drinking it. Am I right? Am I right?"

Aiden staggered, and the rest of them laughed.

"You're drunk," Arion said.

"But that's not why it failed." Aiden pointed at Makareta. She'd been one of Arion's students as well. A mousy introvert with a wonderful talent for sculpting stone. "She took too long getting the features just right. Perfectionist, you know."

Makareta scowled and blushed at the same time. They were all drunk.

"You tapped the Shinara River for a sculpture?" Arion asked. "Here. In the square?"

"Genius, am I right? We were gonna have it smile and wink as people walked by."

Behind them, an elderly Fhrey coughed as she got to her feet. She struggled to drag hair from her face as she stared across the plaza. "My stand. It's gone."

"Do you see what you've done?" Arion asked the students. "If I hadn't been here, if I hadn't intervened, she might have drowned!"

Aiden looked at the old Fhrey and shrugged. "Who cares? She's not Miralyith. Lothian proved how insignificant, how useless the other tribes are now. If they can't take care of themselves, they don't deserve to live."

Makareta must have had less to drink than the others,

or perhaps she'd paid more attention in Arion's classes, because she took a quick step back.

With a hiss and a squeezed fist, Arion summoned light and turned Aiden into a living torch. He shrieked, and the square glowed with brilliant fire as tongues of flame slithered up and down the ringleader's body. The others fell over themselves trying to get away. Looking back, they cringed at the sight of their accomplice burning to death. Even the elderly Nilyndd crafter looked aghast, one arm raised to protect her face, eyes wide in horror.

With a quick puff of air, as if she were blowing out a candle, Arion extinguished Aiden. The ex-student shook but appeared unharmed.

"Illusion," Makareta whispered.

Arion took a step closer to Aiden. "Not so drunk now, *am I right*?" She glared at him, and when she spoke again, her tone was cold. "Here's the problem with the young: You think you're invincible. Just because Ferrol's Law prevents me from killing you doesn't mean you're impervious to harm." She crept closer. "How painful do you think it would be to live three thousand years without skin? *That* I *can* do. And I *will* if I hear you speaking in such a way again. Any of you! We are *all* Fhrey. Do you understand?"

All heads nodded but none as vigorously as Aiden's.

"Now clean up this mess and make restitution for anything you can't restore, or Ferrol help me I'll—"

They were moving before she finished. Arion caught Makareta before she could set off to join the others.

"I expect better from you. You're smarter than that. You should stick to your sculptures and paintings. They're lovely, and the world can always use more beauty. There's plenty of ugly to go around."

Makareta couldn't quite look her in the eye but managed to say, "I'd like to think the Art is for greater things than pretty pictures and carvings."

Arion nodded. "Perhaps, but certainly nothing so wonderfully pure of purpose." Then she allowed herself to look back at the tomb of Fenelyus. "And a thing wrought in stone is a beauty and a truth that lasts forever."

The next morning things had calmed down. The celebrants were sleeping, and Arion was looking forward to her first day as the prince's tutor. Passing through the Garden of Estramnadon, she spotted her mother sitting on a bench directly across from the Door. Arion hadn't seen Nyree in at least five hundred years, but little about her had changed. She still wore her cloud-white hair long and loose, still sat straight and proper, and dressed in what could have been the same white asica Arion had last seen her wearing. The garment's folds enveloped Nyree in a monochromatic pile of silk. The elderly Fhrey presented an image so ancient that it appeared she'd outlived color.

"Hello, Mother."

"Oh, it's you," Nyree said with an indifferent tone that nevertheless translated as disappointment.

Arion expected something else, something cutting, but her mother merely continued to sit with hands clasped in her lap, looking past her daughter at the sacred Door.

"That's it?" Arion asked. "You haven't seen me in half a millennium and *oh, it's you* is all you can say?"

Nyree turned and faced Arion. She tilted her head up, squinting as she studied her daughter. "You look ridiculous, shaving your head like that. Also, you're too thin and pale, but I suppose they don't let you out much now that you're a famous magician."

"An Artist, Mother. Miralyith are Artists, not magicians. Magicians perform tricks using sleight of hand. Artists raise mountains, control the weather, and reroute rivers."

"You use magic. That makes you a magician."

Nyree's gaze left Arion again and returned to the Door.

It isn't only the asica that hasn't changed, Arion thought.

She sat down beside her mother, who frowned and shifted over despite having plenty of room. For no reason Arion was willing to admit, she, too, sat unusually straight and adjusted the folds of her asica, regretting that morning's choice of bright yellow with ornate blue piping.

The two sat for several minutes in silence, listening to songbirds in the trees and the trickle of streams and the miniature waterfalls that skilled artisans had crafted to perfection over the centuries. After a minute or two, Arion also looked at the Door on the other side of the path. Painted and repainted bright white, the Door was an otherwise nondescript gate in a solid, circular wall supporting an enclosed dome. Ivy and flowering vines had covered the dome and sides ages ago, but nothing encroached on the Door's surface. Before it, several stone benches had been placed for visitors to sit and contemplate the simple white threshold.

"You're looking well," Arion offered. "I like your asica. Is it new?"

"No."

Arion waited. Nyree remained silent.

"How is Era?"

"I don't know. I haven't spoken to your father in centuries."

"Oh, I hadn't heard." Arion tucked a tiny edge of piping out of sight. "I recently separated from Celeste. So it's just me in my little house again."

"I'm sure it was the filth that drove him out."

"*Her*, Mother, not *him*. Celeste is a—never mind."

Arion found herself slouching and straightened up again.

Why do I let her do this to me? I'm not a child in my first century. Nor am I insignificant. I am—

"I've been appointed to tutor the prince," Arion said.

"But not in the faith of our lord Ferrol, I take it," her mother responded without looking away from the Door.

"Of course not, Mother. I'm Miralyith now. I have been for nearly a thousand years."

"Oh, you're right," she said without a bit of surprise in her voice. Instead, a colorless, odorless poison coated her words.

"You know, most mothers would be proud to have a daughter rise to such an important position in the fane's court."

Nyree made a sound with her nose, less than a snort and more than a sniff but most certainly unfavorable. "If the fane were a devout member of the Umalyn tribe rather than a godless Miralyith, I'd agree."

"We aren't godless, Mother. At least no less so than the other tribes."

"Oh, no? I've heard the rumors. Miralyith claim the Art has elevated them above everyone else. Some even declare themselves gods. I've never heard a member of any other tribe making such blasphemous claims."

"The Rhunes believe the Instarya are gods. Why aren't you complaining about them?"

"That's different. The Rhunes aren't Fhrey. They're barely one step above rabbits. They see gods everywhere. The only Fhrey they've ever met are the Instarya, and I've never heard of anyone from that tribe claiming to be gods. I can't say the same about the Miralyith. Besides, what a Rhune believes is of no consequence. I'm sure ants consider mice to be gods, too. Such notions don't diminish Ferrol."

"If you took the time to talk to a few Miralyith rather than basing assumptions on hearsay, you might discover any ideas of divinity are in the minority."

"And are *you* in this *minority*?" Nyree asked.

"No."

Nyree smoothed nonexistent wrinkles from her asica. "Well, I'm sure it won't be long before you join their ranks, what with you becoming so *important* and all."

"I don't want to fight," Arion said.

"Fight? Who's fighting?" Nyree leaned back, folded her arms, and lifted her chin so that she was looking down her nose at the Door.

"I came here for a few moments of tranquil contemplation. Nothing more," Nyree added.

Superior even to it, Arion thought.

They sat again in silence, and Arion wondered if she should leave. She hadn't expected to meet her mother that morning, although she should have. All the Umalyn high priests and priestesses were in the city of Estramnadon to witness the coronation of the new fane, and her mother always took every opportunity to visit the Door. Given that Nyree was a morning person prone to early-dawn meditations, Arion could have calculated her mother's Garden visit down to the minute, but she hadn't. Nyree spent countless hours contemplating the disappointment otherwise known as her daughter, but Arion gave no thought to her mother. This stab of guilt prompted her to make one last attempt before departing.

"Is there nothing positive you wish to say to me?" Arion asked.

Nyree appeared surprised by the question. She didn't look at Arion, but she no longer stared faithfully at the Door. Her sight fluttered across the ground while she thought. After a long moment, during which Arion's heart sank with each passing second, Nyree nodded, straightened, and smiled. Arion suspected the grin wasn't born from pride in her daughter but from the pleasure of beating a dare.

"I'm pleased to see you in the Garden. I wouldn't have thought you came here. It's good to find that despite turning away from your tribe to join the ranks of the new ruling class, you still revere the faith enough to contemplate the mysteries of the Door."

As backhanded a compliment as it was, Arion simply nodded. She didn't have the heart to tell her mother she had been cutting through the Garden because it was the shortest route to the palace.

Perhaps Nyree wished to leave her daughter on a positive note or wanted to quit while ahead, but whatever the reason, she stood up. "And I'll leave you to do just that, as I wouldn't wish to deprive you of what is certainly the high point of your day."

"Will you be here again tomorrow?"

Nyree shook her head. "I'm only here to grant blessings on the new fane, which we did yesterday. We witnessed that ridiculous ceremony and watched as the new fane planted his *exalted backside* on the Forest Throne. Then we saw the whole city go insane in celebration. A bunch of your deranged Miralyith flooded Florella Plaza; did you know that?"

"Those were students, and they were trying to make a sculpture of Fane Lothian out of the waters of the Shinara River. They weren't successful."

"No, they weren't, because success is only achieved through physical labor, faith in Ferrol, and determination of the spirit. I still pray that one day you'll come to understand those truths."

She walked away before Arion could say anything more, even goodbye. Arion lingered on the bench, watching her mother go.

I'll never see her again. I wonder if she cares.

Neither Nyree nor Arion was young. Nyree was pushing twenty-five hundred, and Arion had recently turned two thousand. Fhrey rarely lived more than three thousand years. Since the previous fane had ruled for nearly twenty-six hundred years, and it had taken a coronation to bring Nyree into the city, both of them would likely be dead before another opportunity arose. Of course, Arion could visit her mother, but she saw no point in traveling for days to repeat this encounter.

Arion sighed, flopped against the back of the bench, and looked at the Door. She couldn't help it; the thing was right across from her. She walked by the relic every day, but she hadn't really looked at it in more than a century. Like her mother, it hadn't changed.

Most people wondered what was on the other side, and Arion was no different. This unknowable truth was the reason for the benches. Fhrey would come to the

Garden to sit and contemplate the transcendent world beyond.

Maybe it was guilt brought on by her mother or perhaps because she hadn't done so in such a long time, but Arion closed her eyes, cleared her mind, and prayed.

"She's wrong."

Arion was pulled from her meditation when she heard the voice and opened her eyes. Sitting on the next bench over, a fellow in a dingy, brown robe leaned forward, elbows on knees, staring at the Door as people usually did, just as she had done.

"Success," he continued, "is achieved most consistently through cruelty and deception. Determination of the spirit certainly helps, but faith in Ferrol is a currency as valuable as a pair of shoes two sizes too small."

"It's not polite to eavesdrop," Arion replied. "That was a private conversation."

Arion stood to go. She'd already lingered too long and might be late for her first instruction with the prince. The lad was only twenty-five years old and in desperate need of training in the ways of the Art. His previous instructors had been too lenient, leaving the prince with a woeful lack of skill. Before Fenelyus's death she had asked Arion to take over her grandson's education. *He'll rule one day, and I fear he will be a curse if something isn't done,* Arion's mentor had said.

It had come as a surprise when the new fane agreed to honor his mother's wishes. Arion had been convinced that Lothian disliked her and was jealous of his mother's attention toward someone who wasn't related. *You should be more like Arion,* Fenelyus used to say, oblivious to the insult to her son and unconcerned about the possible trouble it might cause Arion once Lothian assumed the throne. So far, the new fane had surprised her.

Arion took a step toward the palace, but the fellow spoke again. Pointing across from them, he said, "That Door can't be opened. Ever try? You could cleave it with an ax, ram it with a tree, or set fire to its wood, and nothing would happen. Even a master of the Art can't breach it. Such a small simple door, but all the power of nature is useless against it. So the question is, how did she do it?"

"How did who do what?" Arion asked.

"Fenelyus. How did she get inside? How did she get past the Door?"

"I don't know that she did." Arion didn't care for this stranger. A full head of hair indicated he probably wasn't a Miralyith, which made her wonder about his comment, *Even a master of the Art can't breach it.*

How does he know what the Art is and isn't capable of? Arion wondered.

"Oh, she did. Trust me."

Arion didn't trust him, not in the least. Her discomfort wasn't merely because he was a stranger; his appearance was disturbing. She prided herself on proper grooming, and he was the most unkempt person she had ever seen. His brown robe was frayed, torn, and stained in more than a few places.

He has actual dirt under his fingernails. She shuddered at the sight and turned away.

"No one saw her go in or come out," he went on despite Arion's obvious avoidance. "The visit was all very hush-hush, and she denied it—or rather avoided the subject—for the remainder of her life."

"Then she didn't go inside," Arion declared. "Fenelyus was an extremely honest person. I knew her well."

"I know."

Arion looked back at him then. "You know what?"

"She was the mother you always wished you'd had, instead of the pompous, pious, prejudiced prude who just left. Nyree still considers your decision to leave your birth tribe and join the Miralyith an act of heresy. She can't understand why you turned your back on the priesthood to become one of *them*."

Arion felt uneasy. She was certain she'd only referred to Nyree as *Mother*, yet this man had used her name.

Since her mother lived in seclusion, it was unlikely the two were acquaintances. Even more disturbing, Arion didn't remember seeing this man while talking to her mother. For that matter, she hadn't seen anyone around them during their chat.

Has he been spying on me? And if so, why?

"Who are you?" she demanded.

He smiled. "You don't have time for me to answer that; you have a prince to teach. The only reason you stopped was because you accidentally stumbled on your mother while cutting through the Garden on your way to the palace."

The uneasy sensation turned to a chill.

If he'd somehow overheard their conversation, he would know about tutoring the prince. It's even possible he could have known about her history with Nyree—a lot of people did. Even if he didn't, he could have guessed as much after listening to them. But thinking more carefully, she was now certain no one had been around them during their conversation.

And how could he know why I'm here?

"Who are you?" she asked again.

"For the sake of expediency, let's limit the answer to a name. You can call me Trilos."

His cavalier attitude made him even more of an enigma. Although her mother wasn't impressed with Arion's accomplishments, almost everyone else was. Being a ranked member of the ruling tribe demanded respect in and of itself. But the Art made Miralyith practically invincible—as demonstrated during the recent challenge—and most Fhrey avoided any contact with practitioners of the Art if at all possible. Those who *did* summon the courage to speak would do so reverently, carefully avoiding anything that might provoke ire. And Trilos had said more than enough to get on her nerves. Ferrol's Law prevented Fhrey from killing Fhrey, but as she had reminded Aiden, it didn't prevent inflicting pain. Miralyith were called Artists because of the creativity needed to manifest magic, and when that creativity was applied to acts of retribution, the results could be terrifying.

Maybe she had been premature in her assessment of his tribal status. Most Miralyith kept their heads shaved in the belief that knots and snarls impeded the flow of the Art, but even Fenelyus had maintained a luxuriant mane that grew wavy and thick down to the middle of her back, but that was Fenelyus. Being the first to wield the Art, she didn't know the impediments knotted hair created. Once she found out, she was too old to care.

I've done well enough in ignorance, wouldn't you say? the old fane had told Arion. *And I admit to my vanity. I wouldn't look nearly as beautiful without hair as you do.*

Using the Art, Arion performed the mystical equivalent of a harsh stare, examining Trilos. Most often this revealed only a person's demeanor represented in the form of colors, which wasn't terribly useful. One didn't need the Art to detect emotions or moods, but if the subject was an Artist, the scrutiny would provide insights about his or her proficiency. What Arion discovered was nothing—nothing at all. According to the Art, Trilos didn't exist.

"*What* are you?" she asked.

He smiled. "Fenelyus was no more capable of opening the Door than you or even I, so a more interesting question is *how* did she do it?"

You or even I?

Arion felt an unfamiliar twinge of fear. Trees had gone from seeds to towering giants since the last time she'd felt afraid. Fear was a childhood monster banished to a distant memory after she'd discovered the Art—at least the life-threatening brand of terror.

But this isn't life threatening, is it?

A person brandishing a blade was an obvious threat. The truly unknown, when it arrived uninvited and used your mother's name, possessed a horror all its own. Arion was Miralyith—the next best thing to a god according to some ardent practitioners—but what sat beside her was beyond her ability to fathom.

"The answer is obvious when you think about it," Trilos said, and bit into an apple. "I'm sure you would have figured it out if you weren't so preoccupied. The answer is this . . . Fenelyus didn't open the Door."

Did he have the apple before? She couldn't remember. *Maybe it was in his hand all along and I just— Wait, where did he get an apple in early spring?*

She watched him chew, the juice of the fruit slipping over his lower lip and running down his chin. When at last he swallowed, he said, "The Door was opened *for* her."

He smiled as if expecting her to care, or maybe he thought she would be impressed or intrigued. Instead, she focused on the impossibility of the juice dripping from his chin. Arion was an accomplished Artist, probably the fourth most powerful in the world now that Fenelyus had passed, but she couldn't manifest creation. As far as she knew, no one could. Not even something as simple as an apple.

"Now you have to ask yourself, who opened it for her, and why?"

"What do you want with me?"

"Do you know what's inside?"

He wasn't going to answer any questions. She considered walking away and wondered if he would let her.

Let me? The thought was odd, irrational.

She had no reason to believe he would interfere or cause harm, and Arion was far from helpless. So it was strange that she felt threatened. She remained standing in front of the bench—her curiosity battling trepidation. Curiosity won out, and she replied, "The First Tree."

Trilos nodded as he chewed. "Your mother would be proud. Yes, the oldest living thing is currently encased in a sarcophagus of stone accessible only by a small white door that can't be opened."

"Is there a point? I need to leave."

"History repeats itself. Frequently, in fact, but not by

its own doing." Trilos looked at the Door. "Once does not make a pattern, so the world is about to change again, about to go for a spin. You'll be at the center, I think, able to influence the tilt, much like Fenelyus. You need to be heedful of strangers. Strangers and doors. Then we'll both find out."

"Find out what?"

"Who opened that Door."

CHAPTER SIX

Rumors

*That spring, we had a new chieftain named Konniger.
We also had a new mystic. Her name was Suri. Konniger
had a talent for drinking, boasting, and the ax, but Suri
could talk to trees.*

— THE BOOK OF BRIN

For the past twenty years, Persephone had sat in the Second Chair beside her husband at every general meeting of the clan. That morning she entered the lodge as a visitor. It felt strange walking into what had been her home—into a world of memories—as a guest. Her eyes were drawn to the changes. The woodpile had been moved to the east wall and the bear rug brought down from the bedroom upstairs. Konniger's ax hung from a winter pillar. Of all these changes, the one she couldn't help staring at was the addition of Reglan's shield to the pantheon of past chieftains' weapons hanging from the rafters.

The inhabitants of the dahl clustered around the central fire, sitting on the floor. Konniger sat in the First Chair, waiting for the crowd to settle. Although he had suffered no wounds from his duel with Holliman, he still bore the gash on his head from the fight with the bear. The bandages were gone, but the bright-pink marks were slow to fade. From the way Konniger avoided looking Persephone in the eye, she imagined the injuries were trivial compared with the deeper pain of failing to protect his chieftain and friend.

Beside him was his wife, Tressa, wearing Persephone's

silver torc and ring. A circlet of spring flowers adorned
her elaborately braided hair. Persephone had been terrified her first day on display; Tressa didn't look the least
bit frightened. She rubbed the arms of the chair, squirm-
ing like an excited child; a great smile hoisted her round
cheeks.

Persephone felt sorry for her. *She has no idea what
she's in for. She sees it as a grand party, but that won't
last.*

A few in the crowd looked over at Persephone and
smiled awkwardly, unsure how to act. Her presence
made the gathering uncomfortable. Everyone saw Konniger's first official meeting as an end to the mourning
period, and she was the leftover debris of a once beloved, but now ruined, reign. She purposely sat in the
rear to give Konniger and Tressa the chance to establish
themselves. Persephone's plan was to remain silent and
invisible.

The lodge filled, causing everyone to shift and press
tightly together. Some from the outlying villages had
come, and the room had never been so packed. Everyone was there, including Adler and Hegner, the two men
maimed in the bear hunt. Adler had gained the nickname One-Eye. Hegner, having lost his hand, was now
called The Stump. Persephone didn't use either moniker
out of respect for those who had received their wounds
in defense of her husband. Like Persephone, they had
sequestered themselves since Reglan's death but had
come out for this. Even Tope, who farmed the high ridge
and was late getting his field tilled due to sickness and
heavy rain, had pulled his family away from work so
that they could all be present. Parents brought their children, who sat cross-legged near the fire pit, the light of
the flames dancing on their cheeks. The younger ones
smiled; the older ones knew better. This wasn't a story
night; there would be no feast or songs.

The new chieftain had called a full meeting to discuss
the rumors that had obsessed the dahl's residents for
several days. Two troubling stories had arrived, one on

the heels of the other. Both had come from the north. The first, clearly impossible, hadn't been believed at all—until they'd heard the second. The second rumor was so unimaginably terrifying that it had to be true.

"Are the gods coming to kill us?" Tope shouted over the murmurs. The farmer, as well as everyone else, was understandably impatient.

Konniger stroked his beard and frowned in irritation at the question, even though he'd called the meeting to discuss exactly that. Perhaps he'd planned some opening statement. This was his first official address as chieftain, and he probably wanted to make it momentous.

Konniger was a handsome man with a thick black beard, long loose hair, and a Rhen-patterned leigh mor pinned over his left shoulder. The cloth was bright and looked to be new. He sat with both hands gripping the arms of the chair, his feet flat and back straight. The model of a chieftain, he appeared strong and fit, firm and solid, a rock for his people to latch onto. Persephone spotted her husband's ring on Konniger's finger and felt the familiar falling sensation in her stomach that made her wonder why she was still there. She was the floating oar after the boat had sunk, the marred, wooden handle of a shattered stone ax.

"It can't be true," Maeve responded with her indomitable tone of absolute confidence. The Keeper of Ways stood slightly behind and between the two chairs. Hood up, white hair tucked away, face as stern as weathered stone, the old woman—all that remained of the previous leadership—lent legitimacy to the pair. "The gods have always treated us fairly. The rules by which we live peacefully were agreed upon in ancient treaties. So long as we pay our tribute on time and in full, don't cross or dam the western rivers, or otherwise bring harm to the Fhrey realm, we are protected from their wrath. This was promised by their Chieftain Fenelyus."

"And what does this ancient tweety say will happen when one of us kills a god?" Gifford asked, his twisted lips mangling the word *treaty*. In a different setting, it might have elicited smiles or even a laugh.

Gifford had been born wrong. His back was twisted like ivy on a post, making walking across the dahl an achievement worthy of praise. His head, which always tilted to one side, looked as if a giant had squeezed it, leaving one eye in a permanent squint and his lips squished. His mother had died giving him life, and many had questioned the wisdom of letting Gifford live. His father had been convinced Gifford would be a great man. Everyone knew he spoke out of grief for his wife rather than from sense, but no one had the heart to intercede. Besides, leaving the infant to the mercy of the forest spirits probably wouldn't be necessary; the boy hadn't been expected to last a week. Gifford's father had died seven years ago, and some of the people who'd advocated abandonment had also died over the years. Gifford, however, was still alive, and at the age of twenty was the best potter in the seven clans.

Maeve's face hardened, if such a thing were possible. "It doesn't say anything. Because a man can't kill a god."

"Trader Justen of Split Road swore it was true," Brin said, her youthful voice piercing the grumbling din. "Said he'd met Raithe and saw the broken copper. *And* the god's blade, he—"

"Hush, girl," Sarah whispered to her daughter.

Brin caught the stern look and diminished, settling back on her heels.

"That's right," Atmore said. "I've known Justen for most of my life. He's never lied to anyone. If he says it's true, then it is. Why else would the gods turn against us? What else could draw such a punishment?"

"A man can't kill a god," Sackett said. At the sound of his low voice, the room quieted. Sackett rarely said much, so when the new Shield of the chieftain spoke, people listened. People believed.

"What have *you* heard, Konniger?" Adler shouted

from the door, his new eye patch granting him a veteran's importance.

Konniger looked over to where a group of strangers stood, ten men wearing solemn faces and the predominantly brown Nadak pattern. "Although I agree with Sackett that a god can't be killed, there is no doubt they have turned on our kind. The gods have destroyed Dureya."

A confused silence followed.

"What do you mean, *destroyed*?" Farmer Wedon asked.

"These men"—he gestured toward the strangers— "are from Nadak. Five days ago, they saw smoke in the north. They crossed into the highlands of Dureya, but the dahl was gone. Men, women, and children butchered. Their lodge and all the outlying villages are nothing more than burned-out shells, only the wind left to howl."

The entire hall murmured in disbelief. No words followed, only gasps and curses, which died on stunned lips.

"How many survived?" Tope asked.

"Dureyans?" Konniger took a long breath. "None. Even the livestock were slaughtered."

"How do we know it was the gods?" Delwin asked. "Maybe it was the Gula-Rhunes."

The men near the door shook their heads. One with a black leather band wound around his forehead said, "The bodies were in neat rows as if they'd been lined up to die. And their weapons had been left. Nothing was taken, nothing looted. Everything was burned."

More murmurs.

"So maybe it was the gods, but Dureya was attacked because Raithe, this God Killer, is from there. We haven't done anything to offend the gods. We don't bother them, and they won't bother us, right?" Delwin said in a tone that sounded more like a wish than a declaration. He had an arm around his wife, Sarah, pulling her close. "This has nothing to do with us."

"But what if it does?" Gifford asked. "What if the gods—maybe they don't see a diff-wence between *Du-e-ya* and *us*?" Gifford using *r*-words in public indicated more than idle concern. "Tell them what you saw this mow-ning, Topc."

Heads turned to the haggard farmer, who wiped his face with a grain sack he usually used as a hat. "I saw smoke to the northwest, right up the valley road. Looked like it was coming from Nadak."

An ominous silence froze the room. The men from Nadak stared at Tope. Then the questions came.

"How much smoke?"

"When was this?"

"What color was the smoke?"

Each voice sounded more concerned than the one before.

"Was a lot of smoke, black smoke," Tope said. "You can still see it if you climb to the top of the Horn Ridge."

Hearing this, the strangers rushed out. The rest watched them go into a deceptively pleasant spring day.

"That doesn't prove anything," Delwin said, but he pulled Sarah closer and placed a hand on his daughter's head.

"Sounds like the Fway punished them, too," Gifford said. "If they come, what we going to do?"

"What do you mean, *do*?" Konniger asked. "What is there to do?"

Several of the faces in the hall looked surprised.

Konniger hadn't exhibited much intelligence over the years, and Persephone figured he didn't understand the question. She pushed up to her knees. "I think they want to know what steps you plan to take to prevent what happened to Dureya, and possibly Nadak, from happening here."

Her comment drew a sharp look from Tressa, whose lips pulled taut.

"There's nothing to do," Konniger replied. "It won't happen here. *We've* done nothing wrong."

"But if a Fhrey has been killed, then—" Delwin started.

"*We* didn't kill him," Konniger said, cutting him off. "They have no reason to bother us."

Tressa smirked. "Dureyans have always caused trouble. Serves them right. I call it justice. They brought the wrath of the divine down on themselves. But we have nothing to fear."

"What about Nadak?" Gifford asked. "What'd they do?"

"We don't know anything about Nadak," Konniger said, then nodded at his wife and drew himself up straighter.

Not the best way to start, Persephone thought. She knew firsthand how difficult it could be, making decisions while everyone watched. When people were scared and looking for someone to take that fear away, it was a mistake to leave them idle to speculate and worry.

"But there are still some things we can do, yes?" Persephone asked.

So much for being quiet and invisible. How long did that last, five minutes? But five minutes ago, Dureya and Nadak still existed.

All eyes shifted between the new chieftain and the old chieftain's widow.

Just say yes. Say, Of course, *and if you can't think of anything, ask me later when no one is looking. But don't leave them lost.*

Konniger declared, "There are things beyond the control of men, and the will of the gods is one of them."

Seriously?

"I agree. We can't control what the gods will do," Persephone said. "But we aren't helpless, either. We could send a delegation to Alon Rhist explaining how we had nothing to do with the actions of Dureyans. And we could send messengers to the other dahls, like the men of Nadak who came here. We should let others know what's going on. At the very least, we should send someone to Nadak to check out the smoke Tope saw.

Maybe they weren't attacked. Perhaps they just had a fire that got out of control. If Nadak has also been destroyed, that's much different than if it was only Dureya. We need to know for sure, as that bit of information significantly changes what we should do."

"Persephone"—Tressa interceded for her husband, straightening in the chair as she spoke—"we grieve for your loss. But Reglan is dead, and Konniger is the chieftain. I think your voice would best serve the dahl by being silent."

Persephone would have ignored the verbal slap if Tressa hadn't mentioned Reglan. At least that was what she told herself afterward. Instead, she said, "If you were paying attention, Tressa, you'd know I wasn't speaking to you."

Konniger patted his wife's hand, probably to defuse the tension in the room. "And if we find out Nadak has been attacked? And if no one at Alon Rhist will talk to us. What then?"

"If this is true, if the gods have declared war and won't negotiate a peace, we need to gather what we can and leave."

"Leave?" He said the word as if he'd never heard it before. "And go where?"

Having me give you all the answers in front of a crowd is no way to instill confidence.

Persephone had hoped Konniger could find his way if she pointed him in the right direction. Apparently, that was wishful thinking. "At this point, I'd say south is a good direction. I'd aim for Dahl Tirre to give us as much time as possible to—"

"To what?" Konniger asked. "In Tirre, we'd have our backs to the sea, without walls or food. And do you think Tirre would welcome us? Such an invasion would spark a clan war. And for what? If the gods are after us, what would a few more miles matter?"

"The time to organize and prepare."

"For what?"

"For war," Persephone said.

A collective gasp escaped from those in the meeting hall. For a few minutes, no one said anything.

Tressa was the one who broke the silence. "Are you listening to yourself? You want to declare war against gods?" She lifted her sight to address the assembly. "Do we take up spears against the Grand Mother of All for not sending sufficient rain? The finest warriors of this village couldn't defeat a bear, and Persephone expects us to make war with the Fhrey?"

Konniger shot his wife a harsh glance she didn't see, then said, "If the Fhrey are set against us, then there is nothing that can be done. Men can't kill gods."

"The God Killer did," Persephone answered.

"That's just a rumor," Konniger replied.

"Why else would the Fhrey destroy Dureya? They use Dureyans to fight the Gula-Rhunes. What else could have angered them enough to turn against allies? If killing a Fhrey is possible, we need to find the one man who knows how to do it. Then, if we can draw all the clans together, including the Gula, we could—"

Konniger shook his head. "It's impossible to unite the clans. The Gula hate us as much as we hate them."

"It's not impossible," Persephone replied. "Ask Maeve. She'll tell you. Generations ago during the Great Flood, Gath of Odeon united the clans, *all* the clans, isn't that right?"

Maeve nodded but didn't speak.

"Under his leadership, our people built boats," Persephone said for her. "We filled them with supplies, and when the waters rose, we set sail and began a new life. Well, this is a new flood, a new disaster. We need to harness the combined strength and wisdom of all our people to survive. When we send messengers to the other dahls to tell them about Nadak and Dureya, we could ask other chieftains to bring their people to meet in Tirre as well."

"You want to abandon everything we've worked hundreds of years to build because the gods saw fit to punish the Dureyans for killing one of them?" Tressa asked, and shook her head, her face bitter.

Konniger sat back, stroking his beard and shifting his eyes while deep in thought. After a few minutes, he straightened and said, "No, such drastic measures aren't warranted. You're overreacting. Tressa is right. We have it good here, better than most dahls, and leaving a place of comfort for the unknown is foolish. You are worried about something that will never come to pass."

Several in the hall were nodding now. Persephone had seen this before. If given a choice between a potentially great hardship and doing nothing, people gravitated toward what was most familiar and comfortable. That was why leadership was needed. To do what was necessary rather than what was easy. Persephone had a history of advocating unpopular ideas and arguing with chieftains. Reglan used to say it was her best and worst trait. If the potential danger weren't so great, if the repercussions of getting this wrong weren't so dire, she would have left it at that. Instead, she said, "But what if it does? Then it will be too late. If we—"

Konniger slapped the arm of his chair. "Tirre won't tolerate us on their doorstep. We'd be as welcome as locusts. Will they share their food? Will there even be enough?" Konniger's voice had lowered to an angry growl.

Maeve finally interceded. "Persephone," she began, clasping her hands and taking a step forward. "Gath of Odeon was renowned even before the flood. Heroes like him no longer walk among us. He was able to win the support of every chieftain. Gathering the clans will do nothing without someone to lead. I fear the chieftains won't kneel before anyone less."

Konniger glanced at the broadax he had lodged in the winter pillar. "I've fought and killed to become chieftain of this clan. I can't take a knee to any man from Menahan, Melen, Tirre, or Warric. The decision is mine, and I say we stay here. This discussion is over and I'll hear no more on the subject."

Maeve locked eyes with Persephone. The old woman shook her head ever so slightly. Maeve wouldn't support her. Persephone couldn't oppose both the chieftain and the Keeper of Ways. Looking around, she saw less anxiety than at the start of the meeting. When she had been talking about leaving, she had seen the eyes of rabbits staring back at her, scared and wanting nothing more than to hide in their burrows. The people feared a mass exodus more than they did the gods. She wondered if even Reglan would have listened to her. Konniger was right about one thing. It was far easier to do nothing than to brave the unknown. She sat back down.

The meeting had concluded with the usual prayer to Mari, the goddess of Rhen, and to Elan, the Grand Mother of All. Persephone filed out with the rest, feeling utterly alone in a crowd of people. Avoiding stares, she walked around the north side of the lodge, away from most of the homes and toward the open space left behind by the depleted woodpile. There, she saw the young mystic again.

"Almost got him that time," Suri told the wolf, whose head was stuffed in a gap between the logs, scratching the dirt and trying to push deeper. "You've lost him now. You're too big to fit in there."

The girl was kneeling on the grass in front of the five-foot-high double-row pile of stacked wood, all that remained of the dahl's winter supply. Both the wolf's and Suri's heads popped up as Persephone approached. The girl frowned. "Don't tell me there's a rule against wolves hunting rats in woodpiles. Is there?"

"What? No," Persephone replied.

"There are rules against everything else here. What you can and can't eat or where you can sleep. Even where to squat in the morning. Everyone here is touched, there's no mistake, but I suppose that's what you get from living inside a wall. Tura always said walls were bad, said the same thing about shoes." Suri looked down at her bare feet. "I didn't understand Tura's scorn of either until now."

Not knowing how to respond, Persephone simply said, "You're still here."

"Your eyes still work," the girl answered with a grin.

If Suri were a normal person, Persephone would have been insulted.

Normal person. Already she had branded the new mystic bizarre. New mystic, new chieftain, there were altogether too many *new*s on the dahl lately.

"Strange game, this stating the obvious," Suri said, shaking her head. She got up and joined Minna at the woodpile. "Pointless, but popular. Everyone plays it. *You're eating our bread. That isn't your bed. You have a wolf.* But as you can see, I'm getting the knack of it. Tura told me to blend in at villages, especially the dahls. She said people who live inside walls are crazy and can be dangerous. Touched animals are, too. Cursed by the gods, sort of like you, and even a tainted squirrel's bite can make you that way."

"I merely meant, well . . ." Persephone hesitated. "I didn't think you'd still be here."

Suri pointed at the treetops visible over the rear wall of the dahl where the gray spears had become a curtain of green. "Was waiting on the leaves."

Persephone laughed. "It's been two weeks."

The mystic twisted her face, thinking hard. "You have two ears." She smiled proudly. "I'm starting to see the fun of this. Using a part of what another person says makes it harder, doesn't it? Probably gets more challenging late in winter when you've been sealed up for months—I assume you can't repeat the same thing twice, right?"

Persephone rolled her eyes.

Suri looked perplexed. "Does everyone here suffer from this eye sickness as well? I've seen a lot of that."

I'm sure you have, Persephone thought.

A pattering sound from the depths of the woodpile sent the wolf thrusting back into the crevice, her claws skittering on the stripped bark littering the stack's perimeter. She sprayed the torn shards across the yard.

Suri sighed. "Minna, you're still too big."

Bizarre might have been an understatement. Persephone decided to get to the point. "When we spoke, you mentioned something bad was going to happen. What did you mean?"

"What do you mean, what did I mean?"

"Ah . . ." Persephone faltered. It hadn't been this difficult talking with Tura, not that Persephone had seen her much. Mystics rarely came to the dahl, and when they did, it wasn't to proclaim *Everything is going to be cream and honey from now on!* Persephone hadn't seen Tura since the season before the Great Famine.

"I mean, well, your prediction sounded implausible at the time. But two of the nearby dahls have been attacked, and I think I should listen to what you have to say."

"I told you, ma'am. I don't know exactly, but the signs were clear." Plucking bark off one of the logs, she tasted it. Then she spat and tossed the strip aside.

"What signs?"

"Near sunset on the first day of spring, I saw lightning in the northwest. The thunder startled a flock of crows that took flight, also in the northwest. The wind was blowing west to east, and a moment later, the sun was blocked out by dark clouds."

"And what does that mean?"

Suri sighed. "Okay, listen. The sun is born in the east, so the east is good. West is bad. That's where the sun goes to die. When signs happen in the west, those are bad omens. Lightning is a judgment of the gods, powerful and violent. Birds are extremely significant, often used as messengers of the gods, and since I saw a whole flock, it means a lot of people will suffer. Blocking out the sun . . . well, even you ought to understand that's not a good turn of events. *Any one* of these signs would have been serious, but all three? Bad news. Very bad news."

"But you can't tell me *exactly* what will happen?"

"Unlike your word game, the gods aren't so obvious, which makes their games a lot more interesting to play. I mean, if Elan came right out and said tomorrow you'll take a walk and be ripped apart by badgers, you'd be terrified and wouldn't go out, right? So she wouldn't tell you that. She might drop some hints, but if you didn't pick up on the clues or couldn't figure them out . . . well, that's really not her fault. Anyway, you go, walking into a horrible badger-ripping death because you didn't know any better. That's the way gods play their games and why I think we need to talk to the trees. So we aren't all ripped apart by badgers."

So very odd.

"Then we *can* change fate?"

The girl shrugged as her attention once again was drawn to the wolf and the woodpile.

"And how will the trees help?"

Suri let out a long sigh. "Minna, did you hear that? I'm starting to see what Tura meant about people living in the walls. Ma'am, haven't you ever talked to a tree?"

Very, very odd.

"I can't say I have. Do you speak to them?"

"Some," the girl said, and then stuck her head into a gap between the logs as if testing her chance of crawling in. It was the wolf's turn to watch with amusement.

"Some?"

"Not all trees like to talk," Suri said, her voice muffled by the woodpile. "Beeches are famous for being unfriendly. They never say a word. Stubborn as can be. You can feel a sense of superiority with them." She pulled her head out of the cordwood and delivered a sympathetic frown to the wolf, followed by a hopeless shrug. "Now, a locust, laurel, or holly . . . well . . . you can't get them to shut up, but they don't know anything. They just chatter. Silly gossip mostly. Willows are notorious for going on and on. And trust me, you don't want to talk to them. Mind. Numbingly. Depressing." Suri dragged out the words like heavy things.

Persephone gave her a skeptical look.

Seeing it, the girl added in a quiet voice, "Seriously, people have drowned themselves after spending too much time under a willow. Which makes you wonder about the gods' motives for putting them near water as often as they do."

She waited, but Persephone remained silent, so Suri continued. "Elms tend to be proud and snooty. Maples are vain. *Look at my leaves, look at my leaves!* Never talk to a maple in autumn. *Unbearable.* You can warn them all you want, you know? You remind them winter is coming and what that means, but they won't listen. Maples have all the memory of a raindrop, which is weird for a tree, don't you think? Now, evergreens, like spruce and cedar, they're nice enough. Most of them are soft-spoken. A cedar on the west ridge knew right where the wind had blown my hat last summer. Every so often you'll find a really sweet old pine. Dear Wogan, you can lose a few days curled up at their feet while sipping needle tea, which they're quite proud of but honestly tastes pretty awful. They'll prattle on about the good old days when the summers were sweeter and the rains wetter."

"And if I wanted to know what the omens you saw meant?" Persephone asked. "If I needed advice about the intentions of gods? Which would I ask?"

"Oh, there's only one tree worth talking to for that—Magda, the old oak."

"Where is this oak?"

Suri hooked a thumb over her shoulder. "There's a glen at the base of the high forest in the fingers of the mountain. She holds court there."

"Holds court?"

"Oh, yes. Magda is highly revered by the other trees. Bushes and plants, too. They all keep a respectable distance and bow before her. It's easy to see why. She's . . . well . . . she's Magda, oldest tree in the forest. And the Crescent is an old forest."

Persephone stared out at the tree-thick hills, which rose well above the level of the dahl's wall. The ridges rolled on, fold upon fold, each a different shade of green, drifting toward blue. The Crescent Forest hugged Dahl Rhen, providing precious gifts of wood and food, but remained a mysterious world fraught with terrors. Dense groves of old trees, caves, and rivers were known to be gateways to the spirit world, and the Crescent had all of them. Persephone had lain in the lodge on many a summer's night listening to the frightening sounds entering the open window. Shrieks and cries, cracks and thumps that could have no mortal origin. The Crescent was a noisy neighbor you knew was up to no good. To live in Dahl Rhen was to dwell on the brink of a leafy abyss.

Persephone's gaze followed the ridgeline to the south, where it rose sharply. "They say the bear that killed my husband and son lives on that mountain."

Suri nodded, and her bright smile faded. Persephone was sad to see it go. Something about the girl's cheerful enthusiasm, as odd as it was, made Persephone feel better—hopeful—as if Suri were spring itself, bubbling and budding with possibility. Now the girl appeared serious for the first time. The tattoos around her eyes and mouth added a grave authority, and for a moment Persephone felt a little frightened. "Grin the Brown makes her home in a cave on a cliff near the top of the tree line. Magda isn't nearly so high, but Grin has a tendency to wander, and she has no respect for the old oak. Grin has no respect for anything."

Persephone looked out at the forest. "I need to speak with her . . . to this tree. Can you take me?"

Suri no longer looked at Persephone; her eyes had shifted to a fluttering butterfly. Persephone waited while Suri watched it land on a sprig of clover. A bright smile filled her face once more.

"Did you hear me?" Persephone asked.

"Did I hear what, ma'am?" the girl replied.

"Can you take me to this old oak? So I can ask her some questions?"

"Do you see the butterfly?" Suri grinned with enthusiasm.

"Yes, I see it, but—"

"So stunning and delicate; it's marvelous. No one can see a butterfly and not stop to admire it. I'd love to be one. To go to sleep and wake up a season later with such beautiful wings and the ability to flutter about. That's the most wonderful sort of magic, don't you think? To change, to grow, to fly. But . . ." She paused. "I wonder what the cost would be." The smile diminished once more. "There's always a cost when it comes to magic. I suspect there is a great price to go from lowly caterpillar to glorious butterfly."

Definitely not a normal person.

Still, Persephone had to admit she liked Suri. "Can you take me to—?"

"Of course I can." Suri smirked. "Why do you think I've risked my sanity staying in this terrible walled place? Oh, is this another game?" She turned to her wolf, which was sitting but still eyeing the woodpile. "Can you get that rat, Minna? Would you like me to move the wood so you can catch it?" Suri looked back at Persephone and smiled. "How's that?"

CHAPTER SEVEN

The Black Tree

The Crescent Forest was our neighbor. A place so vast no one knew all its secrets. From its trees, Dahl Rhen was built. From its animals, Dahl Rhen was fed. And from its darkness, a hero was made.

— THE BOOK OF BRIN

Raithe and Malcolm were nestled in the eaves of a forest just outside Dahl Rhen, a fortified settlement built on a hill and surrounded by a circular wall of logs. The hill itself was dreamlike, so high, so green. Raithe had never seen such lush land. In Dureya, everything was bleached, the only color painted in sunsets. His father had often spoken about Alysin—a paradise where the spirits of brave warriors went after death, a place of green fields, foaming beer, and beautiful women. Seeing Dahl Rhen, Raithe wondered if his father had simply heard rumors of *this* place.

"So that hill is a dahl?" Malcolm asked, sitting with knees up, twiddling a twig between two fingers.

Raithe once more marveled at Malcolm's lack of rudimentary knowledge about how people lived. He'd given up asking how Malcolm had become a slave. Any inquiry resulted in vague responses and a change of subject. Raithe concluded Malcolm had either been taken by the Fhrey as a baby or was born in captivity.

"Yes, that's a dahl."

"A little too symmetrical. Did they make it?" Malcolm asked.

Raithe nodded. "Sort of. Comes from centuries of

building over previous villages." He was in the brush on his knees and had already trimmed a cross branch, constructed the gateway for the snare, and was working at tying the loop. Usually he had trouble with that last part; his fingers were too big. "After a fire or a razing, people rebuild on top of the rubble. Easier than going someplace new, and the well is already there. Do it enough times and a mound builds up."

"So Rhen is a clan? How many are there altogether?" Malcolm asked.

"Seven. Not including the Gula-Rhunes."

"Why not include them? They're human, too, right?"

"Rhulyn-Rhunes and Gula-Rhunes don't get along." Raithe finally got the little knot pulled. "We've been warring for centuries."

"Are they who your father fought against with the Fhrey?"

"Yep. Every year there would be a battle or two and every decade a full-scale war. My father survived more than thirty years of fighting."

"So how is it he never saw a dead Fhrey?"

"The Fhrey don't bloody their hands. They plan the battles, pick and train the men, then send others off to fight. There were plenty of deaths but only among the Rhunes."

Malcolm nodded as if he understood, but Raithe knew he didn't. Few did. Even he had a hard time understanding. His father didn't seem to question any of it. Herkimer accepted war as readily as he acknowledged water being wet. But then Dureya was a different place, certainly nothing like this.

"Usually, the higher the hill, the older the dahl," Raithe said, looking across the field of sunlight. "That's why it's shaped that way. In a real sense, it's a burial mound. By the look of it, Dahl Rhen must be quite old."

The ex-slave reclined but continued to study the dahl. "It doesn't look that big."

Raithe had been thinking just the opposite. The dahl rose majestically in the distance, sun-drenched and luxurious with its abundance of wood. "It's much bigger than Dahl Dureya and mammoth when compared with Clempton, the small village where I grew up."

"I lived in Alon Rhist, remember," Malcolm said. He hooked a thumb at the village. "That's not suitable for a cattle pen when compared with Fhrey standards. How many people do you think live there?"

Raithe shrugged and tied a second knot into the loop as a precaution. He didn't want his dinner getting away. Nothing was worse than finding an empty sprung trap. "Here? I don't know, a thousand maybe. Where I grew up we had close to forty families, about two hundred people, but that was a little village, not a dahl."

"What's the difference?"

"Dahls are the oldest and most populated village of a given clan. It's where the chieftain has his lodge. You know what a lodge is?"

"What beavers live in?"

Raithe stared at him incredulously.

"Yes, I know what a lodge is," Malcolm said with a smirk.

"Well, you don't seem to know much else."

Malcolm shrugged. "I never claimed to be smart." He focused back on the hill. "So there's a thousand people in there?"

"Maybe. This place is twice the size of Dahl Dureya."

"How many Rhunes, I'm sorry, *humans,* are there?"

"Including the Gula?"

Malcolm nodded.

Raithe shrugged. "I don't think anyone knows."

Raithe stared up at the great green mound. Morning fires burned inside the wall. He couldn't see the homes but counted scores of smoke columns rising straight on a windless day. The only structure visible from where they sat was the peaked roof of the lodge. Made of raw logs, it looked huge.

"I don't see why we can't go in," Malcolm said.

"We don't need to. After I finish this snare, we'll go back over to the cascade where we set the others. Hopefully, our first rabbit will be waiting for us. So we'll have plenty of fresh water and roast rabbit for supper. It'll go along nicely with the rest of the bread."

"Bread's gone," Malcolm mentioned.

"Gone? All of it?"

"Last night."

"But we only ate a little bit."

"And the night before we had a little. It's not magic bread, you know."

Raithe frowned. He'd been looking forward to rabbit and grease-soaked bread. Thinking about food when he didn't have any was miserable.

Malcolm pointed to a flock of sheep barely visible on the far side of the dahl. Two men and a pair of dogs urged them up a grassy slope. "They probably have lamb stew in Dahl Rhen, fresh bread, maybe even milk, eggs, and butter. Bet they're having breakfast right now. I love breakfast. Are you familiar with the concept?"

"Don't start that again. If you wanted steady meals, you shouldn't have hit Shegon with that rock." He looked over at Malcolm. "Did he really do those things? Did Shegon feed women to dogs and cut off the hands of a child?"

"No." Malcolm shook his head. "Shegon was a self-indulgent, arrogant fool—most of them are—but he wasn't a monster. He was a hunter. The Instarya are another matter, and they're the ones after us. They're warriors who command the outposts, the tribe charged with keeping order out here on the frontier."

"I thought Alon Rhist was the home of . . ." Raithe stopped before revealing his own ignorance.

Malcolm smiled, not a gloating grin or pretentious smirk but a look of understanding. Raithe reconsidered his earlier impression about Malcolm resembling a weasel. The man did have a pointed nose and narrow eyes, but other than that he wasn't weasel-like at all.

"No, Alon Rhist, though far more impressive than that dahl over there, is small by Fhrey standards. The Fhrey's homeland is Erivan," Malcolm said. "A vast and beautiful country of ancient forests more than a week's hike to the northeast. It's on the far side of a great river called the Nidwalden. Few Fhrey ever leave Erivan. Significant portions of their population have never left the capital city of Estramnadon. They see Erivan as the center of the universe, the source of all things good, so there's no point in going anywhere else. Alon Rhist is the largest of five fortresses built during the Dherg War. The Fhrey out here patrol these lands and ensure there's a safe buffer between people like us and them. It's actually a source of some friction in their society. The Instarya don't like being the only ones forced to live in what most consider a wasteland."

A breeze picked up. All around them leaves rustled, whispering to one another a gentle sound. Across the field, the pillars of cook fires began to lose shape, blurring as they blew to the south.

"I don't know why the Instarya complain. It's really quite beautiful," Malcolm said.

Raithe stood, taking his snare with him. He cut down a small tree, pruned off the branches, and laid it across the opening of a tiny path. The trail through the brush was the perfect size for a rabbit, and little pebble droppings were everywhere. He hung the loop down from it, keeping the noose off the ground. Then he stuck pruned branches in the dirt before the hoop, ensuring that the rabbit would need to jump over them and would land in the snare.

"Bless me with three rabbits, Wogan, and I'll make a burnt offering of the last one to you."

"Bargaining with the gods again?" Malcolm asked. "Wouldn't it be more enticing to offer the *first* rabbit in order to prove your faith?"

"Wogan isn't a god; he's a spirit, a guardian of forests."

"There's a difference?"

"I know you were a slave for a long time, but did they keep you trapped in a hole, too? *Is there a difference?* Is there a difference between a cow and a goat, between the sun and the moon? Tetlin's Witch! I swear—"

"Don't." Malcolm's tone was abrupt and serious.

Raithe paused. "Since when are you against swearing?"

"I'm not. Just choose another name to swear by."

"Why? Using a god or a spirit would be far worse."

"Call me superstitious."

"You? Malcolm of the Rhist, who scoffs at the idea of manes and leshies? You're afraid of the Tetlin Witch?"

Malcolm didn't reply. He pulled his legs up tight to his chest and stared out at the hill and the walled village of the dahl. "You know, rather than praying for rabbits we could just check out the dahl. It worked out all right at the roadhouse."

"You call that all right? Did you forget Donny?"

"What if I promise to keep my mouth shut?" Malcolm asked.

"Is that possible?"

Malcolm frowned. "I meant no storytelling. Aren't dahls supposed to be generous to strangers? Isn't that a thing? They'll at least give us a little to eat, right?"

"Maybe . . . if they follow tradition. Hard times among the clans these days. And it could be dangerous for us. What if someone from the roadhouse is there? A group of traders might welcome the God Killer, but dahls are different. Dahls have chieftains tasked with keeping everyone safe, men who agreed to live by the Fhrey's rules and force others to do the same."

"But I don't see that we have a choice. We can't keep running like this, especially without food."

"Our only hope is to keep moving south and stay ahead of the Fhrey. We do that and we'll stay alive."

"No man can escape death," Malcolm said. "But it's *how* we run that defines us. And aren't you getting a bit—" Malcolm stopped, and his eyes narrowed as he stared at the sunny field between them and the dahl.

"What?" Raithe whispered, trying to see what Malcolm was looking at.

"I think they're women." Malcolm pointed out a pair of figures coming from the dahl and heading their way.

They *were* women. The taller one wore a long black dress that made tramping through the tall grass a struggle. She had wavy black hair that whipped behind her, exposing a lovely face. Beside her walked a girl with painted markings, short hair, and a battered cape dyed the color of red clay. Bounding by their side was a white wolf.

It's just a forest, only trees, Persephone assured herself as they approached the meadow's edge.

But people have died inside it.

Her son had been killed while hunting deer with his two best friends—both able men. And an entire war party had accompanied Reglan.

I should have brought someone along. I could have asked Konniger to send Sackett as an escort, but what would I have said? "I'm afraid of the forest, so I want to borrow the Shield of the chieftain. Oh, and by the way, the reason I'm going into the woods that terrify me is because I feel it's important to talk to a tree. For the good of the dahl, of course." Yeah, that would go over well.

The murky forest grew larger as they approached. Persephone had hoped the trees would appear smaller than she remembered. Things usually shrank when people grew older. The steps of the lodge used to seem mammoth and the stone foundation it sat on had been a veritable cliff when she was a child. But the trees hadn't gotten smaller. If anything they looked bigger. Since her son's death, Persephone hadn't left the dahl, and after Reglan died, she rarely left Sarah and Delwin's roundhouse. But the forest was another matter, and she hadn't entered it, not since . . .

It's just a forest. Only trees.

When Persephone was seven, she and the other children would goad one another to venture deeper into the wood and touch certain trees. Everyone managed to reach the white birch, but only she and her best friend, Aria, had managed to touch the elm beyond the shade line. Then one of the children, perhaps Sarah, dared them both to touch the black tree. No one knew what sort of tree it was. They could barely see it from where they stood in the safe warmth of the afternoon sun. Sarah, if it had been Sarah, hadn't been serious. Everyone knew it. That tree was too deep, farther even than where the grass turned to ferns. It lived where the undergrowth loomed and darkness reigned. The whole idea was silly—crazy, really—and Persephone had laughed. Choosing that tree was a sort of revenge because they'd all been humiliated by Persephone's and Aria's courage.

It couldn't have been Sarah, Persephone concluded. *We're so close now, and I hated the little girl who made that dare.*

She hated her because Persephone had laughed but Aria hadn't.

It didn't matter that Aria was two years older; they were best friends and had always agreed on everything, but this time was different. Aria had taken Persephone's hand and said, "We'll do it together." Her friend had been serious. Persephone, shocked at the words and frightened by the prospect, ripped her hand away. She could still see the disappointment in Aria's eyes, inside of which Persephone's reflection became smaller.

"Just me, then," Aria had said, disappointed.

Persephone had tried to stop her, saying it was stupid and dangerous. She wanted to believe her attempts to hold Aria back stemmed from fear for her friend's life. The truth was she didn't want to be second best. She wanted to be brave but felt like a coward—embarrassed and ashamed.

Aria had entered the forest alone.

No one believed she'd do it, but as they watched, the small girl crept deeper and deeper into the branches and leaves until the underbrush swallowed her. They waited, then called out, but she didn't answer. Hours passed, or so it seemed. To children, time—like the sizes of things—wasn't constant. Persephone eventually panicked and ran back to the dahl to get help.

If only I had run the other way. If only I had run into the forest to save my friend, everything would have turned out so different.

She'd gone only partway up the hill when Aria reappeared. Persephone had heard the cheers behind her. Some called Aria crazy, but there was also awe in their jibes, and Aria had laughed with them. Persephone watched from a distance. She didn't join them. She couldn't, couldn't meet her best friend's eyes, couldn't face seeing herself grow smaller still. Instead, she walked home alone. Aria had called out. Persephone pretended not to hear. Aria shouted she was sorry, but Aria had nothing to be sorry for.

After that, Persephone avoided Aria. Every time they saw each other, Persephone was reminded of her failure and cowardice. A decade had gone by before she spoke with her friend again. The occasion had been Persephone's wedding, and Aria, who was pregnant at the time, stood in the long line to congratulate the new bride. Like all the others, Aria took Persephone's hand, and their eyes met. She expected to see anger, maybe even hatred, but neither waited for her. All she saw was the unbridled happiness of a married woman waiting for the birth of her first child and who wanted the same joyful life for her childhood friend. Aria had forgiven Persephone even if Persephone hadn't forgiven herself.

She had made plans to go to Aria after the baby was born, using the birth as an excuse to visit. She'd apologize for all the years of avoidance and bring a gift for the baby. They would laugh again the way they used to, and all the troubles of the past would fade away. That day never came. Aria died giving birth to her son, Gifford. Maybe the boy inherited his mother's courage. Cursed by the gods, twisted into a tragic wretch, he'd proved them all wrong by living. With awkward hands, he did the impossible over and over, fashioning clay masterpieces that were the envy of every artisan. In his own way, Gifford dared to touch the black tree every day.

Aria died before Persephone could say she was sorry. Sorry for ignoring Aria for years, sorry for pretending not to hear her shouts when walking home, sorry for not running into the trees to save her, but mostly for not accepting her friend's hand and going into the forest.

It had been three decades and Persephone was finally ready to touch the black tree.

"You live out there, don't you?" Persephone asked Suri while her wolf raced ahead of them. Minna paused to smell something before darting off again.

"Yes, ma'am." Suri walked with long easy strides, swinging Tura's wooden staff, which was slightly shorter and infinitely older than the girl.

"How do you do it? Live all by yourself, I mean. Aren't you scared?"

"I'd be more frightened of living where you do." Suri looked back over her shoulder at the dahl.

"I don't live alone. There are over two hundred families on the dahl."

Suri laughed.

"Did I say something funny?"

"Do you know how many families live in the forest, ma'am?"

"Families live in the forest?"

"Oh, yes. There are far too many to count: squirrels, foxes, badgers, spiders, rabbits, hedgehogs, snakes, deer, raccoons, bluebirds, woodpeckers, moose, grouse, owls, weasels, moles, skunks, doves, butterflies—can't forget the butterflies."

"But they aren't *people*."

"Exactly," Suri said with a wink. "You're starting to see my point, aren't you, ma'am? I mean, who wouldn't prefer a family of bunnies, robins, or raccoons as neighbors? And look at the place you live! So much wood decaying around you. Dead bodies aren't a suitable home. The best neighbor you can have is a tree, a *living* tree. They listen more than they talk, provide shade on hot days, give you food and shelter, and don't ask for anything in return."

"What about the dangers? Bears, for example?"

"Oh," Suri said with a knowing nod of her head. "Well, we'd have something to worry about if we were a couple of lilies."

"How's that?"

"Bears love to eat lilies, berries, ants, and mice. If you're not one of those, bears can be quite nice. Playful, but also known to cheat."

"Does that include The Brown?" Persephone asked with more bitterness than she had intended.

"Grin is . . . *different*."

They were at the bottom of a hill, entering a pretty hardwood grove that was still open enough to be dappled by plenty of sunlight. This was where the bright birches of Persephone's youth had grown. They were still there, chalk-white trunks of peeling bark and fresh, bright leaves.

Looking to their left, Suri did a little twirl and waved. Persephone didn't see anyone.

"Who are you waving to?"

"Huh? Oh, there's a holly bush over there I had a conversation with on the way in." She lowered her voice. "Normally I don't care much for bushes. Most are mean and standoffish, with their thorns and prickles. I suppose they have their reasons. I mean, absolutely everyone steals from them. But that holly was nice."

With that, Suri strode onward.

They passed the birches, and the undergrowth changed to fiddlehead ferns. The elm tree had been near there, but after so many years, she couldn't pick it out. Persephone's steps slowed until, without realizing, she stopped. A few steps later Suri also halted, as did Minna. Both of them looked back at Persephone with a puzzled expression.

Persephone stood with her hands clenched as she stared at the dark trees ahead. From this point, the land sloped upward. The undergrowth and the forest canopy cast everything in shadow. "This is as far as I've ever been."

Suri started to laugh but covered her mouth. "Sorry."

"No, you're right to laugh. It's stupid. I've traveled north as far as Alon Rhist and south to the Blue Sea. I've visited all the dahls and have even seen Mount Mador, from a distance, of course. And although I've looked at the forest every morning from my bedroom window, I haven't gone in, not beyond where the sunlight shines. Not that I needed to. I don't hunt, or cut trees, and there's nothing of interest inside."

The tattoos above Suri's eyes lifted in shock, but Persephone was too scared to be polite.

"They're just trees, aren't they?" Persephone said the words to reassure herself, but the fear was still there. The old terror clawed, tightening her stomach and making it hard to breathe. "Even a child . . . even a seven-year-old girl knows that."

"Good." Suri took three more strides, but Persephone still hadn't moved. "Still coming?"

"Can I ask a favor?" Persephone reached out. "Would you . . . would you take my hand?"

Suri narrowed her eyes and glanced at Minna skeptically, then shrugged. "Ah . . . okay."

Suri crossed back through the fiddleheads. The delicate plants quivered and bobbed at her passing, but she never stepped on any. Persephone felt the mystic's tentative clasp.

"Lead on, Aria," Persephone said.

"Who's Aria?"

"A girl I used to know."

Suri looked up. "You're very odd, aren't you, ma'am?"

CHAPTER EIGHT

Asking the Oak

Magda was an ancient oak tree that grew in a glade on a hill deep in the forest. It was said she could tell the future and would answer any question posed beneath her leaves. For most people, "asking the oak" was a simple thing, an afternoon's walk. For Persephone, the trip took a day and a night and cost more than one life.
— THE BOOK OF BRIN

In her mind, Persephone always imagined that the forest beyond the black tree was a gaping maw of darkness filled with malevolent demons, ghosts, and cruel raow that ate people, starting with their faces. Stories told on winter nights spent in a circle around the lodge fire were to blame. Huddled with her feet toward the eternal flame, she had listened while the winds howled, rattling the doors as if something were trying to enter. Most often, stories were told as if they had happened to the speaker, or to a close friend if the hero died, a frequent occurrence. Few of the forest stories were pleasant. No one found fortune or their lost love. Each ended in misery or death. Little wonder, then, that Persephone was amazed by what she found beyond the forest eaves.

Trees with trunks larger than a roundhouse soared to astounding heights, supporting a vast green roof. Shafts of golden light pierced the canopy, painting complex and shifting patterns on a carpet of needles. Moss-covered rocks and beds of old leaves lent a softness similar to Sarah's wool-filled home. At one point, Persephone spotted a pair of deer; delicate and beautiful they stood with heads raised and ears cocked. She glanced away for a moment, and when she looked back, the two had vanished as if they had been apparitions. Suri was right: This was a home—a home of gods—and the best was still to come.

The two had been climbing steadily since entering the trees, and Persephone wondered how they would be able to go much farther if the pitch grew any steeper. Then Suri led her to a crevice in the slope where water sprayed down a tumble of rocks where dirt had been washed away by a falling stream. The water splashed and gathered in pools that overflowed to create a tall, wet, and rocky staircase. A dreamy mist rose, watering lichen and turning the stone a glossy black.

"It's beautiful," Persephone shouted as she followed Suri up an irregular set of slick stone steps.

Climbing the steps was easier than navigating the dead leaves and thornbushes covering the hillside, but the ascent was steep and arduous. Persephone had to stop several times to rest, making Suri flop down on a rock above her where she'd sit, swinging her slender legs impatiently. When they were near the top, Persephone took a moment to look back down. They were quite high, and the cascade appeared smaller somehow, less majestic. Still, the play of water among the rocks was lovely. Movement near the bottom caught Persephone's attention. Three men were in the process of climbing up.

Sackett was easy to identify. His beard was short and his dark hair hung straight and reached well past his shoulders. The other two were just as easy to recognize. One had a patch over a missing eye, the other lacked a hand. Adler's patch was small enough to reveal part of the scar where the bear had gouged him. He continually shifted his head from side to side, making up for the loss of vision. Hegner had it the worst of the three. He was heavier, and lacking a hand he couldn't scramble up the rocks.

"What are you doing out here?" Persephone called down cheerily. Although the forest wasn't as frightening as she'd expected, Persephone appreciated the company. The bear was still out there.

"I was about to ask you the same thing," Sackett answered.

Suri, who nimbly climbed back down to where Persephone stood, asked, "You know these men?"

"Yes. They're from the dahl. Brave men who were with my husband when he hunted The Brown."

"Minna doesn't like them." Suri bent down and stroked the wolf. "She is an excellent judge of character."

Persephone looked at the wolf. "Probably just doesn't like the spears. Sackett is our new chieftain's Shield. We'll be in good hands with him." Looking back down the cascade, she shouted, "Are you out hunting?"

"Yes, we are," Sackett shouted back.

"I don't suppose I could persuade you to travel with us for a while. I'd love an escort."

"Certainly. Just wait for us to catch up," Sackett said.

Persephone waited as they struggled up the wet stones, using the butts of their spears for stability. Their progress was made more difficult by the large wooden shields slung on their backs.

"The trees are talking," Suri said. The girl's head was tilted up, watching the leaves overhead.

"They are? What are they—"

Suri held up a finger to stop her, then narrowed her eyes, listening. Persephone listened, too, but all she heard was the wind rustling branches.

"What *are* you doing out here?" Sackett asked. The man had given up trying to avoid the pools and waded through knee-deep water, soaking his sandals and matting the hair on his legs so that it looked like fur.

There is such a thing as being too hairy, Persephone thought. Despite his luxuriant black mane, Sackett wasn't a handsome man. In addition to all the hair, his deeply sunk eyes beneath a jutting brow gave him a serious, gaunt appearance.

"I know it sounds ridiculous, but we're going to talk to a tree," Persephone explained.

Sackett stopped just two rocks down, catching his breath.

"Did you say, *talk to a tree*?"

"Yes." Persephone pointed at the girl. "This is Suri and her wolf, Minna. She's our new mystic, who studied under Tura. She's listening to them right now."

The tattoos on Suri's face made her look serious again. She stared at Sackett, and like Minna, she didn't appear happy.

"Yeah, well, I think it would be best if Suri and her wolf were on their way," Sackett said.

"Oh, there's no need to worry," Persephone said. "Minna is perfectly tame, and Suri's our guide."

"She's not from the dahl. She needs to go."

"The trees say they know these men, murderers who can't be trusted," Suri told Persephone.

"Suri, hunting animals isn't murder. We rely on the meat they bring in. We'd all starve if they didn't."

"I said *get*!" Sackett shouted in a sharp tone that was frightening enough to cause Persephone to jump, but Suri remained oblivious.

Minna was not. With bared teeth and raised fur, the wolf growled.

Sackett sighed. "Can't say I didn't try." He pulled the shield off his back and looked down at the progress of Adler and Hegner, who were almost up to them. "Adler, go 'round left. Stump, go right. We're gonna have to kill this wolf."

"Don't call me Stump," Hegner told Sackett.

"You aren't killing anything!" Persephone exclaimed. "Your weapons are making Minna nervous, that's all. Suri, can you calm her down?"

The men kept advancing. "Adler, you come up. Hegner, stay where you are. I'll block it in; then Adler can slay it. He has the best angle."

"I order you to stop!" Persephone yelled.

Sackett and Adler chuckled, looking at each other, amused. Persephone had always known laughter to be a warm, friendly sound, but this was cold—the noise a raow might make when tucking itself in for the night on a bed of human bones.

"Don't care what you do with the wolf or the girl. We can move their bodies after," Sackett said. "But no cuts on Persephone. When her body is found, it has to look like an accident. I'm guessing she took a bad fall on these rocks."

"What?" Persephone couldn't believe her ears. Her mind struggled to make sense of the absurd and failed.

Adler fanned out to flank Minna.

Suri finally took her eyes off the canopy and looked squarely at Adler. She pointed at him and announced, "The trees say *you'll* die first. They told me you offended Wogan. He doesn't appreciate killing in his woods."

Suri turned to Sackett. "The trees tell me *you* will die second. Not because you deserve to live longer but so you'll have time to understand. They say you won't be going to Alysin or even Rel. The paths to paradise are shut to you. Your spirit will enter the darkness of Nifrel."

Sackett's eyes narrowed. "I don't need to be a mystic to predict the future. I'm not the one about to die, little girl."

"Yes, you are," Suri said. As usual the girl's tone was wildly out of context. She sounded pleased, almost giddy—a child excited to have been called upon because she knew the answer. "And I get to watch."

"She's crazy," Sackett said. "Go on, Adler. Kill the wolf."

"Now, Minna," Suri whispered.

Adler was shifting his weight to his back foot and raising his spear when Minna sprang. A hundred pounds of snarling teeth and claws landed on him. Perched on a ledge of slick stone, the man went over. Shield and spear clattered on the rocks, swept away by the water. Adler and Minna both fell one shelf down; Adler landed on a boulder. The back of his head struck the rock, making a hollow sound, a muffled crack. Whether he was dead or merely unconscious was impossible to say, but the one-eyed man wasn't getting up.

Sackett raised his spear to throw it at Minna, but Persephone grabbed the shaft. Although she had hold of it with both hands, Sackett jerked it free and slammed the pole of the weapon into her stomach. Persephone collapsed to the rocks, gasping for air.

"Sackett!" Hegner shouted. The one-handed man used his stump to gesture wildly down the cascade.

Still gasping to fill her lungs, Persephone saw two more men coming up the rocks. Both were strangers. The man out front was tall, beardless, slender, and dressed in shimmering robes, with a silver torc around his neck in the fashion of a wealthy chieftain. But Persephone knew every chieftain of the seven Rhulyn clans and hadn't seen anyone like him before. The second man was as different from the first as a wolf was from a dog. Large and muscled, he had a tempest of black hair and a bristling beard. His clothing was as intriguing as his friend's. Dressed mostly in leather, he also wore a black-and-white-checkered leigh mor bearing the pattern of Clan Dureya.

Sackett tracked Minna's movements, but the wolf didn't attack. She leapt back to Suri's side. The two women looked past him toward the strangers.

Persephone shouted, "Help! They're going to kill us!" With her newfound breath, she started to crawl away from Sackett as best she could.

"This is a private matter," Sackett called out to the approaching men. "None of your business. Be on your way."

"The lady just invited us," the slender man said as he passed Hegner without incident.

"You're a stranger here. Best keep it that way."

"I'd rather not, so allow me to introduce myself. My name is Malcolm." The man approached quickly as he spoke, brandishing a spear with both hands. Behind him, the larger man struggled to keep pace. "By what right or authority do you plan to harm these women?"

The two strangers navigated the last of the rocks that Hegner hadn't yet bothered with and stood on equal footing with Sackett, albeit across a shallow pool. The big man had a hand on a naked sword wedged in his belt.

A sword!

Persephone had never seen a man with a sword. They were the weapons of gods, and this elaborately decorated one shone brightly. On his back, she spotted the hilt of another.

Two swords! Grand Mother of All, who are these men?

"Well, *Mal*-colm," Sackett said. "You must be hard of hearing, so I'll say it again. This is a private matter and none of your concern."

"You, sir, are a coward, preying on the weak. You're not particularly handsome, either. I'd go so far as to say you're genuinely ugly. Now, let me tell you what I think about your mother. She's—"

Sackett took a splashing step through the pool separating them and jabbed out with his weapon. Malcolm stepped back, knocking the spear aside with his own. Sackett advanced, shuffling his way across the cascade, fighting the thrust of water as he sought to close the distance, but Malcolm backed up just as quickly.

The man wearing the Dureya-patterned leigh mor rushed forward, donning his shield and pulling the sword from his belt.

Sackett raised his shield, expecting a strike that didn't come. The Dureyan didn't swing. Instead, he stepped in front of Malcolm and planted his feet on firm ground. Malcolm moved aside, choosing to watch the fight he'd started.

"Who are you?" Sackett asked, looking nervously at the metal blade.

The big man said nothing and stood in a slight crouch, shield up, sword back.

"This doesn't concern you," Sackett repeated once more.

"Didn't say it did," the Dureyan replied.

"Then go away!"

"So you can murder these women?" Malcolm asked. "I think not. Perhaps it's you who ought to *go away*."

"Be careful," Persephone said, having regained her feet. "He's skilled with a spear."

Sackett sneered at her, then lunged toward the Dureyan.

The big man blocked the thrust and brought the sword across his body. The blade caught the end of the spear and cut through the wooden shaft. The sharpened stone tip clattered onto the rocks.

Sackett leapt back in fear. "Hegner, get around behind—" he started to say, but stopped after seeing what the rest had already noticed. Hegner was climbing down and was already close to the bottom of the cascade. "Tetlin's Witch! You lousy cul!" Sackett shouted after him.

Throwing the remainder of his spear at the Dureyan, Sackett turned and started his own retreat. Behind him, Minna growled menacingly. Perhaps he thought the wolf was about to leap or maybe that Malcolm would throw his spear. Either way, Sackett rushed his descent over the slime-covered rocks.

Persephone cringed even before he fell.

Sackett slipped and dropped more than five feet, hitting his back on one edge and then another. His body continued its way down the water-sprayed staircase, falling four times. He grunted with each slap against the rocks. The third ledge caught his right foot and spun him, making the last fall headfirst. His skull didn't crack like Adler's, but the blow bent his neck sharply.

Sackett lay in the froth of the stream, groaning and shaking his head in agony. His eyes were squeezed shut and his mouth pulled into a grimace, showing teeth. He didn't try to get up. Except for his head, he didn't move at all.

"Help!" he cried as the force of the water pushed his

body, inching it toward another drop. "I can't move! I can't move!"

Persephone took a step down. Bent over, she used her hands as well as her feet. Where the water flowed over the rocks, they were slick as ice. She inched down knowing she'd be too late. In the back of her mind, she wondered how the death trap of a cascade had seemed so beautiful on the way up. She descended only three ledges before Sackett screamed. The ceaseless flow of water had pushed him down one more ledge. He didn't fall far, but he ended up in a good-sized pool.

Landing on his back, Sackett couldn't lift his face far enough above the water to breathe. Only his forehead and eyes breached the surface. Persephone moved faster, scrambling over the rocks. Then, like Sackett, she, too, slipped. Her foot came off a stone, and Persephone fell on her back. Her elbow and hip took the worst of it, sending jolts of pain through her side. Slipping farther and hurried along by the push of the stream, she cried out, desperately clawing at the slick stones for a nonexistent hold.

A hand grabbed her wrist. She felt fingers latch on. A moment later she was dangling by one arm. Persephone came off the rocks, pulled upward. Her feet continued to scramble for traction. It didn't matter. The arm lifting her wasn't letting go and had no trouble drawing her up. Another arm wrapped her waist. Pulled tight, Persephone was pressed against the soft kiss of white-and-black checkered wool.

Below them, Sackett peered back like a terrified pond frog. His head jerked once, then twice, and slowly his eyes closed and his head disappeared below the surface.

At the top of the slope, Persephone sat in the fingered roots of a huge tree. Wet from the fall, her black dress stuck to her skin. The big man had offered his checkered leigh mor, and she wrapped it around her shoulders. The wool was rough, nothing like the plush cloth Sarah wove. But it was warm, warmer than expected, and she held it close. She continued to look down the course of the cascade that sprayed below. Persephone thought she could still see Adler's body lying across the rocks, a dark form causing the water to froth. Adler was dead, probably had been from the moment his head hit the rock. Hegner was gone.

What just happened? It was a thought repeated more than once while she sat there.

Persephone was still trying to puzzle it out, still trying to make sense of insanity. Sackett, Adler One-Eye, and Hegner—whom Persephone no longer had any trouble thinking of as The Stump—had tried to kill her. Although she wouldn't describe any of them as friends, they certainly weren't enemies. They were neighbors and clan members, which meant they were family. If it had been only one, she could have reasoned he'd gone crazy. But they had been working together.

Since the attack, no one had said much, except Suri, who had coaxed everyone to follow her up the ridge. Persephone hadn't needed much prompting. She wanted to move, to get off those deadly rocks. By the time they reached the top, she was shaking so badly she needed to sit down.

I almost died, was almost murdered!

The idea took a long time to root in her mind. Once it had, the realization stole the strength from her legs. Bruised, wet, confused, and frightened she hugged herself, shivering. The Dureyan must have thought she was cold, because that was when he had given her his cloth.

"You're all right, then?" the big man asked.

She nodded, clutching herself. "I don't know why they did that. They attacked for no reason. Do you think Hegner will come back?"

"No. He looked pretty scared. That's probably the last you'll see of him."

Persephone let out a breath. "You're right. In all likelihood, he's on his way to Warric. He'd never show his face again in Rhen. Konniger would cut his head off."

"Your husband?"

"No," she told him. "Konniger is the chieftain of Dahl Rhen."

"I thought his name was Reglan."

"Reglan was the chieftain, and my husband, but he died and Konniger rules now."

The big man nodded, then crouched on one knee to scratch behind Minna's ears. As he did, she noticed a circular bronze medal dangling from his neck. Bronze was the metal of the gods; she'd never seen a man with any, and this was finely engraved with the image of interwoven vines or branches. So far the Dureyan hadn't offered his name, but Persephone was convinced she knew who he was.

"Thank you. I . . ." She looked at the mystic. "We owe you our lives. I'm Persephone. This is Suri, and you are . . . ?"

"Men who value our privacy," the Dureyan said quickly, and shot a stern glance at his companion. "Just wayfarers on our way south."

It has to be him.

"Traveling a bit light, aren't you?" she asked. Between them, they had only one blanket and a small sack that couldn't hold much food. What they lacked in supplies they made up for in weapons. Over the big man's shoulder was an *extra* sword—a copper sword.

It's definitely him!

"We live off the land," he replied, looking away.

"Are we still going?" Suri asked. The girl was sitting cross-legged on the ground, playing a child's game with a loop of string, weaving patterns between her fingers.

Persephone again glanced down the slope at the cascade. She didn't know what to do. The thought of plunging deeper into the forest—

"Where are you going?" Malcolm interrupted Persephone's thought.

"Well, we *were* going to . . . ah . . . well . . . it's actually hard to explain."

"Is it far?"

Persephone looked at the mystic. "Is it?"

Suri shook her head as she continued to weave patterns with the string looped between her fingers.

"Well, if it's not far, I suppose we could escort you," Malcolm offered.

This brought a scowl from the big man, which his companion ignored.

"And if we did, do you think you could repay our kindness with some food?" Malcolm gave a hopeful smile.

"Yes, of course. When we get back to the dahl, I'll see that both of you get a good hot meal and a place to sleep for the night."

"Then we'd love to help," Malcolm said.

Persephone got to her feet while momentum was on her side. She continued to clutch the leigh mor to her neck. She wasn't cold but figured her rescuer wouldn't be inclined to run off as long as she kept it.

Maeve's words returned to her: *Heroes like him no longer walk among us.*

Suri put her string away, picked up Tura's staff, and scampered back into the deep wood, running ahead but stopping frequently to look at flowers and birds. The wolf mimicked her, or perhaps it was the other way around. With Suri, it was difficult to tell.

Malcolm, his friend, and Persephone walked side by side when the forest allowed, which was often in an area of thick canopy and scarce brush. They continued to climb, the land always sloping upward. Before long, Persephone realized they were following a vague trail. In the open areas, it vanished, but Suri didn't hesitate or doubt. Soon they were on a ridge where beds of old leaves sloped down to either side.

"So where are we off to?" Malcolm asked Persephone.

"Well, Suri is a mystic and augur. She's taking me to an old oak somewhere up here."

"Mystic?" the big man said. His voice betrayed both surprise and awe.

"Yes. I know she looks young, but she was raised by

Tura, a well-respected augur. Tura was ancient. The last time I saw her, she didn't have a single hair that wasn't white. She knew everything—or could find the answers for you. She recently died, and Suri says the old oak can answer some of my questions."

"May I ask what questions you have that would cause you to risk life and limb as you have?" Malcolm inquired.

The thin man had a formal way of speaking that she liked. Even when she was the wife of the chieftain no one had ever said, *May I ask.* The most surprising thing, though, was that he didn't find it strange that she was off to talk to a tree. Regardless of how he said it, Persephone was grateful for the door he'd opened. She'd been looking for a means to bring a subject up, and this was the perfect opportunity.

"We've recently learned the gods of Alon Rhist might have plans to attack us—all of us. All Rhunes." She paused, trying to determine how best to present the next part. "I'm looking for an answer, for guidance, a way to save my people. I'm also hoping this tree can lead me to the man named . . . Raithe."

This drew the Dureyan's stare. "What do you want with him?"

"Rumors say he has killed a Fhrey. People are calling him the God Killer."

"And what? You want to turn him over to the Fhrey? You think that will prevent a slaughter?"

"No, no! Not at all," she said more loudly than intended, and both Suri and Minna paused to look back. "Some call the Fhrey gods, but it'd be impossible to kill one if that were so. I've had some dealings with them, and I know the Fhrey don't respect us. We're ants to them, and if an ant bites you, do you seek out that one ant? Or do you set fire to the whole colony to make sure you're not bitten again? I want to discover if this Raithe really did slay a Fhrey, and if so, how it was done. If one man can kill a Fhrey, others can learn as well. Our only hope might be to fight."

She caught a look between the two. "Such a hero would be welcomed in Dahl Rhen."

"I've heard rumors about this Raithe person, too," the big man said. "But I don't think they're true."

"Of course they are." Malcolm frowned at his associate. "We were at the roadhouse when Raithe told his story."

"*Raithe* didn't tell a story. A rather unpleasant traveling companion of his did. And I'm sure most of that story was lies."

"Really?" Malcolm replied. "See, personally, I found it to be a beautiful tale. It moved me."

Another look, this one more irritated than the others.

"Let me tell you something that I know to be true," the big man said to Persephone. "The Fhrey are deadly. They wear metal and have weapons that can cut through ours."

"Like the way you cut through Sackett's spear?"

The Dureyan didn't respond and merely continued walking along the ridge, looking out at the trees. Talking to him was like fishing. Reglan had tried to teach Persephone. The goal was to get a hooked fish to a net, but if you pulled too hard, the fish would fight back, break the line, and get away. The process was one of give-and-take, letting the fish have time to realize the cause was lost before pulling it in. Persephone decided to skip the topic and let out more line.

"In ages past, during a great flood that threatened to kill our ancestors, a man named Gath united all the clans. He organized everyone in a common cause."

"You're speaking of the keenig," the man said. "The one who wore a crown. The chieftain of chieftains."

"Yes, and I believe we are facing another similar crisis, but if the clans unite under the leadership of another keenig . . . well, there are more of us than Fhrey in Rhulyn."

"How would you know?" the big man asked.

"I told you. I was married to Chieftain Reglan. We

visited all the dahls together. I've also gone to Alon Rhist for the yearly meetings. Alon Rhist is . . ." She hesitated, trying to think how to explain.

"Impressive beyond words," Malcolm helped her.

She smiled and nodded. "Yes, but I didn't see many Fhrey. I think there are only a few hundred."

"She's right," Malcolm said. "I'd estimate the population at the Rhist to be about three or four hundred."

Persephone was growing quite fond of Malcolm.

"We have nearly a thousand people in Dahl Rhen alone," Persephone said. "And there's twice that in the surrounding villages."

"But how many *men*?" the Dureyan asked. "Not boys or the elderly."

"Three fifty, maybe four hundred."

"And how many are trained to use a spear and shield? And I'm not talking about hunting, either. Rarely do deer fight back, and bears don't plan and fortify. How many of your men have more experience fighting than farming? Fifty? A hundred? Any? To win against the Fhrey, in order to be any use at all, a man would have to train for years. And where are they going to get their weapons?" He grabbed the spear from Malcolm. "These are useless against them. What you are talking about is impossible."

"Maybe," she said as if a veteran of a thousand battles. Everything she was about to say made sense in theory, but she guessed the man before her didn't deal in theories. "Yet no one says it's impossible for men to hunt large game like bears and big cats. A bear is far more powerful than a man, faster too. We win because we hunt in groups. What if ten men fought one Fhrey?

"And yes, there may only be a few hundred good fighters in Dahl Rhen, but there are close to two hundred villages in Rhen alone. And who knows how many more in Menahan, Melen, Tirre, and Warric. We're talking thousands. And our women could fight, too. I know I could learn to hold a spear butted against a charge.

We'd be fighting for our lives, and that's a pretty good incentive, don't you think?"

The big man frowned. "Women can't fight."

Persephone shrugged. She wanted to disagree, but that was an argument for another time. "Okay, but there are female Fhrey in Alon Rhist, too. So if our women can't fight, neither can theirs. Is it impossible to think a thousand men can kill a hundred Fhrey? And how many do the Gula have? If we all band together, we could overwhelm them with sheer numbers."

"Not likely to happen." The man shook his hairy head. "The clans would never join together. They're more likely to fight each other."

She let out more line to her fish. "I see your point. It would take a man like Gath. Someone renowned, someone everyone would agree was the bravest, strongest warrior among them. Someone who all the chieftains could kneel to and not lose the respect of their people. It would take a hero."

Time to set the hook.

"It would take someone who'd already proved himself by killing a Fhrey," she said.

Persephone and Malcolm continued ahead but stopped a few steps later. The Dureyan had halted. "You want this Raithe person to be the keenig?" he said.

Persephone nodded. "I think it might be our only hope to survive."

"That's crazy."

"Doesn't sound at all crazy to me," Malcolm said.

I love you, Malcolm! He was practically holding out the net for her fish.

"You be quiet," the man snapped.

"You are Raithe, aren't you?" Persephone asked. "Raithe of Dureya, the God Killer, wielder of the copper sword."

Raithe glanced over his shoulder at the pommel, sighed, and then glared at Malcolm. "I blame you for this," he said, and walked on.

* * *

After drawing out Raithe's identity, Persephone backed off, satisfied with her progress. The three walked on in relative silence. Ahead of them, Suri had stopped, Minna beside her. The girl seemed transfixed, staring off through an opening in the trees. When they reached her, Persephone realized they had climbed higher than she'd expected Below them, the view was breathtaking, forest-covered hills stretched out for miles. The shadows across the landscape indicated the hour was later than she'd realized.

"That's the home of Grin," Suri told them, pointing at a rocky face where the sun revealed a large cave.

"We aren't going up there, are we?" Persephone asked.

"No, ma'am," the girl replied. "Magda is just ahead."

"Magda?" Malcolm inquired.

"The old oak," Persephone said. "Suri says it's the oldest tree in the forest."

"Who or what is *Grin*?" Raithe asked.

"A bear or demon or maybe both. She killed my son, my husband, and several other men from Rhen."

"Sounds like a good thing to avoid, then," Malcolm said.

They continued on, and Suri led them off the ridge and into a shallow basin. As tranquil a place as anything Persephone could imagine, the valley held a flower-filled meadow. In the center stood a massive tree. Lower branches, each as thick as any regular oak's trunk, rested their elbows on the ground as they extended out hundreds of feet. Her gnarled and ribbed trunk, partially covered in green moss, was mammoth. A pair of huge knots gave the tree the appearance of a gentle, wrinkled face that looked down on them with sad eyes.

It was easy to see why Suri had described Magda as *holding court*. Nothing but flowers grew near her. That was Magda's field, and her boughs extended the width of it like a fine gown.

Suri stopped under the tree's leaves and knelt. Minna lay beside her. The others hesitated, unsure what to do. Slowly, Suri lifted her head to the leaves. "Say hello to Magda, the oldest tree."

Malcolm walked to Magda as if in a trance and laid a hand on the oak. "She is indeed a *very* old tree."

"Magda told me once she has lived for three thousand years," Suri declared.

Malcolm continued to let his hands glide over the tree's bark, which was thick and gnarled with deep lines of age. "She would have seen it all."

"What do I do?" Persephone asked Suri.

"Just ask her what you want to know."

Persephone stepped forward and, looking into the knots as if they were eyes, she inquired, "Are the Fhrey coming? Will they attack Dahl Rhen?"

She waited, listening, expecting to hear a booming voice.

All was silent, and she looked at Suri.

The mystic shrugged. "Try something else."

Persephone glanced at Raithe. "How can I save my people?"

They looked up at the leaves, Raithe wearing a nervous expression. In turn, each of them, even Minna, looked at Suri, who scowled.

"What?" Persephone said.

Suri shook her head in irritation. "Magda's being a beech."

"A what?" Raithe asked.

"She's being quiet."

"Maybe she's thinking," Malcolm said. "Or she doesn't know the answers. Those are pretty weighty questions for a tree that doesn't, you know, travel much."

"She talks to the other trees. They tell her all they've heard," Suri explained. "That's how she knows so much. She hears news from everywhere."

"But how can a tree know the minds of gods?" Raithe asked. "Or the lay of the future?"

"The more you know about the past, the easier it is to divine the future." Suri stood up. "Magda!" she shouted, causing Minna to start. "Wake up! You have visitors! This woman is an important lady. She needs to know what to do. She needs to know . . ." Suri looked at Persephone.

"How to save our race from extinction at the hands of the Fhrey," Persephone provided.

Suri looked her way for a second, licked her lips, and then turned her attention back to the tree. "Yeah, that."

Again they waited. Suri's face scrunched up into an elaborate frown. "I don't understand. Normally—"

A breeze stirred the leaves overhead, and Suri's head snapped upward. Her eyes grew wide, and a smile spread across her face.

"*Welcome the gods,*" Suri said formally.

"What?" Persephone asked, but Suri held up a hand to silence her.

"*Heal the injured,*" the mystic went on.

"I don't under—"

Once again Suri waved for silence. "*Follow the wolf.*"

The breeze died.

They waited.

Suri finally nodded with a happy look. "There you go. The answer to your questions."

Persephone blinked. "That's it? Welcome the gods; heal the injured; follow the wolf? What does any of it mean?"

Suri shrugged. "I have no idea."

CHAPTER NINE

Tight Places

Life on the dahl was dangerous. We lived in fear of everything: spirits, sickness, famine, wolves, and bears. That spring there was less sickness and famine and more wolves and bears.

— THE BOOK OF BRIN

Raithe and Minna were friends from the moment they met, but then he'd always gotten along better with animals than people. In Dureya, some of the less aggressive wolves made a living off discarded scraps. The animals were tolerated because their yipping warned when trouble came to visit. As a boy, Raithe had grown fond of many of them, but few had been as friendly, and none so large, as Minna. In Dureya, animals didn't grow big for the same reason the people didn't smile—a lack of everything. Raithe held a similarly high opinion of Suri, who reminded him of his younger sister, the only sibling he loved. That she was a mystic despite her young age was astounding. Mystics were about as common as two-headed unicorns. The few who existed lived apart from the world of men, remaining untainted by influence and corruption. Having a wolf as her best friend demonstrated the sort of wisdom he appreciated.

Persephone was another matter.

He couldn't decide about her. She was attractive for her age; he guessed her to be about ten years older than himself. But she had been a chieftain's wife, the worst sort of woman, and he hadn't liked the way she'd tried to manipulate him. Using others was the way of those who slept in lodges. They thought nothing of deciding the lives of others. Then there were the three men who had tried to kill her. That sort of thing didn't happen by accident. If people wanted you dead, there was likely a reason. Also, she had acted stupidly on the cascade, risking her life for a man who had tried to kill her. Still, it showed more decency than he would have expected, which gave him pause. So did the fact that she'd spoken to him—a Dureyan—with respect. Such behavior would have been unusual from a farmer's wife, but she had been married to a chieftain and lived in a wealthy dahl. Although it was easy to assume her actions were designed to beguile, there was a genuineness about her. Raithe was far from worldly and no expert when it came to the ways of powerful women, but he'd always been able to tell the wolves that would bite from the ones that wouldn't.

"Minna?" Suri raised her brows when the wolf settled next to Raithe, nuzzling his leg. "That's no way to act. You just met him."

"She's friendly." Raithe bent down and scrubbed the wolf's coat.

"No, she's not, are you, Minna?" Suri smirked at the wolf, then shrugged. "Okay, from here follow the ridge back the way you came."

Persephone, who was still staring back at the old oak, turned sharply. "Wait. You're not coming with us?"

The mystic shook her head. "No, ma'am. I live over that way." She pointed through the blur of trees.

"But . . ." Persephone said, confused. "I thought you came to the dahl to stay."

"Did you hear that, Minna? She's a strange one. We only came to tell you the news. Then there was the whole business of waiting on the trees to wake up, but that's done. You have your answer, so we can go home."

Suri took a few bounding steps, causing Minna to leap from Raithe's side and chase after her. This made the girl grin. "Still likes me best!" She took two more steps, then stopped and looked up at the sky. "Better be quick, ma'am. Night appears to be in an awful hurry."

Then, without so much as a wave, the girl ran off, the wolf chasing her through the trees.

"Ah, good . . . bye," Persephone called after her. "And thank you." She continued to stare until the mystic vanished, swallowed by the green.

Persephone looked back at the big oak, and said, "That's it? I nearly die and all I get are riddles? Not even good ones." Raithe wasn't certain if she was speaking to him, the tree, or herself. Taking a breath, she sighed. Unfolding Raithe's leigh mor, she pulled it over her head like a hood and walked forward. "This way, I guess."

Raithe followed Persephone through the trees. Malcolm had been slow to join them, lingering a while longer by himself.

"If we hurry, we can have a hot meal," Persephone said, following the faint trail they had made in the grass on the way in. "You two like mutton? Sarah is working her way through a ewe Delwin butchered. I've lived with them since my husband's death, and I'm sure you'd be welcomed. She's down to the shank, which isn't the best, but—"

"It sounds like a holiday feast," Malcolm said, running to catch up.

"I take it you're hungry."

"Famished, good lady, famished. We've been living on a sparse diet of nuts, mushrooms, and the rare squirrel or rabbit, which between us doesn't amount to much more than a bite or two."

Back up on the ridge they traveled in a line, their feet plowing loudly through dead leaves. The light cut through the gaps at a sharp angle. Trunks and plants were splashed with brilliant gold, and long shadows stretched out from the base of every tree.

"I've heard of your husband," Raithe told Persephone as he walked behind her. "They say he was old."

She nodded. "Over sixty years."

"But you're not so old."

"Thank you." Persephone glanced back at him with a curious look. "I think."

"I'm just saying your husband was a lucky man. Not only did he live a long time, but he was blessed with a young wife."

She laughed—a nice sound. "I've not known Dureyan men to be so charming."

"Ha!" Malcolm scoffed.

Persephone turned to peer at the slender man marching along at the rear of their parade. "Why do you laugh?"

"Raithe isn't what most would describe as *charming*."

"How would you know?" Raithe asked.

"I've been with you night and day for who knows how long now, and you've never struck *me* as charming."

"You're not a beautiful woman," Raithe replied.

"Beautiful?" Persephone said. "Charming or not, you are certainly most kind, but there must be a terrible shortage of girls in Dureya if you—" Persephone froze in place, and her hand flew to her mouth in horror. "I'm so sorry. I didn't mean . . . I . . ." She bit her lower lip in agony.

Malcolm looked at Raithe with a bewildered expression as the three stood listening to the wind in the leaves.

When she didn't say anything else, Raithe asked, "What?"

She stared at him a moment longer as embarrassment slowly shifted to surprise. "You don't know?"

"Know what?"

"Dureya—the Fhrey." She shook her head, her hand still lingering over her lips. "They destroyed Dureya and we think Nadak as well."

Raithe stared at her, puzzled. People often said things that didn't make sense. Those who talked a lot were the most prone to the practice. Words spilled out of their mouths with little thought behind them. Persephone might be one of those. But she didn't seem the sort to lie, and there would be no point in making up such a thing. "What are you talking about?"

Persephone looked to Malcolm for help, but he remained silent, leaning on his spear. "A group of men from Nadak came to Rhen. They said they saw it themselves. The Fhrey killed everyone." Then, more quietly, she added, "They burned the villages as well as the dahl."

"The Fhrey did that?" Raithe asked, trying to picture such a thing in his mind. The gods had never attacked Dureya before, but he found it disturbingly easy to imagine. He looked to Malcolm. "Is this possible? Would they do that?"

"I . . . I expected them to come after us, not your people. But I suppose it's possible."

"How many villages? Which ones?" Raithe asked Persephone.

His question made her cringe. "All of them. The report I heard said . . ." She frowned.

"What?"

"They found no survivors. None. You might be the last living Dureyan."

She said more after that, but Raithe had stopped listening. Malcolm spoke, as well, but Raithe walked away. He had a vague sense of trudging down the ridge with them following. He wanted to think, needed to think, but couldn't. Once, when Herkimer had been training Raithe, he was struck in the head with a wooden mallet. He'd collapsed but was still conscious, his father looming above. Herkimer yelled, but Raithe couldn't hear. The words were faint and muffled, Raithe's thoughts lost in a fog. That's how he felt now. The world had stopped, and when it started again, his first thought was that Persephone must be mistaken. Dureya couldn't be gone. As poor as they were, his people numbered in the thousands. They lived in hundreds of settlements from the Forks to the High Spear Valley. They couldn't *all* be gone.

Why would anyone destroy a place as insignificant as Clempton?

"Raithe, do you know where you're going?" Malcolm asked.

Raithe stopped. They still traveled along the ridge, but the hardwood trees had given way to spruce and cedar as the three plodded uphill.

"Are you all right?" Persephone asked.

"I'm fine."

She looked at Raithe for a long moment as if she were going to offer a dissenting opinion.

"We're going back to Dahl Rhen, right?" Malcolm asked. "I don't remember walking downhill at any point when we were on our way to the oak."

Persephone paused and turned around. "You're right; we didn't."

They were in the middle of an endless group of trees that were different from the ones Raithe remembered passing through earlier.

"We should have turned off the ridge at some point, I think," Malcolm said.

The world beneath the canopy was darkening. The conifers blocked more sun than the hardwoods but not enough to account for the growing gloom. The piercing shafts of sun were gone, night was coming, and it was already hard to tell where one tree stopped and another began.

"I suppose we should head back to where we started going up again, then—" Persephone was interrupted by a not-too-distant howl.

"Do you think that's Minna?" Malcolm asked, his voice concerned but hopeful.

"Came from the other way," Persephone replied. "Out there." She nodded her head at the forest to their left.

Another howl echoed from slightly to the right of the first.

"Maybe we should go this way." Persephone walked briskly in the opposite direction of the howls. Raithe followed after her with Malcolm in tow.

Soon they were skidding down a steep slope, plowing through brown needles still damp from a recent rain. The deeper they went, the darker the forest grew. Near the bottom, the air became noticeably cooler, and the floor of the forest was green with ferns. They waded into a grove of knee-high fiddleheads, where they discovered a creek.

"Is this the stream that goes to the cascade?" Persephone asked.

"Maybe," Malcolm replied. His voice sounded strained.

Persephone followed the flow of water downhill. They trudged onward, but nothing looked familiar.

Howls continued, closer than before. Down off the ridge, the eerie sounds bounced off tree trunks and echoed back. Raithe couldn't determine where the howls came from, but he was certain of one thing—there was more than one.

Persephone picked up their pace as they continued downhill through brush and over stones. With each step, it seemed the world grew darker and the forest changed. Evergreens transformed into black curtains; scattered birches became slender, staring ghosts. Rocks and boulders hidden in shadows took on the shapes of crouching animals waiting to pounce. In the growing dark, he felt closed in, blinded and trapped by the closeness of the trees.

"I'm not sure I know where we are," Persephone told them while pausing beside the creek.

"I don't think any of us does," Malcolm said.

Persephone rubbed her arms. "Well, at this point I'm—" She stopped.

Movement. Creeping figures emerged from the undergrowth.

Three wolves, all black, with sharp, white teeth snarled through curled lips. The trio came out slowly, too slowly.

"Get behind me," Raithe ordered, drawing the Fhrey sword and backing up.

Malcolm clutched the spear in front of him. "Just point and stick, right?"

Before Raithe could answer, Persephone screamed. He whirled around in time to see another wolf rush up from behind. Her shriek frightened the animal. It skidded to a halt. Raithe swung, but the wolf retreated out of range.

"Take my shield." Raithe pulled the wooden board off his back and handed it to Persephone.

More wolves approached. Raithe saw ferns quivering all around them. This was a large pack, more than a dozen.

"Put your backs to each other!" Raithe shouted. "Stay close. Don't run."

The wolves closed to within a few feet, swarming, circling; their tongues hung and dripped. The bravest, a big black wolf with some gray in its coat, inched closer. It snapped, then darted back when Raithe swung. This generated a round of loud yipping.

"Dammit!" Malcolm shouted, missing his wolf, which had darted in at the same time.

Persephone was the first to land a solid blow. Using the edge of the shield, she struck one hard on the snout, causing the animal to yelp and scuttle away. Another wolf lunged at Raithe. He was ready and caught fur, maybe a bit more. The animal yelped.

The pack looped around them in a constantly moving circle. Then, abruptly, one would dart in, snarling and snapping. The lunges and feints caused their tiny triangle to shift. Uneven ground hidden beneath ferns caused Raithe to stumble more than once. If he fell—if any of them did—the wolves would be on them. One deep bite and the smell of blood would put the pack into a frenzy. Bloodlust would overpower fear, and they'd attack as a group. That would end it. Raithe was certain he could kill two, maybe three, but the wolves would win.

"Ah-rou! Ah-rou!" A howl echoed in the forest.

A pair of lights darted through the trees. The flickers appeared, vanished, and then reappeared, closer.

"Ah-rou! Ah-rou!"

The wolves hesitated, backed up, and turned toward

the noise—a howl not made by any wolf. Then the lights burst out of the forest. With a torch in each hand, Suri raced at the wolves, leaping fallen trees and running along their trunks. She sprang over ferns and ran straight for the thickest part of the pack, howling, barking, and swinging the torches. The pack scattered in a panic, splitting apart to let her pass.

"Follow me!" she shouted, racing by.

The three of them didn't hesitate. They turned and chased the mystic through the trees. The pack followed, the leader spearheading the pursuit.

"Keep running. Follow the stream!" Suri shouted as she slowed and dropped to the rear. Raithe stayed back with her as Persephone and Malcolm raced on.

The big black wolf with the splash of gray charged. Ignoring Raithe, it went straight for Suri, who stood her ground and waved torches to no avail. The leader neither stopped nor slowed and launched its full weight at the girl.

A flash of white shot out of the darkness. Minna caught the pack leader in midair and bore him to the ground where the two rolled apart. Before the lead wolf could get up, Suri was on it, stabbing with the torch's fiery end.

The black wolf yelped and fled, its singed fur smoking.

"Ha-ha!" Suri shouted before darting off again.

Raithe followed her, struggling to keep up with the lithe girl as she and Minna sprinted, splashing through the little stream. Persephone and Malcolm stood in a patch of moonlight, looking back.

"There's a drop!" Persephone shouted to them, pointing down at the edge of the cliff they stood on. "Oh, Grand Mother of All! It's a waterfall!"

"Jump!" Suri called.

"What?"

"Jump!"

Raithe slowed as he neared the drop. Suri didn't. Together, the mystic and her wolf leapt off the edge. As she fell, as she disappeared from sight, Suri let out a loud *whoop!*

The wolves were still after them. Barks, yips, and growls filled the forest. Persephone and Malcolm looked back at Raithe, both wide-eyed.

"Better than being eaten," Malcolm said, and surprised Raithe by being the first of the three to jump.

"Oh, Grand Mother, be with me," Persephone prayed, and she, too, leapt.

Raithe looked over the edge, but in the growing darkness all he saw was a cloud of moon-kissed mist rising from blackness. The wolves closed in, growling. They knew the ledge was there and slowed their approach. Six animals fanned out in a semicircle, teeth bared, saliva seething from their mouths.

"Oh, Tetlin's Witch!" Raithe turned and followed the others.

The fall nearly killed Persephone. The impact was only water, no jagged rocks or partially submerged trees. And she was able to get back to the surface easily enough after pushing off the bottom, but the fall itself, that blind drop through total darkness, had almost scared her to death.

She had spent twenty years carrying official news to the other dahls and was one of the few people who'd visited Alon Rhist. The tales of her travels had impressed everyone. But the sum total of two decades paled in comparison with what she'd been through in the last few hours. Persephone had conquered her fear of the forest, survived a murder attempt, received a cryptic message from an ancient tree, battled wolves with nothing more than a wooden shield, and leapt blindly from the top of a waterfall. In one day, her life had gone off its own cliff, and she suspected the bottom hadn't yet been reached.

Once everyone broke the surface, Suri shouted for them to swim behind the curtain of falling water, where a massive hollow of bare rock suggested that the little stream had once been much bigger. Snow wasn't such a distant memory, and the pool was bitterly cold. Still, Persephone barely noticed. Her pounding heart generated its own heat. After swimming to retrieve his floating shield, Raithe was the last one out.

"Whoa!" Suri shouted, shaking the water from her hair. The wolf did the same, but without the exclamation. "We showed ole Char, didn't we?" she said to Minna. "Gave him a mark he'll remember. Now his name *really* suits him. Ha!" The girl was grinning, beaming with enthusiasm. Throwing her arms around the wolf, she praised her. "And you were great, Minna. Slammed him good, you did. Sure showed him this time. You're *my* hero, Minna!"

"You've fought them before?" Raithe asked. The big man's hair was flattened, slick and sticking to his forehead. His beard rained on the stone.

"All the time. Char is a rude neighbor. He and Minna don't get along. He's jealous because Minna loves me more."

The falls drowned out most of the night's sounds, but Persephone heard howling. "Can they reach us?"

Suri nodded. "They'll be here shortly," she added with a bright smile. "Always takes them a while to run back around the ridge. I keep waiting for them to try jumping, but they haven't yet. Char isn't very bright."

Persephone worriedly looked at Suri's soaked torches. "What are we going to do?"

"Disappear," Suri said with a wink.

"What?"

The girl laughed. The sound was high and childlike, not the sort to provide reassurance when facing a ravenous pack of wolves while trapped behind a waterfall. Persephone looked to Raithe but found little comfort in his eyes. The Dureyan warrior looked back with a tense expression.

"This way," the mystic said, and stepped into a crack in the rock. Persephone discovered it was more than just a crack, a cleft wide but low. Everyone except Minna had to duck as they moved through. Behind them, the howls grew louder.

"Where are we going?" Persephone asked as they shuffled between walls of stone.

No longer muffled by the hills and trees, the crisp yips of the pack carried clearly. Then she heard a splash. *They're here!*

"Over here," Suri said, and an eerie, green glow pierced the darkness as a door opened in the rock. The mystic waved for them to follow, and once more she led by example, stepping inside.

With the sounds of splashing right behind, no one hesitated. Heedless of what new horror she might find, Persephone rushed through the stone wall into the new world of green light. Suri shut the door.

All four of them, plus Minna, stood in a chamber not much larger than a roundhouse. Hewn from solid rock, the room was grander than Dahl Rhen's Great Hall. Thick pillars carved from natural stone formed sturdy supports. Austere blocks formed a fortified hall of strength, precision, and uniformity. The clever use of space and tapering angles of square columns and ribbed archways possessed a grace and beauty that awed Persephone. Running in a line around the ceiling, down the edge of walls, and along the borders of the floor were chiseled markings—strange patterns forming an unbroken chain. Stylized pictures were carved on every surface, short people fighting taller ones. Embedded in the center of the floor, where a roundhouse's fire would have been, a large green stone glowed with a steady light. Although not bright, it shone enough to fill the room with an eerie radiance.

"What world have we stumbled into?" Raithe asked. His head turned left and then right while he gripped his sword.

"An old one," Malcolm replied.

"Is this your home?" Persephone asked Suri.

The girl's face reflected the absurdity of the question. *"Nooo."* She dragged the word out. "Stone walls are almost as bad as wooden ones. I live in Hawthorn Glen, one of the loveliest little places you'll ever see."

"Is this one of those crimbal doors you spoke about? The ones that lead to Nog?"

Again the mystic shook her head.

Sounds of growling and the scrape of claws on stone startled everyone except Suri and Minna. Raithe pulled his sword and slipped on his shield.

Suri chuckled. "They can't get in."

Raithe moved forward and touched the stone's decorative border that marked the place where they had entered. Except for the carving, no discernible evidence of an opening remained—not even a crack.

"How did you open it?" Raithe asked, returning the weapon to his belt. "And how is it sealed?"

"The door will open if you press the diamond shape in the design at the top. On the outside there's no design, just a little rock sticking out a bit. You have to feel around to find it, and it's too high for the pack to reach."

Persephone looked around and saw no other exit. "We're trapped, then."

Suri pulled off her cape and draped it over a horizontal pole mounted in the wall, which seemed put there for that exact purpose. Minna sniffed around the chamber. Neither appeared concerned. "The pack will eventually get frustrated and leave. We have a while before they do. Char is stubborn. We'll spend the night to be sure."

The scratching and barking continued at the door, but it became clear the pack wasn't getting in. Persephone relaxed and allowed her shoulders to droop. Now she noticed the cold. She removed Raithe's leigh mor and wrung water from it and her hair. Snapping the blanket-sized cloth, she wrapped herself again.

"What made you come back for us?" Persephone

asked, moving closer to the glowing stone and hoping it would be warm like a fire. It wasn't.

Suri untied her deer-tooth belt. "Got your message."

This caused them all to glance over.

"We didn't send any message," Raithe said, shaking the water from his hair and stroking more from his beard.

Suri stripped off her vest and skirt, hanging both alongside her cape, leaving her naked. Persephone glanced toward Malcolm and Raithe. They had discreetly turned their attention to the marks lining the room. Persephone appreciated the gesture even if Suri didn't seem to care.

The mystic's tattoos weren't confined to her face. Similar designs graced her whole body. A pair of twisted tendrils ran along Suri's collarbone, and another line ran straight down the center of her chest before curling around her back. Thick swirling bands like a tree's roots encircled her arms from elbows to shoulders.

"If you didn't send a message, then Wogan must have been in a generous mood," Suri said. "I wasn't even to the pines when I saw a squirrel drop his acorn and run back down the tree to get it. So Minna and I raced back as fast as we could."

The girl wasn't as thin as Persephone had expected. Suri's hip bones did stand out and ribs were easily counted, but the weight the girl did have was all muscle.

"Took me a while to find you," Suri went on. "Where were you headed to, anyway? I thought you were going back to the dahl."

"We were," Persephone said. "But we missed a turn."

"I'll say. You were going *exactly* the wrong way. Being touched as you are from living where you do, I figured you were hunting Grin. I followed your trail, and you were heading straight for her cave."

"That wasn't our intention. We were lost," Persephone said.

"Should have thrown a bit of salt on your trail. That would have kept the leshies away."

Raithe sent a sharp look at Malcolm, who shrugged.

"How did you find this place?" Malcolm asked, still looking at the chiseled markings that lined the room.

"Tura showed me." Suri busied herself by squeezing the wetness out of her clothes. "Not many secrets in this forest that old Tura didn't know. There's five of these stone rooms under the Crescent. Most are nicer than this. Pretty metal shirts are inside some. I tried one on, real heavy and too small. Another one has horns, pipes, and a box with strings that make wonderful sounds when you pluck them."

Satisfied with her clothes, Suri walked behind one of the pillars and returned with her arms filled with blankets. She handed them out—thick soft cloths, one of which Persephone draped around herself. Suri wrapped one over her shoulders and lay down beside the green stone. Minna snuggled up alongside the mystic.

"This is a rol—a Dherg safe house." Malcolm pulled his blanket up like a cloak, complete with a hood. "A remnant of the Belgric War."

"The what?" Raithe asked.

"A war between the Fhrey and the Dherg, who used hidden places like this to retreat to or stage attacks from. That's where the term *Dherg* comes from. It means 'vile mole' in the Fhrey language."

"How do you know that?" Persephone asked.

Malcolm shrugged. "I lived with the Fhrey."

"You fought for them?" Persephone asked, focusing more on his spear than on the man.

"No, nothing like that. I was a slave." Malcolm touched the metal band around his neck.

"Oh," she said, not knowing what else to say.

"Wasn't so bad. Alon Rhist is a beautiful place. I suspect my life was better than it would have been in one of the Rhune villages. I was warm, safe, had plenty of food, and a lot to learn."

"You ran away?"

"Yes." Malcolm paused, his eyes betraying a faraway thought. "Funny how being well cared for isn't enough.

My labors were light, and as long as I performed my tasks, I wasn't poorly treated. In some ways, I was living a princely life, but . . ." He pulled his blanket tighter. "Raithe and I haven't had a decent meal in days. We're always wet, cold, hungry, and dirty beyond belief. And yet I much prefer my new life over the days spent in Alon Rhist."

He sat down near the glowing stone. "Fulfillment comes from striving to succeed, to survive by your own wits and strength. Such things make each of us who we are." Using the blanket, he rubbed his hair. "You lose that in captivity, lose yourself, and that loss saps your capacity for joy. I think comfort can be a curse, an addiction that without warning or notice erodes hope. You know what I mean?" He looked at each of them, but no one answered. "Live with it long enough and the prison stops being the walls or the guards. Instead, it's the fear you can't survive on your own, the belief you aren't as capable, or as worthy, as others. I think everyone has the capacity to do great things, to rise above their everyday lives; they just need a little push now and then."

Minna's head lifted. Her ears tilted toward the door.

Outside the growls grew louder, though the scratching had stopped. A yelp was cut short. A thunderous roar followed, making them all jump.

Another wolf cried out and then a third.

Suri startled everyone by shouting, "Don't be a stubborn fool, Char! Run!"

"What's going on?" Persephone asked, but Suri was too focused on the sounds beyond the door.

Another wolf yelped, and Suri got to her feet. So did Minna. Neither left the light of the green stone, but both stared fearfully at the closed entrance.

Silence. Not a sound from inside or out.

Suri's tattoos masked much of her expression, but tears ran down her cheeks. "You should have run, you stupid, stupid fool," she whispered.

Persephone could hear her breathing as they waited. "Suri, what just—"

BOOM!

Each of them jumped as something powerful struck the stone door.

Raithe drew his sword again. It flashed green, reflecting the glow of the stone. Malcolm grabbed his spear, letting his blanket fall.

BOOM!

Dust and bits of rock flew.

They all got to their feet then.

"What is that?" Raithe asked.

"Grin," Suri replied.

For the first time, Persephone saw unabashed fear on the girl's face.

"Can she get in?"

Suri hesitated, and everyone knew the answer before she replied, "On her hind legs, she's twice as tall as me."

"Is there any way to brace the door?" Persephone asked.

Suri shook her head.

BOOM!

"Will it hold against the pounding?" Malcolm asked as another cloud of dust and stone chips flew from the wall.

"It *is* just a bear, right?" Persephone asked. "Why would she try to get in here?"

"She wants us for dinner, I think," Raithe replied.

"But why? I'm pretty sure she just killed more than one wolf. Should have plenty of food already. More than she can possibly eat."

BOOM!

Persephone felt the power of the blow shake the room. A small metal shield that she hadn't seen earlier fell off the wall. It rolled, wobbling faster and faster before coming to a noisy stop.

BOOM!

"Why would a bear ignore a feast to throw itself against a stone wall?" Malcolm asked.

They braced for the next attack. Instead, the roar came again.

They waited.

Silence.

Suri walked to the door, her cheeks still wet. She placed her hands against the stone.

They all waited.

Then Suri turned. "She's gone."

CHAPTER TEN

The Galantians

There is an old clan saying: When a stranger comes to the door, always be generous because it might be a god in disguise. In my experience, gods do not use disguises. They are too arrogant.

— THE BOOK OF BRIN

The next morning they found six dead wolves outside the rol. No sign of Grin the Brown, only the bodies and the blood spattered on the crevice's stone walls. Suri paused for several minutes beside the wolf with the burn mark on its fur.

The men kept their blankets but Persephone and Suri put the others back. Raithe also took the metal shield that had fallen during Grin's attack. Remarkably light, it was decorated with the same fancy circles and designs as those on the walls of the rol. Raithe offered to draw straws with Malcolm for it, but the ex-slave declined. He preferred the spear and needed both hands to wield it.

A morning mist filled the forest. In the days he and Malcolm had spent in the Crescent, Raithe had seen it many times, but the haze was still unnerving. There were no forests in Dureya, and the few trees that managed to grow were stunted, emaciated things. He'd grown up in open, rocky highlands of grass and lichen-covered stone, and it felt unnatural to be surrounded by trees and wrapped in fog. The haze further supported Raithe's belief that they were walking in a perilous world of guarded secrets and murky mysteries. Trees appeared and faded in the mist as if by choice—silent watchers, sentinels of spirits and gods. Caught early enough, the waking forest had no time to disguise itself into something mundane. This was a place of enchantments, a place where anything could happen.

Suri led them back through the falls and up to the ridge, taking time to explain where they had gone wrong. The mystic pointed at trees as if one could be distinguished from another. When she was done all three nodded, even though Raithe remained clueless. By the time they returned to the cascade, the mist was in full retreat and lingered only in isolated low-lying areas.

The men's bodies were gone. Persephone scanned the rocks with apprehensive eyes. Raithe created a mental list of who or what might have taken the men: spirits, more wolves, Grin the Brown, Wogan, or perhaps the inhabitants of the dahl. That last one troubled him, but his empty stomach concerned him more. He wanted to ask Persephone if she intended to make good on the promise of a meal, but he refrained. They hadn't spoken much that morning. The quiet of the wood demanded silence.

When at long last they cleared the tree line and returned to the open field, all of them except Suri gained a spring in their step. Once more the blue of a peerless sky stretched above, and the unhindered face of the sun shone down. The great wooden wall of Dahl Rhen crowned the hill of spring flowers. Wet grass soaked their legs as they climbed the slope where already Raithe could smell food. As they neared the top, a horn announced their approach.

"That's an *all clear*, right?" Raithe asked Persephone.

She nodded, holding the hem of her dress up and exposing sodden sandals speckled with bits of grass. "It would be two blasts for an alert and three for a call-to-arms threat."

"Same as in Dureya," he said.

Persephone nodded, smiling.

"I'm just so glad to be back. I don't think I've ever missed this place so much. It feels like I've been away for a year rather than only a day. A long and incredibly frightening year. I'm going to sleep well tonight."

Suri stopped. "I expect you can find your way from here, ma'am?"

"Yes, Suri." Persephone rolled her eyes. "I don't think I can get lost within sight of my home. But won't you please come in with us? The least I can do is get you a meal. You saved my life. You have to let me do that much."

The girl hesitated, then glanced at Minna. "What do you think? Their food was pretty good."

"Come. Eat. Spend the night," Persephone told her. "You can leave fresh in the morning."

The girl whispered to the wolf, "One more night won't make us touched, Minna. But if you see me wearing shoes, bite me."

Raithe discovered that Dahl Rhen was nothing like Dahl Dureya. Inside, the village was huge and packed with roundhouses built with the luxury of logs sealed with daub. The thickly thatched roofs formed tall, cone-shaped peaks. Torches lined gravel paths that snaked between the homes, and a broad gravel avenue ran up the center of the village to the lodge and the common well. Filling gaps between dark-soil gardens were fire pits and woodpiles.

Woodpiles!

In Dureya, wood was more precious than metal. Here, the villagers burned it even though it wasn't night or winter. The series of vertical logs surrounding the village were crucial for protection, and even inside, wooden fences bordered gardens. *Probably the only way to keep the goats and pigs out.* Along with chickens, the animals wandered freely underfoot. Raithe checked Minna, but the wolf paid no attention to any of the livestock and stayed at the mystic's side.

Dominating everything was the lodge. The huge building sat in the middle of the dahl at the opposite end of the gravel pathway. Perched on a foundation of stone, the big wooden house was four times the size of Dureya's lodge. Squared beams braced the peaks and framed great doors. Pillars formed by binding together the trunks of six giant pine trees stood on either side of the porch.

On the left side of the path leading to the lodge, two braziers flanked a stone statue of a god. The sculpture stood only three feet tall and had vaguely human features dominated by large breasts and wide hips. Dureyans had their own gods, the Mynogan, who were actually three gods—the gods of war. Dahl Rhen's god looked friendlier.

There were more people there than Raithe had ever seen gathered in one place. As many as a hundred walked the pathways, worked the well, or tended gardens. Most were women and children. One of the few men he saw was a potter, a cripple who sat huddled over an odd spinning table, shaping wet clay.

A cripple? Raithe pondered this. *How wealthy is this place that it can afford to feed a cripple?*

His answer was visible in the healthy faces of those around him. In Dureya, those who survived the winter looked like skeletons. These men and women were downright pudgy. Well dressed, too. Done up in neatly tailored tunics, thick woolen leigh mors, and breckon mors large enough for double folds. Most of the clothes were dyed or patterned in one fashion or another, and Raithe felt embarrassed for his crude leather and thin checkered cloth. His shame was compounded by all the stares greeting them.

Raithe had expected looks. Everywhere he and Malcolm went there had been stares, but these were more pronounced. The people of Dahl Rhen dropped gourds filled with water and bundles of wood. One stared so hard that he walked into a fence post and nearly fell. Those working on roofs climbed down, and those swinging mattocks in the garden stopped. Everyone watched in shock as if the members of his group each had three heads and a tail. What surprised Raithe was that they weren't restricting their attention to Malcolm and himself. As Persephone led them up the gravel path toward the lodge, people stared at her most of all. And there were whispers, lots of whispers, her name muttered more than once.

They were nearly to the lodge's steps when a woman called from a roundhouse's doorway. "Seph!" She frantically motioned them closer. "Where have you been?"

Persephone gestured toward the woman. "Raithe, Malcolm, Suri, this is Sarah. The one I told you about. She's one of Rhen's best weavers. Her husband, Delwin, is—"

Sarah grabbed hold of Persephone's wrist and pulled her inside. The men and Suri followed. The roundhouse's wall was covered in paintings, and the room was filled with rich wool. A spinning wheel and a large loom dominated the space. Inside were two more people: a young woman working a spinning wheel and a girl beside her, carding wool. Both stopped their work the moment the group entered.

"What really happened? I don't believe it, any of it, not for a second." Sarah wrung her hands as if strangling an invisible chicken.

"What are you talking about?" Persephone asked. "Sarah, what's wrong?"

Sarah, whose braided hair framed a kind but troubled face, glanced nervously at Raithe and Malcolm. She took hold of Persephone's hands. "Hegner has accused you of murdering Sackett and Adler."

"*What?*" Persephone's voice registered somewhere between a yell and a scream. "Hegner? Hegner is here! I thought he had run off."

"He said you tried to kill him, too," Sarah said. With another glance at Raithe and Malcolm she added, "And that you had help."

Persephone seemed too dumbfounded to speak. She stared at each of them in shock.

"Why in the name of the Grand Mother of All couldn't you have killed The Stump, too?" the woman working the spinning wheel asked.

Long, black hair wreathed a face of high cheeks, a sensual mouth, and a delicate nose, all of which paled in comparison with her eyes—big, dark, deep, and intense. To look into them was to peer over the edge of a sheer drop. The woman wore a simple, thin dress, but draped over *her* curves, it came alive. Dureyan women were valued for strong backs rather than their looks, and even the most beautiful of them never looked this way. In legends, women like her would either lure men into disaster or raise them to fame. The dilemma for the would-be hero was determining which.

"Konniger is making me marry that cretin," she announced, and scowled.

"Moya, please!" Sarah snapped.

Outside the open doorway, people gathered. They spoke quietly to one another and pointed to the group inside Sarah's roundhouse.

Persephone finally regained her composure. "I didn't kill anyone. Hegner attacked me! All three of them did."

"That's not the story he's telling."

"What possible reason would I have to—? I need to get this cleared up." Persephone turned and walked out.

Raithe followed the others out even though he was as uncomfortable in crowds as he had been in the forest. Too many people were like too many trees. In Dureya, villages consisted of only a few families. But here, nearly two hundred people now gathered in front of the steps and more were spilling out of roundhouses.

All of them had the same rosy-cheeked, well-fed faces. Faces without pockmarks or the deep lines cut by blistering winds. Also missing were the scars, broken teeth, and severed fingers that a life of warfare bestowed. And not one carried a weapon. Instead, they held hollow gourds, chisels, and mallets. One fellow carried a basket of eggs.

Raithe expected Persephone to confront those just outside Sarah's house, but instead she pushed through them and marched down the broad pathway past the well and on up the steps of the lodge. At the top, she stopped, pivoted, and faced the people of the dahl.

She waited for a moment while the crowd gathered. Then in a loud voice she said, "Yesterday, Sackett, Adler, and Hegner tried to kill me in the forest." She paused, probably for the full weight of the statement to settle in. "They chased me up a cascade, and Sackett and Adler both died when they slipped and fell on rocks. I don't know why they attacked me. They didn't—"

"That's not how Hegner tells it." A stocky man stepped through the lodge's doorway behind Persephone. He wore the silver torc of leadership.

Raithe's first thought was that the man's beard was short for a leader, and he disliked the chieftain's eyes. They didn't seem even, the left one being slightly higher than the right. The only visible scar was a recent one, still pink and healing—hardly the mark of an experienced warrior. Walon, Dureya's chieftain, had a beard down to his chest, few teeth, and a face like beaten copper. That was the mark of experience, the sign of a survivor. The Rhen chieftain did have one thing no one in Dureya had. He carried an ax.

At the sight of it, Raithe pushed to the foot of the steps. This wasn't his clan, and this man wasn't his chieftain. Raithe didn't have a stake, other than a promised meal, in whatever dispute was about to start, but he had come to like Persephone. Undecided only a day before, he knew if there was a fight he'd back her.

Persephone turned to face her chieftain. "Then Hegner's a liar, Konniger."

"Is he? If Sackett, Adler, and Hegner sought to kill you, why aren't you dead?" Konniger folded his arms and glared. "Do you expect anyone to believe two experienced hunters slipped and fell? Are you saying you had nothing to do with their deaths?"

Persephone opened her mouth to speak.

"Hegner!" Konniger called to the darkened interior of the lodge. "You were there—you're the one she's accusing—tell everyone what you witnessed."

The one-handed man appeared from the shadows and stepped onto the porch. "We were out hunting and found her on the cascades with those two fellas there." He pointed with his good hand at Raithe and Malcolm.

Eyes shifted toward them, and those closest inched away, which was fine by Raithe.

"We thought Persephone needed help. Him being Dureyan and all. Could have been in trouble. She must not have seen us yet because she kissed the big one."

A woman sporting a circlet of flowers over braided hair also emerged from the lodge. She stood to the side and slightly behind Konniger. Hearing Hegner's words, she began shaking her head while looking at Persephone. "Reglan isn't dead a month and you're already carrying on with another man. Or were you seeing this lover *before* our chieftain died? Were you stealing away into the forest while your husband was out avenging your son?"

"You lousy, lying cul!" Moya burst out, and pushed forward. She might have reached the steps if Sarah and a few others hadn't caught her.

"Watch your mouth," Konniger snapped.

"Outbursts like that are why we ordered your marriage," said the woman with the circlet, whom Raithe concluded was the Second Chair, Konniger's wife. "You're a wild animal, Moya. Hegner will beat some respect into you."

Moya thrashed but was held back.

"Go on, Hegner," Konniger said.

"Yeah, well, like I was saying, they were kissing, but we still wanted to check things out. She certainly looked willing, had her arms around him and stuff, but you never know. He might have been forcing himself on her. We climbed the cascade, and when Persephone saw us, she told them we couldn't be allowed back to the dahl. She said it would *ruin everything* if people found out. That's when these two attacked. The big one has a sword, two in fact. And we didn't stand a chance. He killed Sackett and Adler. Woulda killed me, too, if I hadn't run."

"Why are you saying these things?" Persephone asked Hegner. She didn't seem angry. If anything she sounded hurt, but most of all her tone and the shake of her head expressed bewilderment. "You know none of that is true."

The crowd had expanded out beyond the well and the stone god. Most of Clan Rhen filled the broad pathway leading from the lodge steps to the front gate, where they stood shoulder-to-shoulder on the crushed gravel. A few kids were out near the closest roundhouses, standing up on roughly cut benches near fire pits to try to see over the heads of their parents. The crowd murmured as people talked among themselves.

Konniger raised his hands to quiet them. "It's your turn, Persephone. What motive do you put forth, for I can see no reason why three of our most distinguished men would attack you without provocation."

Persephone shook her head. "I don't know. I've been trying to figure that out since it happened. But these three were with me, and they can testify as witnesses on my behalf."

It was Konniger's turn to shake his head. "It's reasonable to assume they'll take your side. We would need someone impartial. Was there anyone else?"

Persephone clenched her fists. "No. But can't the same be said of Hegner? Who are his impartial witnesses?"

The chieftain stroked his beard. "You make a good point. But two men are dead; that fact isn't in dispute. I find it difficult to accept that two experienced hunters would merely fall to their deaths." He focused on Raithe. "And Dureyans are well known for their murderous ways."

Raithe shoved the two people in front of him aside and climbed the steps to stand before Hegner. "He called me a murderer." The words rolled out in a growl. "In Dureya, an accuser will defend their claims in battle. I imagine this custom holds true in all dahls." He glanced at Konniger. "I demand that he take it back, *and* his lies against this woman, or we'll let the gods decide the truth. We can settle this matter right now." He let his hand rest on the handle of the sword.

"You challenge a one-handed man?" the wife said. "How like a Dureyan."

"What does that matter?" He pointed at Hegner. "If he tells the truth, the gods will award him victory even if he had no hands and just his vile mouth. Or don't you believe in the gods?" With a disdainful shake of his head, he added, "So like a southerner."

"You are violent, disrespectful, and no doubt a liar," the wife declared, shaking her head. "Don't you see how you're proving Hegner's point? You don't think we can see what is *really* going on?" She lifted her voice to the crowd. "What more proof is needed? The killer who helped Persephone is a Dureyan!"

"The gods will tell the truth of it," Raithe barked, and moved toward Hegner.

Konniger stepped between Raithe and the one-handed man. The angry murmur of the crowd rose.

Raithe had hoped to get a meal, a decent night's sleep, and maybe some food for the road. Instead, he found himself accused of murder and facing off with a dahl chieftain on the steps of their lodge in front of a herd of pampered villagers. Perhaps Shegon wasn't a god, but he sure must have been favored by them. Since he had killed the Fhrey, Raithe's life had been cursed. His only consolation was that it couldn't get any worse.

Then the horn sounded. It blew once, twice, then three times.

Everyone's attention turned toward the far end of the broad pathway, as men scrambled to seal the gate with a thick wooden beam.

From the wall came the shout, "The gods are here!"

Persephone watched as fear ripped through those gathered. All eyes turned to their chieftain, but Konniger didn't inspire confidence. He stared at the gate and swallowed hard.

"Turning at the crossroad!" Cobb shouted from his perch on the wall beside the gate. "Definitely coming this way."

"What do we do?" Bergin the Brewer asked. He twisted the dirty towel in his hands.

Even Tressa looked to her husband expectantly, but Konniger didn't move, didn't speak.

"How many are there?" Persephone shouted across the dahl.

"Nine," Cobb yelled back. "Well, there's seven gods and two . . . other things."

"What do we do?" Tressa whispered to her husband.

The chieftain ran a hand over his mouth. He looked left and then right, breathing heavily.

"Konniger, you need to go out there," Persephone said. "Meet them on the road before they reach the dahl. Talk to them. I'll come with you to translate."

Konniger looked at her then. She expected anger, a seething glare; maybe he would hit her now. Persephone would have preferred a slap to what he gave, a terrified bewildered expression.

He thinks we're already dead.

"I'll do no such thing." Konniger shook his head. "That would be suicide. Our walls are thick and our gate strong. We'll be safe here."

Persephone searched the crowd and found Malcolm. She came down from the steps and grabbed him by the arm. "Will the walls hold them?"

Malcolm shook his head. "Your walls are made of wood. Even stone would only slow them down."

Persephone looked out at the faces. Mothers took the hands of children, their heads turning back and forth between the gate and Konniger. Husbands held their wives close, and tears formed in the eyes of many as hope faded. They all began to understand that their chieftain wouldn't save them.

There are things beyond the control of men, and the will of the gods is one of them.

"They're at the grazing line," Cobb shouted, his voice starting to shake.

Persephone turned away from Malcolm and focused on Raithe. He stood on the steps, one hand still on his sword. He was big, his shoulders broad, his face stern.

God Killer.

"Everyone!" she shouted, climbing back up the steps. "Listen to me. This is Raithe of Dureya. The God Killer!" She looked at him, trying to determine their chances in his expression. He was definitely angry, maybe even furious, but she saw no fear.

"Cobb says there's nine of them. How many did you fight last time?" Persephone asked Raithe.

He didn't answer.

"Thirteen," Brin said. "According to the stories, he faced Shegon and twelve of his men. After he defeated the leader, all the others fled."

"Fewer this time. Can you do it again?" Persephone asked.

Raithe exchanged a hard look with Malcolm. "There's a big difference between that story and what really happened."

"Perhaps, but if they plan on repeating what happened at Dureya, then you'll die with us," she said.

"You're sure the gate won't hold them?" Raithe asked Malcolm.

"No more than a garden fence."

"So there really isn't a choice, is there?" Raithe sighed in resignation. "Tell them to open the gate."

"No!" Konniger came to life. "You can't let them in!"

"Didn't you listen?" Gifford said, hopping forward and leaning on the crutch Roan had made. "They'll smash the gate." He looked at Malcolm with his squinted eye. "Maybe being gods they might just tell it to walk away and up it will go."

"We have the God Killer," Brin said. A smile bloomed across her face. Hers was the only one. "They'll probably run when they find out he's here."

"Brin, for the love of Mari, be quiet," Sarah pleaded with her daughter.

Raithe started down the steps. The crowd parted to grant him a path.

"Open the gate!" Persephone shouted, and then returned to Malcolm's side. "He can do this, right?"

"I guess we'll see."

"They're gods!" Konniger shouted. "Men can't fight gods!"

Along with everyone else, Persephone watched the God Killer walk alone down the pathway. "You better hope you're wrong."

Raithe kept his eyes focused on the gate.

The worst that can happen is you'll die. A favorite saying of his father's. He'd heard it countless times. During the Long Winter, when his mother became creative with their meals, even she had used it. *Try it. The worst that can happen is you'll die.* For a Dureyan living on a plain of burning rock and freezing snow, death wasn't feared. *Might even be a step up,* his father also used to say. Everyone died anyway, and in Dureya most died young.

Raithe didn't fear death, but he had hoped to marry someday and become a better parent than his father. He wouldn't spend his life off fighting, leaving his family to fend for themselves.

Coming so close to Dahl Rhen had been stupid. He could have veered around it and been miles away if only he'd stayed in the forest's eaves and pushed south as planned. Staying with Malcolm had been an even bigger lapse of judgment. He could have, should have, abandoned him at the roadhouse. Traveling would have been faster with a child in tow. But getting involved with Persephone was his worst mistake of all.

How did her problems become mine?

Raithe's father wouldn't have been trapped so easily. He knew better than to let emotions cloud judgment.

Raithe hadn't learned that lesson, despite hearing it so often. After trying for years to avoid following Herkimer's footsteps, it was ironic Raithe would die in the same foolish way. He'd be just one more stupid Dureyan slain by a Fhrey. There would be a difference, though— he would be the last.

Despite Konniger's order, the men at the gate lifted the rough-hewn log free of the hooks and tossed it aside when Raithe approached. They didn't push it open. Once their responsibility was done, the pair bolted like rabbits.

Raithe looked back. Persephone stood next to Malcolm, clutching his arm and whispering into his ear. The shakes of the ex-slave's head and the look on his face verified what Raithe already knew—he didn't stand a chance.

With a sigh, he pushed the heavy gate open and left the dahl. Outside, the Fhrey party approached in two lines, walking side by side. Raithe expected exact duplicates of Shegon, but these Fhrey were different.

He didn't care for the changes.

They wore yellow armor that shone like gold in the afternoon sun. Many had Shegon's blond hair and draped blue capes of the same shimmering cloth over their shoulders, but these Fhrey had sunbaked skin and bodies of lean muscle. Two weren't Fhrey at all, nor were they human.

One was easily the largest being Raithe had ever seen. Twelve feet tall or more, he had a bald head and flat brutish features. The giant wore only a skirt of leather and straps of hide, and he carried a mammoth sword. The other one walked on two legs but looked more like an animal than either a man or Fhrey. Its sickly-yellow eyes seemed too large for its head, and it loped along on short legs. With its hunched back and incredibly long arms, its claws dragged along the ground. The thing's skin was dark and leathery, and the ears were pointed, though much longer and sharper than those of any Fhrey. Worst of all was its mouth, which was filled with so many rows of needle-sharp teeth that it couldn't contain them all. They stuck out at odd angles, and Raithe wondered how the creature could eat without tearing its lips to pieces.

"What a helpful fellow you are. Opening the door for us like that," the nearest Frey said with a smile. His blond hair was cropped shorter than Shegon's, his pointed ears standing out. Unlike Shegon, this Fhrey's shoulders were broad and his build muscular. Aggressive sky-blue eyes noted Raithe's every movement.

"Sorry, but you can't come in," Raithe said, standing in the center of the path and realizing just how stupid that sounded, even to himself.

The short-haired Fhrey's smile became a grin. "And why is that?"

Raithe didn't like the grin. The Fhrey had a gleeful, eager expression; he was hoping for trouble.

"Because I said so." Raithe let his hand settle on Shegon's sword.

The Fhrey's eyes followed the movement and narrowed with interest.

The rest of the party advanced and came to a stop behind the first, where they fanned out to get a better view.

"What do we have here?" another Fhrey said. Except for the giant, he was the tallest of the group. His hair reached his shoulders, but like all the Fhrey, he had no beard. "A welcoming committee of one?"

"On the contrary," the first replied, "he says we can't come in."

"Can't? How rude. I mean, even for a Rhune that's ill mannered."

"And he has Shegon's sword."

This revelation caught all of their attentions. Looks of surprise ran across their faces, followed by expressions of delight.

"So this is the famous *God Killer* we've heard so much about," the tall one said. Like all Fhrey, he had beautiful, delicate features: flawless skin, straight teeth, and those brilliant blue eyes.

The entire group was relaxed, weight back on their heels, shoulders loose, not a hand on a weapon. Raithe wasn't sure if he was pleased or worried about that. Maybe they weren't there to fight. Or maybe, like Shegon, they knew he wasn't a threat.

"Tell the truth. Did you kill Shegon?" the tall one asked.

"Yes," Raithe said. "And I'll do the same to any Fhrey who tries to enter this dahl."

"Well, well. Aren't you the bold one." The tall Fhrey took a step closer, and Raithe realized they were the same height. Raithe glared back, refusing to blink.

"So you're a great warrior, then? Do you think you could kill me?"

He didn't reply. The Fhrey was sizing Raithe up, and he wanted to keep him ignorant.

"There are stories about you all along the road. I'm a little disappointed. I expected you'd be taller—the tales certainly are."

The others laughed.

"Do you know who *I* am?" The tall, long-haired Fhrey held his hands out, palms up, and slowly pivoted to give Raithe a full view. Sun glared off his brilliant armor, and the wind blew his golden hair. "I'm Nyphron, son of Zephyron, leader of the Instarya tribe, and captain of the Galantians, these nice fellows with me. They are the elite of the Instarya, and as there are no greater warriors than the Fhrey, these Galantians are the best of the best."

"Being their leader, I suppose that makes you the best of the best of the best?" Raithe spoke with a cavalier tone. He wanted to show he wasn't impressed, which was difficult since he was certain the Fhrey told the truth.

Nyphron shook his head. "No, I'm actually not." He clapped the short-haired Fhrey's shoulder. "Sebek is."

This brought a round of moans from the rest of the troop.

"Well, okay, each of us has specific fields of expertise. *But . . .* " He paused, holding up a finger and glancing at the others. "I'd still say Sebek is the best overall warrior. Anyone dispute that?"

Sebek grinned.

No one said a word.

Nyphron returned his focus to Raithe. "I suppose you think you're something special now that you've killed one of us, yes? Before you get too full of yourself, look at the sword you carry. See all the fancy decorations on the hilt? The encrusted gems? Lovely, isn't it? Do you think that's a warrior's weapon? Shegon was a member of the Asendwayr tribe, a hunter. They provide food for our kind. Although they're skilled trackers and excellent in forests and fields, they don't know much about *real* combat. That sword is merely decorative. A pretty toy. He received it as a gift from an admirer. Some idiot in Estramnadon who doesn't know the first thing about battle made it."

Nyphron drew his sword. He did it slowly, making a point not to threaten. Nevertheless, Raithe took a step back and gripped the hilt of his weapon more tightly.

"This"—he presented his weapon—"is *Pontifex,* one of the names we have for the wind. It's a custom-crafted, curved cleve I designed myself—simple, short, and fast. Not as austere as Sebek's more traditional twins, but as you can see it's definitely not a toy. So tell me, Rhune, do you think you can kill me?"

"I'm not a Rhune. I'm a man."

Nyphron smiled. The cheery, simple look disturbed Raithe more than anything that had happened so far. He didn't know what it meant.

"Let's find out exactly *what* you are. Go ahead, draw that pretty sword."

Nyphron waited until Raithe had his blade clear. "And your shield, slip it on. We need to do this right."

Raithe wasn't certain if it was a trick. The Fhrey saw

his apprehension and took a step back, providing him room to safely arm himself.

"That's an odd shield," Sebek said, and glanced at Nyphron. "Did Shegon have a weird little decorative Dherg shield?"

Nyphron shrugged. "Who knows?"

The Galantian leader also had a shield, and in one blindingly fast motion it moved from his back to his forearm. The action was beyond impressive—like magic. Raithe couldn't help being intimidated, even as he realized that had been the point.

The rest of the Fhrey stepped back, and when they were both ready, Nyphron bowed while touching the sword's pommel to his forehead. Raithe returned only a nod.

He expected the same lethal speed as before and wasn't disappointed. Nyphron was faster than Shegon, but not exceedingly so. If Raithe hadn't already faced a Fhrey—if he hadn't seen the lightning-quick strikes before—he would have been dead in an instant. But Raithe was ready this time. He gave himself over to instinct and caught the stroke with his new shield. He had no idea what to expect and was shocked when the power of Nyphron's blow rang the metal and jarred the buckler from his grip. With no supporting strap, it fell to the grass.

"No protection," Sebek muttered. "Just decorative."

A following stroke was inevitable. Raithe acted in anticipation rather than in reaction. Nyphron struck, aiming to decapitate him. If Raithe had been an instant slower, he would have lost his head. His blade clashed with Nyphron's, and Raithe feared a repeat of his failure with his father's copper, but as the metals kissed, Shegon's weapon—toy or not—held.

Nyphron wasn't one to pause. Momentum was in his favor and he pressed hard, striking again—first low then high. Raithe caught the strokes an instant before they would have cleaved off his leg and arm. He had no time to counterattack as the Fhrey forced his advantage.

He's fast, so incredibly fast.

Raithe's brothers weren't this quick. They were brutes, big and heavy. Raithe was the swiftest among them, and he used that to his advantage. If they caught him, Raithe was beat, so he perfected his ability to dodge. Speed had made all the difference in the past. Speed and balance, but Nyphron was better at both.

Stretched to his limit, Raithe fell back, holding on to life by his fingertips as he managed to barely place his sword in the path of Nyphron's hammering. The blades had no time to stop singing before the next toll sounded.

Defeat was inevitable. Raithe only needed to make one mistake, and it wasn't long before he did.

The Fhrey's sword came across in a blinding sweep, and Raithe batted it aside, but with too much force. He lost precious time recovering his balance and wouldn't be able to catch the next stroke.

From somewhere behind Raithe came a gasp of fear. He wasn't the only one to see what was coming. In anticipation of the killing blow, he gritted his teeth.

Miraculously, Nyphron slowed. The Fhrey looked up, distracted by something near the dahl's gate. Something behind Raithe. The lack of concentration was brief, but enough. Knowing he couldn't counter Nyphron's attack, Raithe didn't bother. Instead, he made a dangerous gamble. For the first time, Raithe went on the offensive. He swung down instead of across. They would trade blows, blood for blood.

The move might have worked, but the Fhrey raised his shield—another first.

Before his stroke was through, Raithe was already shifting for his next. He had the upper hand now and intended to keep it. Spinning, Raithe cut upward. Nyphron was forced to dodge. Again and again Raithe pressed his attack, knowing he couldn't allow the Fhrey to catch his composure or the tide would turn again. Raithe hammered his opponent, desperate to weaken the strength in Nyphron's arm.

Sweat formed on the Fhrey's brow, and his gleaming eyes weren't so bright. Remembering his brothers' tactics, Raithe moved in close to mitigate the Fhrey's ability to dart clear of attacks. When he saw his chance, Raithe stomped down hard on his opponent's foot. Surprise flashed on Nyphron's face and Raithe took the opportunity to punch him hard in the jaw with the hilt of Shegon's sword.

The Galantian staggered backward, stunned and off balance. Blood dripped from his chin, and his shield lowered.

Seeing his one clear chance to win, Raithe stabbed out—

Clang!

Raithe's attack was parried away. A second stroke hit the hilt of Shegon's sword, breaking Raithe's grip and throwing the weapon to the ground.

Sebek stood before him, holding a cleve in each hand— violence in his eyes. Bold, confident, powerful. Despite Malcolm's assurances, Raithe believed that what stood before him was indeed a god. He waited, but Sebek didn't advance. He merely stood with one foot on Shegon's sword.

Nyphron was bent over, panting for breath and wiping blood and sweat from his eyes. Raithe, also struggling for air, took a step back, and drew his father's hunting knife. It wasn't much, but it was slightly better than Herkimer's broken blade.

Of course, how fitting that I'll die holding the same knife. The gods are nothing if not poetic.

Nyphron waved a dismissive hand at them both. "We're done."

What does "we're done" mean? Is this where they kill me?

Raithe didn't mind the break; he needed a rest. The chance to clear his eyes and take in much-needed air was welcome. Waiting for what would come next, Raithe glanced behind him to see what had distracted Nyphron. Persephone and Malcolm stood together, watching wide-eyed from the open gate. Persephone had hands over her mouth. Malcolm appeared just as apprehensive but managed to offer Raithe an approving smile.

"How did you learn to fight like that?" Nyphron asked.

"My father taught me."

"*Your* father?" He glanced over at Sebek. "Did you see?"

Sebek nodded. "Hard not to."

"My father fought in the High Spear campaigns," Raithe explained. "He was taught by your people."

"He wasn't taught by my *people*," Nyphron said. "He was taught by my *father*. Those are *his* techniques."

Raithe didn't know what to say. He decided *nothing* was the best course and focused on breathing. Whatever came next, he would need air.

"Why did you do it?" Nyphron asked, and then spit a bit of blood. "Why did you kill Shegon? Was it for sport? To see if you could? To test your mettle?"

Raithe shook his head. "I thought you heard the stories. He killed my father."

"That was true?" Nyphron looked surprised.

"Killed him right in front of me."

Nyphron stared hard at Raithe, and for another long moment no one moved or spoke. Then the Fhrey nodded as if understanding something. "Thing is, Shegon was a *brideeth eyn mer.*"

"I've heard that about him," Raithe said.

"If it wasn't forbidden, I'd have killed him centuries ago." Nyphron ran an absent hand through his long hair and looked at the sword beneath Sebek's boot. "Give it back to him. He's earned it."

"We going again, then?" Raithe asked.

"No." Nyphron held up his free hand as he sheathed his sword. "I found out what I wanted to know."

"Which was?"

"That it's possible."

"What is?"

"For a Rhune to kill a Fhrey."

"Glad to have helped."

"Can we come in now?" Nyphron asked.

"Sorry." Raithe shook his head.

"Not very courteous of you."

"Neither is slaughtering thousands of people and burning down Dureya and Nadak."

Nyphron nodded. "You make a good point. But would it make a difference if I told you *we*"—he gestured toward his group—"had nothing to do with that? In fact, we're outlaws . . . rebels . . . because we refused to take part in that reprehensible affair. We went against the edicts of our ruler and declined to butcher defenseless Rhunes. We're in flight, like you, and from the same pursuers. If you have been offered shelter, couldn't we receive the same?"

Raithe was stunned. He had imagined the conversation going differently. "It's ah . . . it's not my decision to make." He turned to look at Persephone again. She blinked then nodded.

"It would appear the lady approves," Raithe said. "Welcome to Dahl Rhen."

"Wonderful." Nyphron smiled. "Where is Maccus?"

"Maccus?"

"He's the leader here, right?"

This time Persephone spoke from the shelter of the open gate. "Chieftain Maccus . . . was . . . that is . . . he is . . . dead. He's been dead for, ah, seventy years, I think. He was my husband's great-great-grandfather."

"Oh," Nyphron said. "Well, do you still make that marvelous wine? The pale red one, with a hint of nuts? I've boasted about it all the way here."

"There *was* a vineyard once, up on the slope of the Horn Ridge," Persephone said. "But it was lost to drought decades ago."

Nyphron scowled. "Doesn't anything in this place last?"

"Hardship," Persephone replied. "We always have an abundance of that."

The god looked directly at her. Their eyes met and he smiled. With a nod, he replied, "Well . . . at least you have that."

CHAPTER ELEVEN

The Tutor

There were seven clans of the Rhulyn-Rhunes and three for the Gula-Rhunes. Each clan had a chieftain. When it was necessary to unite, a single leader was named and we called him the keenig, which eventually became the word king. The Fhrey had tribes instead of clans and no chieftains. Instead, they had a single ruler who was called the fane.

— THE BOOK OF BRIN

The three stones clattered to the marble floor. One rolled toward Arion, who picked it up and handed the smooth egg-sized rock back to Mawyndulë. The fane's son acted as if the little stone weighed a ton—every movement dramatizing extreme effort. Even his breathing appeared labored, each exhalation a long sigh. He stood before her, frowning, head bowed and shoulders slumped so that the sleeves of his asica slipped down and covered his hands.

"I can't do it," he told her.

"Try again," Arion insisted.

"I don't want to."

The two were in the palace's entrance hall, which Arion had chosen for its high ceiling. She'd chased away the servants to give them privacy, and it was there, before the grand staircase and among the lavish frescoes, tapestries, polished stone, and vases filled with flowering plants, that the two faced off in a battle of wills.

"I don't care. Do it anyway." Arion folded her arms in a gesture that should have ended the debate, but this was no typical student of the Art. Mawyndulë was the prince, the twenty-five-year-old son of Fane Lothian, and every one of those years had been spent isolated in the Talwara Palace. Surrounded by servants and those eager to curry favor, the prince had developed an inflated sense of himself.

He glared back defiantly, his anger unmistakable.

Most people wouldn't risk antagonizing the son of the only Fhrey endowed by the god Ferrol with the power to kill or order the death of another of their kind. But being too lenient wouldn't help Mawyndulë or the future of their people. After spending time with him, Arion was sure Fane Fenelyus wanted her grandson schooled in more than just the Art. And she was going to do exactly that.

You may be the prince, she thought, *but I've lived more than two thousand years. Which well do you think goes deeper?*

If she was going to teach him anything, she had to establish respect. As far as Arion knew, the only person Mawyndulë held any respect for, other than his father, was First Minister Gryndal. Not a surprise, Gryndal was a legend and held in awe by nearly every Miralyith.

Arion didn't waiver. She stood with folded arms, staring directly back. After several minutes, the prince's ire turned to bafflement. Servants who'd been with him since birth weren't likely to lock eyes with him for long. This was only their third meeting, his second lesson, and the prince was testing her boundaries. Centuries of meditation and training gave her a considerable edge. Arion didn't so much as blink. The prince struggled to mimic her resolve. The lad was stubborn if nothing else. That was good. It showed a strength of character. She could work with that.

In the stillness of their silent war, Arion could hear the rustle of leaves and the songs of birds entering an open window accompanied by a pleasant spring breeze. Deeper in the palace, she could make out the muffled music of the Estramnadon Choir practicing for their performance before the fane. She settled in for a long battle and focused on her breathing, each inhalation and

Age of Myth · 163

exhalation evenly paced. Arion was just becoming comfortable when Mawyndulë's glare wavered.

The prince huffed, and with a scowl picked the stones up again—two in one hand, one in the other. He threw the first, but with too much force. Arion was grateful she had insisted on practicing under the high ceiling of the entrance hall. Mawyndulë quickly threw the second stone, too quickly. The height and timing were both off.

Is he really so inept or feigning incompetence out of defiance?

The stones came down like projectiles, and Mawyndulë chose to dodge rather than catch. She didn't criticize his reluctance. From such a height the rocks would hurt.

The stones hit the floor again with loud cracks.

"See!" Mawyndulë shouted, putting hands on hips. He pursed his lips so tightly that they went white.

"Yes, yes, I see. You've proved me wrong. That's wonderful. Now, if you'd actually juggle the stones, I'd appreciate that even more."

"It's stupid, and I don't see what this has to do with the Art." He hummed, and with a tension-filled flick of his fingers the stones rose and chased one another in a circle like a wheel spinning in the air. "Why should I use my hands when I can already do this with the Art? Your lessons make no sense."

"Yes, you're very clever, but that isn't today's lesson," she said.

Arion picked up a wineglass from a nearby table. She'd been enjoying the light, delicate ambrosia while waiting for the prince. The glass was empty except for a dry red ring at the bottom.

"Catch," she said, and tossed it at Mawyndulë.

"What?" Panic flashed across his face. The prince reached out with his control hand, and the crystal goblet bounced off his fingers. He tried to make a grab with the other, almost had it, but the glass slipped away, as did

the stones. Everything struck marble. The stones clattered; the glass shattered.

"Hmm," Arion mused, tapping her upper lip. "Something seems to have gone wrong there, didn't it?"

"Yeah, you threw a glass at me!"

"Imagine if it had been a knife, a javelin, *or a ball of fire*. And instead of stones, what if those rocks were people's lives?" She looked down at the mess at his feet. "Perhaps if you had learned how to concentrate on more than one thing at a time, they wouldn't all be dead right now."

"Arion," the boy said, looking down. "They aren't people; they're stones."

"Lucky for you, or should I say lucky for them? Now pick up those poor dead bodies and try again."

"And the glass? That was—"

Arion coughed, and the eight large pieces, seventeen shards, and two thousand three hundred and seventy-four grains of powdered dust leapt off the floor and reassembled themselves into a glass, sitting on the table, perfectly restored. Even the residue stain remained.

"Whoa." Mawyndulë stared at the goblet. "How did you do that?"

"By paying attention when others were teaching me and not questioning their methods."

The prince contemplated this. His eyes shifted between the glass and the stones while he rubbed the stubble on his head. Like all Miralyith, Mawyndulë shaved his head, but it had been a few days, and a dark shadow was forming. Arion couldn't understand how he could allow that. She couldn't go two days without shaving. It didn't feel clean.

As Mawyndulë bent to pick up the stones, the doors of the Grand Entrance burst open and boomed as they banged against the walls. Arion didn't need to look to know who it was. Gryndal's aversion to touching doors bordered on obsession. He avoided touching most things, preferring to cultivate lavish fingernails long enough to curl. Instead, he used the Art to punch doors open and always overdid it. Arion knew the excessive force wasn't due to a lack of skill or control, just one of Gryndal's many idiosyncrasies. His issue with doors was among the least peculiar.

Gryndal didn't offer so much as a glance in their direction as he marched across the hall. The jingling of tiny chains draped between piercings in his ears, cheeks, and nose accompanied each step. A long golden cape flowed in his wake. Arion rolled her eyes. Gryndal was using the Art to summon a breeze to make his mantle billow. He maintained a second weave to enhance its color, which was brighter than any dye could achieve. Mawyndulë had a different reaction. He watched the First Minister with wide-eyed eagerness.

As Gryndal passed them without breaking his stride, he barked out, "You. Follow."

"Do you think he means you or me?" Mawyndulë asked Arion, unable to contain his excitement.

"I suppose we should find out. Go on. You won't be able to concentrate now, anyway."

The boy sprinted after the First Minister, toward the throne room. Arion bent down, picked up the rocks, and placed them in her satchel. Although ordinary, the stones were the same ones she'd learned with. Arion kept few keepsakes, but these were three of her most prized. She had hoped they would somehow make things easier with the prince by instilling the same sense of wonder in him as mastering them had in her. So far things weren't going as she'd hoped.

When she looked up, Mawyndulë was already out of sight. Arion sighed. Gryndal was a tough act to compete against. As the winner of the Grantheum Art Tournament each year as far back as anyone could recall, he was the idol of every Miralyith. Arion was in the minority; she couldn't say she cared for him. Although Fenelyus hadn't mentioned anything, Arion suspected that the old fane had shared Arion's opinion.

I wonder what she would have made of Trilos.

Who, or what, he was remained a puzzle. She hadn't

seen him since that one meeting, and even though she inquired about him everywhere she went, no one had heard of anyone by that name. Her failed efforts to unmask the stranger deepened the mystery to the point that she almost doubted the encounter altogether.

Arion caught up to the pair outside the throne room. Even Gryndal didn't dare blast open *that* door, but she was surprised he had waited for her.

"Your flawless magnificence, I have news," Gryndal said to the closed doors, and a moment later they opened. Gryndal entered, his cape whipping like the tail of a cat nervous about getting it caught. Arion and Mawyndulë followed.

The throne room was precisely that—a room for the throne. The chamber needed to be massive because the Forest Throne consisted of six extremely old and intertwined trees of different varieties—each representing one of the six original tribes of the Fhrey. A mass of roots formed the room's floor, and the ceiling was an impenetrable canopy of branches and leaves. The fane's "chair" predated everything except the Door. The Forest Throne was the second oldest thing in Erivan and perhaps the world. The room, the whole palace, had come later.

"Your Majesty, a bird has arrived with confirmation from Alon Rhist on the matter of Nyphron and his Galantians," Gryndal said. He and Mawyndulë stood at the foot of the Forest Throne, where Fane Lothian sat listening. "They have indeed refused to obey your edict and assaulted Petragar before escaping to the wilderness of Rhulyn."

"How is Petragar? Did they kill him?" the fane asked.

The Fhrey's supreme ruler—and divinely chosen voice of the god Ferrol—sat with one leg over the tendril arm of the magnificent throne, absently strumming a seven-string vellor. The Great Chamber wasn't designed for music, and the soft notes were lost to the expanse, making weak, wistful sounds. Fane Lothian wore a green robe and the familiar gold-cast circlet of leaves, the same one that had graced Fenelyus's head for as long as Arion had lived. Seeing it on his bald head, she conceded Fenelyus's argument that hair had its beauty.

"No," Gryndal reported. "Petragar is alive but seriously injured."

"So where are they now?"

"Unknown. I don't expect they'll return to Alon Rhist. Not on their own, that is. They'll have to be brought to justice."

Lothian sighed. "I didn't want it to be this way."

"Excuse me, my fane, but I'm a bit lost," Arion said. "Exactly what are we talking about?"

"Nyphron, son of Zephyron, was the commander at the Alon Rhist frontier outpost."

"Son of Zephyron? The Instarya who challenged you for the throne?"

Lothian nodded. "I doubted his son would give me his unwavering loyalty, so I replaced him with Petragar. Nyphron took the change worse than I expected."

"Indeed, after beating the new commander bloody, he deserted," Gryndal added.

"That's horrible," Arion said. "I had no idea conditions out there had become so atrocious."

"Few do," Gryndal told her. "And we need to keep it that way. All these centuries stationed on the borderlands, all these years living among savages, has bred dissent among the Instarya. They have grown wild and insubordinate, and the Galantians are the worst example of this. They're more Rhune than Fhrey now."

Arion frowned as she noticed how Mawyndulë stood with hands grasped behind his back in the same stance as Gryndal.

"Uncivilized barbarians." Gryndal's usual voice could make *Good morning* sound like a death sentence, but he spoke now with even greater brutality.

Arion thought Gryndal saw himself as the epitome of culture. Dark eye makeup, half a dozen facial piercings, and an obsession with wearing only gold were all attempts to demonstrate his refinement. As fastidious as he was about his appearance, the Art was his true addiction. Fenelyus had warned about the temptation to overindulge. *Power has a way of seducing by saying what you want to hear. Remember, it's easier to believe an outlandish lie confirming what you suspect than the most obvious truth that denies it,* the old fane had said.

"Such insubordination is dangerous to leave unchecked, my fane. I advocate execution," Gryndal said.

Lothian considered this, then shook his head. "I don't agree. They only beat Petragar. They didn't kill him. If they had crossed that line—"

"They haven't crossed it . . . yet. Are you willing to take such a risk?"

"I may be the fane, but I still need justification. Ferrol's Law grants me the power, but I must be judicious in its use."

Gryndal looked irritated, more so than usual. Seeing any expression beneath all the rings and chains was difficult. Arion suspected that he walked carefully through the thickets of the Garden so he didn't catch the hoops or chains on any branches.

Maybe that's the point. His way of displaying he's above such mundane concerns.

Given the length of his fingernails, he certainly couldn't juggle her rocks or—she smiled—open doors.

"Ferrol's Law was created for ordinary Fhrey, *not* the Miralyith," Gryndal said. "The Art has elevated us, and we cannot be bound by the law of a god when we have become gods ourselves."

Arion saw Mawyndulë nodding, a look of wonder and admiration in his eyes. He would be the next fane, and it was her responsibility to make sure he was a good ruler.

She stepped forward. "How wonderful! I wasn't aware we had achieved divinity. When *exactly* did that happen?"

Her tone caught them all by surprise.

"And now that we have," she continued, "please tell me when we'll be having tea with brother Ferrol? My mother would love his recipe for vegetable soup. As for myself, I'd like some advice on how to create my own race of people, for that ability has eluded me."

Gryndal's chains rattled as he turned to glare, his look so venomous that she prepared to weave a shield. He wasn't beyond abusing his power. There were those who accused Gryndal of excessive violence during tournaments and told stories of him using the Art in romantic encounters. One ex-lover claimed their tryst had resulted in her death and resurrection, which proved that not all the rumors were true. Still, Arion once had seen Gryndal torture another Fhrey, a simple Gwydry farmer. As far as she could tell, he'd done so for the thrill, seeing how far he could go without killing the man. Not unlike holding one's own hand close enough to a flame to almost burn.

"Gryndal didn't mean it that way," Lothian said. A flip of his hand revealed how oblivious the fane was to the cataclysmic eruption pending only three feet away. "But he makes a valid point. Miralyith are a breed above everyone else. It's foolish and outdated to think otherwise. We might not be gods, but compared with the other tribes we might as well be."

"Then we should seek to be benevolent gods, yes?" Arion said. "Treat other tribes the way we would like Ferrol to treat us?"

"Exactly," Lothian said. "We have a responsibility to our own, and the Instarya are monsters of our making. They want to return. Did you know that?"

"You can't allow it," Gryndal said, reluctantly pulling his gaze away from Arion. "They can't hope to assimilate into Fhrey society any more than a Rhune could. They would be a terrible disruption."

Arion noticed how the First Minister used the term *Fhrey* as if it no longer applied to himself.

"Come now, Gryndal. It's not quite as bleak as all that," the fane said. "Rhunes are vile, filthy beings living in makeshift dwellings of dirt and rocks. They wallow in their own waste."

"You've seen them?" Mawyndulë asked excitedly. "You've crossed the Nidwalden River?"

"Yes, once. Many centuries ago."

"You left Erivan?" Arion asked. "Why would you do that?"

"My mother required it. During the Dherg War, she wanted me along to see it for myself."

"And you saw a Rhune?" Mawyndulë asked again.

The fane chuckled. "Not a Rhune, many Rhunes. They multiply at a ridiculous rate. A single female can give birth to a brood. Some mothers have as many as twelve or fourteen offspring."

"Fourteen?" Arion said, shocked.

"Yes . . . well, not at one time, at least I don't think," Lothian explained. "But they have been known to bear a single litter of two or three, possibly more."

"There must be thousands," Arion said.

"Tens of thousands," Lothian corrected. "We actually don't know how many."

"Are they dangerous?" Mawyndulë asked.

"No more than any other animal," Lothian said. "In fact, a bear or big cat is far worse. The Rhunes are terrified of us. They would scatter if we came near."

"You are correct, my fane," Gryndal said. "I shouldn't have grouped the Instarya so easily with the Rhunes, but it doesn't change the fact that centuries among the barbarians have made the Instarya unfit for Fhrey society. Similarly, I don't think the Instarya at Alon Rhist are capable of dealing with Nyphron and his Galantians."

"So you have no confidence in Petragar?" the fane asked.

Gryndal looked at Lothian as if he'd made a bad joke. "Nyphron is dangerous, my fane, and one of your best warriors. I think you would be wise to send a Miralyith. The Instarya revere Nyphron and his Galantians. The longer they avoid judgment, the greater the risk becomes they could fuel a rebellion, as we saw with Zephyron."

"But that wasn't a rebellion," Arion said. "Zephyron followed the law and acquired permission from the Aquila to blow the Horn of Gylindora and challenge for the throne."

"It was *legal*," Lothian told her. "But it revealed a mindset, a propensity for dissent against the rule of the Miralyith, that I don't appreciate."

"I'll go!" Mawyndulë announced, eyes shifting between his father and Gryndal. "I'll bring this Nyphron back on a leash."

"The frontier is no place for a child," Lothian declared.

"I'm not a child."

This united them all in a smile, all except Mawyndulë.

"Actually, this is why I invited you to this meeting, Arion. I think you should be sent to subdue this Artless rebel," Gryndal said.

Arion was stunned and not at all pleased. "I have responsibilities here. I need to continue Mawyndulë's lessons. He's woefully behind."

"I can fill in for you," Gryndal said.

The delight on Mawyndulë's face was unmistakable.

"Besides, as tutor to the next fane, wouldn't you agree that crossing the Nidwalden and seeing the greater world would enhance your ability to educate the prince?"

A good argument. Too good.

She didn't have a response.

"It shouldn't take long," Gryndal assured, most likely to preempt any objection. "Certainly not for one such as you."

"I don't see how I'm any better suited than any other Miralyith," Arion said.

"You're too modest. Were you not handpicked by the great Fenelyus to be Mawyndulë's tutor? And didn't she bestow upon you the honorific of Cenzlyor? Surely you possess talents that impressed her. Why else would she choose you over me? Here is your chance to utilize such skills."

He's maneuvering me out of the way.

What she didn't know was how long Gryndal had been planning the move. The comment about Fenelyus choosing her over him was troubling. He hadn't shown any interest in teaching the prince, but that didn't mean he hadn't been harboring resentment. Arion had the nagging sense that she ought to resist the invitation, but Lothian was nodding with a smile in her direction. The decision had been made already, and her opinion no longer mattered.

CHAPTER TWELVE

Gods Among Us

Although I still see the days of my youth as warm and sunny, I realize now that before the gods came, life on the dahl was a monotonous routine of drudgery. Afterward, nothing was the same.

—THE BOOK OF BRIN

"What are they doing now?" Moya asked Brin, who peered through the open door of the roundhouse. "Where are they?"

"Haven't moved. Still in front of the lodge steps. They're setting up a little camp, laying out beds for the night. I only count eight, though. One's missing."

They were all in Roan's home. Although no smaller than Sarah's roundhouse, it felt cramped, stuffed with all manner of things including: piles of antlers, string, branches, stones, boxes, tusks, bones, sticks, reeds, plants, and an abandoned beehive. Since returning, Persephone no longer felt comfortable imposing on Sarah's hospitality. Her husband, Delwin, had appeared less than enthusiastic at the prospect of their one guest turning into five. It certainly didn't help that one was a Dureyan, another a wolf, the third a mystic, the fourth an ex-slave from Alon Rhist, and that Persephone had been accused of murder. In contrast, Roan and Moya were delighted to have them. Roan even rushed out and enlisted Padera's help to fix their meal. Roan hadn't entertained before and was clueless about what to do. She wanted everything to be perfect.

"The missing one is probably up on the wall somewhere," Malcolm said. "The Instarya are a militant group and always post a sentry."

"The gods are making beds?" Moya asked.

"Yes," Brin said, acting as everyone's eyes and ears. "One's setting up a fire. Two others are sharpening weapons."

"So gods sleep?" Moya asked no one in particular.

"They aren't gods," Malcolm said. "Actually, they're not much different from us. Some think the Fhrey, Dherg, and Rhunes are all related."

"Like from the same clan?" Persephone asked.

"Originally, yes."

Raithe, who was sitting on the floor beside Malcolm, Suri, Minna, and a goat's skull, offered a sour chuckle. "We're nothing alike."

Malcolm smirked. "You're worldlier than I thought. Met a number of each, have you?"

Raithe replied with a scowl and shifted the goat's skull to clear a few more inches of room.

"I have," Persephone said. "And although being from the same clan does seem to be a bit of a stretch, I can see the point. There are a lot of similarities."

She sat in one of the net swings that dangled from the roundhouse's main support beam. *Hanging chairs,* Roan called them. Roan had a habit of making unusual things, and her home, in addition to resembling an overstuffed squirrel's nest, was a showcase of oddities.

The house had been built by Iver the Carver, who had been a part-time peddler. As a result, the place was always filled with a scattered assortment of trinkets. Having been Iver's slave since birth, Roan had grown up as one more bit of scrap. Iver had died the previous winter, and Roan was still trying to figure out life as a free woman. Moya had moved in with her a few weeks after Iver's death. Given Moya's outgoing nature, everyone expected her to be a positive influence on the shy ex-slave, and Roan did seem a little better. But the improvement hadn't extended to the house. Neither Roan nor

Moya, it turned out, could be called tidy. The only thing not in abundance was floor space.

"How are we similar?" Raithe asked.

Persephone shrugged. "Well, we all sleep. I wouldn't think a god would have a need for that."

"So do rabbits."

"Yeah, but rabbits don't wear clothes, have language, or use tools."

Moya nodded in agreement. She, too, was in a hanging chair and was using both hands to sip tea from one of Gifford's beautifully crafted ceramic cups. His creations were delicate, perfect works of art that everyone treated with care. "What about Konniger, Brin? Any movement from the lodge?"

"Both doors still closed," the girl replied with professional brevity.

"I'm going to have to go up there," Persephone declared.

"Why?" Moya and Raithe said together, each with the same shocked tone.

"I have to tell Konniger what's going on. He's the chieftain and needs to know. Can't imagine what he's thinking with nine Fhrey on his doorstep."

"Seven," Brin corrected. "Seven Fhrey, one giant, and . . . I can't tell what the other one is."

"What *is* that ninth one?" Raithe asked Malcolm. "Do you know?"

"Goblin," Padera said. The old farmer's wife was deftly working the glowing coal bed in the fire pit. She was boiling water in a suspended skin sack and showing Roan how to bake bread wrapped in soaked leaves.

"Goblin?" Moya leaned over, dangling precariously in her swing and trying to look out the door Brin was holding open. "How can you see anything with those old, tired peepers of yours?"

Persephone had wondered the same thing. The old woman's squinting eyes were so lost in the folds, creases, and wrinkles of her mushed-melon face that they all but vanished. When Padera spoke, one—and only one—

would pop open with a powerful glare while the other squeezed tight as if she were taking aim.

At that moment, the old woman had her sight on Moya. "These old eyes can still thread a needle faster than you can explain why you're hanging there and dangling your breasts in front of two men."

Moya scowled and sat back in her swing.

"I don't think you should go near the lodge," Raithe told Persephone. "Before the Fhrey showed up, your chieftain was siding against you. Didn't seem too happy afterward, either."

"Konniger isn't the problem," Persephone said. "It's Hegner who's lying."

"Maybe so," Moya said. "But if Konniger wants to know what's going on, he can come out and talk to the Fhrey himself."

"This shouldn't be about Konniger and what he should do or hasn't done," Persephone replied. "For the good of the dahl, the chieftain needs to know what is happening."

Roan carried another Gifford cup of hot tea and handed it to Persephone.

"Thank you, Roan."

Roan didn't reply. She just nodded and made her way back through the debris to where Padera was working over the pit fire.

"I wish the Fhrey had accepted your invitation to stay in the lodge," Moya said, grinning mischievously over her drink. "Can you imagine? Konniger having to move back into his family's house? He hates them, you know. Tressa has been bragging all over the dahl about how wonderful it is to be out of that *overcrowded pit*. When she was safely in the lodge, Tressa called Autumn and her husband pigs and said she didn't know how she managed to live there."

"You *really* don't like him, do you?" Persephone asked.

"What part of *Konniger is making me marry The Stump* don't you understand?"

"'Bout time you married someone and stopped tempting every man from here to the Blue Sea," Padera said, slurring the words through toothless gums. "You know, wars have started over women like you."

Moya scoffed. "You're so full of crap, old woman."

"Brin?" Padera called.

Brin tore her eyes away from the doorway. "Augusta of Melen, daughter of Chieftain Fisol, started the Battle of the Red River when she refused to marry Theo of Warric. When Theo's father was killed in the fight, Theo vowed vengeance and summoned all of Clan Warric to his banner. This resulted in what became known as the Ten Year War, which claimed the lives of a thousand men and instigated a famine that lasted two years."

"See," Padera said. The old woman handed the dead chicken she'd brought with her to Roan. "Pluck it."

"I'm sorry," Persephone sat up, making her seat rock. "But I have to side with Moya on this one. Konniger is making her marry a man who tried to kill me."

"Why *is* that?" Padera asked, once more peering out at her with one eye.

"I wish I knew," Persephone said. "I wouldn't say we're *friendly,* but I'm not aware of any ill will between us. I hadn't had any trouble with any of them until yesterday."

Roan, who stood next to Padera, struggled to yank feathers from the dead chicken, which she held by its feet. The old woman sighed. She took the dead bird and submerged it in the skin of water, which by then was boiling. She jiggled it vigorously up and down, waited a few seconds, pulled it out, and then submerged it again. The old woman did this several times, then plucked out a tail feather and smiled. "There," she said, handing the chicken back. "Try it now."

Roan pulled the first feather, and it slipped free without effort. "You're a genius."

Padera grinned, or more accurately her eternal toothless frown stretched wider. "*You're* the genius. I'm just old. When you've raised six children, a husband, and dozens of cows, pigs, sheep, and who knows how many chickens, you learn a few things. Just remember, there's always a better way."

Roan nodded with fierce conviction, her eyes serious and focused as if Padera had charged her with a crucial task. "There's always a better way. There's always a better way . . ."

"Well, if you have to go, I'll go with you," Raithe told Persephone.

The big man stretched out his legs, which extended across a third of the room.

"Thank you, but I'm not sure that's such a good idea. If I bring you into the lodge, it might start a fight." She took a sip of tea.

"You can't go up there alone."

"Wasn't planning on it. I'll bring Delwin and maybe someone else I trust, like one of the farmers."

"What are they going to do if he decides you're guilty and wants to execute you right there in the lodge? You might need someone who can fight."

"Maybe that's how things are done in Dureya, but there's a process here. Our Keeper of Ways will insist."

"Your Keeper is a big man, is he?"

"A frail old woman, actually. But our chieftain respects our traditions and will listen to her. No one is executed without a public hearing."

"Uh-huh, sure. I'll be outside just in case. If you have trouble, yell."

Flattered by Raithe's concern, Persephone took a quick sip of tea to hide a self-conscious smile.

"So, Brin"—Moya leaned over the edge of her suspended netting—"what happened? To the woman who started the war?"

Brin took a second to think, and her eyes shifted in focus. "After Theo of Warric successfully besieged Dahl Melen, he burned it and killed everyone she ever knew and a good deal of livestock. Then Augusta of Melen killed herself."

"Oh," Moya said with a suddenly sour look.

"Raithe, Malcolm," Padera barked. "Fetch us some water. Take those empty gourds by the door."

Without a word, the two men got to their feet. Raithe bent low. The ceiling was too high for most to touch, but Raithe was tall and there were plenty of plants, gourds, and fish hanging from the rafters to bang his head on. They grabbed the containers and headed out.

"You sent *Raithe* to fetch water?" Persephone and Brin asked in concert the moment the two had left.

"Was just sitting there," Padera replied.

"But . . . but . . . the man saved us . . . and he's killed a god!" Brin declared, crawling back toward the fire and rising to her knees in protest.

"Then he ought to be able to handle carrying some water, don't you think?" The old woman fixed her with a one-eyed stare and a misleading toothless frown that Persephone knew to be a smile.

"I can't believe how fortunate it was, running into him in the woods," Moya said to Persephone. The young woman clutched the teacup to her breast. A wicked smile crossed her lips. "He's handsome."

"You're spoken for," Brin reminded her.

"Shut up, will ya?" Moya scowled, huffed, and slammed her head backward on the netting, making a *thrum* sound. "The Stump can go hang himself. Got any spare rope, Roan?"

Roan paused in her chicken plucking. "Of course I do. I always keep—"

Moya sighed. "Roan, I'm not serious."

"Oh . . . sorry."

"Don't need to apologize, Roan."

"Sorry."

Moya sighed again. "Never mind."

Persephone loved Moya for her forthright, honest, speak-her-mind openness. She didn't know anyone who was braver or more helpful. But secretly Persephone wondered if Konniger, Tressa, and Padera were right about Moya taking a husband. Not that she should be forced to marry The Stump, but Moya, looking the way she did and refusing every proposal, had started fights among suitors. The gods had blessed her with beauty beyond mortal bounds, just as they had given mankind fire. Both gifts had the ability to leave destruction in their wake, but no one was foolish enough to swing a torch at every tree. Moya, on the other hand, was an uncontrollable flirt and oblivious to the devastation she caused.

Brin resumed her vigil at the door, her eyes intent on something. "Raithe and Malcolm are at the well."

"The Fhrey doing anything?" Moya sat up.

"A couple looked over, but they're still just sitting there."

"Keep an eye out," Moya told her, then turned back to Persephone. Drumming her fingernails on the cup, she asked, "So what *were* you doing out in the forest? You never did say."

Persephone looked embarrassed.

"You weren't really secretly meeting Raithe, were you?" Moya sat up, her brows rising. "You weren't, you know . . . what The Stump said?"

"No!"

Moya frowned and settled back in disappointment. "What, then?"

Persephone sighed. "I went to talk to a tree."

Moya, Roan, Brin, and Padera looked at one another.

"Come again?" Moya said.

Persephone nodded toward the mystic, who sat cross-legged on the floor between a stack of flat stones and a battered basket stuffed with dusty pinecones. With Minna's head on her lap, Suri appeared oblivious to everything around her, playing intently with her string again, a spider-like pattern forming between her fingers.

"Suri came to me a while ago saying she saw signs of a terrible catastrophe, something worse than any famine. I didn't think much of it at the time."

"But then the Fhrey burned Dureya and Nadak," Moya said.

Persephone nodded. "Suri told me the old tree could

help. Would answer questions and is the oldest tree in the forest. And she *is,* too, huge and ancient."

"How's Magda doing, anyway?" Padera asked. The old woman was fanning the fire beneath the water sack.

"You know about the oak?" Persephone asked.

The old woman nodded. "Melvin and I, we first . . . um. We were *married* under her leaves. Beautiful spring day. Songbirds filled her branches and sang to us. A good sign."

"Probably a sapling back then, eh, Padera?" Moya grinned.

"Hard to tell," the old woman replied. "Sun hadn't been born yet."

They all laughed, except for Roan, who paused in her plucking to study the old woman with new interest.

Raithe and Malcolm returned, carrying an array of gourd jugs hanging from a pole.

"Into the large skin over there." Padera pointed.

"So you actually spoke to this tree?" Moya asked.

"I asked questions," Persephone clarified. "Suri told me what the oak said."

Roan, who was making a little pile of wet feathers at her feet, stopped plucking. She stared at Suri. "You understand the language of trees?"

Suri nodded without looking up from the web between her fingers, tongue sticking out as she worked the string thoughtfully.

"And what *did* it say?" Moya asked.

"A bunch of gibberish, really," Persephone replied.

"Not gibberish." Suri spoke for the first time. "You asked Magda for answers; she gave them. Problem solved."

"But none of it made any sense," Persephone said.

Suri shrugged. "Not Magda's fault you can't understand. She kept it simple for you. And she was right, but she always is."

"She was right?" Persephone asked, confused.

Suri nodded.

"What *exactly* did she say?" Padera asked.

Persephone shrugged. "Something about . . ." She looked at the mystic. "Suri, do you remember?"

"Welcome the gods. Heal the injured. Follow the wolf," Suri recited without looking up. "Can't get much simpler than that."

Persephone spilled some of her tea. "That's right! For the love of Mari! *Welcome the gods!*"

Everyone looked toward the roundhouse's open doorway, where the evening sun cast a patch of light across Roan's floor mat. For Persephone, the light looked a little more golden, a little more magical than it had a moment before.

"I just got a chill," Moya said.

Padera looked at her. "More clothes might help. Oh, wait, I forgot who I was talking to. How about we try this instead. Less jawing and more work will warm you up. Get off that swing and cut up a bowl full of potatoes and set them in the sack to boil." Then the old woman turned to Suri. "You staying for the meal?"

"I invited her," Persephone said.

"That's fine, but it's gonna take a while," Padera explained. "Any chance you could help Persephone discover why Sackett, Adler, and Hegner tried to kill her yesterday?"

Persephone looked at Suri. "Can you do that?"

"I'd need bones," the mystic said.

"Got a dead chicken right here." Padera pointed at the bird Roan held. "Or do you need to kill it in some ritual?"

"Bird die today?"

"Wrung its neck an hour ago."

"Should be fine." The mystic pulled a loop around with two fingers and grinned to herself.

Raithe finished dumping the water, set the gourds down near the door, then turned and surveyed the interior, looking for a place to sit. "You're certain it's all right, us staying here tonight?" Raithe asked. "Might be a bit cramped."

"We'll make room," Persephone said, then put a hand to her forehead. "Oh, I'm sorry, Roan."

Roan, who was still only halfway done with the chicken, paused. "What for?"

"For being rude. This is your place, not mine. I shouldn't have spoken on your behalf."

Roan tilted her head, then looked to Moya.

"Forget it, Seph," Moya said, shaking her head with a sympathetic frown. "I'm still trying to convince her it's okay to sleep in the bed. Every night she curls up on the floor mat."

"The floor mat?" Persephone looked over at a thin sheet of reeds that, being daytime, was rolled up and out of the way. "Why?"

Moya looked to Roan.

Roan rolled her shoulders. "It's Iver's bed."

"Iver's dead," Persephone said. "You understand that, right? It's your bed now."

Roan offered only an embarrassed grimace.

"See?" Moya sighed in resignation.

Roan let the half-plucked chicken droop so that the bird's neck brushed the ground. "I've always slept on the floor."

"But you own this place now . . . everything, including the bed, is yours," Persephone said. "You could at least sleep in one of these hanging chairs. These are very comfortable, by the way."

Roan stared at her, breathing faster, her eyes tense, her hands wringing the chicken's legs.

"Relax," Padera told her. "Calm down and give me that bird before you ruin it." Padera took the chicken back from Roan. The old woman finished plucking the second half of the bird in a pair of minutes. Once stripped, she chopped off both feet and pulled the crop and gizzard out of its severed neck.

"Roan," the old woman said. "Go to my house and bring back a bag to collect these feathers. You can save them and make a nice pillow. You'll find a couple in the back next to dear old Melvin's clothes box."

Roan nodded once more with fierce conviction, the welling panic forgotten in light of the new task. She headed for the door but halted abruptly before stepping out. "Whoa!"

They all looked over and saw that Roan had nearly run into the giant who had arrived with the Fhrey. He was standing in front of the roundhouse, blocking the entrance as he bent down and peered in.

Persephone scrambled to her feet, and Raithe moved to her side. The giant didn't say a word. Didn't look at the rest of them. His eyes were fixed on Padera, who worked at removing the chicken's viscera.

The old woman peered up through her left eye, a hefty scowl on her collapsed mouth. "You're blocking my light."

The giant glanced down at his shadow and shuffled over a step.

"It's easier for you." The giant's voice surprised Persephone. She expected a loud booming roar, but his words were soft. "Your hands are small. There aren't birds big enough for me to clean that way."

Again Padera looked up, this time focusing on the giant's hands. "You need a hook." She glanced toward Roan. "My Melvin's hands were too big for delicate work, too. Roan can make one that even your paws could manage. Can't you, Roan?"

Roan, who'd been looking at the giant with as much wonder as the rest, narrowed her eyes and furrowed her brow. She wound a lock of hair, put the strands in her mouth, and chewed. Then she shocked everyone by walking up to the towering brute and grabbing hold of his right hand. Tilting it up to catch the sunlight coming in through the door, she studied it and placed her own hand against his palm. The difference was striking; Roan's looked like a doll's. The giant said nothing. Roan muttered to herself, nodded, and then scurried to the back of her house, where Iver's workbench was buried beneath a pile of assorted sediment.

The giant watched her for a second and then turned

his attention back to Padera and the chicken. "Stuffing?" he asked, struggling to see.

Padera nodded and raised the chicken up in the air. "Filling her with bread and thyme."

"Garlic?"

"Of course."

"Butter?"

Padera scowled.

"Okay, stupid question. I don't always have access to any. What about pepper?"

Padera did her one-eyed glare, this time sucking in both her lips. "Do I look like a Dherg queen to you? Do you think Drome bestows great riches upon me? And before you ask, I won't be adding saffron, gold, or emeralds, either."

The giant lifted his shirt. Beneath was a line of pouches on a long string. He opened one, pinched some of the contents, and held out his hand.

Padera waddled forward, and the giant sprinkled a dash into her palm. One brow went way up.

The giant grinned.

"What's your name?" Padera asked.

"Grygor."

"Grygor, would you care to stay for supper?" Padera asked. Looking back, she added, "I think we're going to need more chickens."

The wall of Dahl Rhen was twenty feet thick, framed with wood, and filled with dirt. Grass grew on the top, but the constant traffic from men patrolling the wall had created a worn path that circled the entire dahl. After the evening meal, Raithe had walked the course from one side of the gate to the other, watching the sunset. The height gave him a nice view of the surrounding landscape. The expanse of the forest loomed to the west as a black outline with jagged edges. The eastern side of the dahl was gentle rolling hills of green. Even in the fading light, he could see the north–south road cutting through the fields.

Raithe walked with his leigh mor tied over one shoulder. The evening wasn't cold. Spring had let go of winter's hand and was reaching out toward summer. The transition was most evident in the sounds of crickets and the oscillating din of tree frogs, which was even louder on the forest side.

Traveling will be easier now.

Hearing the ladder's creak, Raithe turned and was surprised to see Persephone climbing up. Trotting over, he extended his hand to help her up. The act was instinctive, but after feeling her fingers, the intimacy of the moment struck him. Hands could be such expressive things; hers were incredibly warm.

"Malcolm said you were up here. He thought I should let you know I was heading over to speak to Konniger," Persephone said as she reached the top. "But honestly, I don't think there will be any trouble."

Persephone faced him with hands folded, still wearing her black mourning dress. Her head tilted down as her eyes looked up; that tilt made up his mind.

"Nice up here on a night like this," she said. "I've walked this circle hundreds of times."

"Not many places where you can see so far."

"You haven't been to the top of the tower in Alon Rhist then, have you?"

He shook his head.

"But you've seen it, right? The tower?"

He nodded. "Dahl Dureya is near Grandford. The tower is hard to miss, but it's not like the Fhrey give tours."

She looked north as if trying to see the great spire. "Did you have family in Dureya?"

"No," he said, "not anymore. I used to have three brothers and a sister. Heim and Hegel died together in the High Spear Valley, fighting the Gula-Rhunes. They're buried there in a mass grave."

"Sorry to hear that."

"Don't be. I didn't like my brothers. Not even Didan, who was the nicest and closest to me in age. Even he was a bastard. Stabbed me in the hand once because I was playing with his new dagger. Held me down and put the point right into my palm and said, 'So you want to know what the blade feels like, do you?'"

She grimaced as if Didan's stab had just occurred. "How old were you?"

"Six," he told her. "So yeah, I had some pretty awful brothers, but my sister and mum were terrific. Luckily for us, my father and brothers weren't around much. When they were gone, we'd stay up late, singing songs and telling stories. Kaylin, she was my sister, had an incredible imagination. Almost every tale had a ghost or dragon and a hero who rescued a beautiful girl. We'd be in the house around the fire with the winter gales shaking the walls, listening to her go on. She helped us forget how low we were on dung bricks and how cold the night would be. Kaylin could do that sort of thing with her stories, take you someplace else, someplace warm, someplace wonderful. Best times we had were when everyone else was off to war and it was just the three of us."

Raithe stopped talking and gritted his teeth, feeling his throat tighten. He squeezed his left hand, the one Didan had stabbed.

"We tell stories here, too, but most aren't so pleasant. The heroes are usually lost in the forest and either eaten or sucked away into the spirit world forever. We tell them to keep children out of the forest, but it makes winter nights bleak. I think I would have liked your sister's stories better." Persephone brushed back her hair and looked out at the fading light. "Malcolm says the two of you are leaving in the morning."

"Yeah," Raithe replied. "At least *I'm* going. Can't speak for Malcolm."

"Why are you leaving?"

Raithe looked to the north again. "I don't think it's safe having the God Killer here, well, in any village, really. Best if I find a little out-of-the-way place of my own."

"But I was hoping you'd—"

"Yeah, I remember what you were hoping, but I'm not keenig material."

"You're a great warrior, and you have tremendous courage."

"No. I'm just a stubborn Dureyan, which I guess is another way of saying *stupid*. You don't want a stupid keenig."

"I don't think you're stupid. You're brave, kind, and decent."

"You don't know me."

"I know you fought for me at the cascade and against the wolves. You stood up against Konniger and faced the gods when no one else dared."

"Whose point are you trying to prove?" He smiled.

She smiled back and was prettier for it, younger looking.

"Listen," he said. "I sort of made a promise to myself. I come from a family of warriors. All my father and brothers ever did was fight, one battle after another. It's all they knew, so that's what they did, kill and burn. They were good at it, good at destroying things, but they died fighting. None of them ever accomplished anything . . . well, positive . . . or lasting. They never built something or made a difference. I want my life to amount to more than years of bloodshed."

"But being keenig is—"

"Is just more killing. Don't you see? You want me to be like my father. You want me to lead people into battle, to kill and destroy. I want something else."

"What do you mean by *else*?"

"Better."

"Better?" Persephone chuckled. "What could be better than being the leader of our entire race?"

"To live somewhere safe and raise a family. To teach my sons to do the same. That would be good and lasting." Raithe allowed himself to look directly into her eyes. He always did this with men; anything less was disrespectful, even cowardly. But with a woman, the same action felt indecent somehow. Maybe because he enjoyed it. He couldn't hold his gaze and still say what he planned, so he looked back out at the hills.

"I was thinking . . . hoping . . . you might consider coming with me."

"With you?"

He kept looking over the wall. "I don't see how you can stay. Your chieftain is siding with Hegner, and he'll have to administer justice. If you stay, he'll punish you. What do they do to killers here?" He didn't wait for her to answer. He wanted to get it all out. "Whatever it is, be hard to do if you're not around. Besides, you're like I am: You don't have a family, not anymore. You don't even have a home to call your own." He let his eyes return from their exile and look back into hers. "I've enjoyed your company, and it sounds like you've done a lot of traveling and know your way around. It'd be nice having you along. I'm thinking we can find someplace where we could both start over."

Her brows were up and her mouth open even before she spoke. "Are you asking me to run away with you?"

Her tone sounded just short of laughter.

Raithe's heart sank, and he sucked a breath in through his teeth. "I'll take that as a *no*."

Persephone's eyes weren't so bright now, and Raithe shifted his focus to the grass at their feet. He felt a burning desire to be anywhere else than where he was. His face was hot, and he felt a prickly heat where leather covered skin. He took a couple of steps away.

"Wait." She stopped him with a hand on his arm. "I'm sorry. I'm flattered. I am, but . . . don't you think I'm a little old for you?"

"Obviously not or I wouldn't have asked." He didn't like the sound of his voice. It came out with a bite. That wasn't the way he wanted to leave things, but—

I should get away before I say something to make this worse.

Instead, he blurted out, "Is it because of Nyphron?"

Persephone looked puzzled. "Nyphron? Why are you bringing him up?"

"He's interested in you, right?"

"Interested in me? A Rhune?" She looked at him, amazed.

"When he saw you at the gate, he lost concentration. Nearly got him killed. I guess I could see how you might—"

She rolled her eyes. "Oh, please."

"There are lots of stories where gods become infatuated with mortal women."

Looking over her shoulder, she smirked. "They're not gods, remember? Besides, I don't think that's going to be a problem. If anyone is likely to catch one of their eyes, it will be Moya." She put a worried hand to her brow and sighed. "Now that I think about it, I ought to talk to her about staying away from them."

Raithe drew away again.

"Raithe." She stepped forward, her face pained. "My husband was killed less than a month ago. We were married for twenty years. I loved him. I *still* love him. Can you understand?"

In his head, he told her she wasn't helping. He wanted to explain that loyalty and devotion were virtues he rarely found, and he wanted to be as fortunate as Reglan had been. In his head, he also apologized for intruding on her grief and for presuming someone like him had a chance with someone like her. He was Dureyan, after all. He imagined telling her all these things, but when he finally opened his mouth, all he said was, "Okay."

The word hung there, heavy and sad. Perhaps she didn't want that to be the last word between them because she spoke again. "You're wrong about me not having a family. Padera is like a mother to me, the way she has been to everyone since her children died. Brin is like my daughter or at least a niece because I consider Sarah my sister. Moya is like a troublesome but irresistible cousin, and Gifford . . ." She reached up and wiped her eyes. "You see? I do have a family, and they're in trouble, serious trouble. I can't leave. I'll be able to convince Konniger of my innocence. I've known him for years."

She performed a more thorough wiping of her face, then stepped forward and hugged him tightly. "I want to thank you for all you've done for me and everyone here. You saved my life more than once. I wish you would stay. You don't have to be the keenig if you don't want. You can still help. You've already helped so much just by being here. And maybe . . . maybe you could build a happy life in Dahl Rhen. What do you say?"

She released him and stepped back, hands clasped before her.

Raithe didn't feel *quite* so foolish anymore. He was far from happy, but the hug was nice. He'd never wanted much. Dureyans didn't have dreams the way others did. Food and warmth were all they cared about, and until that moment Raithe's plan was to be alone in the wilderness. But now he saw how lonely, how empty that would be. He found himself nodding.

"And as for the Fhrey . . ." Persephone looked over her shoulder at their camp near the well. "Who knows how long they'll stay. To be honest, they scare me. They scare everyone . . . except you."

She was wrong. The Fhrey scared him plenty. Why they hadn't killed him, he wasn't sure. The Galantians appeared impressed by the novelty of a Rhune who refused to give in, a Rhune who would fight. Leaving before the novelty wore off was the smart thing to do, but the idea of going without her made his stomach sink.

Perhaps given some time, I'll be able to convince her to come.

Persephone sighed and looked at the lodge. "Well, I suppose there's no point in delaying any longer. Best get at it."

"Be careful in there," he told her. "I mean it, Persephone. If you have any problem, yell. Yell real loud and then get out of the way. I'll do the rest."

"Thanks, but attacking the chieftain probably isn't the right approach, and I doubt it would help my case."

"Works in Dureya." He smiled.

She started back down the ladder and paused. "It'll be okay; you'll see. I've known Konniger for years. He was my husband's Shield, after all. I just need to explain my side of things. Oh, and you can call me Seph. You've earned that."

"The Galantians said they'll help us," Persephone declared, standing before the chairs in the center of the lodge's Great Hall. Delwin and Tope Highland had come along. The two men stood beside and slightly behind her. Tope's boots were muddy after a day spent turning soil on the ridge. He wasn't known as a fighter, but years working in the high fields had made him strong. Delwin held his shepherd's staff in one hand and a big floppy hat Sarah had made for him in the other. He wasn't a warrior, either, but as close to a brother as Persephone had. Both men were eager to get home after a long day's work but had agreed to come with her.

"Help us how?" Konniger's tone was more than skeptical but shy of sarcastic, a low smoldering growl of reluctant tolerance.

Konniger and Tressa sat in the First and Second Chairs, wearing stone faces. Maeve and Krier stood to either side as was proper for the chieftain's Shield and the Keeper of Ways. The formality was grating. She was being received like a stranger. Worse even, Persephone smelled cooked meat and baked bread, but the food had been cleared before she entered. Even a stranger would have been invited to dine with them.

Persephone refused to look at Hegner, who stood in the back. She also avoided Maeve's and Tressa's eyes and kept her focus on Konniger. "If other Fhrey come, come to destroy Dahl Rhen, they'll speak for us. They believe it's possible to prevent what happened in Dureya and Nadak from occurring here."

There were others in the hall, including Riggles, who farmed the fertile southern fields, and Devon, the huntsman who had been Sackett's close friend. All of them had something in common—she didn't know them well, and some, like Krier and The Stump, she didn't like. There were others, too, new faces that clustered in the shadows behind the First Chair.

Not one of them greeted this news with a smile.

"Why would they do such a thing?" Konniger asked.

"Because these Fhrey oppose what the other Fhrey are doing. They disobeyed their leaders and refused to burn Nadak and Dureya, and—"

"And yet Nadak *was* burned," said one of the strangers who stood behind the chairs, a man with a grizzled face and an accusing stare. She didn't understand where all the hostility came from until she noticed the hammer broach pinned to his shoulder. He was from Nadak.

"True, but *they* didn't do it," she explained. "They tried to stop it. These nine are renegades. They don't want to hurt us. They can't return to Alon Rhist, so they're looking for a place to shelter. But if the others do come, these Fhrey will speak on our behalf, convince their kind to spare us. Don't you see that if—"

"If the Galantians are outlaws, why would anyone listen to them?" Konniger asked. "And since they are criminals, won't their presence put us in greater danger? Harboring fugitives will prove to Alon Rhist that we're troublemakers. Allowing these renegades to stay will make matters worse."

Persephone clapped her hands against her sides. "If the Fhrey do intend to burn Dahl Rhen to the ground and kill every last man, woman, and child, how could matters get worse? Don't we stand a better chance with these Galantians as allies?"

"*If* is the important word in what you said. What *if* the Fhrey have already enacted the full extent of their retribution? *If* they have no plans on attacking us, we'll give them a reason to change their minds," Konniger said, a stern look on his face.

"Our best option is to appease them," Tressa said. "Maybe if we handed over these outlaws. Could we do that? Could we send word to Alon Rhist and tell them they're here? Wouldn't that prove we're not like Dureya?" Tressa's eyes widened with excitement. "We could hand over the God Killer, too! I'm sure it would impress them. They would see we aren't a problem. They might even reward us."

"According to Nyphron, the Galantians' leader, the Fhrey of Alon Rhist have been ordered to eliminate all Rhunes. This goes beyond retribution for one Fhrey's death. They are bent on killing all of us."

"Nyphron?" Konniger stopped her. "So you're on a first-name basis with this Fhrey?"

"He told us his name, yes."

"He told *you* is what you mean," Tressa said. "Why hasn't this Nyphron presented himself to Konniger? Why hasn't he come before the chieftain?"

"I don't know. Maybe they're expecting someone from the lodge to come out to speak with them."

"And I'm wondering why these outlaws are so willing to help us. Why would they go against their own kind?" Tressa asked. "What's in it for them?"

"I'm not sure. Which is why you should *go talk to them*." Persephone was getting frustrated now. "I would think you would want to find out such things."

"And I think you can't help butting in. You can't accept it's me, and not you, sitting in the Second Chair. You forget who rules Dahl Rhen now." Tressa's face had turned red.

"Tressa," Persephone said in a quiet voice. "People who lead don't need to remind others who the leader is. All I want is for you to do your duty."

"All *you* want from *me*! How dare you stand there and demand—"

Konniger patted his wife's hand, apparently trying to calm her. "I think there is a bigger point being overlooked." He gazed sternly at Persephone. "Up until a few days ago, everything was fine. Now two of the dahl's most capable hunters are dead and we have been overrun by not only the famed *God Killer* but a contingent of Fhrey warriors whom you invited in against my orders. The whole thing seems a bit too convenient for my taste."

The others in the lodge were nodding and exchanging knowing looks. Something was going on—had been going on—since before she had entered. While she talked, the men scowled. Persephone had expected to find relief or appreciation; although she could have understood finding concern, worry, or fear. Instead, she saw agreement on the faces of the men gathered in the Great Hall.

What has Hegner been saying about me?

"You don't think I see what you're doing?" Konniger accused. "If you wanted to rule, you should have made a proper challenge like Holliman did. Oh, but you couldn't, could you? You didn't have anyone here strong enough to act as your champion. So you had to plot and wait while you maneuvered outsiders. Now you have your own personal army of Fhrey."

"Konniger, you've known me since you were a boy and protected me and my family for a decade. You *know* me. You can't possibly believe I'd kill or arrange for others to kill Adler and Sackett. You're jumping to conclusions. I know you're in a difficult position, and it's Hegner's word against mine. But look at the sources. I'm a respected chieftain's widow who helped lead this clan through the Great Famine and the Long Winter, whereas Hegner's claim to fame was when he stole Wedon's prized calf. Who deserves your trust?"

"I didn't steal no calf!" Hegner shouted.

"You've also said you didn't take a jug of Bergin's beer, but you were caught with it."

"Yeah, well, okay. I took the beer, but I didn't steal no calf."

"There," Persephone said. "This is who you are listening to? Do you really think I've been having secret meetings in the forest? You know damn well I haven't set foot in the forest in all the years you've guarded me and my family. And except that one time, I haven't left Sarah's house since Reglan's death. I was gone for one day . . . just one. As for the Fhrey, they aren't my personal anything. But if they were, why would I come here and try to convince you to step up and go see them? The only reason I've talked to Nyphron at all is because no one else was."

"So what *did* you tell this *Nyphron*?" Konniger asked, folding his arms over his chest.

"I told him he had permission to speak on behalf of Dahl Rhen if more Fhrey arrive."

This brought a wide smile to Tressa's face and made Konniger's head nod along with the rest. They all seemed pleased, with the exception of Hegner, who slunk back into the shadows.

"You didn't think you should ask your chieftain before making alliances?" Krier asked. Until then he had leaned against a winter post, but at that moment he took a step toward her.

Krier was an ugly man who'd first come to Persephone's attention for beating Gifford. The bully often taunted and threw rotten vegetables at the potter. The matter had come before Reglan, and Krier defended himself by saying the cripple had attacked him with his crutch, but witnesses said Gifford had simply fallen on Krier after tripping. *Gifford is cursed by the gods. Having him around invites bad luck,* Krier often said. Although no one was ever accused, someone had tried to set fire to Gifford's house, and it was no secret whom most suspected.

Tope, who was no friend of Krier, straightened up and spit in his direction.

"You have a problem, Tope?" Krier asked.

"Yeah," Tope replied. "You're too far away."

Persephone put a hand on the farmer's sleeve, trying to calm him. Then said to Konniger, "Would you have said differently? Would you have refused their help and tried to keep them out of Dahl Rhen?"

"That's not the point," Tressa nearly shouted, and

slammed her hand down on the arm of the chair. "You had no right! Reglan is *dead,* dead and buried. You aren't in charge anymore!"

"Enough!" Konniger raised his hands. "I'm the chieftain of this clan, and I need time to figure this out. One thing I do know, the Galantians represent a threat. Maybe they are in league with Persephone, or maybe their kind will attack us because we are providing shelter. Either way, we would be safer if they weren't here. So this is my decree . . ." He looked directly at her. "Persephone, you'll go out there and tell the Fhrey you had no authority to speak on behalf of Clan Rhen. Then, you'll inform them we don't want their help and tell them to leave. As for this matter between you and Hegner, I'll decide that later when I can address it properly."

Persephone looked at Delwin and Tope. The two stood rigid, their eyes shifting nervously.

"You have a problem with that?" Konniger asked.

Persephone nodded. "Yes, yes, I do. I did what I thought was best to save this dahl. It was not my intention to challenge your authority but rather to encourage you to exercise it. You're the great chieftain—so act like it. If you want the Fhrey to leave, you go out there and tell them yourself, and I'll go back to living off the kindness of friends. Maybe I'll start knitting a shawl. I think I'll need one come winter . . . if you haven't killed us all before then, that is."

Persephone turned and walked away so abruptly that Delwin and Tope were momentarily left behind.

As she left, she heard Tressa say, "See, what did I tell you?"

CHAPTER THIRTEEN

The Bones

Suri had a wolf named Minna. They were the best of friends and roamed the forest together. She had tattoos, was always filthy, afraid of nothing, and could do magic. From the first time I met her, I wanted to be Suri . . . I still do.

—THE BOOK OF BRIN

The bones were excellent . . . for a chicken.

Suri would have preferred a crow or, better yet, a raven. Gods frequently chose them to be messengers and spirits often inhabited their bodies. Not that Suri would dare kill one to get at its bones. The divine rarely appreciated the murder of a faithful servant. And of course there was always the risk of actually wringing the neck of a spirit in bird form, and that was just a bad day for everyone involved. The chicken bones would work even if the connection through the veil was hazy and intermittent. At least she wouldn't fear offending anyone. No god, goddess, or spirit would ever inhabit or employ a chicken.

Suri planned to call on Mari. She didn't know exactly what she was looking for, but Mari, the goddess of wisdom, was the patron of Persephone's home, and so Suri figured Mari would be the best overall choice. Suri was outside the palisade on the western side of the dahl, the highest point she could find. Minna lay quietly on the hill a few feet away, giving her space. The wolf was considerate that way. The mystic built her little fire and waited for the sun to descend. It was best to begin a reading at dusk, when the doors between the worlds were open the widest. They wouldn't remain open long. While waiting, she divided the bones into groups. Those taken from the right side of the chicken referred to the "us," the ones on whose behalf she performed the reading. Bones from the left represented the "others," those in opposition.

As the sun dipped behind the distant trees, Suri dropped the two sets of bones into the flames. She waited as the black line of forest trees swallowed up the giant orange ball. She didn't count or use any physical measurements. Suri was an instinctive augur. She performed her rituals by feel. Tura had taught Suri everything the old mystic had known, but she admitted no one could teach interpretation. You were either born with the talent or not.

Suri had the gift.

Tura had spotted it right away. The old mystic told Suri how she had called songbirds as a toddler. After placing the child in a clearing of daisies, violets, and bluebells, Tura would hide in the nearby forest eaves. Before long, Suri would be surrounded by a flock of birds—a multicolored gathering of unrelated songsters: goldfinches, red-winged blackbirds, blue jays, magpies, yellow- and black-throated warblers, bay wrens, robins, mockingbirds, and song sparrows. Suri would sit among them, delighting in their symphony. Gathering birds wasn't her only talent; she also talked to fire spirits, knew when it would rain, and could predict the arrival of the first hard frost. Suri had the gift, but Tura gave her the tools to use it.

As the sky shifted hue from orange to purple, Suri felt the moment and doused the fire. Fire spirits hated water. All the children of the fire god, Outha, did. This one was no different, and it hissed at her.

"Sorry," she told it, and wished she knew its name. She wasn't even certain all spirits had names. The most important ones did. Wogan, the spirit of the Crescent Forest, for example, and Fribble-bibble the spirit of the

High Stream, whose name she loved saying. The little fire spirits were like the rock and breeze spirits, too many to keep track of. She wondered if Elan bothered to name them all.

Gathering the bones, Suri laid them on a woven mat and began looking for the fire-born cracks and tiny holes. The way Tura had explained it, searching for truth in bones was a lot like guessing a person's intent from the tone of his or her voice. In this case, it would be the voice of Mari, and the language was that of the divine. As such, much was left to interpretation. Still, Suri had a knack for divination that wasn't restricted to just reading bones.

Tura had marveled at Suri's ability to find her way in the forest. Initially, the older mystic attributed this skill to an excellent memory, but tossed that idea aside when Suri demonstrated the ability to find places she hadn't been to before. After more than fifty years in the Crescent, Tura had discovered two of the underground rooms—the ones Malcolm had called Dherg rols. Suri found the other three in a week.

But communing with fire spirits is where Suri excelled the most. By the age of eight, her game of talking to fires and making the flames dance and change color had grown into something more. While watching Tura struggle to light kindling by spinning a stick with a bow, Suri ignited her own pile of wood with a few words.

"How did you do that?" Tura had asked.

Suri shrugged. "I asked a fire spirit to come, and it did. Isn't that right?"

Tura nodded, but Suri had seen the confusion in the old woman's face along with apprehension and maybe even a little fear. Tura began talking about malkins after that and mentioned how Suri might have come from the land of crimbals.

Suri stared at the bones, reading them as best she could in the fading light. That was always a problem with sunset readings. Such things needed the light of day to decipher, and it faded so fast. As the sun set and the night took hold of the world, Suri read a number of things. They weren't the answers she was looking for, nothing about the men and why they had attacked, but what she saw was even more important.

Suri finished studying the patterns on the right leg. The holes were close together and near the top, indicating the forecast would be impending rather than concerning some distant future. Looking at the cracks, she saw there were two lines, which suggested two separate tales.

First and foremost, the chicken was flooded with bad omens in the same overwhelming manner that Suri had seen just before coming to Persephone. Little had changed on that score. Looking deeper, searching for specifics, she saw that all the bones agreed that the full moon would be the time of reckoning—the pivotal moment. The bones didn't say how because the bones didn't know, most likely because she was reading a chicken. They only showed a convergence of powers that, depending on the outcome, would change the world. Three of the bones told of a terrible danger to both the "us" and the "them." One of the bones fascinated Suri because it suggested that a great secret was hidden in the forest and guarded by a bear. That bone also said this secret would play a significant role in the conflict to come. But it was the last bone that shocked her more than any other. The largest and clearest, only its tip had been marred by the fire. This bone declared that a monster was coming to Dahl Rhen to kill them all.

Suri cursed the fading light as she stared at the cracks and smudges. She would have guessed the *monster* referred to the Fhrey, but no. The marks indicated a single creature rather than a host of enemies. And the markings were so clear that Suri knew the monster's name. More came after that but was lost to charring. It didn't matter; Suri had all the hints she needed.

"Grin," she said aloud.

A moment later, a bear roared in the distance, startling a flock of dark birds. They flew away toward the setting sun—toward the west.

Minna's head came up, her eyes peering at the forest. She whispered to Minna, "That's not good."

CHAPTER FOURTEEN

Into the West

So many of our words originally came from either the Dherg or the Fhrey. The Fhrey word for "primitive" being Rhune, *it became their word for humans.* Rhulyn *then means "Land of Rhune."* Avrlyn *means "Land of Green." And* dahl *was the Fhrey word for "wall." The suffix* -ydd, *in Fhrey, translates to "new." Which is why on the map I have named this region* Rhenydd.

— THE BOOK OF BRIN

Because of its name, Arion expected the frontier of Avrlyn to be green, but for the last several days all she'd seen was brown. Brown rocks, brown grass, brown mud; even the trees were dingy. She'd also been disappointed by the lack of fields. Arion had seen paintings of open valleys—large expanses of flat land or rolling hills—that granted visions of massive skies and wondrous sunsets. Instead, since crossing the Nidwalden, she had walked through an endless tunnel of forests, and the vast woodlands known as the Harwood weren't anything like the ancient groves of Erivan. They didn't invite guests to wander in dappled shade. Instead, dense thickets shunned the light and barred passage with thorny brambles. Forests here were wild, hostile things, and she imagined secrets cloaked in moss, leaf, and needle.

She followed Thym, who rode on a cream-colored horse. Gryndal had offered to supply her with a guide, but she had declined. It wasn't due to any concern about him harming or spying on her. She simply didn't want to spend several days of isolation with one of Gryndal's toadies. Still, she recognized the need for a guide.

To her surprise, Arion learned that no living Miralyith, aside from the fane, had set foot outside of Erivan. That forced her to pick a guide from one of the other tribes, which widened the choices, but not by much. Few Fhrey besides the Instarya had ever crossed the Nidwalden River, and none of them could be found in Estramnadon. Eventually, she narrowed the choices to six. They included an Eilywin architect who had once been employed by the Instarya to do some repair work on the northernmost fortress of Ervanon after it had suffered an attack from a band of giants. She'd asked three times about the giant attack to be certain she'd heard correctly. She had. There was also a trio of Nilyndd builders, the same ones the Eilywin had brought with her to do the actual repairs. Another possibility was an Asendwayr hunter, who had served for several hundred years at each of the four Avrlyn frontier outposts, but he was ill when Arion visited. And then there was Thym, an Umalyn who was charged by the tribe of Ferrol's faithful to spend the warm months ministering to the outer reaches.

Arion chose Thym because she felt comfortable with one of Ferrol's faithful, having grown up among that tribe. After two thousand years, Arion recognized almost everyone living in Estramnadon, and Thym was no different. Still, he had been just a face and a name. And although she'd probably met him before, she couldn't recall any conversations. Thym was in the process of preparing for his yearly trip west when she explained about the fane sending her to Alon Rhist, and she asked if he would act as her escort to the frontier. He replied with a stiff smile and a dutiful nod, then introduced her to the horse she would ride.

Arion had never ridden a horse; few sane Fhrey had. The skittish animals were known to bolt or throw their riders. Ferrol had blessed the Fhrey with three thousand years of life, and given that falls often resulted in permanent injury or death, the idea of getting on the back of even the most docile animal was reason for concern.

"Can't we walk?" she had asked when meeting the horse for the first time.

"It's nearly a hundred miles over rough terrain to Alon Rhist," Thym replied. "And forgive me, Your Eminence, but you don't look like you do much hiking."

She conceded, accepting the logic that there was little point in obtaining a Green Field Guide's services if she didn't take his advice. And that's how Arion came to be precariously perched on the back of an extremely tall white horse named Naraspur when she and her guide reached the edge of the Harwood. The long tunnel of trees ended, and Arion beheld a wondrous sight. Leaving the forest, she discovered they were at a great height, on a ridge that afforded a breathtaking view. Having lived her entire life under Erivan's canopy, Arion was amazed.

So this is the sky!

The entirety of it was so broad and deep, it appeared endless. There were inexplicable white wisps floating above them, and a brilliant light. Previously, she'd experienced the sun only filtered through layers of leaves and needles. Looking straight out, Arion saw her first horizon. She could see for forever. Hills rose and fell in blue ridges. Even more impressive was the monstrous mountain that towered over them. Cone-shaped, it appeared to challenge the vast blue of the sky for dominance, its peak a brilliant white. From it flowed a river, which snaked below them, glistening silver. But not even the mountain could rival the awe-inspiring sight of the sky.

Thym waited patiently, his horse's tail swishing. The Umalyn were a patient lot, but he also must have known the effect of that bend in the road. She imagined that everyone he traveled with paused in that exact spot.

"It's beautiful," she said.

"From here on, you'll need to travel with your hood up to guard against the sun. Cover your skin except during early morning or late afternoon. Otherwise you'll burn."

"Burn?"

Thym nodded. "If you limit your exposure, your skin will gradually darken. Then you won't have to worry. A lot of sun too quickly will burn you." He patted the top of his head with the flat of his palm. The priest had a full head of curly brown hair, so full and buoyant that he might have been wearing a furry hat. "My hair protects me, but you won't fare so well, so do as I say and keep your hood up." Thym urged his horse onward.

Arion did as he said, but sneaked tentative peeks skyward from under the lip of her garment. She wondered if Thym was lying to make a fool of her. That marvelous sense of freedom that had come with such a wide view was lost within the confines of the hood, but she followed Thym's advice. Her guide hadn't spoken much, and she didn't think he'd break his silence if the danger wasn't real.

"How far are we?"

"Still a few days out, but you'll be able to see it once we reach the top of that next ridge."

"Really?" she said skeptically. "I'll be able to see the distance of more than one day's ride?"

He laughed and caught himself with a hand over his mouth. "Forgive me, that wasn't very respectful, Your Eminence."

"I told you to call me Arion."

"Of course, Your Eminence, but do understand that not all Miralyith are as nonchalant as you. Should I fall into the habit of familiarity, I might find it a habit hard to break. If I slipped up with someone else, someone less inclined to dispense with the honors of your tribe's station . . . well . . . I don't even want to consider what could happen."

She sighed. "Fine. But I'm curious, why did you laugh?"

He looked down, embarrassed. "Please forgive me. That was rude."

"But why did you do it?"

Thym's eyes came up, and a bit of his smile lingered. He pointed to the rows of hills. "You already see more than a day's ride. Those distant peaks are the Fendal and Adendal Durat, mountain ranges that cross the west side of Avrlyn and are easily a hundred, maybe a hundred fifty miles away." He pointed at the mountain looming over them. "Just to reach the peak of Mount Mador would take you days."

Arion gazed out amazed. "But it looks so close."

"Distances are deceiving, especially when climbing is involved."

The two followed a constricting path that twisted back on itself, descending the ridge into a shallow valley.

"And all of this is uninhabited?" she asked.

"Of course not." Thym had moved ahead as the path narrowed, and she couldn't see his face any longer. "These hills are filled with all manner of creatures."

"Rhunes?"

"No." Thym shook his head. "Down there, over that river is the High Spear Valley; that's the farthest north we allow the Rhunes to travel. Most live in Rhulyn, that big area beyond. Over there"—he pointed to mountains in the far north—"are where the Grenmorians live, and there are all manner of goblins, of course. They live everywhere: hills, swamps, forests, even the sea. There are other things as well. These lands run deep, and no one has explored it all."

"What about the Dherg?"

Thym shook his hairy head. "The Dherg live underground in the far south. Extremely rare to see one of them."

Arion peered southwest, where he had indicated Rhulyn was. "How many Rhunes are there?"

"No one knows. When they were nomadic, their numbers were small. Parents could only carry so many children, you see. Once they entered Rhulyn, they must have finally eluded the goblins that had been driving them, and they started settlements. They spread out in villages, and that's when their population exploded. We deny them the land across the Bern River to keep them from encroaching farther into the west."

"I heard a single mother can have fourteen offspring. Is that true?"

"I imagine more than that, but I'm no expert on the Rhunes. All I know is what I've gleaned from listening to the Instarya's stories. They do have such wonderful tales. Life out here isn't like life in Estramnadon." He looked at the valley below. "This isn't a tame world. The Instarya patrol it, watch the roads, and ferret out the threats. They live lives of high adventure, and they're riveting to listen to."

"Or maybe they're just good at making up stories."

Thym looked back. "Of course. But it's different for you, isn't it? All of this." He waved at their surroundings. "You're not concerned at all, are you?"

"Should I be?"

"I always am."

"You're a member of the Umalyn, a Priest of Ferrol. Have you no faith in our god?"

"I have every faith in Ferrol," Thym said. "I trust Ferrol will do as Ferrol chooses. I spend my life working to increase the odds that He *won't* rain misery upon us as a people. That is enough to ask. I don't expect Ferrol to notice me personally, much less protect me from a rampaging giant, a life-threatening storm, or a horde of goblins."

"You don't look terribly frightened."

Thym looked back. "Well, not this trip, of course. You're with me."

"And why does that matter?"

"You're Miralyith," Thym said, and turned around, leaving his back to her. Whether he meant her to hear or not, she caught the words said under his breath. "You're the scariest thing out here."

They reached the bottom of the valley, where a small stream ran through a chasm between scarred hills. There were few trees, and the rocky land was covered in a felt of grass. *Green fields*. It was as if they were in the middle of a massive bowl. All around, hills rose, and to the south one huge tooth speared that wondrous sky—

Mount Mador. She knew the tale of how Fenelyus had created the mountain during the war with the Dherg, even though Fenelyus didn't speak much about that time. The old fane avoided mentioning anything about the war, talking about it only in vague terms. To everyone else, the Great War had been her finest hour, but Fenelyus treated it as a shameful thing. "Mistakes of my youth," she often called it. Mount Mador didn't look like a mistake. The towering behemoth was astounding. The fact that Fenelyus had ordered the land to rise to such a height was beyond impressive.

I could never manage anything like that.

The sheer power and force of will required was more than Arion could imagine. She felt privileged just to see the mountain, to be inspired by it. Gryndal had been right: This trip was good for her.

Reaching a stream, Arion was forced to urge her mare to follow Thym across. So far, the trip had been along a fairly clear trail. Crossing looked to be dangerous, and neither Arion nor Naraspur liked the idea. The horse shifted from side to side, voicing her apprehension with unmistakable body language. Arion lay forward, clutching the horse's neck with both arms as at last Naraspur moved forward. They made their way through the stream, which turned out to be shallower and easier than expected. Arion sat up and chided herself for being so concerned. Like most Fhrey, and certainly those who populated Estramnadon, she had lived a life of isolation, one that lacked adventure. She was starting to regret that.

"What are the Instarya like?" she asked as the trail widened enough for her to come alongside Thym.

He looked skeptical. "You haven't met anyone from the warrior tribe?"

"Of course not. I grew up in the temple and then sequestered myself in the towers of the Miralyith. Oh, by the way, what's that big light in the sky again?"

He rolled his eyes.

"That was a joke," she told him with an encouraging smile.

He squinted his eyes, a hint of suspicion added to his face.

"You know what a joke is, right?"

He nodded. "Oh, yes. I just haven't heard a Miralyith make one."

"Given how well that one went over, I'm not surprised."

He studied her a moment longer, then shrugged more to himself than to her. "The Instarya are . . ." He paused, searching the horizon. "You have to understand that they've been out here, left to guard the frontier, since the Dherg War. Lothian will be the fourth fane they've served under. After the conflict ended, they weren't allowed to return home. Generations have been born and died, some without setting foot on our side of the Nidwalden. So over the centuries they've adapted."

"Adapted?"

"Life out here is different. Luxuries are few, the weather is awful, there's no culture to speak of, and everything is potentially dangerous. Even some plants are poisonous. The Instarya have developed a more robust outlook, a set of values that might appear crude to you at first. They're more akin to the ancients in that they hold honor and courage sacred. To them these are not just ideas, not mere concepts or metaphors. The Instarya are a proud people and . . ."

"And?"

Thym looked uncomfortable. Refusing to face her, the plump priest wrapped in his white asica kept his focus up the trail. "And, well . . . they don't like the Miralyith."

Like all Fhrey in Estramnadon at the time, Arion had been at the Carfreign Arena to witness the challenge. At Fenelyus's death, the leader of the Instarya had returned to Erivan and had been awarded the right to challenge Lothian for the throne by blowing the Horn of Gylindora.

The battle had been horribly one-sided. Zephyron had come armed with sword and shield; Lothian had used the Art. It had been the first time a challenge had been fought between a Miralyith and a member of another tribe. Lothian had sought to make an example and didn't merely beat the Instarya leader—he made the contest a spectacle.

First, Lothian enveloped himself in a shield of air, rendering Zephyron's weapons and fighting ability useless. Next came humiliation. Using the Art, Lothian turned his opponent into a puppet. Zephyron stripped, danced, and humiliated himself before the crowd. Lothian forced the Instarya leader to crawl on all fours, bark, howl, roll in mud, and eat grass like an animal. Then the show started a long walk into darkness as Lothian began his second act by forcing Zephyron to mutilate himself. The first offense was making him bite off and swallow each of his fingers.

At that point, Arion had risked admonishment by leaving. She had only reached the rear of the arena before vomiting. Later, she heard that the "battle" had continued for another two hours and that by the end of it she hadn't been the only one to get sick. When Lothian finally granted the Instarya death, Zephyron had become unidentifiable as a Fhrey. No wonder the Instarya didn't embrace the Miralyith as benevolent leaders.

Coming around a bend, Arion saw another stream. It looked much the same as the first. This second branch flowed even more lazily, and with newfound confidence she remained upright as Naraspur crossed. Although it wasn't much deeper, the current was stronger, and as the horse was climbing out the far side, one of her hooves slipped. Arion felt the odd shift of balance. A stuttering step followed, bouncing Arion harshly and tilting her to one side. The fear of a dozen warnings and tales of tragedy flashed through her mind as she reached for the horse's mane. Naraspur, who likely had quite enough of the river's current, chose that moment to leap the remaining distance to the far bank. Arion failed to go with her.

With a horrified cry, the tutor to the prince fell. She struck rock and river, certain her life was over. Her last thought was how it was embarrassing to die in such a fashion. A painful moment later, she realized she wasn't dead. Her hands, hip, left knee, and elbow hurt, and she was soaked, but other than that she was fine.

Thym turned his horse and rode back, staring at her in shock.

The pain was bad, the embarrassment worse, but it was the fear the river had caused that made her angry. Standing in the water and the shadow of Mount Mador, Arion began a weave. Recognizing the signs of magic, Thym retreated, taking Naraspur with him.

A whirlwind erupted, and the ground groaned, cracked, and screamed the way rock did when suddenly awakened. The river continued to laugh at her. Creeks and streams were overly light-headed things and had a tendency to laugh and chuckle over rocks, even when no one fell into them. This one had made the mistake of laughing at a Miralyith.

The whirlwind vanished, the ground settled, and the stream disappeared, rerouted far to the east. In its place she left a smooth bluish-stone walkway bordered by short rock walls. Nestled in alcoves, flower boxes over-flowed with beautiful yellow blooms that had once dotted the river's bank. In one recessed opening, a statue of an elegantly robed woman poured water from a pitcher into a cistern, the level of which remained constant. Arion's clothes were dry once more, and she walked up a set of stairs that followed the slope to where Thym waited with a gaping mouth. She didn't stop after reaching him and continued walking without saying a word.

"Your horse, Your Eminence," he called.

"No, thank you. I'm walking from now on."

They reached the top of the next ridge, Arion on foot, Thym riding his horse and leading Naraspur with a rope. From this new vantage point, Arion felt she could see the whole of the world. The sun was nestling on the backs of the distant mountains, bathing a vast valley in a sharp light. Where the sun kissed the hills, they were a brilliant orange. Everything else faded into dark purple. Night and day shook hands across eternity, and there, on a dominant hill overlooking a wide river, a singular tower rose beside a dome, both of them ringed by a great wall. Looking as if all the structures had sprouted naturally out of the crest of the promontory, the fortress and a small city stood watch over the massive plain below.

"There it is," Thym said. "Alon Rhist, the Bern River, and Rhulyn."

As they approached Alon Rhist, a light rain began to fall, and Arion had an unsettling feeling that she'd forgotten to latch the front door to her home back in Estramnadon. She imagined it swinging open and rain getting in. Rugs and drapes were no doubt getting soaked, and yet the poor flower in the pot on her table was probably dying of thirst. All the power of the Art couldn't help any of it. She consoled herself with the knowledge that not much could be damaged. It wasn't a grand house, certainly not as majestic as one would expect for someone of her stature, but she didn't need much. She was rarely at home, which contrary to her mother's belief was the real reason Celeste had left.

Since joining the Miralyith, it was the same reason everyone had gone. Even Anton had complained of neglect, and he was a Miralyith. The problem was that Arion placed the Art before all else. Living alone wasn't a problem for Arion. At least that was what she'd told herself since Celeste's departure.

Still, twenty years with Celeste hadn't been a total loss. In that time, Arion had managed to learn a bit about construction. Celeste had enrolled in the Atro Elendra School of Architecture with dreams of gaining a seat on the Estramnadon Design Council. Arion thought

Celeste had about as much chance of landing a director's seat as Arion had of becoming fane. But when helping Celeste with her studies, Arion had learned a great deal about the Eilywin tribe's philosophy of structure.

The number one tenet of Fhrey architecture required all structures to take inspiration from their surrounding landforms. Adherence to this doctrine bordered on religious conviction. To construct a building that defied the land, that ignored the flow of creation, was tantamount to rejecting the divine. Such hubris would doom the inhabitants to a cursed existence. In Erivan, homes were built of stone for permanence and because harming a tree of Erivan was forbidden. Despite the building material, each house was fashioned to appear as a natural part of the forest. The Airenthenon, where the high council met, had been built as an extension of a rocky hill. The Talwara Palace was fashioned in much the same way, on an opposing outcrop that had swallowed and surrounded the Forest Throne. Then there was the tower of Avempartha, which Arion had only recently discovered when crossing the Nidwalden River. The structure rose high above the great Parthaloren Falls and mimicked an upward explosion of water. Seeing that tower, another of Fenelyus's creations, Arion had stared in awe for so long that Thym became weary and pleaded to move on. Alon Rhist's tower wasn't as amazing as Avempartha, but it was still striking.

Built on an already impressive pinnacle of rock alongside a river-cut chasm, the Rhist continued the upward thrust of stone, amplifying it with a sky-piercing tower. The jagged-toothed spine of the crest was mirrored in the sharp archways supporting the transom between the great dome and the towered keep. From a distance, Arion had thought the place pretty. Up close, the fortress, which marked the edge of the fane's reach and formed the premier bulwark for civilization, was impressive. The sheer height of the spire was difficult to comprehend, because the barbican that formed the fortified entrance was itself seven stories tall. Even so, it appeared to be but a footstool to the soaring keep behind it.

Inside, the Rhist was less remarkable. Stark walls of stone remained unadorned except by weapons, of which there were many. For the Instarya, decorations were shields crossed with swords. Furniture displayed the same single-minded military focus. Assembled from wood, chairs lacked cushions or padding. Everything was neat but sterile, ordered but lifeless, cold, hard, and unforgiving. What struck Arion the most was the lack of greenery. The architects of the Rhist had taken the Eilywin philosophy to the extreme and built a cave of stone to fit in a rocky realm.

In contrast with the cold building, Arion was greeted with as much warmth and fanfare as the Rhist's commander could muster. Escorted by eight pairs of honor guards in front and behind she walked past lines of Fhrey adorned in full, polished armor. They snapped salutes in a precision wave as she passed. A pair of drums rolled and two long horns blared, and from every window the Miralyith purple and gold banners flew in her honor. Arion felt a tad awkward at the fuss. She was the tutor of the prince, not the fane.

The commander received her under the dome, where he sat in a hard chair with mismatched pillows. Petragar rose as she entered. He was dressed in a formal asica adorned with Asendwayr colors but worn in the Miralyith style, lacking knots and crisscrosses. Arion knew his name but little else. She was unlikely to learn much more since his face was wrapped in bandages. He whispered to an assistant standing beside him, who said, "Welcome to Alon Rhist. I am Vertumus, Legate of the Post. May I introduce the most esteemed patriarch of the Asendwayr, former senior counsel to the Aquila, the fane's personally appointed commander of Avrlyn and Rhulyn, his grand and worthy lordship Petragar of the Rhist."

The two bowed.

She returned their bows. "I'm Arion," she said.

Vertumus hesitated, looking out of sorts as if she'd tripped him. The assistant to the commander was a little Fhrey with a receding hairline and enough gray to suggest he was well into his second millennium. He was dressed in formal Asendwayr garb, a green-and-gold tunic with a long cape.

"The commander is extremely honored to have such an esteemed person as yourself visiting Alon Rhist," Vertumus went on, finding his rhythm once more. "He regrets that due to recent events he cannot speak as clearly as he'd like, and he has asked me to aid him in this matter." They bowed again.

Arion didn't bother to return it. She was far too tired and dirty for formalities. All she wanted was a bath and a bed. Even a meal could wait.

"Where is Nyphron now?"

Petragar looked at Vertumus, who replied on his behalf. "We believe he has gone south to hide among the Rhunes."

Petragar whispered once more, and Vertumus spoke up. "Certainly these unpleasant matters can wait until another day. It's late, and you've traveled a long way. You must be tired."

"I'd greatly appreciate a bath." The grit from traveling was horrible. Twice she had ordered Thym to stop at clear mountain pools so that she could clean up. She had used the Art to turn each into a luxurious hot spa, but it had been two days since the last one.

"Of course. I'll have one prepared immediately. Afterward, we will feast in your honor." Vertumus looked over Arion's shoulder, and at the snap of his fingers, a soldier ran off. "Commander Petragar insists that you occupy his quarters while you are here. I'll have your bags brought up and the bed turned."

"I don't know that a feast is necessary, and I only have the one bag," she said.

The two seemed a bit relieved, relaxing slightly.

They don't like Miralyith.

"Anyway, I can carry my bag, unless . . ." She looked

out the western windows. "My room isn't at the top of that tower, is it?"

"Of course not," Vertumus said. "Elysan, escort Her Eminence to the commander's chambers."

Arion was nearly out the door when Vertumus asked, "Will you be staying long?"

She paused and shook her head. "I expect I'll be leaving in search of Nyphron in the morning."

"In the morning?" Vertumus's brows rose. "So soon? But we have no idea where Nyphron and his Galantians are."

She smiled. Arion rarely dealt with non-Miralyith, and those she did speak to were well aware of their capabilities. Out on the frontier all they had was rumors, and she could imagine the sort of stories told after the spectacle of Zephyron's death. "Did he leave anything personal behind?"

Vertumus glanced at Petragar, then said, "Well, yes. Most of his things are still in his room."

"And does he have hair?"

"Nyphron? Hair? Oh, yes, long and blond. But I don't see—"

"Well, then." Arion clapped her hands together as a sign of *problem-solved*. "If he's left any behind in a brush or on a pillow, I'll have no trouble finding him."

"Oh," Vertumus said. "Then I'll see that Nyphron's quarters are scoured for strands. But we, ah . . . we expected you'd be staying longer than—"

"No reason to delay. Thym tells me he knows nothing of the Rhune villages, so I'll be continuing without him," Arion went on, her weariness making her curt. "He'll be staying here. I assume that's all right."

They both nodded, and Vertumus said, "He usually stays here or in one of the other outposts in the summers."

"Good. Also, I'll need you to keep and care for the horse I brought with me."

"You won't be taking it?"

"No."

The two looked at each other, puzzled. "But you might be several days on the road. You'll need supplies and—"

"In an unpleasant rage on the way here, I nearly obliterated the poor beast. I ended up rerouting a river instead. So no, for the good of the animal, my own safety, and the protection of nature itself, I won't have anything more to do with horses."

At her raised voice, Petragar took a step back. Vertumus remained frozen, staring at her; he didn't look to be breathing.

Petragar elbowed his servant.

"As ... as you wish, Your Eminence," Vertumus managed to choke out.

The commander whispered to his assistant, who nodded and then said, "We will, of course, provide you with whatever you need, but ..." He bit his lip. "Exactly how many soldiers should we have prepared for the morning?"

"Soldiers?"

"Yes. How many do you think you'll need to subdue Nyphron and his Galantians? Will fifty be enough? Would you prefer more?"

Now was her turn to be puzzled. "Why in Ferrol's name would I need soldiers?"

CHAPTER FIFTEEN

The Lost One

When I was born, the name Moya had no meaning or significance in the Rhunic, Dherg, or Fhrey languages. It does now. And in all three it means the same thing— brave and beautiful.

— THE BOOK OF BRIN

The people of Dahl Rhen had gone without drawing water for as long as they could. Once the Fhrey had settled next to the well, no one was willing to go near it except Raithe, and Persephone refused to make him the village water boy. The women decided to go together, hoping there was safety in numbers, and a herd of women would be less likely to spark a problem than a troop of men. Tense husbands and sons watched from doorways as their wives and mothers gathered all the containers they could carry.

Persephone led the expedition since it had been her idea. All told, they had more than twenty women, each laden with poles and gourds. Tressa was notably absent. No one from the lodge had ventured out, and Persephone wondered what they were drinking in there.

The former chieftain's wife lined everyone up single-file along the outer wall in front of Bergin the Brewer's row of aging clay jugs. She offered words of encouragement, telling them to be calm and quiet. They were to fill their containers and then head back the way they had come. Delwin, Tope, Cobb, Gelston, and Gifford stood alongside Bergin, watching. Each looked about as relaxed as a turtle without a shell.

"You be careful," Delwin told Sarah. "And if there's trouble, you drop that pole and run back to me as fast as you can. You understand?"

Persephone wondered what Delwin, or any of the men, thought could be done if trouble arose. Raithe was the only one capable of standing up to the Fhrey, and even he didn't stand a chance against so many. Not that there were nine at the well. Each day a few of them left the dahl and went into the forest. No one knew where they went or why, but she took advantage of the daily excursions when planning the "well raid," timing it for when the fewest Fhrey would be present.

Brin had been one of the first to volunteer to haul water, but her parents had refused.

"If it wasn't for the good of the dahl, do you think *I* would be going?" Sarah asked her. "This is dangerous. We have no idea what they might do." Sarah was trembling, and Delwin gave his wife a long, tight hug.

Persephone, Moya, and Sarah led the column across the byway on the far side of the lodge. They passed the newly turned black soil of the Killians' garden, where green beans were already sprouting. Then they moved past a pile of green wood Viv and Bruce Baker's boys had stacked. As they neared the lodge and the well, Persephone saw Raithe and Malcolm not far from Sarah's roundhouse, watching the procession.

The Fhrey watched as well.

There were only three in their camp near the well, and Persephone was disappointed that neither Nyphron nor Grygor was among them. She had talked to those two before and wasn't sure if any of the others knew Rhunic. Persephone spoke Fhrey, but she wasn't confident in her ability. Knowing their language was a requirement of all chieftains because the Fhrey held meetings to review treaties and discuss grievances. Reglan had learned it from his father, and she learned the vernacular when Reglan had taught their son. Konniger didn't realize it yet, but he was going to have to learn the language from her.

Thankfully, the goblin wasn't there. The assortment of Galantians who ventured into the Crescent Forest each day was different, but each party always included him.

Aside from their daily outings, the Fhrey stayed mostly in their camp: stitching clothes, sharpening blades, polishing armor, and speaking quietly among themselves. That morning the tall one who carried the spear, a gigantic pole with a fearsome blade, sat rubbing it with a cloth. Next to him was the quiet one, who braided his hair and had a fascination with tying knots in lengths of rope or in the frayed threads of his clothes. The last was the one called Tekchin.

Persephone had heard his name from several of the others, usually when they told him to be quiet. Tekchin was a scary-looking Fhrey with short-cut hair, intense eyes, a scar cut along the side of his face, and a sneer that seemed just as permanent. The scar was easy to see as none of the Fhrey had beards. Persephone had previously thought Fhrey were like women in that respect, but since their arrival, she'd seen them scraping their faces with blades.

As the line of women approached the well, Tekchin stood up and moved to the edge of their path. Sarah faltered at his approach, and Persephone grabbed her hand, squeezing tightly to keep her walking. The Fhrey folded his arms and glared as they neared. So merciless was his gaze that the whole line slowed. Sarah tugged backward, and even Persephone had trouble keeping her feet moving forward.

From behind her, Moya shouted, "What are *you* looking at?"

Moya!

Persephone thought her heart might have stopped at that moment. Her feet certainly would have if they weren't in a procession, and it was hard to stop twenty people moving as one.

"I'm looking at *you*," the Fhrey growled back in Rhunic, and moved toward her.

The line did halt then, jostling to a standstill. This

time it was Sarah who squeezed Persephone's hand, and she did so with enough force that it hurt. Persephone guessed the only reason the women hadn't scattered was that they were too scared to move.

Then Moya did the unthinkable. She stepped out of line and closed the distance between herself and the sneering Galantian. She walked so forcefully that the empty gourds dangling from the pole over her shoulders bounced together making hollow *clunks*.

"Well, this ain't a show, you know?" Moya said with the same saucy disdain she'd used when Heath Coswall asked her to dance last Wintertide. "We need water. So why don't you help us out and put your eyes back in your head."

No one breathed for a moment as the two faced off; then all three Fhrey began laughing. Tekchin nodded and held out his hand. Moya looked confused. She obviously had meant for the Fhrey to help by getting out of their way, but he'd taken her words of assistance literally. When she didn't react, he reached out and lifted the pole off her shoulders. Moya stood still, as if a bee were buzzing around her. Tekchin took her gourds to the well, where he began pulling water.

The women just stared.

"*Get over here and give me a hand,*" Tekchin demanded of the others in the Fhrey language.

The one with the spear set his weapon down and began working the rope, tying it around a gourd and lowering it. The Fhrey with the braided hair approached Persephone and took both her and Sarah's sets of jugs. He brought them over to the well, and Tekchin filled each.

"What's your name?" Tekchin asked Moya.

"Who wants to know?"

Don't push it! For all that's sacred, don't push it! Persephone thought. She was ready to kill Moya yet wanted to kiss her at the same time.

"I'm Tekchin," he said, exchanging an empty gourd

for a full one. "The handsomest and most skilled of the Galantians."

This brought an immediate and loud moan from the other Fhrey.

"That scar suggests otherwise," Moya replied. "On both counts."

More laughter, louder this time.

"*Pretty and smart,*" Tekchin said to the others in Fhrey.

Persephone was thankful Moya couldn't understand their language. A comment like that would have been tantamount to putting torch to tinder.

"This?" Tekchin returned to Rhunic and touched his cheek. "Naw, this is a beauty mark given to me by a special friend. He's dead now, of course, but he was a gifted opponent and aiming for my throat. I can assure you it proves my skill. So what's your name, or shall I call you *Doe-Eyes?*"

"Doe-Eyes? Seriously?" Moya rolled her same-said eyes in disbelief. "I would have expected something less sappy from a god. My name is Moya. Call me anything else and you'll receive a second beauty mark."

Tekchin struggled but failed to resist smiling. Behind him, the rest of the Fhrey laughed once more.

"God, eh?" Tekchin said.

"Don't get too excited. Apparently it's only a rumor."

"I like you, Moya."

"Most people do," she replied. Seeing that her water containers were filled, Moya lifted the pole, laid it across her shoulders, and walked away.

The raid on the well had been a huge success, and Persephone received praise for coming up with the idea, despite Moya being the true hero of the hour. With stores of fresh water once more at hand, meals were made, animals watered, and songs sung. Not everyone was pleased. Konniger and Tressa were reportedly livid. Later that afternoon the new chieftain summoned Persephone to the lodge, a demand she chose to ignore. When Maeve was sent to ask why she had failed to appear, Moya answered for Persephone. "Tell Konniger she's taking a *bath*."

This unleashed uncontrolled laughter in Roan's roundhouse, drawing a huff of indignation from Maeve before she left. No one knew whether Maeve actually delivered the message because a few minutes later the dahl's horn blew again, three long wails. The singing and laughter stopped.

"Fhrey!" Cobb shouted once again.

The gate stood open, as it did most days from dawn till dusk, and Cobb looked to Persephone for direction. She turned to Nyphron, who along with the rest of the Galantians had returned from their hike in the forest.

No one sought Konniger.

The Galantians said nothing. They merely gathered their weapons, slung shields, and marched out the gate. Not all of them went. The goblin stayed behind.

Persephone climbed the ladder to stand on top of the wall. She leaned out on the logs and looked down as the two groups converged just below. This new troop was remarkably similar to the Galantians. They wore brilliant golden breastplates, studded war skirts, plumed helms, and long blue capes. Despite the uniformity, Nyphron stood out. He was taller than the others, had no helm, and his golden hair blew in the breeze. But it was more than that. The swagger of his walk, and the way he folded his arms and stood waiting for the others to approach, made him greater than the rest—a god among gods.

"What's going to happen?" Cobb asked her. "Are they going to fight?"

"I don't know."

"Similar in numbers. What if they do? Do we help?"

"I don't know."

"What if they lose?"

"I don't know, Cobb! Be quiet, will you?"

The ladder creaked, and a moment later Raithe and

Malcolm climbed up. They all leaned on the sharpened tips of the log rampart, peering down, waiting for the clash.

A terrible thought crossed Persephone's mind. *What if Nyphron has been waiting for reinforcements before starting a slaughter?*

The two groups exchanged hand gestures—nothing threatening, greetings perhaps—and then they came together and began talking in Fhrey. Persephone did her best to understand the exchange.

"*What are you doing here?*" the leader of the other group asked.

"*I was going to ask you the same thing,*" Nyphron replied.

"*We're looking for the Rhune that murdered Shegon.*"

"*Not here.*"

"*You sure?*" the other Fhrey asked.

"*We've been here for days. I think we would have noticed.*"

The other leader nodded thoughtfully, and there was a long pause.

"*Why'd you do it?*"

It was Nyphron's turn to nod thoughtfully. "*You're not looking for Shegon's murderer, are you?*"

"*We are, but Petragar also asked if we could find you.*"

"*And what will you tell him?*"

"*I don't know.*" The Fhrey sighed. "*Fleeing just made matters worse.*"

"*Fleeing?*" Nyphron laughed. "*Sikar, tell me honestly, have you ever known me to flee?*"

Although there had been a formation of sorts on their approach, both groups had broken their lines. They didn't exactly mingle, but they weren't prepping for combat, either. Sikar stood in the forefront with Nyphron. Smaller, thinner, with shorter hair and a weaker posture, Sikar appeared no match for the leader of the Galantians.

"*So what would you call it? Petragar said you refused orders, broke his jaw, and ran off.*"

"*First of all*"—Tekchin paused to belch—"*Petragar, the little ass-ica that he is, was unconscious at the time. So he doesn't know Tet.*"

Sikar kept his attention on Nyphron. "*Are you saying you didn't defy orders?*"

"*Oh, we disobeyed,*" Nyphron said, and glanced back at the Galantians with a wry smile. "*That part is true. And we have no intention of returning to the Rhist.*"

"*You might want to reconsider,*" Sikar said. "*Petragar has sent word to Estramnadon.*"

"*What a brideeth,*" Nyphron said. "*That's the kind of overreaction I'd expect from someone like him and it's exactly why Lothian shouldn't have turned over the reins of the Rhist to anyone but an Instarya.*"

"*Nyphron, you refused a direct order from the fane, and you broke the commander's jaw. What did you expect?*"

Nyphron shrugged.

Sikar stared at him in disbelief, then looked back at his troops and shook his head, clapping his hands to his sides. "*Nyphron, the fane could order your execution. Why did you do it?*"

"*I thought you'd met Petragar,*" Nyphron said, and smiled.

Sikar sighed. "*This isn't funny. When I go back, I will have to report finding you.*"

"*If you feel you have to, go ahead.*"

"*And then what? I don't want to be the one getting the order to bring you in . . . or worse.*"

Nyphron smiled. The Galantian appeared to find this entertaining, but he seemed to be the only one. "*Do you think you could?*"

Sikar stared at him, his face hard. "*I wouldn't have a choice. Nyphron, your father is dead. Lothian won. He's the new fane and can't be challenged again for another three thousand years. So you're going to have to live with that fact. Even if he dies before the Uli Vermar,*" *his son will take over, and then what will you do? Challenge him? Repeat your father's mistake? Swords can't defeat the Art. You were there. You saw what happened in that arena."*

Nyphron no longer looked so jovial and began walking around Sikar.

"*A Rhune killed Shegon,*" Nyphron said. "*It proves Rhunes can fight.*"

"*According to Meryl, Shegon was unconscious when he was killed.*"

"*I hadn't heard that, but it doesn't change the fact that the Rhunes know what is possible now. Fhrey can't kill Fhrey, but Rhunes can. If provoked, they will fight back.*"

Sikar shook his head. "*I hope you know what you're doing.*"

"*Let's just say I don't intend to make the same mistakes as my father.*" Nyphron stopped and clapped Sikar on the shoulders, leaving his hands there and looking into his eyes. "*What do you say? Why don't you join us?*"

"*You can't be serious. What you're suggesting is unthinkable. It's not our place to question the fane. Our lord Ferrol appointed him—*"

Nyphron shoved him backward. "*Don't give me that crap! Ferrol didn't pick Lothian. He was the son of Fenelyus; that's how he got the Forest Throne. Before the Art, challenges were fair. But now it doesn't matter who the Aquila picks. From here on we're doomed to be ruled by the Miralyith, and Lothian just happened to be the next in line. He's a privileged, self-centered elitist who thinks anyone from another tribe is a lesser race. We're nothing but slaves to him. My father was the only one willing to say so and back it up with a sword.*"

"*And now he's dead,*" Sikar said, stepping forward to regain the ground he'd lost.

"*I think I'd rather die than be a slave,*" Nyphron shot back.

Sikar looked up at the wall lined with spectators. He

sighed. "*You might be put to that test sooner than you think.*"

"*What do you mean?*"

"*I mean it might not be me who is sent to retrieve you. The Rhist is expecting a visitor from Estramnadon.*"

"*A visitor?*"

"*Her name is Arion.*"

The Galantians looked at one another. No one appeared to recognize the name.

"*Rumor has it she's the tutor to the prince,*" Sikar said.

"*Miralyith,*" Nyphron said gravely.

"*Tutor to the prince,*" Tekchin added. "*That can't be good.*"

Sikar nodded. "*Petragar was falling all over himself making preparations of welcome. Running honor guard drills, hanging banners, scrubbing walls. Nyphron, her nickname is Cenzlyor.*"

"*Swift of mind?*"

Sikar nodded. "*It was given to her by Fenelyus— Fenelyus!*"

"*You think she's coming after us?*"

"*Why else would a palace-level Miralyith pay a visit to the Rhist?*" Sikar's face filled with sympathy. "*The only way you could be in more trouble is if Gryndal or the fane himself was on his way.*" Sikar sighed. "*Listen, I wasn't in Estramnadon for the challenge. I didn't see it, but I heard what happened—what Lothian did to your father. You should run. Just disappear.*"

Nyphron shook his head. "*It wouldn't help. No one can hide from a Miralyith.*"

Sikar nodded and extended his hand. "*Any idea where we can find Shegon's killer so this trip won't be a total loss? Perhaps it will appease Petragar if we come back with something.*"

Nyphron turned and looked up at Raithe. "*I'm pretty sure he's southeast.*"

"*What? In Menahan?*"

"*That's a possibility.*"

"*Great. I love the stink of sheep. Okay.*" Sikar sighed. "*Good luck to you.*"

Nyphron gripped Sikar's forearm and the two clapped shoulders.

"*I hope we never see any of you again,*" Sikar said, then turning to Tekchin, he added, "*Especially you.*"

"*Sikar, you sound like a spurned lover.*" Tekchin laughed.

Sikar laughed with him, and as he turned around and walked away, he called back, "*You forget how many of us owe you gambling debts, Tekchin. Farewell!*"

Tekchin stopped laughing as he watched them leave.

Suri had slept through the morning events, missing the well raid and the confrontation at the gate. Certain things could be done only by moonlight, and recently Suri had discovered many tasks to do. It wasn't until late afternoon that she woke, unable to sleep through the screaming.

By the time she crawled out of Roan's house, the noise had stopped. The man lying on the grass in front of the lodge was a twisted heap of blood-soaked rags—no longer breathing. Parts of him were missing. Most of him was missing. Suri had seen similar sights dozens of times in the forest: deer, wolves, foxes, and opossums left mauled and partially eaten by hunters who'd had their fill or whose meal had been interrupted. The bulk of the dahl gathered around to see the sight. Even the Fhrey looked on with interest.

Konniger was out of the lodge, standing on the raised porch and declaring, "This was the work of the bear that killed Reglan, Mahn, and Oswald. Krier had been cutting wood at the edge of the forest." Konniger pointed up toward the tree-covered mountain. "He was bucking a log. The men he was with went to get the sled. They weren't gone more than a few minutes. When they got back, Krier was gone. They followed a blood trail and found him where he'd been dragged to."

Krier's wife wailed in the crowd, held on her feet by others.

Suri reached into her pouch, pulled out the blackened leg bone of the chicken, and rubbed it thoughtfully with her thumb. "What do you think?" she asked Minna, who sat dutifully beside her and refused to engage in idle speculation. "You're such a wise wolf."

The marking on the bone had said a monster was coming, and it had given Suri its name. Rarely did a chicken render that level of detail, but Suri was certain she'd gotten it right. There wasn't any doubt about Grin the Brown, but the bone had revealed that she was no mere bear. It had to be a demon.

It wasn't uncommon for evil spirits to possess people and animals. Tura had fought a raow after they stumbled upon its bed of bones. She was certain the raow had once been an unfortunate woman lost in the woods. Starving, the woman had been taken over by a demon, which was how most raow came to be. Grin was no raow. Suri had narrowed the choices of demons down to three: a yakkus, morvyn, or bendigo. She was leaning toward a morvyn, since they were the result of an animal eating human flesh. The Brown seemed to have a fondness for the taste of people. Still, Suri had to be sure. As mystic, it was her responsibility to hunt and kill this demon for the good of the region, and an incorrect identification could prove disastrous.

Konniger returned inside the lodge.

Suri didn't like the log building. Entering it felt like climbing inside the dead rotting body of old friends, but she had to find out more about what kind of demon she was dealing with, and this was as good a time as any. The mystic climbed the stone steps and ducked into the wooden cave.

The fire was still burning in the big room's pit. She searched for Konniger but guessed he'd already headed up the stairs. She could hear creaks and shuffles overhead. Suri crept along the edge of the fire pit, inching toward the steps. Twelve pillars, four rows of three, held up the ceiling.

They line their halls with the dead bodies of noble beings.

The place stank of smoke and grease. On the walls hung square shields painted different colors and long spears with ribbons and feathers tied to the necks. The skins of animals lay on the floor: deer, bobcats, and two bears—one black, the other brown. Suri stepped around them, grimacing. As she looked back at the entrance, the bright light of day was being strangled by the doorway. The place was the lair of predators, murderers, and thieves.

Little wonder the demon assumed a bear's shape.

A boy dropped a log on the fire and peeked at her and Minna. He offered a smile. Suri smiled back.

"I understand! I told you I understood. Now leave me alone!" Konniger's voice boomed overhead, a sort of inferior thunder.

The mystic headed toward the stairs with Minna padding along behind.

Overhead, a door slammed.

"Where do you think you're going?" Maeve appeared at the top of the steps, glaring down. Her face was flushed, and there was anger or perhaps fear in her eyes. Suri often had difficulty distinguishing between the two, at least with people.

"I need to speak to Chieftain Konniger."

"About what?" Maeve remained on the steps with her hands on the rails, blocking the way up.

"I've done a reading from bones. Several now. The thing that murdered that man out there, Grin the Brown, isn't a bear at all."

"Of course not!" Maeve's voice jumped in pitch and volume.

Suri took a step backward at the old woman's outburst. Minna took two.

"So you know. Good. That's why I need to speak with Konniger. It's a powerful demon. He said so the day he brought back Reglan's body. He's fought it. If I can ask him some questions to learn the demon's true nature, then I'll be prepared. The demon is coming at the light of the full moon, but I don't know exactly what kind of demon we're talking about. If I could—"

"Get out!" Maeve snapped, and pointed to the door. The old woman was furious. "Konniger is too busy to see you. We have Fhrey camped just outside the hall and men being slaughtered on the eaves of the forest. He doesn't have time for mystic nonsense."

"It's not nonsense."

"Out!" she cried, coming down the stairs.

Suri and Minna retreated.

"You don't understand."

"Out, I say!"

Suri stood her ground at the bottom of the stairs. "But Konniger—"

"Konniger doesn't know nothing about anything—nothing about the bear, especially."

"Come the full moon, that bear will kill everyone, even the Fhrey, I think."

"Shayla would never do such a thing. She's a good girl."

"Shayla?" Suri asked, puzzled. "You call Grin *Shayla*?"

"If you don't leave, I'll call Hegner. He's Konniger's Shield now. He'll—"

"Shayla means 'lost one.'"

Maeve's face hardened. "I want you gone. Not just out of this lodge but off the dahl. I'll have Konniger banish you." She looked around but only found Habet and scowled. "Hegner!"

"Why would you call Grin the Brown *Lost One*?"

Maeve came down from the stairs and rushed to the wall. She pulled one of the spears from the hooks and whirled at Suri.

"I wouldn't do that," the mystic said. "Minna doesn't like it when people point sticks at us."

To emphasize this, the wolf began to growl, fur rising.

Maeve stopped. "Hegner! *Hegner!*"

"Come on, Minna."

The two left the lodge. Behind them, the doors slammed, hard.

The mystic glanced down at the wolf. "Well, what do you make of that?"

The wolf looked back at the closed door but again kept her own counsel.

"You are so smart, Minna. You must be the smartest of all wolves."

CHAPTER SIXTEEN

Miralyith

To the Fhrey we were little more than dust, as unnotice-
able as pebbles along a path. It gave us an advantage,
but not for long.

— THE BOOK OF BRIN

Arion left Thym and Naraspur in Alon Rhist and traveled south alone. For her, loneliness wasn't a problem.
She reminded herself of this twice. The second time she
added the adage about how Miralyith were trained to
live inside their heads and being with people was the
real hardship. The third time she considered how, being
alone, she could stop and rest when she liked, walk
when she wanted, sleep where she wished. By the fourth
time, she wondered why she had to keep reminding herself that she was better off alone. Then she faced the
obvious realization that she wasn't just alone with her
thoughts. She wasn't isolated in her home, away in the
Garden, sitting in a quiet room of the palace, or studying at the art academy. Arion was completely alone.
There wasn't another Fhrey for miles and no Miralyith
at all on this side of the Nidwalden. Those thoughts
were sobering.

Before being appointed as the prince's tutor, Arion
had taught at the Estramnadon Academy of the Art.
One of the hardest things to teach, after students learned
the basics, was that Miralyith weren't invincible. Everyone in Erivan treated them with respect, deference, and
even fear. Such behavior made it all too easy to believe,

as Gryndal did, that they were above others. Such thoughts led to a number of serious and sometimes fatal accidents. Arion knew of one student trying to fly who had nearly died from jumping off the roof of the Airenthenon. Another student, grieving over a lover's death, had entered the afterlife to save him and never returned.

Being a Miralyith wasn't the same as being allpowerful. The fall from Naraspur had been a reminder of just how vulnerable she was. If Arion had landed on her neck or slammed her head on a rock, she'd be just as dead as anyone else. A more immediate concern was that she couldn't create or summon food and water. She had to carry supplies on her back and hope more would be found before her provisions ran out. And while she wasn't worried about being attacked when awake, she would need to sleep. While unconscious, she couldn't maintain even the simplest weave. As she often told her students, a Miralyith was like a diamond—harder than anything, but if hit in just the right place, it shattered like glass. And there she was, alone in an unfamiliar wild wilderness, a diamond in the rough.

At least she had her string.

String patterns were taught at the art academy to boost concentration, creativity, and dexterity, as well as to familiarize students with the idea of weaving patterns out of interconnected threads. The Art was all about recognizing and making delicate patterns, and string games were as much an illustration as a tool. Such games were used only briefly, early in a Miralyith's training. Most gave up their strings as soon as they touched their first deep chord and discovered the addiction of the real thing. Arion still used her string more than two thousand years after learning the technique. Teaching students had reintroduced her to the simple joys of the game, a series of repeating chords representing the circle of life that could be bent, twisted, and looped to create new patterns, new paths.

A particularly elaborate web was forming between her fingers when she noticed a crude wooden fort on a hill, rising ahead of her. She'd passed two others—charred ruins on blackened mounds. This one looked to be the first inhabited encampment. Arion had used Nyphron's hair to track him. A simple location weave accompanied by burning a strand produced smoke that drifted in the target's direction. The color gave an indication of distance. Judging by the last reading, Nyphron and, probably, the rest of the Galantians were inside. She might have cast another location check, but the weave she had going was beautiful, and she was having fun with the string. The warrior Fhrey she had met at Alon Rhist didn't impress her as being overly intelligent, which was reason enough to assume the son of Zephyron was hiding in the most obvious place.

She heard a horn when she was still a quarter mile away, three blasts in quick succession. With a sigh, she unwrapped her fingers and let the string once more return to a simple loop. She slipped it around her neck and began a weave of another sort.

Nyphron and his band of warriors were known to be excellent combatants. One named Eres was deadly with a thrown spear. Another, called Medak, could throw a knife with accuracy for several dozen yards. Neither of these could harm her at such a distance, but Arion was a cautious sort. The weave she made was a simple thing, which required little concentration, the magical equivalent to putting a hand out in front of her. It probably wasn't necessary; Fhrey didn't kill Fhrey. But that didn't mean they couldn't hurt one another, and Nyphron had battered Petragar easily enough.

She hoped Nyphron wouldn't make a fuss. She had no desire to harm or embarrass him, especially given the way Lothian had treated Nyphron's father. In her eyes, the fane had shown poor judgment in making such a spectacle. No one could challenge again until Lothian's death or the start of the Uli Vermar, which wouldn't occur for three thousand years. But, of course, the memory would linger. In the future, only another Miralyith would ever challenge, which was the real point of the show.

Arion had weak ties to her parents, but she recognized the Instarya might feel differently. Thym had suggested as much. Nyphron must hate Lothian, which would account for his recent rebellion. He'd likely feel the same way about the fane's emissaries as well. She would try to be as gentle as possible. He only had a party of six Fhrey, and Vertumus had assured her the Rhunes wouldn't interfere. *More docile than inebriated sheep* is how he had described them as she left Alon Rhist. And, of course, their belief that the Fhrey were gods would work in her favor. Despite this, she felt uncomfortable; far too many people were thinking of themselves as gods these days.

When the horn blew, Persephone came out of the roundhouse with everyone else.

The sky was blue, the sun bright, and the breeze warm. A perfect spring day for shearing. Delwin and Gelston, who spent all year with the flock, directed the operation and did most of the actual clipping. A number of others had gone to help round up and wrangle the sheep. Raithe had been one. He'd asked Persephone for work, and there was plenty of need. On that day, he'd gotten up before dawn, split wood for the boiling, and went with the other men to fetch the flock.

Wedon, a farmer and occasional leather worker, was the gate's guard that morning. He shouted down from the wall through cupped hands, "Fhrey!"

"Again?" Moya said, coming out of Roan's roundhouse to stand beside Persephone, hands on hips. Staring out the open gate, she shook her head.

Wedon was looking down at Persephone, who once again looked to the Galantians. All nine were there, forming up beside the well and donning their weapons. Nyphron was speaking to the goblin in another language that she couldn't understand; it sounded like he was mostly coughing and spitting. He spoke quickly, earnestly, and wore an expression more serious than she'd yet seen. The little creature nodded and ran off behind the woodpile.

Konniger came out of the lodge along with The Stump and stood on the top of the steps.

"Should we seal the gate or leave it open?" Persephone asked Nyphron.

"How many are coming?"

"Wedon?" Persephone asked.

"Just one."

Nyphron ran a hand through his hair and looked at his fellows. The expressions on their faces made Persephone nervous. The last time they were all smiles and laughter. This time no one joked; no one laughed; no one smiled.

"Should we seal the gate?" she asked again.

"That depends on how much you like your gate," Nyphron replied.

Wedon looked to Konniger, who remained on the steps, now flanked by Tressa and Maeve. Konniger, in turn, stared at Persephone, who finally replied with a shrug, "Leave it open, I guess."

"Why do we even have these walls?" Moya asked.

Roan appeared on the other side of Persephone, shifting to one side to allow Gifford a better view. The potter still wore his leather apron, which was soaked and smeared with clay. No one said anything. No one moved, and at nearly midday Dahl Rhen came to a stop. The only sounds were distant birdsong and flapping banners on the lodge.

Out of that silence, a figure appeared, framed in the open gate. Dressed in flowing robes of white, which billowed in the breeze as if made of gossamer, she appeared ghostly. Tall, thin, and more delicate than one of Gifford's best vases, she didn't seem of the same world as everyone else. Too elegant, too perfect with eyes of bright blue and pale, thin lips.

She made no sound.

It's as if she floats, Persephone thought.

The lady in white entered the gate. Drawing back her hood, she revealed a bald head. She walked until reaching the center of the dahl, then stopped—just a few feet from Nyphron and Persephone.

Behind the lady Fhrey, Delwin, Malcolm, Raithe, and a few other men entered, each of them out of breath. Delwin still held his shears and Raithe the prod stick. The bald Fhrey didn't turn her head or look around; she remained focused on Nyphron.

"You are Nyphron, son of Zephyron, of the Instarya?" the bald woman asked in the Fhrey language.

"Yes," Nyphron replied. He stood where he was, stiff and still, his hands hanging at his sides.

"I'm Arion of the Miralyith. I have been sent by Fane Lothian to request your return to Estramnadon."

"Request? In that case, I'll decline the offer."

The lady took a step closer. *"Your fane insists."*

"I no longer recognize Lothian as my fane. So I see no reason to care if he insists or not."

Persephone didn't understand why the lady in white was such a problem. There were seven strong Fhrey warriors, a giant, and the creepy goblin thing, presently hiding behind the woodpile, arrayed against her. And yet the Galantians' apprehension was palpable.

"Please don't make this harder than it needs to be." The lady Fhrey took a breath and another step forward. *"I was at the arena and saw what happened to your father. I'd like to spare you any more humiliation and pain."*

"And how do you propose to do that? If I appear before Lothian, do you think he will treat me any different? I won't go back with you."

The Galantians gathered around Nyphron with hands on weapons.

Arion granted them a cursory glance. *"I have no instructions concerning the rest of you. Don't involve yourself, or you'll share Nyphron's fate."*

"We're Galantians," Sebek said. *"And Instarya. Sharing fate is what we do."*

"*Touch him and you're going to have to fight all of us,*" Tekchin declared.

Arion didn't appear concerned. If anything, she looked sad. "*I'm trying to be kind. We both know what's going to happen. Wouldn't you prefer to follow me out of here with dignity? You can explain yourself to the fane. Tell him you were distraught from witnessing the death of your father. He's not without compassion.*"

"*No? I thought you said you saw what happened in the arena?*" Nyphron replied with a growl in his voice. "*Were those acts of compassion? Had the situation been reversed, my father would have made Lothian's death quick, painless, and honorable. Don't stand there and tell me to throw myself on a tyrant's mercy. All of you Miralyith are the same. Since Fenelyus became fane, you've lorded over the rest of us, set yourselves up as gods. The war with the Dherg ended centuries ago, but the Instarya are still condemned to serve in the wilderness while you, all of you, bask in the security we provide. Why is that? What are we doing out here? Why only Instarya and a handful of Asendwayr? Why don't the great Miralyith send a few to serve? Why are there no Eilywin? During the war, when Alon Rhist was fane, other tribes were out here with us, wielding hammers and shovels. They built the Rhist, but not one of them remains. Where are the Nilyndd? Ferrol knows we could use them. And the Umalyn—*"

"*I came here with Thym of the Umalyn,*" she said.

Nyphron rolled his eyes. "*Yes, once a year, two or three of the most unfortunate Umalyn priests condescend to visit and find fault. What a great help they are. We have been forced to live and die out here, denied the rights of every other Fhrey to cross the Nidwalden and go home. We aren't good enough to be a part of Erivan, we are only fit to suffer defending it. Protecting a fane who treats us without respect. No, I won't willingly return with you, not while I have breath in my body. Lothian is your fane, not mine. I no longer serve him, for he no longer values me.*"

Arion sighed. *"I'm sorry, but you are Fhrey, and you are coming with me. I just want you to know that I'll take no pleasure in this."*

The lady Fhrey gestured with her hand, and Nyphron's wrists came together in front of him as if they'd been bound. Then, she twitched her finger, and he jerked forward. At the same time, Persephone heard an odd sound. Someone was singing. Less a song than a chant, and all the words were in another language.

Arion staggered then, shoved back several steps as if blown by a powerful wind. She nearly stumbled into Malcolm. Nyphron stopped walking forward.

"Now!" Nyphron shouted in Rhunic. "Do it now!"

Persephone heard a loud roar and watched in amazement as Arion caught fire. In an instant, her whole body was engulfed in a pillar of flame that swirled and coursed up twenty feet into the sky. Those close cried out, backing away.

The Galantians drew weapons and ran at the blistering column of fire. One threw a javelin, another a knife. Then everything stopped.

The javelin and knife froze in midair and fell. A moment later seven of the nine Galantians slammed into an invisible wall. Three hit so hard they bounced and collapsed, dazed. The giant staggered and reeled, blood running from his nose. The woodpile was swept aside, revealing the yellow-eyed goblin chanting and dancing until he, too, stopped. With a wave of Arion's hand, the goblin froze and the fire surrounding her vanished. She was still dressed in pristine white; not so much as a thread of her wondrously white robe had been singed.

"Sit down, all of you!" Arion ordered. The Fhrey, as well as the creature near the woodpile and the giant, were thrown to the dirt. *"I've had enough of this foolishness."*

The remainder of their weapons flew from their hands and scabbards, clattering into a pile near Arion's feet. *"This is why you're treated poorly. You dare to attack your fellow Fhrey?"* She pointed at the goblin. *"You've enlisted practitioners of the Dark Art! You've become wild and are too dangerous to be allowed back into society. Association with the Rhunes has distorted your ideals of loyalty and honor. What virtue is there in living like an animal? What honor is there in rebellion? You've become feral—no, worse—you've become rabid! It isn't for you to decide whom you serve or the wisdom of the fane's actions. Lothian is fane because Ferrol has decreed it. Your father died because our god knows who will make a better fane. When you disobey Lothian, you're defying Ferrol's will. Who do you think you are to—"*

Arion crumpled, sprawling face-first on the gravel where she lay awkwardly twisted, her cheek pressed against the little rocks of the path. She didn't move. Her robes billowed up briefly with a breeze then settled as lightly as dandelion tufts. Everyone stared in shock at the pool of white robes and the bright-red blood that began to stain them.

Behind her, holding a rock in both hands, stood Malcolm.

"We *really* need to talk about this habit of yours," Raithe told Malcolm as he stared down at the pile of cloth and the frail Fhrey at his feet. "This wasn't our fight."

"Shegon wasn't my fight, either, but you didn't seem too upset then." The ex-slave continued to stare at the bleeding Fhrey with a look of sadness so pronounced that Raithe wondered if the man would vomit. As he thought about it, Raithe realized Malcolm had looked the same way after hitting Shegon.

The Galantians rushed forward. Nyphron stopped, looking down at her. "She's breathing." Then to Raithe and Malcolm he said, "She's still alive. You need to finish her."

"What?" Raithe asked, stunned.

"You're the *God Killer.*" Nyphron looked squarely at

him. "You have two swords. Use one of them and kill her."

"She's defenseless," Raithe said, hoping Malcolm didn't say anything. This was not the time to be admitting past transgressions.

"I know." Nyphron took a tentative step closer, a step wide of her pretty white robes. "Which means it'll be easy."

"I don't kill women or children."

"That's not a woman. That's a Miralyith."

"I don't even know what *Miralyith* means."

"It means she's too powerful and dangerous to live."

Sebek looked at Malcolm. "You do it. Kill her. You don't attack a Miralyith without finishing the job. Leaving her injured is suicide for you, us, and pretty much everyone."

"Don't lay this at our feet. If you want her dead, go ahead and kill her yourselves," Raithe said. "We can't stop you."

"We can't. Fhrey can't kill another—" Nyphron looked irritated. "Where's Grygor?"

"No! Don't hurt her!" Persephone cried, rushing forward. She held her skirt above her ankles and muscled her way into the ring surrounding the fallen Fhrey.

"Grygor, get over here," Nyphron called, and the giant lumbered toward them, pausing to pick up his sword. "I need you to kill this bitch."

"Don't let them hurt her!" she shouted at Raithe.

Raithe wondered when, and how, he had become the arbiter of all things. He hadn't even been the one to use the rock. "Why?"

"Protect the injured," she said, looking deep into his eyes as if this was a magic spell she was casting. "*Protect the injured*, remember?"

He didn't. Not at first but then it hit him, and he understood what had lit a fire under her. "You *are* kidding."

Persephone stood before the giant, holding up a palm to stop him. Then she faced the Galantian leader. "If you want to stay with us—and since you can't go back to Alon Rhist, this might be the only place you are welcome—I forbid you to harm her."

"You, you, what?" Nyphron asked. The Fhrey blinked repeatedly, as if trying to get a clear view of her. For the first time, Nyphron appeared genuinely and unequivocally dumbfounded.

"Persephone!" an enraged Konniger shouted from the doorway of the lodge, a fortress of wood he'd retreated to. "Stay out of it. This isn't our affair."

"It is! This lady *cannot* be harmed. Raithe, help me," Persephone pleaded. "Don't let Nyphron kill her."

"Nyphron can't kill her," Malcolm said, his voice a refuge of calm assurance. "Fhrey can't kill Fhrey."

"That's why *you* have to do it," Nyphron told Raithe. "Or let Grygor."

Raithe had no intention of killing anyone. He had nothing against the lady, and she was pretty, which made the idea even more distasteful. It was always more difficult to snap a rabbit's neck than crush a spider. He found himself agreeing with Konniger. This was none of their business. Around them, the inhabitants of the dahl inched closer, closing a hesitant circle. Children were pushed back or held close as parents watched with worried eyes.

Persephone pressed on, ignoring everyone. She bent down and touched the face of the Fhrey. "Delwin, Cobb, Wedon, take her into the lodge. *Gently*. Carry her upstairs and put her in the bed in the loft."

"Are you insane?" Nyphron asked. "You don't understand. *She's Miralyith*. If she wakes up . . ." He shook his head, at a loss for words. "She'll—she'll erase Rhulyn from existence, and all of you along with it."

"I don't care." Persephone tilted the delicate, bald head and grimaced at the blood leaking into the dirt. "It's what the tree said to do."

"The what? Did you say the *tree*?" Nyphron asked.

"She's right." Malcolm was nodding.

Nyphron focused on the ex-slave even as Delwin and

Cobb crept in, moving like cats terrified of the Galantians and not terribly thrilled with the Miralyith.

"Go on, pick her up—gently," Persephone instructed. "Be very careful. She's bleeding badly. We need to stop it or she'll die."

"Good, let her die!" Nyphron declared.

His outburst caused the men lifting the Miralyith to flinch, but Nyphron wasn't looking at them; he hadn't taken his eyes off Malcolm. "You'll be the first one she'll come after, you know? You and your rock."

The path to the lodge was blocked by the giant. "What do you say, boss?" Grygor asked. The giant was still holding his sword. Not that he would need a blade to kill the delicate Miralyith.

"I mean what I said," Persephone told Nyphron sternly. "Leave her be, or you won't be welcome here anymore."

Nyphron broke eye contact with Malcolm. "Never mind. Forget it. You heard the woman. We don't want to jeopardize our welcome."

"You sure?" Grygor asked.

Nyphron shot the giant a look.

"Just asking."

"Stryker! You lousy goblin," Nyphron shouted at the creature still near the fallen woodpile. "Get over here. We need to talk."

The giant turned sideways, letting the men carry the Miralyith past him toward the lodge.

"Dammit, I said no!" Konniger shouted. "You aren't bringing her in *my* house."

As the lady Fhrey was borne up the steps, Hegner and Devon joined Konniger's side, spears at the ready. The three stood, blocking the entrance, a wall of muscle and stone-tipped sticks.

Raithe caught Persephone by the arm. "Does it have to be in there?"

"It's the best place, the most comfortable, and it will be quiet and safe."

Raithe nodded, then looked at the chieftain. "Move out of the way."

"This is no concern of yours, Dureyan," Konniger growled.

"Your maimed friend and I have unfinished business. I'll be happy to include you in the fun if you like." He drew Shegon's sword. "So we can settle everything now, or you can get out of the way."

Konniger didn't move, but he also didn't attack. The man appeared just as trapped in his position as he was in that doorway. Instead, he repeated himself, speaking louder. "This is no concern of yours!"

"Well, it certainly is *my* concern," Nyphron said as he and the other Galantians came up. This included the goblin, who had escaped the woodpile and was wiping blood from its hooked nose. "If we aren't going to kill her"—Nyphron shook his head in disgust—"then she's going to have the best bed possible. Maybe that will make a difference when she wakes up. I doubt it, but we can hope."

Konniger was still frozen. Only his eyes moved as they darted between Raithe and Nyphron.

"Grygor, give him some help, he looks stuck," Nyphron said.

The giant took a step forward, traversing half the lodge's steps in one stride. That was all it took to make Konniger move. "C'mon." The chieftain grabbed Tressa's wrist, abandoning both the porch and the lodge while Hegner and Devon followed close behind.

"You just better hope she dies," Nyphron told them. "You're putting a dragon to bed in there, and when she wakes up—Ferrol help us."

Tekchin sighed. "I wouldn't count on it. Ferrol will be on *her* side."

By the time they laid Arion on Persephone's old bed, the bald Fhrey had a purple bruise covering the back of her head and a bump roughly the size and shape of a small apple.

"Open the window and light the lamp," Persephone ordered. "Wedon, run get Padera and Roan. Oh, and Suri the mystic, too."

Cobb opened the window without saying a word, and Delwin lit the lamp without question. People were used to following Persephone's orders. They'd been doing it for twenty years, and when gods fought within the dahl's walls—for surely this bald Fhrey *was* a god—doing what felt normal was the next best thing to feeling safe. Persephone didn't pause to question if she *should* be taking control. Things needed to be done, and the stakes were too high to leave matters to a novice chieftain.

"He bashed her good," Padera said with a whistle when she arrived. The old woman tilted the Miralyith's head to one side. A small cut near the crown bled more than Persephone would have thought possible. Bright splashes of red were on the floor, and the sheets and pillow were starting to soak. "Need bandages."

"Suri, there's a sheet in that chest," Persephone told the mystic. "At least there used to be. Go ahead and tear it into pieces."

"Strips," Padera corrected. "*Long* strips. Need water, too." The old woman peered at the wound with her squinting eyes. Persephone grabbed the lamp and held it up.

"Cobb, get water," Persephone told the man, who looked happy to have an excuse to leave.

"Gonna need your needle and thread, Roan." Padera held her hand out to the woman expectantly, while Roan dug into the purse on her belt. As she did, Padera eyed the injured Fhrey. "You sure you want me to fix her, Seph? I'll do my best if you say so, but"—she turned and looked into Persephone's eyes—"in my experience, when you find a mountain lion caught in your rabbit snare, it's best to accept good fortune and spear the thing rather than let it loose. Might be better off putting a pillow over her face."

The Fhrey lady was so small, her skin so pale against the brilliant explosion of red.

Protect the injured.

"We *have* to save her," Persephone insisted.

The old woman nodded. Getting the tools from Roan, she went to work.

It didn't take long for Padera to sew and bandage the Fhrey. Roan stood beside her, passing threaded needles, wet cloths, and the bandages Suri had prepared. Now that things were beginning to settle, Persephone had time to think, and doubt. She felt sick.

Maybe I'm wrong. What if it's all just a coincidence? What if the tree meant something else, or if Suri can't hear trees at all and is simply delusional? Am I killing all of us? Grand Mother of All! I challenged the leader of the Galantians and threatened to throw him out of the dahl! And I defied Konniger . . . again. If he didn't have a reason to side against me before, he does now.

Everyone was against the idea. Nyphron, Konniger, even Padera had questioned the wisdom of healing the Fhrey woman. Although merely a poor farmer's widow, who likely hadn't traveled more than ten miles from the dahl, the old woman knew everything. *Maybe not everything, but certainly everything worth knowing.* Padera understood how best to lay out a garden and knew what to do when a little girl like Persephone ate a handful of poisonous berries. In all her long years, there wasn't anything the old woman hadn't seen. If the world operated logically, Padera would have been made chieftain years ago. So if the old woman felt it was best to let the Fhrey—

"Heal the injured," Suri said, and punctuated the words by ripping another sheet.

"What?" Persephone asked.

Suri tore the sheet again. "Magda's instruction. You said it wrong outside. It wasn't *protect* the injured. She said to *heal* the injured."

"Did I say it wrong?" Persephone couldn't remember. *Does it even matter?*

Persephone stared at the Fhrey woman, so slight and fragile. She didn't look like a monster. If Magda was to be believed, this woman's fate was tied to that of Persephone's people. Her path was clear. *Heal the injured.*

Persephone turned to Padera. "This woman must live. Will she?"

The old woman nodded. "Whether to praise or curse, she'll live. Question is, will we survive her waking?"

CHAPTER SEVENTEEN

The Boulder

We once thought that Alon Rhist comprised the entire Fhrey world. We'd never heard of the Nidwalden River and what lay beyond. If we had, we wouldn't have believed. At that time, we couldn't. How can a fish understand the aerie of an eagle?

—THE BOOK OF BRIN

The forum of the Aquila was packed, every council member in attendance. The frescoes of Gylindora Fane and Caratacus stared down from the ancient dome of the Airenthenon as the great room filled to capacity with spectators. The counselors were uniformly dressed in their finest asicas; even Gryndal had suspended his love of shiny yellow and wore the purple-and-white counselor robes. Under the dome, only the fane wore gold.

The Airenthenon was one of the oldest buildings in Estramnadon, held aloft by a ring of giant columns. Its age was painfully obvious to Gryndal as he sat on one of the torturously hard stone benches on which all except the fane were forced to perch. Efforts to introduce any change or a bit of luxury into the Aquila's council chambers had always been struck down. Serving on the Erivan high council was believed to be a sacred privilege, not a reward. Gryndal planned to erase the building along with its miserable benches. No sense leaving old symbols lying about. He'd replace it with a park.

"I wish to offer my congratulations on this, your first day in the Aquila as fane." Curator Imaly was on her feet, addressing Lothian. Apparently, she found the stone benches just as unpleasant.

The fane sat on pillowed cushions, but his smile faded all the same. Imaly had that effect on people.

"I do hope you'll be making the plight of the Instarya one of your top priorities," she went on. "How go your plans in that regard?"

This was the first official meeting of the Aquila, the high council of Erivan, since Lothian's victory. Its intended purpose was to be an uneventful opportunity for handshakes and back-slapping, a social gathering with no agenda, debates, or demands. Yet that didn't stop Imaly from straying from the program. She'd always been an irritant, but since her election to Curator she'd graduated to a genuine problem, one of the many Gryndal had marked for disappearance after he replaced Lothian.

"Well enough," the fane replied from his chair in the center of the chamber.

"Well enough?" Imaly asked, standing obnoxiously straight and appearing five times more regal than Lothian.

"Proper planning takes time and consideration. Nothing happens overnight. If that's what you're thinking, you will be disappointed."

"Actually, that's not at all what I'm thinking."

Gryndal didn't know how she did it, but at that point Imaly managed to stand even straighter. Being a direct descendant of the Fhrey's first ruler, Gylindora Fane, Imaly possessed an unerring stately demeanor, which, thankfully, wasn't complemented by beauty. The Curator was large for a female, endowed with brutish shoulders, thick fingers, gathering jowls, and a square jaw. Her voice was equally harsh but also loud, clear, and commanding—the exact opposite of the fane's. Although she was nothing to look at and certainly had no future in any choir, she possessed one of the shrewdest minds in the council, making Gryndal pay attention whenever she spoke.

"I was thinking," Imaly said, "that you have no plans at all, nor will you be setting the matter as a priority at any time in the near future. Like those who have come before you, you're content to maintain the status quo."

"This is the first day of the new council, Imaly. I'm here to learn names, not set policy."

"Yes, of course." She nodded. "Forgive me. Would you like to begin by learning the name of the Instarya senior council? I know I would." She went through the drama of looking around. "Where is the Instarya senior council? Oh, that's right, we don't have one. Their seat was replaced by the Miralyith some two thousand years ago, wasn't it? Makes it easier to ignore them that way."

Lothian glanced at Gryndal, who said nothing and wouldn't speak up. Imaly knew that, too. Everyone in the Aquila knew it. The council had Gryndal on a chain—for now. Plans were in motion to break those links. In the meantime, he was making lists.

"As I said," Lothian resumed, raising his voice and adding a hint of displeasure, "today I'm not here to set policy."

"No, of course not. Why would you? There's certainly no rush. The Dherg menace was vanquished, what, a thousand years ago? What difference will another thousand years make? Still, I have to wonder . . . Why are the Instarya still out there? And why only them? Is it so the rest of us will forget they even exist? Or is the warrior tribe no longer wanted? After all, if they returned, where would we put them? With no more wars or battles to fight, would they be content to lay down their swords and pick up hammers or lutes? Do you expect them to enter the priesthood? Awkward, uncomfortable issues are often pushed to the back of the line, dropped in some dirty basket and shelved indefinitely. Given enough time, such things begin to stink."

She raised a finger to her chin, thoughtfully. "Which brings me to my next question. What of Zephyron's son? I have reports from Alon Rhist that Nyphron and a handful of followers are in open revolt. Is this what you mean by *well enough*?"

"It is going well enough *to suit your fane*," Lothian

said, leaning forward in his chair. "Or are you suggesting that isn't *well enough* for *you*?"

Imaly hesitated.

The pause was so long that even Gryndal sat up to watch. Imaly was too smart not to back down. The fane had raised the stakes beyond her means, and she was just making a good show to save face. She continued to wait, impressing Gryndal with her fortitude. Someone coughed. Sandals scraped on the stone and parchments shuffled.

"Of course not," Imaly replied at length. "As I said, I merely wished to offer my congratulations." She made a modest bow and sat down.

If not for the Law of Ferrol, Gryndal would have reduced Imaly to a black spot ages ago, yet he couldn't deny that at least on this day she'd unwittingly helped him. The fane would be seething over this embarrassment when Gryndal broke the news of Arion's capture.

The other counselors kept their distance as Fane Lothian and First Minister Gryndal descended the broad steps of the Airenthenon to Florella Plaza. Imaly had shaken the beehive, and no one wanted to get stung. Gryndal alone played the role of beekeeper.

"I thought you handled yourself well in there," Gryndal said. "Imaly can be—"

"You'd best have good news from the frontier," Lothian told him, lifting the hem of his asica as he descended the steps.

"I'm afraid not," Gryndal replied. He made no effort to cushion the news with his tone. Imaly had set the spark to kindling; now he would gently blow on the embers. "Things have worsened."

"Worsened? How could they be worse? The council already fears Alon Rhist is on the verge of revolution."

"Arion has been taken captive."

"What? By whom?" Lothian stopped on the bottom

step to glare at him. Several of the council members slowed their retreat, looking over their shoulders.

"Nyphron and his Rhunes."

"*His Rhunes?* What do you mean *his* Rhunes?"

Lothian had a wonderful tic that twitched the right side of his upper lip whenever he was irritated. As puppets went, Gryndal couldn't have asked for a more accommodating one. But Gryndal wasn't interested in a puppet.

"It would appear Nyphron is in open revolt and has set himself up as a protector of the barbarians. He and his Galantians have taken refuge in a Rhune dahl. When Arion arrived to extradite Nyphron, she was captured."

"Captured?" The fane stared at him incredulously. "How can they capture her? She's *Miralyith*!"

Gryndal suppressed a smile that threatened to tug up the corners of his mouth. His efforts resulted in a grimace, which Lothian appeared to interpret as disgust for the crime. "But, she's not the fane."

The march of withdrawing counselors came to a complete stop as everyone within hearing paused to listen. Gryndal began walking again, urging the fane away from the steps and farther into the plaza. He wasn't concerned about them overhearing. Listening to the conversation might even be good, but eventually he'd lead the fane to the heart of the matter, and he'd rather be alone for that.

Lothian followed as expected. He always did.

"Arion was at a disadvantage, because Nyphron has forsaken the laws of his ancestors and embraced the wickedness of the barbarians."

As part of the ceremonial opening of the first council meeting under the new fane, the plaza was filled with celebrating craftspeople and entertainers. A thin crowd ebbed and flowed around artisan stands while dancers followed musicians; storytellers gathered flocks with promises of thrills and adventure.

All of them so easily amused by silly things, like children, Gryndal thought. No, not children. He'd thought

of other Fhrey that way when he'd graduated from the
Estramnadon Academy of the Art, but they'd dropped
lower in his estimation since then. Now it was his fellow
Miralyith who were the children, Lothian being a prime
example. The rest were industrious little beavers that
were busily building their dams and scurrying in the
sun.

"What did they do to her?" the fane asked.

"Bludgeoned her in the head with a rock."

Lothian halted again, his eyes wide in astonishment.
"No! Are you serious?"

"I saw it myself this morning," Gryndal explained. "A
Rhune crept up when she wasn't looking. Got in behind
her shield."

"*Saw* it?" Lothian stared at him, baffled. "That's
clairvoyance. You can do that?"

Gryndal began walking again, forcing the fane into a
trot to catch up. "I certainly didn't just return from a
trip west."

"Your abilities never fail to amaze me, Gryndal. I'm
grateful you're on my side."

Gryndal allowed himself a smile this time. Lothian
was blind in more ways than simply magical sight.

"So what happened? Is she all right? Will she live?"

"My *observation of her progress* revealed that Arion
entered a Rhune village and spoke to Nyphron. The
conversation didn't look to have gone well, since she
had used the Art to subdue him and his Galantians.
Then, a Rhune bashed her over the head with a rock. I
saw a great deal of blood where she lay in the dirt."

"Blood? Lay in the dirt?" Lothian's face hardened.
"She is the teacher of my son. Handpicked and beloved
by my mother!"

Gryndal struggled to keep from smiling—Lothian had
never liked Arion. The fane had expressed jealousy on
several occasions before his ascension. He worried that
Fenelyus cared more for Arion than for her own son.
And the tutor's self-righteous, reproving attitude was
too much like his mother's. At times like these, Gryndal

wished for a peer, for someone he could talk to and share such luscious moments. If only Imaly weren't the enemy. Perhaps he would tell Trilos, though he might not fully comprehend the sublime humor and beauty of the moment. Trilos cared only about the Door.

Noticing that Lothian was slowing down, both physically and mentally as emotions drained him, Gryndal blew across the hot coals. "If Fane Fenelyus were alive . . ."

"Oh! My mother would have incinerated the entire frontier. How dare they touch her beloved Arion! Everyone remembers my mother as this sage, peaceful leader, but—do you remember how she was in the war?"

"Better than you, I suspect. You were only what . . . ?" Gryndal made a twirling motion with a finger, trying to recall the exact age. Several passersby cringed at the action and quickly moved away.

"I was young, but I remember," the fane said. "I recall there was once a plain where a mountain now stands. She could be so cruel. She did it on purpose, you know."

"It was war."

"There is war, and then there's what she did to the Dherg. She could have burned them or rained down hailstones, but no, neither would have been ample punishment. They have such an affinity for the land, and she knew it would crush their spirits as well as their bodies to have rock and stone rise against them. Everyone speaks of her empathy and how she allowed the Dherg to live. But I was there at the battle when she met the Dherg army on the Plains of Mador. She had only recently received the Art, and none of us knew what she was capable of. The vile moles with their iron blades and armor had crushed every force we'd sent against them. I'm not proud to say I was scared. My mother might have been, too, since the Dherg had killed the last two fanes before her. In the end, I was more frightened of her than I had been of them. More than a hundred thousand were crushed and buried beneath a snow-capped monument to her power and ruthlessness."

"And you are your mother's son." They finished their walk across the plaza and arrived at the palace, where the gate was promptly opened.

They were inside the grounds now, away from uninvited ears, and it was time to add fuel to the fire.

"What will you do, my fane?"

"I want this rebellion crushed. And I want those responsible made an example."

"A wise course, but I fear Petragar might not be up to the task."

"Petragar isn't up to the task of strapping on his sandals."

Gryndal nodded. "In hindsight, I think you might have made a mistake sending Arion. She's too kindhearted for this sort of thing."

"She only knew my mother in the later years, after she'd softened. I need someone who isn't afraid to use the necessary force to ensure obedience." Lothian stopped and turned. "What about you?"

"Me?" Gryndal worked hard to present the perfect marriage between surprise and flattery.

"Yes." The fane smiled. "You'd be perfect."

"Sadly, I'm afraid I'd suffer the same fate as Arion if I can't retaliate against—"

Lothian waved his hand. "I'll grant you power to act in my stead. You will have absolute authority to do whatever is necessary to bring the traitors to heel. Order must be restored."

"Does that include *executing* those Fhrey who are disobedient?" Gryndal wanted to be clear on this point, and the moment he said the word *execute,* he saw Lothian hesitate. "I'd hate to die bleeding in the dirt like Arion."

"She's dead?"

"She had her head crushed with a large rock and collapsed. I can't imagine she survived, given the amount of blood I saw. And I just don't want to be—"

Lothian's face darkened, his mouth flattening into a level line. At that moment, Gryndal could see the family resemblance with Fenelyus. "You are hereby granted the authority to carry out my will. I furthermore extend to you the right to use deadly force if you feel such is necessary to restore order on the frontier. This right will be in effect until your return."

One down. One more to go.

"I'll gladly do your will, my fane, but I'm also tutoring your son, and . . ." Gryndal shook his head. "No. I don't suppose that would be advisable."

"What are you thinking?"

"Just that Mawyndulë has lived such a sheltered life, and if . . . no . . . never mind. It would be too dangerous."

"You're thinking of taking him with you? That's a wonderful idea. He *has* been coddled too much, isolated in our corner of civility. He should see the world and learn of its blemishes, discover firsthand the realities of power. My mother took me with her to the Battles of Mador and Cradock's Keep. I learned more in those two trips than I had in centuries. No, you're right, Mawyndulë should go."

"If I'm taking the prince, it might be wise to bring a contingent of soldiers—just in case."

"Of course. Draw what you need from my personal guard. Just remember, Gryndal, I want this to be over. I don't care how you do it, but I want it done."

"You can count on me, my fane. I'll bring the thunder."

Gryndal left the fane and headed uphill toward the spiritual heart of Fhrey society. The highest point in the city was a fitting place for the Garden; all great things should be raised higher than lesser entities. He believed that with all his heart. It made perfect sense. Problems arose when that axiom was challenged. When the weak tried to yoke the strong and fools attempted to restrain genius, that was when the world suffered. A natural order dictated right from wrong, just as it caused water to run downhill. Gryndal refrained from assigning that design to a god—even Ferrol, whom he had revered for the first thousand years of his life. He'd also idolized his father and the fane, but that, too, had been when he was a child. As he grew older, the distinctions between himself and others had diminished. His father was nothing special, and he couldn't respect someone lesser than himself. The same was true of the fane. In her last years, Fenelyus had grown feeble, and Lothian wasn't half the Miralyith his mother had been. Recently, Gryndal noticed even Ferrol's stature dwindling.

What can a god do that I can't?

Approaching the bronze gate to the Garden, Gryndal spotted Imaly. Sadly, she spotted him as well.

"Nice evening for a stroll, isn't it?" she said with a flirtatious tone meant to lull him into a false sense of camaraderie. Even if Imaly had been young, thin, and beautiful, it wouldn't have worked. Not that failure had ever been a deterrent for her. The brittle-haired Curator of the Aquila had always been a pain, but lately she seemed to relish nettling him.

"You embarrassed the fane this evening," he said with his own disarming smile.

"Did I?" She looked down at the hem of her asica, scowling and still playing the innocent female. "The streets should be kept cleaner. My wardrobe is getting ruined."

She clutched three scrolls, records of the meeting. As Curator, she not only presided over the Aquila but was responsible for keeping and preserving what had transpired. Why records were kept, Gryndal didn't know, sentimentality perhaps.

"Don't be coy. You know you did, and he didn't appreciate it."

Imaly looked up with an amused smile. "Lothian shouldn't do foolish things. Then he wouldn't be embarrassed by awkward questions."

"And, likewise, foolish people shouldn't ask awkward questions that will make the fane their enemy." Gryndal stood straighter and slipped his hands into the sleeves of his asica in the fashion of the Umalyn priests. He felt it gave him a more intimidating, pious, not to mention learned, posture.

"I don't worry about that. We in the Aquila have you as our champion now, don't we?" She took a step closer. He wondered if she were merely proving she wasn't afraid or actually trying to intimidate him, a mistake of epic proportions. "You wouldn't let anything bad happen to us. We council members are a weak and cowardly bunch, ruled by self-preservation. Under stress, we're likely to forget our oath of office and blurt out the names of those who applied to challenge. Given the outrage Lothian demonstrated when dealing with the Instarya leader, can there be any doubt about his reaction if he learned a fellow Miralyith and trusted adviser sought the throne?" She looked down at the scrolls. "I don't think that's ever happened before. Imagine his surprise."

She leaned in close, stared into his eyes, and whispered, "It was a misstep petitioning as you did. You should have known we'd refuse."

"Why *is* that?" Gryndal answered without moving. This was going to be an intimate conversation of whispers. He was tall, taller than average, but so was she, and the two faced off without blinking.

Imaly shrugged with a wary smile. "The rules were designed to give all tribes a chance to rule. Pitting two fellow tribesmen against each other, especially from a tribe that has ruled for so long, would suggest the Miralyith were circumventing the spirit of the law. We could be accused of favoritism, of admitting the future of Erivan will be one of continued Miralyith dominance."

"Which it will. Nothing can change that. No other tribe can defeat us as long as we retain the secrets of the Art. So why—"

"Appearances are more important than reality. As distasteful as it is, I can't deny that your tribe shows every sign of retaining control indefinitely. But unless you intend to rule by subjugation, it's important the people believe they live in a society where anyone can become fane. Religion and tradition remain allies in a system that's still perceived to be fair. Truth be told, I wouldn't mind seeing a division in the Miralyith and the trouble it would cause. Plus, watching two Artists battle in the arena would be quite entertaining. But as the Curator of the Aquila, I'm dedicated to protecting the Fhrey, even from themselves."

She explained all this with a friendly smile as if they were best of friends. Maintaining an affable expression, she added, "Besides, we all know what you'd do if you sat on the Forest Throne, and none of us would ever let that happen."

"Careful, your overconfidence is showing," he told her. "I'm not done yet."

She laughed. "You won't live to see the Uli Vermar. You're older than Lothian."

"But that doesn't mean a challenge won't occur sooner. Alon Rhist was older than Ghika."

"Yes, but Ghika was killed in the war."

"As was Alon, and after only five years." He feigned an innocent look.

Imaly narrowed her eyes. "We're at peace, Gryndal. What's more, there's no nation capable of threatening us, so the ..." Imaly paused, staring at him. "Fhrey can't kill Fhrey, Gryndal. Only the fane has such power. Remember that."

"Are you sure?" He inched in closer still until he could feel his breath bounce back, and he whispered, "There's nothing that prevents it."

"The Law of Ferrol will eject you from Fhrey society and the afterlife will be closed to you. Would you sacrifice eternity for the chance to be fane for just a few years?"

"I have a theory about that." He put his cheek to hers and spoke into her ear. "The Umalyn tell me the only requirement for blowing the Horn of Gylindora is that the challenger must be of Fhrey blood. Nothing else.

Ferrol wasn't a stickler for piety or virtues. You could be a murderer, but as long as a single drop of Fhrey blood runs in your veins, the horn will sound for you. Then, if successful in the challenge, well, how could the fane of the Fhrey be excluded from the society he rules? And how could Ferrol's chosen be denied absolution?"

Gryndal grinned as Imaly pulled back, her friendly smile gone at last. He enjoyed rocking her; he so rarely managed it. Now that Jerydd was permanently seated as the kel of Avempartha and Fenelyus was gone, Imaly was his only worthy adversary, and she wasn't even a Miralyith. As a descendant of Gylindora Fane, leader of the Nilyndd tribe, and Curator of the Aquila, Imaly remained the only obstacle, other than Lothian, who stood in his way.

"That's a lot to risk on a theory," she said, her tone losing the playful lilt. "And a dangerous thing to admit."

"I didn't mean to suggest *I* was going to kill Lothian. You're right; that would be too much to risk on a theory. But someone else might. Should that happen, if Lothian were to die prematurely, I'll seek to blow the challenge horn again. And . . ." He let his smile fade. "I highly suggest you don't stand in my way a second time."

Gryndal waited until Imaly had disappeared around the Fountain of Alon before he passed through the bronze gate and entered the Garden. A few others strolled the pathways, but this was a place of reflection and meditation so it remained quiet—a world apart. Gryndal had spent days in there, practicing concentration and widening his inner eye. He learned to connect to the world with deeper, more powerful chords. He also spent a good deal of his time staring at the Door.

The entrance was so unassuming, so austere. It could have been a door to any ordinary house, but instead it provided the only entrance to The First Tree. No artistry adorned the threshold, no hinges or lock, not a sign or a clue. Plain and rectangular, the wooden Door didn't sport a knob—just a rather crude latch. In all the centuries of daily pilgrimages, Gryndal had never been able to determine a way to open it. He'd knocked once as a boy; it was a rite of passage. The Umalyn frowned on the tradition, considered it disrespectful to their god, but even they tried to find a way in.

Trilos, the only person more obsessed with the Door than the priests, was once again on the stone bench, staring at the Door. Leaning forward with elbows on knees, his long hair hid his face, a good thing. Trilos wasn't the most handsome Fhrey.

"I'm going to be leaving in the morning," Gryndal said.

"I know," Trilos replied without looking over.

Long ago Gryndal had given up wondering how Trilos knew things, just as he'd learned to look past the unkempt appearance and utterly cavalier attitude. Most Fhrey trembled at Gryndal's passing, and other Miralyith bowed out of respect. Even Imaly and Lothian became nervous with nothing more than a long stare from Gryndal. But Trilos remained oblivious.

Gryndal often inquired into Trilos's past and his nature, but the unkempt Fhrey maintained his annoying habit of ignoring questions he didn't want to answer. Trilos appeared to know more about the Art than anyone— even more than Gryndal's old instructor, Jerydd, who had been taught by Fenelyus herself. To Gryndal's great amazement, Trilos made claims about teaching Fenelyus. If true, there could be only one explanation. Trilos had to be the avatar of the Art, the singular manifestation of power, self-created and self-aware, that had taken corporeal form to educate the Fhrey. If that wasn't the case, it didn't matter; Trilos was always worth speaking to.

Who or what else could Trilos be?

"Any advice before I leave?" Gryndal asked.

"No."

"No? You've been giving me advice for years."

"Not this time."

Gryndal sat beside the rumpled pile of cloth and

mangy hair, who was his imaginary friend with a Door obsession. "Why?"

"Those are the rules."

"Rules? There are rules? Since when are there rules? Whose rules? Rules for what?"

"My game, my rules," Trilos said.

"I don't understand."

"Of course not."

"You aren't making any sense," Gryndal replied.

"Neither does that Door," Trilos said. "Impossible to open, and yet it was."

Gryndal sighed. "So you've said, *many* times. I just don't believe you."

"Because if *you* can't do it, no one else could have?" Trilos laughed. "I must admit I love your arrogance. I picked well. Still, I'm positive Fenelyus went inside."

"How'd she open it, then? Oh, right, she didn't, did she? You insist she had help, even though Fenelyus was the most powerful person in her day."

"What makes you think she was the most powerful?" Trilos asked.

"Everyone knows that."

Trilos looked at him oddly. "What an absurd statement. Are you drunk?"

"What's absurd about it? Ever hear of common knowledge?"

Trilos grinned.

Gryndal disliked Trilos's smile. There was something disturbing in that expression on that face.

"What exactly do you suppose is *common* about me? And why would you rely on random, unverified conclusions of ordinary people who presume absurd notions like *The sun will rise each day* merely because in their existence it always has? By that same logic, they should live forever. And I can assure you they won't. You disappoint me, Gryndal."

"Fine. So who opened the Door?"

"Was hoping you'd find that answer for me," Trilos stated.

"I told you. I'm leaving to go to Rhulyn in the morning. I can't—"

"That's exactly what I need you to do. You're going to put down the Instarya rebellion. I need you to crush the revolt."

"You're in luck then."

"Luck is only a word. If you act according to your nature, which you can't avoid, that will trigger it."

"Trigger what?"

Trilos shifted to face him better. "Do you know what started the Belgric War?"

"Greed on the part of King Mideon."

"Yes, but more precisely, Mideon was convinced that inside"—Trilos pointed at the Door—"was The First Tree, and that eating its fruit would bestow eternal life. Because Fane Ghika refused to grant the Dherg king access—something she couldn't do because she couldn't open the Door any more than you or I—the Children of Drome attacked the Children of Ferrol. That was partially my fault. You see, I was the one who told Mideon about the tree."

Gryndal narrowed his eyes. "No offense intended, Trilos, but while you're not a beauty, you don't look anywhere near *that* old."

"Appearances are usually deceiving."

"And you expect me to believe that you started the Belgric War with a lie? A war that—"

"What makes you think it was a lie?"

Gryndal glanced at the Door. "Because no one knows what's really in there. Or are you going to claim *common knowledge*?"

Trilos scowled.

"What does any of that have to do with me going to Rhulyn?"

"I gave Fenelyus a gift. To be honest, she already had it. I just showed her how to use it. Fane Alon Rhist was dead, and the Fhrey were losing the war. I was angry with the Dherg, so I intervened."

Trilos did give Fenelyus the Art!

"That should have been the end of it. The Dherg had murdered thousands of Fhrey out of greed. Fenelyus had just cause and more than enough power to erase the Dherg from existence."

"But she didn't," Gryndal said.

"No. She chased them to Drumindor. Everyone expected her to rip it apart and throw the remains into the sea. So did I. Instead, she spared them. The story goes that she left the Fhrey army camped around the base of the Dherg fortress for weeks, and when she returned, she met with King Mideon and offered peace."

Gryndal nodded. "And you think while she was gone, she came here and went inside the Door?"

"Yes. And that saved the Dherg from extinction."

Gryndal stared at the Door with new interest.

"I had set a boulder rolling when I gave the Children of Ferrol the Art, knowing your people would wipe out the Children of Drome, but something stopped it. You might call it luck, but could random chance stop such a thing? What could have prevented a boulder that big from rolling? What unlikely occurrence could forestall the sun from rising? Who opened that Door for Fenelyus, and, more important, where might that person be? That's why you're going to Rhulyn, to separate luck from intent, and this time I'll be watching."

"Watching for what?"

"For an invisible hand to open that Door and once again stop the boulder. You, dear Gryndal, are my boulder."

CHAPTER EIGHTEEN
Healing the Injured

It was like waiting for the sunrise and a chicken to hatch—if the sun marked the end of the world and the chicken was an all devouring demon.

—THE BOOK OF BRIN

The light intensified the throbbing behind Arion's eyes. Both her hands and feet felt numb, and when she tried to move, a sharp pain exploded from the back of her head as if a chisel had been slammed through her skull. She might have cried out, impossible to tell. Between winces and despite the pain, Arion had managed to discern she was inside a crude hut of some sort; the walls were made from thick, untreated wood and the ceiling from bundles of yellowed grass. She was on a bed of sorts—rough wool over straw, stiff and itchy.

What in Ferrol's name has happened to me?

Working that single thought and trying to use her eyes was all she was capable of. Everything else went toward enduring the pain. She felt as if she were drowning in anguish. Panic welled up, but mercifully she drifted off again.

Arion fought to consciousness several more times but never stayed awake for long. Always she was in the same bed, beneath the same grass roof, flooded by the same awful pain. In her haze-filled agony, she sensed the presence of others around her. Conversations in a language she didn't understand. Occasionally hands touched her, mostly around the head. When she was moved, she passed out again. How long this went on was impossible to tell. Time became a vague tangle of dreams, visions, and reality mixed in equal measures and degrees of importance. When she wasn't in the hut, she was talking with Fenelyus about the importance of teaching more than the Art to the next generation of leaders and how power without compassion would destroy them all. On occasion, a wolf would enter her visions, or an old shriveled female Rhune whose head was wrapped in a cloth. Once, she found herself sitting on a bench in the Garden across from the Door with an irresistible urge to try the latch.

"Go on," Trilos told her from where he sat on the other bench. "You know you want to. Everyone wants to know what's on the other side."

Arion stood up and walked to the Door. She placed her hand on the latch, knowing it would do nothing, but what if it—

She lifted. The latch clicked.

Arion's heart raced as she felt the Door give, felt it start to open.

"So you're the one I'm looking for!" Trilos exclaimed.

With Trilos's voice still in her head, Arion woke.

She was once more in the hut, on the straw bed with wool covers. The numbness in her extremities was gone, and though her head still throbbed, the stabbing pain behind her eyes had taken a break. She looked around. Sunlight came through a window. Birds sang, and she felt a gentle breeze brush her face, the only part not covered by a wool blanket. A moment later, Arion noticed she wasn't alone. Across the room, caught in a shaft of mote-filled sunlight, was a Rhune girl.

She sat sideways, legs hanging over one arm of a stiff chair, bare feet moving back and forth, forming little circles in the air. The girl had markings, tattoos that curled symmetrically around the sides of her face like vines. The child was filthy, her hair a ratted mess, the bottoms of her bare feet blackened. Over her shoulders, she wore a tattered woolen cloth the color of clay. Her legs were covered in baked-on mud, stained from splashes of dirty water. Every fingernail was outlined in dirt as if she'd just come from digging with bare hands.

Do Rhunes do that? Burrow underground like moles?

The girl's attention was focused on something in her fingers while a huge white wolf lay at the foot of the chair, its muzzle resting between its forepaws.

The Rhune girl was disgusting, the animal disturbing.

Arion didn't move. Instead, she tried to remember, to think how she had gotten where she was. The last thing she recalled was being in the Garden with Trilos and opening the—

No. That wasn't real . . . was it?

It couldn't be. She had left Estramnadon in search of the rebel Nyphron. She remembered arriving at Alon Rhist and meeting with Petragar.

Yes, I definitely remember doing that—him and his servant. What was his name? Vert, something.

She remembered arriving at a Rhune village and—

Yes! I found Nyphron!

After that, the trail went cold.

The girl noticed her and smiled. She spoke some brutish language that sounded like barking.

Rhunes are animals, Arion thought. *Animals that merely resemble Fhrey.*

She lifted her head, but pushing up to her elbows made her instantly dizzy.

The girl barked once more, but within the beastly yelps she caught what sounded like *Arion.*

"*You know my name?*" she asked in the Fhrey language.

The girl nodded.

Arion was stunned. "*You understand me?*"

The girl nodded again. Arion saw the full measure of her face: homely, inelegant, and misshapen, no doubt the result of a godling left unattended to play with a pile of clay.

"*Tura,*" the girl said. "*She teach divine words.*"

"*Who are you?*" Arion asked.

"Me is Suri."

"Where are we, Suri?"

"Dahl Rhen." The girl continued to sit sidelong across the arms of the chair, feet still making circles in the shaft of sunlight. Lothian had said that the Rhunes were terrified of the Fhrey, that they considered them to be gods and would cower in their presence. In Estramnadon, no one except those in the palace would remain so casual in Arion's presence.

The Rhune girl pointed at the ceiling. *"This is a . . . ah . . . wooden cave. Call it . . ."* She hesitated, then shrugged. *"Place where Rhune leader sleeps."*

"How did I get here?"

"Carried after."

"After? After what?"

Suri pointed at Arion's head.

Arion reached up and noticed something there. A cloth wrapped everything above her eyes.

The girl swung her legs off the chair's arm and onto the wolf, which didn't seem to mind. *"Best leave on or insides fall out."*

"What . . . ?" Arion froze. *"What happened to me?"*

Suri mimicked hitting herself on the head and made a bursting sound as she did. *"Hit with rock. Fixed now. You don't die."* The girl grinned.

"You did this? Wrapped my head, I mean."

Suri nodded. *"Yes. Others help, too. Many help. Keep insides in."*

"Ah . . . thank you for that. But why did someone hit me?"

Suri stood up, detangled her fingers from a loop of string she had been playing with, and placed it around her neck. *"Wait. Me get Persephone."*

The girl said something to the wolf, which got to its feet and moved to Arion's bedside. The huge beast with long white fangs hovered over Arion while the girl scampered off.

Arion instinctively made a ward with her fingers—a simple physical defense—but nothing happened. She hummed, going back to the basics to harmonize with the energy around her, but still nothing, no vibration or even an echo. Her ability to perform the Art was gone. Unconnected and disconcerted, she looked into the eyes of the wolf, and for the first time in centuries she felt mortal fear.

What have they done to me?

Arion pushed away from the animal, at least as far as the wall allowed, a bad idea. The sharp pain returned along with a dash of nausea, but the wolf kept her attention. It didn't growl or bare its teeth, but that hardly mattered. A large, fanged beast standing less than five feet away took precedence over pain. This one appeared to be watching her.

But watching for what? If I try to get up, will it kill me? If it attacks, what can I do?

At that moment, the best she came up with was scream.

The sound of footsteps approached, and then Suri and a new female entered. Arion was disappointed to see it was another Rhune. The wolf drew back when Suri called to it. The two Rhunes spoke to each other in the same guttural language. Arion caught the word *Nyphron*. And the girl left the room.

"*Nyphron?*" Arion asked.

The new Rhune nodded, then spoke in Fhrey. "*I speak your language, not well, but some.*"

She was older and wore some type of disgusting dress made of crudely woven black-dyed wool. She had long hair and a lot of it.

"*I sent Suri to bring Nyphron,*" the Rhune told her, keeping a distance and standing against the doorframe.

"*You're Persephone?*"

"*Yes.*" She nodded many times.

"*The other one, Suri, said that people have been taking care of me.*" Her hand came up and touched her bandages.

More nods. "*You suffered serious injury. Afraid you might die. We knitted you. Stopped bleeding.*"

"Knitted? Do you mean sewed? I was bleeding?" Arion felt her nausea grow.

"Yes. Very much."

Arion inched down off her elbows and closed her eyes. That felt much better. Her head was growing fuzzy again. Already she was exhausted and wanted to sleep, but she couldn't. She had to stay awake. She had to find out what was going on.

"Who hit me and why?"

Persephone didn't respond.

Slowly Arion turned to look at her. *"Did you hit me?"*

"No!"

"Well, who, then?"

The Rhune looked terrified. *"Please not to kill us. Rhune people do no wrong. We people of Dahl Rhen good people, very, very good. Never harmed you or yours. Lived long years by treaty signed in Alon Rhist. Never broke it. Not once. Done nothing wrong. Very peaceful we people be."*

The Rhune's mastery of the Fhrey language suffered when she was nervous.

"Wait. Was it a Rhune that hit me, then?" She saw in Persephone's eyes that it was. *More docile than inebriated sheep,* Vertumus had told her. *Rhunes think Fhrey are gods,* everyone had said. They had left out the Rhunes' odd quirk of worshipping their gods by battering them senseless with rocks. *"Why would a Rhune hit me?"*

"You were fighting with Nyphron. Nyphron good to us . . . ah . . . Nyphron has been good to us."

Arion's eyes went wide. She remembered it now. She had confronted Nyphron. He resisted. The others, the Galantians, tried to interfere, and then—

Once again, the sound of feet on wood approached, and Persephone dodged out of the way as Nyphron entered. He approached hesitantly, shield on his left arm. Behind him came another Fhrey, his arms crossed over his body, gripping the handles of two short swords.

"*You live,*" Nyphron said, his tone decidedly disappointed.

"*Your concern is overwhelming,*" she replied.

"*I'm just a bit surprised. I didn't think I would need to be told when you woke. I sort of expected the news to be apparent when the sun went dark and the ground swallowed us. There's not even lightning or thunder. Isn't that what you Miralyith do just before you murder people?*"

They didn't do anything to me, she thought. *He doesn't know.*

"*Sorry to disappoint,*" she said. "*But I have a headache. It seems someone hit me with a rock.*"

"*Not hard enough, apparently.*"

If you only knew, Arion thought.

Her best hope was to make sure he didn't. She'd never heard of anyone losing the Art, but then again, head injuries weren't a common occurrence among the Miralyith. The injury had to be responsible. If she had a day or two to heal, then maybe—

"*For what it's worth, the Rhunes saved you. You were leaking blood like a punctured wineskin.*" He pointed at Persephone. "*It was her idea to sew you up. Why, I don't know.*"

"*And what did you do?*"

"*Not a thing. I watched you bleed in the dirt and did nothing at all. No, that's not true. I smiled a good deal.*"

His sword-gripping friend shifted uncomfortably.

"*I don't like you,*" Nyphron went on, his tone simmering between contempt and rage, but his hand didn't go near his sword, which Arion was exceedingly happy about.

Arion had never been scared of swords any more than she'd been afraid of wolves. Yet at that moment, both worried her, and the long metal weapons kept drawing her attention.

"*I don't like your kind,*" Nyphron told her. "*You act cowardly—without honor.*"

"*And it was a Miralyith who killed your father.*" She

pointed this out in the hope that her understanding might calm him, but she didn't see a marked difference. If anything, it made him angrier. She wasn't thinking clearly. She couldn't; her head was too fuzzy.

"*My father had hoped to restore the Instarya's rights as Fhrey. Rights your people stole.*" Nyphron paused, then after a breath said, "*You came here to arrest me, to haul me back so I could also be humiliated and murdered before an audience of asica-wearing Miralyith— more entertainment for the fane. I could have let you die. All I had to do was stop her. Just keep the Rhune away.*" He glanced at Persephone, who stood frozen against the doorframe as if she'd been nailed there. "*You would have bled to death facedown in the dirt—and it still would have been with more dignity than your fane granted my father. So to answer your question, I did nothing, and you're alive because of it.*" He leaned closer. "*You owe me and everyone in this village your life. Maybe you should think about that while you dream up whatever destruction you have planned.*"

Arion didn't have any plans for destruction. She was still trying to piece together what had happened and wondering if the two swords Nyphron's friend was keeping warm with his palms would come out anytime soon. The only positive thing was that she didn't have an opportunity to dwell on the throbbing of her head, which hurt so badly that her eyes watered.

"*You might also consider that there is an alternative to slaughtering everyone,*" Nyphron said. "*You could let us go. The Galantians and I will live out our days in the wilds. You won't hear from us again. We'll disappear. If you have to, you could tell the fane you found and killed us. Problem solved, ego served, page turned. I think you owe me that much for letting you wake up.*"

"*I'll consider it.*" She wiped the tears from her eyes. The pain in her head was reasserting itself with a fury.

"*Since each breath you take is a gift we gave you when your head was dangling from your neck like a dead goose, I hope you'll be considerate enough to at least inform me of any decision you make before ripping the sky apart."*

"*I'll see what I can do,*" she managed to say as the pain forced her teeth to clench. She held his stare as long as she could, the pain hammering hard with each second. Arion was relieved when he broke first.

"*Anything can I get you?*" Persephone asked. She grimaced nervously. "*Is—there—anything—I—can—get—for—you?*"

"*I want to sleep. I just need to rest, and I'll be better.*"

She hoped that was true.

The room was dark the next time Arion woke. Outside the window, stars shone. Inside the room, a single lamp—a hollowed-out block of chalk stuffed with animal fat—revealed the same girl she had awakened to before. This time the girl lay on the floor. Her head was propped against the side of the wolf, which lay sprawled across the wooden floor. Once more, Suri played with a loop of string.

Arion wasn't in any immediate pain for a change and just lay still, watching as the girl wove a surprisingly complex pattern. Arion had no idea Rhunes played the same game she taught her students, and seeing it was like watching a dog walk on its hind legs. Arion knew the design. After centuries, she'd likely formed every possible combination. The one between Suri's fingers was what Arion referred to as the Spider's Box, and the girl was doing a lovely job. Her fingers worked with unexpected facility—whirling, twisting, and drawing out the string with nimble grace and uncompromising confidence. Arion realized this Rhune girl, who used a wolf as a pillow, was doing a much better job of weaving than Mawyndulë ever had.

"*The bottom thread,*" Arion said when Suri hesitated.

She expected the Rhune girl to jump at the sound of her voice, but she didn't even look over.

"*No,*" she replied, focusing on the labyrinthine structure. *"Done that one. Was thinking if I . . ."* Suri reached in with both thumbs, hooked the primary strands, and then rolled her wrists. Inverted, the whole architecture of the pattern had turned inside out.

Arion smiled. *"Very clever."*

Suri sighed. *"Dumb. Now stuck."*

"No, no, you're not." Arion propped herself up. *"Come closer."*

Suri sat up, leaning toward the bed. Arion studied the weave. Reaching out, she hooked her fingers inside the pattern and pulled the entire arrangement free of Suri's hands and onto her own fingers. Arion looped two more strings, folded the whole thing inside itself again, and held it out to the girl.

Suri studied the weave, tongue slipping along her upper lip. Then a smile appeared, and she inserted her fingers into the center and pulled. The pattern extended and slipped back onto her hands. With a bend of two fingers the construction changed once more.

In that instant, they both laughed in delight.

"Me never done that one before," Suri said.

"Nor I. But then neither of us has four hands."

After she let the string slip off all but two fingers, Suri saw the pattern vanish, and the string was just a loop again.

"And it's not 'Me never done that one before'; it's 'I have never done that one before.'"

Suri looked skeptical. *"Sure?"*

"Pretty sure."

Suri lay back down on the wolf. *"Feeling better?"*

Arion nodded and realized her headache was still there, just quietly curled up in the back of her head for the time being. She wasn't as dizzy, either. Her stomach had calmed, and she even felt a bit hungry. Buoyed by her general well-being, she closed her eyes and hummed to create a resonance, but she was still blocked. The Art didn't respond. The lack of sensation was distressing, as if half her body were paralyzed.

What if it doesn't come back?

Although she had lived without the Art in her youth, Arion couldn't imagine how. Losing it would be worse than losing her arms and legs. She'd be an invalid. The very idea terrified her. Fear welled up, threatening to drown her.

I shouldn't think about that—not now, not here.

"*Can you juggle?*" Arion blurted, throwing out the question as an anchor to keep herself from slipping off a cliff.

The girl looked at her, puzzled.

Arion saw her belt pouch on a table. "*In that bag,*" she told Suri, "*are three stones. Can you throw them up and keep all of them in the air at once?*"

Suri smiled. She took the stones from the bag and, getting to her knees, tossed them up one at a time with a natural ease. The ceiling was low, but the girl didn't hit the beams. Catching and tossing the stones, she soon had them moving in a tight circle.

"*You've done this before.*"

"*Tura taught me . . . ah . . . she taught I?*"

"*No,*" Arion said. "*In that case, me is correct.*"

"*Sure?*"

"*Pretty sure.*"

Suri once more looked skeptical. Arion smiled. Not because the girl had second-guessed her native language skills but because Suri wasn't watching the stones. They continued to fly one after another, her hands catching and tossing with a mind of their own. The display was impressive. Not that it was a remarkable example of juggling skill, but this was a Rhune, and a young Rhune at that. Arion had been taught they were barely above animals, distinct from Fhrey or Dherg in their lack of intelligence. Rhunes couldn't think the way people did. They acted mainly on instinct. Any resemblance they had to higher beings was simply an imitation or purely a coincidence. But that didn't appear to be the case. Persephone and the girl both spoke Fhrey, and the girl could juggle better than the prince. She even formed complex string patterns for enjoyment. How could that be possible if they couldn't think? *"Who is Tura?"* Arion asked as Suri caught the stones and reached for the bag.

"Was mine friend. She raised I."

"No, you should have said, 'Was my friend, and she raised me.'"

Suri scowled, then shrugged.

"Did you have a fight?"

"Fight?"

"You said Tura was your friend."

"Died."

The casual way she said it shocked Arion. *"What killed her?"*

Suri looked puzzled. *"Nothing. Just died. She old."*

Arion peered into Suri's dark-brown eyes. Seeing her own reflection, she wondered if Ferrol was trying to tell her something.

"Why is it you're always the one watching me?" Arion asked.

"Me not," Suri said. *"Perse—"*

"I am not."

The Rhune girl sighed and rolled her eyes. *"Persephone watches, too, and old woman. Others have work. We, more time. I should be ..."* She trailed off, watching Arion for a correction. When it didn't come, she went on, *"Solving riddle of bone, but I"*—another brief hesitation—*"can think here, too."*

"What's the riddle of the bone?"

"Asked gods tell future. Them answer through chicken bones." Suri drew out what looked like a blackened stick. *"This one very strong. Warned of a terrible monster. Great power coming. Killing all us. I believe it be Grin, a great brown beast that lives in forest. Not bear after all. She demon, but me don't know which. Not knowing, can't stop. Working out puzzle of which. Problem is, only have until full moon."*

The surprise of discovering such a Fhrey-like Rhune was instantly squelched by the girl's superstitious bone-foretelling rituals and belief in monsters and demons. Perhaps the girl wasn't an animal, but she was primitive nonetheless. Arion found this disappointing. For a moment she had been excited to think the differences between Rhunes and Fhrey might have been narrower than suspected. The string weaving and juggling almost suggested that Rhunes had the capacity to learn the Art. The look of shock and revulsion on Gryndal's face if she could prove that would be worth a crack on the head. Yet despite everything, Suri was still a Rhune, still a world apart.

"*Awake?*" Persephone said as she nervously entered.

Suri got to her feet and stretched. "*See,*" Suri told Arion, and pointed at Persephone. "*I time is over.*"

"*My shift is over,*" Arion corrected.

"*Sure?*"

"*Pretty sure.*"

Suri shook her head with a scowl, then spoke to the wolf. It, too, got up and stretched. The two headed toward the door together, and then Suri paused and looked back. "*Not worry. It come back.*"

"*What will?*" Arion asked.

Suri only smiled, then disappeared beyond the doorway.

CHAPTER NINETEEN
Waiting on the Moon

Whenever people ask about Persephone, I tell them how she could not card wool. I think it is important for people to know she was human.

—The Book of Brin

Pings and plops made explosive rings in puddles as Persephone sat on the damp mat, looking out at the rain. A leaf had fallen. With no trees nearby, it must have been blown by the storm's wind. It teetered on the edge of one of the stones that lined the walkway above a puddle of muddy water.

The damp air felt cold again. Spring had taken a step back, retreating as if unsure of itself. Brin had given her a thick wool blanket from her parents' house, the one with poorly stitched flowers outlined in yellow thread. Warm, though, and Persephone wrapped it to her neck.

"So she's awake, and we're still alive," Moya said. The hero of the well raid was back to spinning, trying to finish a skein before she ran out of light.

"She's still in a lot of pain," Persephone said. "And seems a little confused. Who knows what will happen when she heals."

"Suri with her again?" Brin asked. Brin sat on the floor, carding wool. Persephone knew the girl had always enjoyed visiting Roan, but since Raithe had arrived, she all but slept there. Sarah didn't appear to mind as long as she completed her chores. Brin brought them with her, four big bags. The recent shearing provided mountains of wool and plenty of work, and Brin was quick to ask others for help.

"Padera is with her now," Persephone replied, and resumed her own attempt at carding wool.

Persephone had little experience carding, combing, spinning, or weaving wool, although she'd seen each performed countless times. Watching and doing were radically different things. Persephone had managed only the one roving so far. What was supposed to result in a long, uniformly thick strand of clean fibers remained a short, dirty wad. She would have switched to combing, but Brin assured her that carding was easier. The girl had enlisted all of them, even Malcolm and Raithe. No one could turn down Brin's bright smile, and there was *a lot* of wool.

"Padera?" Moya asked. "She's probably just sleeping up there."

"She took some knitting, I think."

"She's definitely sleeping, then."

Brin leaned toward the door, looking out at the rain. "Where is Suri?"

The girl was nearly as fascinated by the mystic and her wolf as she was by Raithe—nearly. Nothing could distract Brin from the Dureyan for long, and she delighted in teaching him to card. Not surprisingly, Raithe got most of her attention, and his rovings were good, whereas Persephone's and Malcolm's suffered from neglect.

"Outside," Moya said, pumping the foot pedal of the spinning wheel and making it hum. "Her and the wolf."

"In the rain?" Brin asked.

"She doesn't like being inside," Persephone said.

This caught Roan's attention. She was the only one not actively employed in the wool chores. Instead, she was on her knees near the cluttered rear of the house, sewing a patch of cloth to the side of her tunic. "Suri or the wolf?" Roan asked with a worried tone.

"Both, I suspect. But it has nothing to do with you,

Roan. Suri is uncomfortable inside any place. She doesn't even like being inside the walls of the dahl."

Roan responded with her hallmark almost-smile, a trait as typical of her as Gifford's walk or lisp. Life had battered them both. Gifford was a cripple on the outside, Roan on the inside, and Persephone wondered if that was the price of divine gifts.

All these people—all these amazing people.

She was haunted by visions of their bleeding bodies lying in the dirt as the dahl blazed. Persephone saw their future as she saw the leaf outside, teetering on the edge in a growing wind.

So much in jeopardy—so much at stake—and yet what can a leaf do to influence the wind?

"So why is she still here?" Moya asked.

"Suri?" Persephone looked up from her carding. "Still trying to work out why I was attacked, I think. Has something to do with bones, she told me."

"Any clues?"

Persephone shrugged. "If she has any, she's not told me. Maybe she wants to get all the facts straight first."

"Speaking of puzzles . . ." Brin said to Raithe as she knelt before him in the creation of another perfect roving. "What's the answer to the riddle?"

"Riddle?" he asked.

"The one you posed to the Crescent Forest." Brin sat up straighter, closed her eyes, and recited, *"Four brothers visit this wood. The first is greeted with great joy; the second is beloved; the third always brings sad tidings; and the last is feared. They visit each year, but never together. What are their names?"*

"You remember all that word for word?" Moya asked, amazed.

"Excellent, Brin," Persephone said. "Just like a true Keeper."

Brin smiled. "I only heard it once, but I keep trying to solve it. Not that I'm wiser than the Crescent. I mean, you asked the forest, and it didn't know the answer, right? So how could—"

"Spring, summer, autumn, winter," Roan said from the back of the room.

They all turned and stared.

Noticing the silence, Roan looked up. "That's right, isn't it? The names of the four brothers?"

"Yes," Malcolm said with a little smile. "Yes, it is."

"Seems sort of obvious once you hear the answer," Moya said.

Malcolm narrowed his eyes at Roan. "Pardon me for asking, but I'm curious. Why are you sewing a patch on your tunic? There's no hole, is there? Not even a wear mark."

"It's not a patch," she replied. "It's a pocket."

"A what?"

"A *pock-et*. That's what I call it. You know, like a poke—a little sack? But this is a tiny one. So it's a pock*et*. See?" Roan picked up a bit of string from her worktable and slipped it in. Then she let go, leaving it there as if she'd performed a magic trick. "Because it's open on top, I can put stuff in and take it out with one hand, and it's always with me."

"That's brilliant," Malcolm said.

"As long as you don't stand on your head," Moya brought up.

"I don't think Roan will be—" Persephone began, and stopped when Moya gave her a surprised look.

"This is Roan we're talking about, Seph. Two weeks ago, I stopped her just seconds before she stuck a needle in her eye."

Persephone looked at Roan, aghast. "Whatever for?"

"She wanted to find out how deep the socket was," Moya answered for her.

"Oh, blessed Mari! Roan, don't ever do that," Persephone said.

"Okay." Roan nodded without the slightest indication that she understood why. She then looked back at Malcolm. "I was thinking of putting a pocket on both sides." She placed her hand on the other hip, marking the spot. "Next time Padera asks for needle and thread I won't have to fumble with a pouch's drawstrings."

"You're a marvel, Roan," Moya told her. "A little batty, but amazing all the same."

"She's not batty," Persephone said. "She's a genius."

Roan shook her head self-consciously and once more displayed the disbelieving look that broke Persephone's heart.

What sort of monster was Iver?

Persephone had liked the man. Strange how it was possible to see someone for years yet still not know him.

"What do you think Konniger will do now?" Moya asked. Her spinning wheel made a little breeze in the house.

"Sarah told me he and Tressa are staying with the Coswalls," Persephone said. "I didn't mean to drive them out. They could've stayed."

"No one will go near the lodge now, not even the Galantians, not while *she's* in there. Well . . . except for you three. 'Course Suri's a mystic, so nothing she does surprises anyone, and Padera would spit in a bear's eye. What's she got to lose, right? The woman's lived the equal of ten normal lives. Probably tired of it all."

"And me?" Persephone asked. "What are people saying about me?"

Persephone knew there was talk. There was always talk. Life in a dahl was filled with endless days of mundane repetitive tasks, and gossip was the only entertainment. After Hegner's accusations, the death of Sackett and Adler, and the arrival of Raithe, the Fhrey, and a Miralyith, there was a lot to talk about. All of it in whispers whenever she was around, so Persephone knew much of it was about her.

Moya slowed down, letting the wool play out. "Don't know how reliable it is, but Autumn told me Konniger is spreading a story about you trying to take over. That's why you drove him out of the lodge. One more step in your master plan."

"My *master plan*? All I'm trying to do is save the Miralyith's life, and this dahl in the bargain. I put her in there because it's warm and dry."

"I'm not the one complaining," Moya said. "And I know everything Hegner and Konniger are spewing is complete rubbish, but . . . what if it wasn't?"

"Moya, you can't possibly think—"

Moya shook her head and held up her hands. "No, I don't mean it that way." She looked around at the others, most of whom saw the seriousness in her eyes and stopped what they were doing. "What I mean is maybe you *should* become chieftain."

"Clan chieftains are men," Raithe said.

"No," Moya replied. "They just always have been."

"Well, yeah, and that's because any member of the clan can challenge a chieftain to combat for control of the clan," Raithe replied. "At least that's how they do it—did it—in Dureya. Not too many women are keen with a spear or ax. And a chieftain needs to be capable of leading men into battle, which means you want the strongest and toughest."

"People in Rhen don't go to battle every week," Moya pointed out. "Never been a battle in my lifetime."

"Still, it helps to have a man in charge to keep order."

Moya's face hardened. "Seems Persephone is the one keeping the order around here, not Konniger. When it comes to keeping order, I'd rather have someone using the head above their shoulders than the one below the waist."

This brought a round of smiles and a few glances at Brin, who looked puzzled.

"But how well would she fare in a one-on-one fight with him?" Raithe asked.

"The ability to kill someone shouldn't be how we choose our chieftain," Moya said.

"What *should be* and what *is* are usually very different. Doesn't change the fact that armed battle is how these things are decided."

"She could have a champion fight for her," Brin said.

Both Moya and Raithe looked at the girl.

"According to the Ways, anyone can have a champion stand in for them so long as that person agrees to fight and has no desire to be chieftain themselves."

"Is that true?" Moya asked.

Brin nodded. "I thought everyone knew that."

"Not everyone studies the Ways like you, Brin." Moya turned to Persephone. "There you go. Have Raithe fight Konniger and take the First Chair."

"I wouldn't ask someone to risk their life for me."

"He fights gods! You're only asking him to kill Konniger. I don't think there's much of a risk."

"The Fhrey aren't gods, and I don't care if it was Cobb being challenged. I wouldn't ask such a thing of anyone, especially someone I hardly know," Persephone said while avoiding looking at Raithe. The man had feelings for her, and she was calling him a stranger. "You just don't want to be forced to marry Hegner."

"Of course. Would you? Would anyone? But that's not the point. Fact is, you'd be a great chieftain. We all know it—those of us capable of thought, anyway. Everyone looks to you in an emergency, and not a single person hesitated when you said to take the Fhrey into the lodge. I was just a kid, but I remember the famine and how *you* saved us. My mother hated you, by the way."

"Oh, thanks for that, Moya." Persephone frowned. "Always glad to add another name onto the long list of people who've hated me."

"Let me finish." Moya rolled her eyes. "She cursed your name every night because you convinced Reglan to ration the grain." She turned to Brin, who had stopped carding to listen. Brin loved stories. "The Long Winter was over, summer was here, crops were looking great, but everyone was hungry because Persephone demanded the granary remain locked."

"A lot of people hated me for that," Persephone said softly, remembering what, at that time, had been the worst year of her life. She had survived back then by thinking life couldn't get any worse. Maybe that was why everything was so upside down on the dahl since Suri's prediction of death—the gods felt the need to prove her wrong.

"My mother said the only reason Reglan appeased you was because you nearly died in childbirth a few weeks earlier," Moya continued. "He was worried about you, and my mother said you used your loss to get your way. She thought you forced the ration because you wanted the rest of us to suffer along with you."

"Your mother said *that*?"

Moya nodded. "And you wondered why I didn't cry at her funeral. Well, it was stuff like that."

"What happened?" Brin asked. "I never heard this story."

"I wish I could say the same," Persephone said, looking out at the rain.

"You were young then, Brin. This was what? Ten years ago?" Moya asked.

"Eleven," Persephone said. "But let's not talk about it."

"Oh, no, you have to finish it," Brin pleaded. "I might be the next Keeper, and this could be important. You know, for the future. In case something like that happens again. Please?"

Moya shrugged. "You tell it, Seph. You know it better than anyone."

Persephone was quiet for a long while; then she sighed and said, "It started with Tura. She had come from the forest and warned Reglan and me about a famine. I believed her, but he didn't. Part of the reason was because Tura so infrequently visited the dahl. For her to come, it must have been important.

"Another reason was because I knew how low our stores were and how much people wanted to gorge themselves after so long on rations. If Tura was right and we didn't take precautions, the entire dahl would have starved. I pleaded with Reglan to seal the granary. People were hungry; they almost revolted. They saw no reason for such measures. I had never fought so vehemently with him before, but I couldn't back down. Maybe Reglan did go along just to calm me. I don't know. But he heeded my pleas." Persephone paused, and the room was silent.

"When spring came, everything was fine. The crops were growing well, and everyone gave me angry looks. I ended up spending the nice weather holed up in the lodge. Then the storms came. Weeks of them. Wind, hail, and rain destroyed everything. After that there was a drought, two whole months without more than a few miserable drops of rain. Just when we thought it couldn't get any worse, winter came early. We went into it with only what we had saved in the granaries. That was the start of the Great Famine. There were a lot of deaths. We stacked the bodies in the snow because the ground was too hard to dig. We waited for spring to bury them. When bodies started to disappear, Reglan and I prayed it was wild animals or even ghouls stealing them."

"But you saved us," Moya said. "*No one* would have survived otherwise, and everyone knew it. People listened to you after that. They still listen to you. You just have to talk to them."

Persephone shook her head. "Konniger is chieftain."

"Sure, now he is, but you could—"

"No, Moya. Don't you see? When Reglan agreed to ration food that spring, what would have happened if your mother had found herself a Dureyan warrior and challenged him for leadership? How would that have been? You wouldn't have liked that, would you? Konniger isn't a great chieftain—not yet—but if we stand by him, he could be. He just needs a little help at the moment, and it doesn't help that Hegner is whispering lies about me."

"Konniger is worthless. Did you know he named Hegner as his new Shield?" Moya said. "What kind of idiot makes a one-handed man their bodyguard?"

"There has to be a reason; he's just not telling us. When I was Second Chair, Reglan and I couldn't always tell everyone everything. We had secrets we had to keep hidden for the good of the clan."

"Like what?"

"Like what really happened to the missing bodies waiting for a spring burial."

"What did happen?"

"Let's just say it wasn't animal tracks we found."

Suri sat in the rain outside Roan's home, her back against the doorposts and legs outstretched to the edge of a mud puddle. Minna lay beside her, the big pile of wet fur rising and falling with the wolf's breath. As always, the animal's heat kept her warm. The mystic had the loop of string in her hands again, weaving another web with the added challenge of the rain, which created pretty liquid jewels on the string.

Suri felt time slipping away, and she had to think. The yakking going on in the roundhouse was distracting, but the rain helped. The gray curtain and the constant patter assisted in blocking out the rest of the world. Not all of it. She still could hear the conversation inside if she listened. That was where the string came in. It helped her concentrate. Strings were like that. So were ponds—hard to find a good thinking pond, though. They needed to be isolated in a deep wood with plenty of cattails and dragonflies and few, or preferably no, biting bugs. A good thinking pond was located on the northern side of the Crescent, but it was too far so she settled for her string.

What is the secret of the bear?

If she'd had a chance to speak to Konniger, she might have learned something. The bear might be a bendigo, morvyn, or yakkus. A bendigo she could deal with; a yakkus would be bad. She didn't think it was a yakkus. They killed with sickness, and so far everyone had been ripped apart. It was probably a morvyn. In fact, it was most likely a morvyn. The eating of people was a big hint, but she didn't want to face a demon on a guess.

Despite the sound of the rain and the distraction of the string, Suri heard Persephone's accounting of the Great Famine. *We stacked the bodies in the snow because the ground was too hard to dig. We waited for spring to bury them. When bodies started to disappear, Reglan and I prayed it was wild animals or even ghouls stealing them.*

That was particularly strong evidence they were dealing with a morvyn, unless Persephone was right about having a ghoul problem. Suri pulled the string through her fingers, thinking about bears and forest spirits. One thing was certain—death was coming unless she could stop it, and she couldn't stop it unless she understood what *it* was.

Inside, the conversation had shifted from famine to a debate about who the chieftain ought to be. Raithe and Malcolm were also in there but said little. She liked that about them. Reminded her of Minna. Fools believe silence is a void needing to be filled; the wise understand there's no such thing as silence.

"Nice wolf," said a young man, hobbling forward assisted by a wooden stick under one arm.

His back was twisted, his face misaligned—one eye and the corner of his mouth higher than the other. His right shoulder was pinched up to his cheek, and his left leg dragged as if one foot were dead. He wore a surprisingly clean tunic, although at that moment it was soaked through. His hair was combed neatly back, which was probably easier since it was wet. In his free hand, he held a beautiful clay amphora with an enamel finish. Around the belly of the pot was the image of a woman with a broken chain in her hands.

"Her name is Minna," Suri replied.

"Fiwst wolf with a name I've met." The man paused. "Come to think of it, I can't say I've met a wolf." He spoke slowly, deliberately, and sounded as if his nose was stuffed. "Pleased to meet you, Minna. I'm Gifwadd."

"What's wrong with you?" Suri asked. "Are you cursed?"

Gifford laughed. "Many times, I suspect."

"Nice stick," Suri said. "I have a staff but never tried using it that way."

Roan came out of the roundhouse. "I call it a crutch."

"She made it fo' me," Gifford said. "Should have named it without an *r*, though." The cripple smiled . . . or the closest thing to a smile that his face could produce.

"I'm sorry, Gifford. I should have thought about that. We could change its name," Roan said.

"No. It's fine." He held out the amphora with his free hand. Rainwater splashed off its sides; the few drops that found the opening made a deep, hollow sound. "Woan, this is a peasant I made you. I think it's my best yet."

Roan didn't move. Her hands covered her face as she stared at the ceramic vase, shocked. "It's . . . it's so . . . it's lovely. And is that the new glaze?"

He nodded. "Inside and out. Difficult to paint the inside, too. Took awfully long to do."

"You can't give this to *me*."

"I don't see why not. I made it fo' you. It has a pict . . . ah . . . an image of you."

Roan bent over and peered closely. "That's me?"

"Who else?"

Roan squinted at the image as raindrops ran down the side of the ceramic. "But . . . but she's beautiful."

"Uh-huh." Gifford nodded. "Exactly. Now please take it. It's quite light, but holding it out like this is—"

"Oh! Sorry." Roan took the vase, continuing to marvel at it. "This is a work of art. I don't understand why you would give such a thing to *me*."

Gifford hesitated a moment. Suri had trouble understanding the expressions of people, and seeing as how Gifford's face was already squished and askew, he was harder to gauge than most. Still, he looked as if he was about to say something, then changed his mind. He made an attempt to shrug, but only one shoulder responded. "Goes with the set of cups I gave you."

"You can't keep giving me things."

"Did the chieftain pass a new law?" He gave another lopsided smile, but Suri imagined all his smiles were that way. "Even if he did, I'd bweak it."

Roan looked flustered. "I meant that I don't deserve this, any of these things. I'm just a—"

"He's dead, Woan," Gifford told her, his voice louder. "You not a slave now. You fwee. And I'd—" The potter bit his lip and sucked in a noisy breath through his nose. "Cups and pots would be the least I would give you. If I could . . . if I wasn't . . ."

Gifford squeezed his lips together and stared at Roan. The two of them stood in the rain, facing each other and breathing hard so that their breaths created a single cloud.

Roan hugged the big amphora to her chest and asked, "Are you all right?"

"No," Gifford said miserably, then glanced at Suri. "She'll tell you. I'm cussed."

Roan looked puzzled.

"Cursed," Suri clarified.

"Yeah, that. Keep the pot. Bweak it. Give it away. You can do what you want, Woan. You can do what you want because you fwee. Wememba that. And you beautiful, too. You should have the best of anything, but all I have to give you is a pot." He offered one last misshapen smile, or maybe that one was a frown.

"Nice meeting you, Minna," Gifford called as he limped away.

The wolf lifted her head at the sound of her name.

"Who cursed him?" Suri asked Roan as she continued to watch Gifford hobble off.

"What?" Roan looked down at her, puzzled for a moment. "Oh. The gods maybe. He was born that way."

"His mother died giving him life," Persephone said, appearing in the doorway. She was looking at Roan, a sad expression on her face. "When he was born, the people of the dahl thought it would be best to leave him in the forest, but his father refused. He said Gifford was a fighter like his mother, and he was right. The son of Aria just may be the bravest man on the dahl."

"What do you mean *leave him in the forest*?" Suri asked.

"Hmm?" Persephone looked over. "Oh, well . . . some children, the unwanted ones, are sometimes given over to the mercy of the gods."

Suri let the string fall from her hands.

The next morning Raithe went to work on the eaves of the forest. His shirt was off and his swords hung from a nearby tree branch. He was still carrying his father's broken blade for reasons he couldn't put into thoughts. The sky was clear blue after the rain, and the light of the climbing sun pierced the leaves in shafts. Out where the forest met the field, out in the stillness of a dewy dawn, it was possible to forget the world was ending.

Or is it?

The question itself appeared up for debate. The doomsayers—and Raithe acknowledged he had been one—believed the Fhrey were coming to kill them all and him in particular. But the Fhrey had come three times, stayed twice, gone once, and everyone was still alive. The whole affair was almost enough to inspire hope . . . almost.

What fun is there in crushing the hopeless? Like with pigs or cows, there is a period of fattening before the slaughter. The gods are just waiting for the right time, and my time is running out. Why am I still here?

The answer was obvious; he just wasn't happy about it.

He wiped his face and remembered the land across the rivers where his father had dragged him. Herkimer had been wrong about many things, but not about that place. While exploring, he and his father had crossed both the Bern and the Great Urum rivers, where Raithe had beheld paradise. On the far side, he'd climbed a hill and seen a new future for himself. A land the Fhrey called Avrlyn was filled with lush fields and rich forests.

That was where he wanted to go, where he hoped to live. Afterward, Herkimer had picked the meadow at the convergence of the two rivers, but Raithe couldn't get the other hill out of his mind.

He couldn't go there alone. Even his father had understood that and brought Raithe along. Probably would have sent Raithe back to get a wife once they were established. Maybe given a year or two, Persephone might change her mind, and if she came, others would, too. He fantasized about her, Malcolm, Suri, and a few of the others joining them. They could do it. Together, they could build something . . . something beautiful.

He picked up the ax again.

Since the death of Krier, there had been a notable lack of volunteers to cut wood and an abundance of talk regarding the community's dwindling supply. When the morning arrived without rain, Raithe borrowed an ax from Roan. She apologized when handing it to him, saying she'd made it the previous fall after the season's wood supply had been cut, so no one had tried it yet. She continued to apologize three more times in the event it didn't work well. Apparently, she had beaten the blade from a chunk of metal she and Gifford had found when searching for glaze materials.

Raithe hadn't used many axes in his life. Trees were rare at Dahl Dureya, but he had gone with his father and some others during their pilgrimage to a forest far to the south. The few axes he had used were straight poles with a wedge of flint jammed into a split on one end and lashed tight with leather strips. Usually a strong man needed an entire day to drop and reduce a tree to usable pieces. Doing so would leave him with aching arms, and the ax heads broke so often that dozens of replacement flints were brought along.

The tool Roan had given him was nothing like the ones he'd used before. It had a long, curved handle that went through a hole in the metal head. When he swung, Raithe cut through small limbs in a single stroke, bark and all. Working alone, he'd already taken down a respectable maple and limbed it in less than two hours. The ax had to be magic.

He dragged the leafy branches out of his way and then rested, catching his breath, leaning with one foot up on the body of the naked trunk. He marveled at the bright nibs of wood the ax had clipped away so cleanly.

"If I were a bear, you'd be dead."

Raithe whirled, lifting the ax in defense. Behind him stood a Fhrey, the one who had disarmed him during the fight with Nyphron.

Sebek stood casually, weight on his heels, back straight, chin high, arms relaxed. He wore only a leather skirt and sword belt; his bare chest appeared just as bronzed, just as indelible, as armor. Sculpted by the morning sun, his body was a series of sharply hewn muscles, a landscape of lean strength. Angled planes formed his face: high cheeks, a broad jaw, and precise lips. Cold and blue, the Fhrey's eyes smiled with a hungry delight.

Raithe didn't say a word. He looked toward his swords still hanging on the tree branch. The Fhrey was between him and his weapons. Sebek saw the glance. He stepped back, picked up Shegon's blade, and swung it menacingly.

"This is a terrible sword," Sebek said. "Gaudy, heavy, and too long. But I suppose you like long blades. They are the weapons of cowards who fear getting close to their enemies."

He tossed the weapon to Raithe. But before he had time to catch it, Sebek had both of his blades drawn. "These are Nagon and Tibor," the Fhrey said, holding the twin cleves up. "Lightning and Thunder. Each forged from the same batch of metal by preeminent Dherg smiths."

"Dherg smiths? Is that why the blades are so short?"

Sebek grinned, and in that toothy smile, Raithe saw danger. *He doesn't just like fighting—he loves it. And he probably has more than a passing affection for those swords.*

"Short swords are fast, and I'm not afraid to get close." Like a big cat, Sebek began to pace. As he did, he continued to take practice swipes in the air. "You made a number of mistakes when fighting Nyphron."

"And yet I won, or would have."

"Would you?"

"No way to know for sure, now, is there?"

Sebek gave a little laugh. "I know."

"Good for you."

That grin again. "You don't believe me? Don't think I can tell the outcome of a fight before it starts?"

Raithe didn't have to *believe,* he *knew.* But showing weakness in front of Sebek wasn't a good idea. Raithe moved to slip the sword into his belt.

"Not yet," Sebek said. "I want to show you where you failed."

"Not interested, chopping wood. You're interrupting."

"You can chop wood later, if you survive."

Raithe was waiting for the attack. He'd expected it since Sebek appeared. He just couldn't anticipate what an attack from Sebek would be like. He was faster than Nyphron; Raithe didn't see the blade. Once more, Raithe acted on instinct and was right—he met Sebek's sword. The moment they collided, the impact jarred the weapon from his hand, just as in their first encounter. An instant later the point of Thunder—or was it Lightning—was pressed against his throat.

Raithe didn't move.

Sebek nodded as if they were having a conversation, then pulled back and walked five strides away. "Pick it up."

Raithe was already in the process, wiping the sweat from his palms on his leigh mor.

"It's not your fault, I suppose," Sebek said. "You're so young. You show promise, but you lack experience. You can trust me on that. I'm senior captain of the guard and master of arms at Alon Rhist. I'm also Shield to Nyphron. I've trained and tested thousands. Now, let's see if you can get Shegon's sword anywhere near me."

The bad news was that Raithe saw no hope of avoiding a fight he had no chance of winning. The good news was that Sebek didn't appear to want to kill him, at least not right away.

Sebek dodged his first stroke with no effort. On his next swing, the Galantian displayed his speed, slamming Raithe in the face with the butt of Lightning—or was it Thunder this time? Raithe staggered. His eyesight blurred, and he tasted the blood running down from his nose.

"Get serious or I'll beat you unconscious. Here, I'll make it easier." Sebek sheathed one of his swords. "Now try again."

Raithe shook his head and spat. Shifting his feet the way Herkimer had taught, he drew in his elbows and then leaned to the right until Sebek shifted his weight. At that moment he spun left, swinging the blade horizontally, and attacked Sebek's undefended side. He expected to slice Sebek across the chest. Amazingly, Sebek deflected the blade with his hand—his *empty* hand. The Fhrey slapped the flat of the blade, driving it down and away.

Raithe pivoted once more and swept high. Again, Sebek slapped the blade aside. Frustrated by the ease with which the Fhrey deflected his attacks with a bare hand, Raithe swung harder and faster. Following one stroke with another, he closed the distance between them. Sebek became pressed enough to use both his hand and a sword to deflect the attacks. But then, when Raithe thrust the sword at his chest, the Fhrey caught his blade with his hand, twisted it, and once again disarmed him.

"Your father wasn't a good teacher," Sebek said, handing the sword back. "You're slow, predictable, as graceful as an ox trapped in mud, and have no strategy for attack. I'm surprised Nyphron had so much trouble with you. But I think he wanted you to win. Still . . ."

Sebek nodded slowly, thoughtfully. "You're much better than I expected. Much better than I would have thought a Rhune could be."

"Are we done, then?" Raithe asked, picking up Roan's ax.

"Yes. I got what I wanted."

"What was that?"

"The truth."

CHAPTER TWENTY

The Prince

We were foolish to think the Fhrey were gods, but it was insanity for the Fhrey to believe it, too. I'd rather be foolish than insane.

— THE BOOK OF BRIN

As he rode alongside Gryndal at the head of a small column of soldiers, Mawyndulë worked hard to hold a stoic expression. Locking his teeth together, he stiffened his lips, which were constantly trying to betray him. His eyes were wide, but there was no helping that. He had no idea how to be casually in awe. Mawyndulë desperately wanted to appear as the unflappable prince of the realm instead of a sheltered youth seeing the magnificence of the world for the first time. The flaw in the plan was that he wasn't and he was.

Since leaving Estramnadon, Mawyndulë had gazed dewy-eyed at the great Parthaloren Falls, the marvelous tower of Avempartha, the snowcapped peaks of Mount Mador, the fjords of the Green Sea, and finally the broad, sweeping vista of Rhulyn. The sheer size of everything was incredible.

And the colors!

The sun playing on the barren hills and stony mountains produced a strange beauty. The harsh landscape sang of adventure and secrets. He saw himself traveling the wasteland alone, climbing the jagged ridges, and peering into lost caves. He imagined discovering Dherg treasure guarded by sleeping dragons, which he would slay. Or perhaps the guardians would be a troop of Dherg, the little monsters with their shining metal weapons lashing out from underground hiding places. In every fantasy, he was victorious—although he allowed himself to *almost* be beaten in a few of his daydreams before making his enemy pay dearly.

When Alon Rhist appeared on the horizon, the sight was beyond boyhood imaginings. Mawyndulë couldn't have dreamed that big. This was the stuff of legends. The great tower looked like an upthrust spear, punching out of the ground, stabbing the sky. The dome might have been the helmet of a giant, hidden just below the surface of the great hill. Such scale wasn't possible beneath the trees of Erivan. This was a place open and free, a land of heroes, a home for adventure. Even seeing it from afar, Mawyndulë fell for the romance, the grandeur, and the excitement he imagined as daily realities.

No one is forced to learn how to make string patterns in a place like this. No one needs to practice juggling inside a thrusting spearhead.

Mawyndulë wondered how often Alon Rhist was attacked. Regrettably, the war with the Dherg had ended long before Mawyndulë's birth. But the little cretins still existed, cowering in their dark places under the earth, seeking revenge and a return to the world of light.

Once a month maybe? Once a month would be good.

Mawyndulë knew Gryndal wouldn't linger at the outpost long, only a week or two, but he hoped they might be around for at least one assault. As the son of the fane, he would, of course, command a battalion of soldiers. And as one of only three Miralyith on the frontier, he would also command their awe.

Mawyndulë imagined hordes of Dherg scaling the cliffs and walls, emerging like droves of armored crabs or hairy spiders from every cleft and crevasse. Mawyndulë's troops would be shrieking in fear, but their young prince would boldly step forward and refuse his counselor's pleas to don armor. Fearless, he would look down at the enemy from the balcony of the—

"Miserable desolation," Gryndal muttered as they began the final climb toward the outpost. Mawyndulë's new teacher was scowling—no, it was more of a sneer. "Look at this." He gestured at the fortress of Alon Rhist. "They practically live in a cave. Little wonder they've become animals. This whole land is worthless, the armpit of the world, an empty, forgotten basin of rock. Even trees shun it." A black scorch mark off to their left caught his eye. "At least some of the vermin have been exterminated."

"Vermin?" the prince asked.

"Rhunes," Gryndal replied.

Mawyndulë had seen Rhunes only in paintings. Renowned artists who spent time in Avrlyn had filled the Talwara and the Airenthenon with frescoes. Most were dramatic, sweeping landscapes of the frontier at sunset or sunrise. Others featured impossibly tall mountains and unimaginably fierce rivers. In several, there were images of Rhunes, docile figures wrapped in blankets beside dwindling fires. But some depictions cast them as ferocious savages. While not nearly as frightening as the Dherg, ghazel, Grenmorians, or dragons, they were still scary with their wild eyes and crude weapons.

Mawyndulë was excited by the prospect of seeing an actual Rhune. Since learning about the trip to Avrlyn, he had compiled a mental checklist of things he wanted to see: bears, mountain lions, ghazel, Mount Mador, giants, the sea, the tower of Avempartha, Rhunes, the Great Urum River, Dherg, and dragons. The last two were actually at the top of the list, ghazel at the bottom. The sinister creatures had always scared Mawyndulë as a child, and the prospect of meeting a real one revealed that the fear hadn't completely disappeared. So far he'd crossed only the mountain and the tower off his list.

Gryndal was nodding. "Yes, Rhunes. One of their villages, I imagine. Petragar was able to accomplish something at least."

All Mawyndulë saw was a mound of dirt on top of which lay blackened timbers.

"I do apologize for dragging you out here to this rat-infested cellar, my prince," Gryndal said. "But your father feels you need to suffer indignities to build character. I don't agree. Such things are remnants of a bygone era—a time before the Art. The Miralyith have no need for such foolishness. We don't require an understanding of those below us any more than we need to experience life as a snail or ant. It's this notion that we are still related to them that hinders us from achieving our full potential. The only reason we are not yet recognized as a pantheon of gods is because we can't manage to allow ourselves to accept the reality that we already are. The absurdity is obvious when you consider how insane it would be to think of ourselves as equal to animals. Can you imagine believing yourself to be merely the most successful tribe of goats or cows?"

Mawyndulë chuckled at the thought of a cow telling him to juggle.

Gryndal nodded. "You see what I mean? It makes no sense. The Miralyith simply cannot be compared to lesser forms of life. We command the four winds to do our bidding. Does a Rhune do that?" He paused a moment and then, fixing Mawyndulë with one of his hard stares to indicate he was about to provide the point of a lesson, added, "Does an Instarya, Asendwayr, or Umalyn do that? Come with me, my prince." Gryndal urged his horse off the road toward the scorched rubble. Turning, he said, "You guards wait here."

Mawyndulë's father had sent twenty Fhrey from his personal staff to provide protection. None were Miralyith, which meant his father had sent cows to guard a god. That thought made Mawyndulë smile as he looked at Hyvin. The captain of the guard smiled back, mistaking Mawyndulë's expression as approval, appreciation, or perhaps even friendship. In truth, he was imagining Hyvin as a cow with drooping udders.

Mawyndulë followed Gryndal, the two trotting until they were amid the burnt ruins, which smelled unpleasantly of smoke.

"You understand what I'm saying, don't you?" Gryndal asked in a serious tone.

Mawyndulë nodded despite his uncertainty. He thought Gryndal was saying that Miralyith were better than everyone else, something he already knew. But he also suspected he was missing a larger point that his new tutor was making. Mawyndulë often felt that way. What he couldn't determine was whether he was ignorant or if people pretended they were smarter just to make him feel stupid. Arion often made him feel inadequate. Juggling rocks and playing with strings were things she claimed had benefits he couldn't yet understand.

Was this her way of pointing out I'm dumb?

But it could be that these things had no greater point, and she was just making a fool out of the fane's son. Arion probably had gone home each night and laughed with friends, telling them what idiocies she'd forced the prince to do. When Gryndal had explained that Arion might be dead, Mawyndulë hadn't felt the least bit sad.

"See, I knew you would understand what I'm talking about," Gryndal said. "You're smarter than your father. You can see what he can't. The fane is hopelessly mired in a fraudulent past. He can't possibly envision a future different from what he's used to because he lacks imagination. Do you know the single most important attribute for greatness in the Art?"

Mawyndulë shook his head even though he remembered Arion saying it was control. Something told him Gryndal was looking for a different answer.

"Imagination," Gryndal said. "The ability to think creatively. We call it the Art for that exact reason. Imagination is power. And I can see great power in you, Mawyndulë. Great power. You won't be limited by traditions and foolish laws invented thousands of years ago by Fhrey who couldn't conceive of the power we wield today. Do you think Gylindora Fane would have agreed to the restrictions she placed on herself and all subsequent Fhrey if she had the power we do? She was a product of her time, and back then the laws were necessary. Intertribal warfare was rampant and threatened to destroy us as a people. But can you honestly imagine any other tribe, or even all the tribes combined, successfully mounting an attack against the Miralyith?"

Mawyndulë shook his head. After seeing what his father had done to the leader of the Instarya and having seen Mount Mador with his own eyes, he knew the power of his clan was indisputable.

"That's why the laws must change or, more precisely, why others must learn that such rules no longer—and never actually did—apply to the Miralyith. Gods have no such boundaries. You see that, don't you?"

Mawyndulë nodded again.

Gryndal smiled, and then a sad look stole over the tutor's face.

"What's wrong?"

Gryndal shook his head. "It's just so tragic."

"What is?"

"That your father rules instead of you," he said, and then gave a wistful sigh. "If you were fane . . ."

"I will be fane one day."

Gryndal looked at him with a sympathetic smile. "Your father isn't that old. He's just over twenty-one hundred. He could rule another thousand years. In the meantime, you might have an accident. You could die on this very trip. Such a sad ending when we need your wisdom so badly."

"Together we might change his mind," Mawyndulë said. "Show him Ferrol has ordained the Miralyith as superior to all other Fhrey."

"I've tried, believe me. My efforts were counterproductive. I convinced him to make an example of Zephyron, but afterward he regretted what happened in the arena, and if anything it has moderated his feelings toward ordinary Fhrey. The fane . . . well . . . it's like trying to persuade a rock to fly. He simply doesn't know how," Gryndal said.

Mawyndulë laughed, and Gryndal laughed with him. They rode in silence through the blackened ruins.

Even after days on the trail, Mawyndulë still wasn't comfortable in the saddle. He didn't know why they had to ride—the soldiers didn't. They walked behind them in double rows. Gryndal had insisted on the horses, but they were merely trading sore feet for a sore seat. Sitting on the animal scared him. There wasn't anything to hold on to except some flimsy hair on the thing's neck. Nothing would keep him on its back if the animal bolted. Three times the horse had stumbled or jerked unexpectedly. Each time he'd nearly screamed. The only good thing about being on the horse was the added height. He could see farther and was well above the soldiers, which he liked. Most of them were taller than he was, but they had to look up at him when he was mounted.

"Your father simply doesn't have the imagination that you do. It's so unfortunate. You're already more capable of ruling than he is, yet you're impotent and treated like a child."

Mawyndulë was nodding. He honestly couldn't agree more. Those same thoughts had come to him on many occasions. "You really think so?"

"Of course. The thing is, it's not hurting us." Gryndal wagged a finger between them. "It's hurting everyone else. Our people could be so much more if we only freed ourselves from the restrictions of the past." Gryndal sidled closer and in a whispered voice added, "I know it's wrong for me to say this, but sometimes I honestly wish some tragedy would befall your father. Not anything fatal, of course, just something rendering him unable to rule so that you could take over. I know that sounds terrible, but I fear your father isn't suited to guide us into the future. His rule will lead to disaster. Trust me, Mawyndulë, your father's reign will threaten our whole way of life." Then he leaned closer still. "It's even possible that someone might take it upon themselves to kill the fane to prevent that."

"Kill? A Fhrey? That would break Ferrol's Law. They would no longer *be* Fhrey."

Gryndal pursed his lips as if to say something, then

stopped himself, looking unsure. Mawyndulë had never seen that expression on his new tutor.

"What?"

Gryndal shook his head, his lips pinched together.

"Are you saying this isn't true?"

"I'm saying . . . It's possible, I think, to gain Ferrol's forgiveness."

Mawyndulë stared at him, confused.

"If, after killing the fane, the murderer were to blow the Horn of Gylindora—you see, only a single drop of Fhrey blood flowing in their veins is required—and if this ostracized person were to win the challenge . . . well, how can the fane of the Fhrey not be a Fhrey?"

"Are you saying—"

"I'm only pointing out one of my many concerns. Your father is my friend, and I fear his own adherence to tradition might cause someone to act rashly."

Something caught Gryndal's eye.

"What is it?" Mawyndulë asked.

"Fresh stones." Gryndal walked his horse over.

At the center of the flat-topped hill, Mawyndulë saw what Gryndal had: new dirt dropped into a burned-out cavity of a building's foundation. Fresh stones had been set upon scorched ones.

"Looks as if Petragar missed a few rats," Gryndal said.

He walked his mount around the debris, peering with a slight squint. His eyes shifted left and then right. A grin filled his face as he trotted forward around a collapsed pile of stone and blackened logs. With a wave of his hand, the logs flung themselves end-over-end, revealing five huddled people.

Rhunes!

They were so caked with soot, dirt, and ash that Mawyndulë could hardly make out their features. They looked nothing like the paintings. Their hair was long and filthy and not just on their heads. Dirty mats also grew on the cheeks and chins of the males. All were dressed in tattered rags, the original color of which

Mawyndulë couldn't begin to guess. They were barefoot, unless mud counted as a covering. Primitive knives and hatchets made from sticks and stones were stuck in strips of animal hide tied around their waists.

"Like rats," Gryndal said. The sound of his voice caused the cowering Rhunes to wail and quiver. "They just come back. Look at them already building their little dens in which to breed."

Gryndal walked to Mawyndulë's side, turning his back to the Rhunes, who whimpered and huddled together with arms wrapped around one another.

"And oh, my prince, do they ever breed. They spit out a new litter of offspring in less than a year—less than a year! This group, even as small as it is, could become twenty-five in five years. In twenty years . . . well, in twenty years, who knows? Depends on how many of the offspring are female, but easily a hundred. In a mere century . . ." He shook his head in disgust. "Before your first centennial feast, this little nest of rodents would outnumber any tribe in Estramnadon, even the Nilyndd."

"How many Rhunes are there?"

Gryndal shrugged. "Ferrol knows. Tens, maybe hundreds, of thousands. Too many for the land to feed. By denying them the fertile fields beyond the Bern River we've been able to keep their numbers down." He indicated the horizon. "Contained, they exhaust the ground they live on and create a wasteland. They end up starving or eating one another. Either way their numbers are controlled to some degree."

"They do that? Eat their own kind?" The prince grimaced.

"Just like your goldfish."

Mawyndulë looked at the little cluster of dirty creatures with newfound revulsion. The feelings of pity he'd initially experienced faded.

"Honestly, I'd prefer rats. They're cleaner. My greatest fear is that some of these"—he nodded in the direction of the Rhunes—"would cross the Bern or, worse, the Urum River. It's a vast country out here, and only two need to slip over. The horde that would result would blanket the world. Then they would breach the Nidwalden en masse. Once inside Erivan, they would act like locusts. All of Elan would be devoured. Nothing would be left except a world like this—a world of dirt, rock, and rubble. This is the sort of trouble I spoke of, the peril your father toys with because he lacks your imagination and vision. It makes me fearful, so very fearful."

Gryndal stared. "The Instarya and a few Asendwayr live among the Rhunes. They think of them as pets and in some cases even more than that. I wouldn't be surprised if some of those stationed out here have taken Rhune females to their beds."

Mawyndulë recoiled. He looked at the filthy, hairy, bony females in the dirt and ash. He shivered. "That's not possible. No one would—"

"Don't be so naïve; of course they would. You need to understand that the lesser tribes have more in common with the Rhunes now than they do with us."

Mawyndulë couldn't help glancing at the soldiers behind them and wondering if they could hear. Gryndal made no effort to speak quietly, but if they heard, they showed no sign of offense. They were the personal guard to the fane and probably had heard worse. Mawyndulë felt awkward.

What must they think?

"The two groups share the same limitations, the same subjection to the dominance of nature," Gryndal went on. "What we use for our delight, they are slaves to. We can tell the sun when to shine and grant the sky permission to rain, but the non-Miralyith Fhrey freeze to death when it gets cold—just like the Rhunes, Dherg, goldfish, and locusts. They are all the same. It's time we understood this. We Miralyith aren't just another tribe, but another being altogether."

A new thought poked into Mawyndulë's mind as once more he looked at the soldiers. *What if the reason they*

*don't take offense is because they don't think the same
way I do?*

Mawyndulë looked over at Alon Rhist, only a short
distance away now. The fortress appeared different, less
majestic, less heroic. The buildings had been hewn from
rock, chiseled from stone by hundreds of workers. If
Mawyndulë had wanted to, he could have made a better
fortress by himself. The whole of Rhulyn, he realized,
wasn't grand or glorious at all. It was nothing but abject
desolation.

"Compared with everyone else," Gryndal told him,
"we are gods."

The prince's teacher glanced over his shoulder and
flicked his fingers. The five huddled Rhunes died in a
burst of blood.

CHAPTER TWENTY-ONE

The Full Moon

I swear, the reason for full moons is so the gods can more clearly see the mischief they create.

—THE BOOK OF BRIN

Nights were warmer. Leaves were full. Fireflies streaked the forest. This was Suri's calendar, her chronological list of things needing attention. The stars announced the time for gathering wildflowers on the high ridge and collecting winter's deadwood. She should have had a large bowl of dandelions soaking already. Tura had always liked the early batch the best. Spring edged toward summer and Suri was behind, but she had more important things to deal with—the moon was just shy of round.

Suri climbed the steps and entered the Great Hall of the lodge. Doing so at night made her think of death. Tura hadn't said much on the subject of dying. Whenever they found a lifeless bird or fox, they'd buried it. "Replenishes the world," Tura always said. But when the old mystic had become ill, she'd told Suri, "When I'm gone, heave my carcass on a pile of wood and set it aflame. Then let the wind scatter my ashes to the forest and field. I want to fly like dandelion tufts."

The part Suri had latched onto was *when I'm gone.* It begged the question of where she was going. Suri asked a few times, but Tura's answers were always vague. The woman knew how many veins were in the average maple leaf and insisted on following an insanely precise recipe for apple butter, but she talked of her death in imprecise generalities. She spoke of Phyre, the afterlife. According to her, it was divided into three sections: Rel, Nifrel, and Alysin. Rel was an indifferent place where most went after they died; Alysin welcomed only the greatest of heroes, and Nifrel took the truly evil. When pressed for specifics such as exactly where Phyre was or how she planned to get there, Tura changed the subject. Suri figured the old woman didn't know. She found this frightening because Tura knew everything. After burning Tura's body in a shallow hole, Suri pictured death not as a mystical place called Phyre but as a fiery pit. She was reminded of that each time she went to watch over the Miralyith.

Entering the dark hall—that pile of deadwood with its eternal fire—was like dying.

Firelight danced on the walls as the mystic crossed the big room, carefully avoiding the furs and refusing to look at the mounted heads in fear she'd see a friend.

That's probably why Tura had me burn her. So these strange people of the dahl couldn't hang parts of her body in their lodge.

Persephone asked her for help because Suri was one of the few who understood the bald lady's language. She didn't mind watching and genuinely liked Arion, despite her obsession with *me* and *I*. So few people knew how to build an interesting string pattern, and most of the time the Miralyith just slept. But there was another, more important, reason she suffered trips into Dahl Rhen's shrine of death. She was looking for Maeve.

Suri hadn't seen the old woman since hearing the conversation between Roan and Gifford. Maeve was as elusive as a unicorn—perhaps more so, as Suri had seen at least two of those. The Keeper of Ways hid herself in the depths of the wooden building that Suri was loath to explore. She had taken her shift looking over Arion while secretly hoping she would cross paths once more with Maeve, but so far . . . nothing.

"We're out of time. I don't suppose you'd be willing to sniff her out?" Suri asked Minna.

The wolf looked up silently.

"Fine. I understand. We'll just have to open some doors."

Suri didn't like the idea of opening doors in the lodge. Given the horrors kept on display, she worried about the things they felt the need to hide.

No one was there to stop her. As usual, the place was empty. The chieftain and his friends had vacated shortly after Arion had been housed on the second floor. They were probably outside the wall again. Suri and Minna had been making a daily escape from the wooden prison to breathe free air lest they go insane. On these excursions, she often saw a group gathered on the east side of the dahl near the standing stone. Konniger, his wife, the one-handed man who had been at the cascades, and a crowd of men—as many as twenty—would be there, but not Maeve. That old unicorn never showed herself.

Suri's bare feet and Minna's four paws padded across the raised wooden floor. They both halted at the sound of a muffled cough. It felt wrong to disturb the silence of the flickering tomb, but she needed to chance it. "Maeve?" she called.

Suri heard a creak and the sound of one of the doors opening.

The old woman shuffled out of the shadows into the wavy light. A bony hand held a robe tight to her neck. She peered at Suri with furrowed brows. "What do you want?" She glanced at the ceiling. "You're supposed to be up there, aren't you? Playing guard, or gatekeeper, or whatever?"

"I need to speak with you . . . about Shayla."

Maeve took a step back as if Suri had pushed her. Fear and fire both ignited in the old woman's eyes. "Leave me alone." She moved to close the door.

"I know how to free her."

The Keeper of Ways stopped. "*Free her?* What do you mean, *free her?*"

"A child left in the wood is irresistible to a morvyn spirit, like a squealing mouse to a night owl. They swoop in and possess the helpless; the innocent gives them the ability to walk the face of Elan, to have a physical presence. But a child can't hope to survive in a forest, so the morvyn turns itself into an animal—wolves or bears mostly. That's why they get such bad reputations." Suri looked down and patted Minna's head sympathetically.

"In most cases, they live an unusually long life and then die. Rarely do they do anything bad because the child is still in there, still fighting for control. But if they taste human flesh, then the spirit of the child is weakened and the morvyn gains the advantage. Seeking to take total control, the morvyn lusts for more human flesh. The more it eats, the weaker the child's spirit becomes and the stronger the demon gets. Should the spirit of the child grow too weak, then the demon becomes all-powerful, able to unleash its evil upon the world."

Maeve cringed in horror with each word. "You said you know how to free her?"

"I read the bones," Suri went on as gently as she could. "Grin the Brown is coming to devour everyone on this dahl. This will happen at sunrise tomorrow. So I'm going to her cave to stop the morvyn by freeing your daughter. Without a body, it can't harm anyone. I was wondering . . . would you like to come?"

When the door opened, the old shriveled Rhune, whose face reminded Arion of rotted fruit, slowly rose to her feet. Someone was going to great effort to avoid making noise, trying not to wake her.

Arion wasn't asleep. There was only so much sleep a person could endure. The first few days she'd been blessed with a body demanding rest, and she'd retreated into unconsciousness whenever possible. She had good days and bad. Good days were when she had trouble seeing and felt like her head was going to explode. Bad days made her look forward to good days. Recently, there had been more good days than bad, a hopeful sign that she was getting better.

With the improvement, she'd lost the refuge of sleep, which had become elusive. Arion spent hours lying on her back, staring at the wooden rafters. Most of the time she lay listening to the world: the breathing of whoever was on watch, the wind above the roof, random thuds from below, or an occasional shout from outside. On that evening, she listened to the whispers of the old woman trying not to disturb her rest.

The guard changed every few hours, always the same three: Persephone, Suri, and the old woman, whose name Arion didn't know. Maybe she'd heard it, but it hadn't stuck. The old woman didn't speak Fhrey, and as a result she was as interesting as the chair she sat in. Arion's eyes were closed, but she knew who had entered the room—impossible to miss the click of claws on wood. The girl with the wolf was back. As much as she feared the animal, which had a tendency to stare while licking its fangs, she looked forward to Suri's shifts.

The girl was fascinating. She made complex string patterns and juggled. Suri understood the Fhrey language and talked to the wolf as if it understood what she said. And although none of those things by itself indicated anything, all of them together suggested a particular inclination. If Suri were Fhrey, Arion would have her tested for entrance into the Estramnadon Academy of the Art. The enigma, of course, came from Suri being a Rhune. Only a small percentage of Fhrey had the talent to be Artists, and Rhunes were known to be akin to animals and incapable of basic reasoning, much less mastering the Art.

Unfortunately, Arion also continued to lack any ability in that regard.

The Rhune girl hadn't explained what she had meant about *it* coming back. Arion had asked, but the girl had feigned ignorance, teasing her with a smile each time the subject was broached.

It hadn't come back.

With each day's passing, Arion grew less confident the Art would ever return. The blow to her head had severed her connection to the natural world. The ability to sense life had gone numb. Like birds that knew when to fly south, Arion used to feel the impending sunrise and experience the shifts in weather and seasons as if they were moods, colors, or music. Once discovered, the Art had opened a previously unnoticed window through which a continuously shared consciousness with Elan passed. The world was a bonfire of power that produced constant heat, but that heat was gone, and she felt horribly cold in its absence. Unlike the numbness in her hands and feet, which had healed quickly, her connection to the world and the ability to tap it in order to wield the Art had not. Arion felt blind, deaf, and numb—imprisoned in her own body.

"*You can stop pretending,*" Suri said. "*Padera is gone.*"

Padera! That was her name.

Arion opened one eye. In the light of the little lamp with its flickering flame, the girl was perched once more on the chair, one foot tucked underneath her, the other thrown over the arm. The wolf curled up beside the chair. Both stared at Arion.

"*How did you know?*"

"*Breathe different when you sleep.*"

Arion carefully pushed up to her elbows. She could feel her fingers, which was good, and her head throbbed with just a dull ache. She was much better, yet knowing this was little comfort.

Why hasn't it come back? If I can feel my hands, why not the Art? What if it never comes back?

"*Did you bring your string?*" Arion asked. Helping the girl with patterns was one of the few things she looked forward to each day.

Suri tugged on the loop around her neck, pulling it out of her clothing but leaving it as a necklace. She still sat on the chair, staring at the floor.

"*Something wrong?*" Arion asked.

"*Might not see again.*"

"*You're going blind?*" Arion asked, dramatizing the girl's purposeful avoidance of pronouns.

The girl scowled. "*Know what I mean.*"

"*You know what I mean, and you should have said, 'I might not see you again.'*"

Arion expected an irritated smirk or maybe an argument. She'd been making a concerted effort to teach the girl to speak proper Fhrey, something Suri reluctantly submitted to but rarely without protest. Suri did look over but showed no hint of resistance. She appeared pensive, even a bit scared.

"*Why? What's going on?*" Arion's first thought was that a village meeting had been held and the mongrel hordes had decided to execute the evil Miralyith. They probably would do it at dawn, a ritual killing, a sacrifice to their sun god.

"*Have to do something dangerous,*" Suri said.

A wind blew in through the window, threatening the lamp's flame, which fluttered but survived.

"*What are you going to do?*"

"*Fight demon for girl's soul.*"

Arion wasn't certain she had heard correctly. Suri had probably gotten the words wrong. She did that on occasion, and it then became a verbal form of the string game as Arion worked to untangle the idea from the sounds Suri made. "*The word* demon *means an evil spirit.*"

Suri nodded. "*A morvyn—an evil spirit—took over an infant. Turned her into a giant bear. She feed on people. Bones show morvyn will come here on morning of full moon. Tomorrow. Greatest power then. Kill everyone if me not stop it.*"

Arion didn't bother to correct the pronoun. She had other more important concerns. "*What do you mean when you say you saw the future with bones?*"

Suri pulled out what looked to be a burnt stick from her satchel. "*The signs are clear. Even know part of the name of the demon, Grin, like a nasty smile, see?*" The girl held out an old chicken bone. The bottom half was scorched black. *"There is an evil bear in the forest called Grin the Brown. Not bear, is morvyn. Think that is what the bones mean. But me never drive out demon before. If fail . . ."*

She glanced at Minna. *"Need to ask favor."*

"From me?" Arion was barely able to sit up and feed herself. *"What?"*

The wind fluttered the lamp again. Suri glanced at it, then continued, *"Going with the mother of the child to a bear den. Not to fight, too powerful. Only hope is to drive demon out. Will have mother call to child. Bear knows mother, sort of knows me, too. Not taking others. Morvyn would attack. That includes Minna."* She paused to scratch behind the wolf's ears. *"Hoping to leave Minna here. Door is only thing that stop her from following."*

The idea of being trapped alone with an angry wolf was only marginally better than the idea of the village executing her. *"This doesn't sound at all wise to me. Forgive me for saying this, but you can't tell the future from bones, and demons don't possess children and turn them into murderous bears. It all sounds like tribal myths, silly stories to frighten children."*

"Can leave Minna?"

Maybe it was the way Suri acted like a Fhrey by playing with string. Or perhaps it was because she watched over Arion every night. Most likely it was the mournful look on the girl's face while asking. Regardless of the reasons, Arion said, *"Yes."*

She regretted it immediately. Arion opened her mouth to take it back when the wind gusted again. This time the lamp blew out, leaving them both in darkness.

Arion could still see; the moon was nearly full and its light spilled in through the window. As such, there was no mistaking what happened next. Suri looked at the lamp, which sat on the table across the room. She rubbed her hands together briskly, murmured a few faint words, and then clapped.

The lamp flared to life.

"*How did* you *do that?*" Arion asked, stunned. She put her emphasis on the pronoun again, but this time it had nothing to do with language lessons. Arion knew exactly how Suri had lit the lamp, and until recently she would have done the same thing in much the same manner. But this girl was a Rhune. She repeated the question. "*How did* you *do that?*"

"*Asked a fire spirit to light lamp. Should have asked wind to stop playing around, but wind doesn't listen.*"

Hearing nothing that made sense, Arion continued to stare in shock. "*You're a Rhune.*"

"*You're a Fhrey. You play that game, too?*"

Arion had no idea what game Suri was talking about and didn't care. "*What else can you do?*"

The girl shrugged. "*Eat, sleep, run, jump—*"

"*I meant like that.*" She pointed at the lamp.

Suri looked puzzled.

"*You don't see a difference?*"

Suri continued to look puzzled.

"*Can everyone light lamps at a distance?*"

Suri thought about this. "*Different people do different things. Tura sang good. Padera cooks tasty soup. Gifford makes pretty clay cups. Sarah is good making blankets. Minna runs fast. You make swords stop.*"

"*Can you make swords stop?*"

Suri shook her head.

"*Can you make it rain?*" Arion asked.

Suri chuckled.

"*Can you open the door to this room without touching it?*" Arion asked.

"*Can you?*" the girl shot back.

Arion glanced over her shoulder at the closed door and sighed. "*Not at the moment.*"

Suri smiled, and Arion caught something odd in her expression, a playful mischievousness. But then Arion knew so little about Rhunes, and Suri was the strangest of them all.

"*How did you learn to make fire? Did someone teach you?*"

"*How you learn to walk?*" Suri asked. "*How you learn to talk? Someone teach you?*"

Arion found she was smiling. What a perfect answer. Not just the point being made but the way she made it—an answer in the form of a question. Statements were ends, and there was nothing closed or final in the Art. This girl, this Rhune, was doing the impossible, thinking and acting like a second-tier Miralyith, and she wasn't even a Fhrey.

Suri left the chair and came over to Arion's bedside. The wolf followed. "*If don't . . .*" Suri glanced at the wolf and then leaned over and whispered in Arion's ear, "*If not come back, explain to Minna. Tell her me had to go.*"

Suri pulled back, and Arion saw tears in the girl's eyes. Suri bent down and hugged Minna's neck, saying something in her crude language. Suri sniffled and wiped her face.

"No," Arion said. "*Suri, don't go.*"

The girl looked up, surprised.

"*Don't do anything stupid. Don't do anything dangerous. You're . . . you're . . . special.*"

"*You special, too.*" Suri smiled.

"No, you don't understand. You have talent, real talent. And you're a Rhune. Do you know what that means?"

"*Know if don't stop Grin the Brown before sunrise tomorrow, everyone dies. Know same way know how to light lamp.*" She stood up and looked at the flickering light. "*Sure not want me to go?*"

Arion bit her lip.

CHAPTER TWENTY-TWO

Curse of the Brown Bear

When the dead betray the living, the victims are memories.

—THE BOOK OF BRIN

One look at the old woman and Suri knew the trip would take forever; she just didn't think forever would take so long. They left before dawn, but the sun was past midday by the time they reached the Third Step. That was Suri's name for the shelf of rock that jutted out from the cliff just up from the base of Talon Rock, which was what Tura always called the mountain. The Crescent Forest had many hills but only one mountain, a steep climb of rocky ledges. The forest was different there, less undergrowth but darker and denser. Trees did what they could to survive among the cliffs, resulting in acrobatic growth around boulders as they reached for sunlight. There were about fourteen steps in all, but that was to the summit, and luckily Grin the Brown made her home in a cave on the eighth step. This was still plenty high, well above the tree line, but not too much of a hardship for a normal person. For Maeve the climb was an epic feat.

Although the two had walked well enough when in the forest, as soon as they hit the incline, the old woman started needing rest stops. Suri gave her Tura's staff to lean on, but she still moved at a creep. Maeve could have lost a race with a tree. Now the path was as vertical as the stairs in the lodge, and Maeve was panting like Minna after a late-summer run. Suri didn't think it was possible, but Maeve's face looked even more like melted wax than before. It drooped, sagged, dripped with sweat, and had a flushed rose color. They would make it in time, and that was all that mattered. Suri was pleased with her foresight in starting as early as they had.

Unlike many of the other bears, Grin hunted during the day—another sign of a morvyn Suri couldn't believe she'd missed all these years. They had plenty of time before Grin returned, and it wouldn't take long to set a trap. Suri just needed to get to where the morvyn slept before it came home.

"This is all my fault," Maeve said as she sat on the rocky shelf of the Third Step. The Keeper of Ways had babbled nonstop as they walked. Suri hadn't paid attention, but sitting still there wasn't anything to do but listen.

"Why did you abandon your baby?" Suri asked. "Was it ugly? Was it like Gifford? I heard people wanted to throw him in the forest when he was born."

"No!" the old woman yelled. "I never wanted to give her up. She was taken from me."

"Someone *took* your child? Was it a crimbal?"

"No." The old woman shook her head. "Chieftain Reglan ordered Konniger to take her away. I was weak. I should have stood against him. I should have made him kill me first."

Wiping the sweat from her face with a white cloth kept in the wrist of her sleeve, she said, "I should have fought. That's the whole of it. I let my little girl down. You know Padera, don't you?"

Suri nodded as she sat cross-legged on the dirt. She could tell this was going to be a longer-than-usual rest.

"I hate her. Oh, Mari, how good it feels to say it aloud. I *hate* her!"

This surprised Suri, who thought the toothless woman with the humpback was one of the nicer inhabitants of Dahl Rhen.

"Do you know why?" Maeve didn't wait for an answer. "Because that old hag raised six children—six! All dead now, including the grandchildren, because she outlives everyone, but each survived to maturity. She saw to that. Padera is a good mother. No, she's a great mother. That little troll is a *perfect* mother. Nearly bald under her scarf, did you know that? That's why she never takes the wrap off. She has a face like a goat stepped in a melon but is too embarrassed to let people see she has no hair. Honestly, who cares?"

Suri felt completely unnecessary in the conversation. Maeve wasn't even looking at her. The old woman just stared at the ground between her knees.

"Padera wouldn't have let Konniger take one of *her* daughters into the forest."

"Is Shayla Konniger's daughter, then?"

Maeve looked up with an expression somewhere between appalled and the brink of laughter. "By Mari, no! Konniger was . . . well, much younger. And if it had been his child, if it had been anyone else's . . ." She looked back down at the dirt. "Konniger was kind about it. Might not think it seeing him today, but back then he was a decent lad. He took Shayla gently. Said he would find a pretty place. A place where the gods would surely find her and keep my baby protected from harm. He did a good job. I owe him for that kindness. When he came back, he told me that after he'd set her down in the forest he'd only taken a few steps, and when he looked back, my sweet little girl was gone and in her place sat a bear cub."

Suri was surprised. She'd never heard of a morvyn possessing and transforming a body so quickly. Her understanding was that it took days.

"When he told me, I went right out and looked. Weeks I hunted. Every day rooting through every miserable thicket, but I finally found her. The gods turned Shayla into a beautiful bundle of brown fur, but I could still tell she was mine. So cute, so perfect. And she needed someone to take care of her. I fed her. Milk at first, then I took some meat from the feasts. Just a little. But then she got bigger. I stole a goat, then another."

Maeve wiped her face and squeezed her nose. "Soon Shayla learned to hunt on her own. That was a huge weight off my shoulders, but then . . . the Long Winter and the Great Famine came. There wasn't any food, not for us on the dahl or for her in the forest. Everyone was thin; *walking dead*, we used to say. When people started to die, we stopped saying it. Even Padera's children died. But I wasn't going to let *my* baby perish, not after all I'd gone through, after all *she'd* gone through. My baby needed meat to live. All the goats were gone. And the sheep were guarded."

Maeve stopped talking and just stared at the ground as if seeing ancient snow.

"You found meat?" Suri asked.

"Yes. I found meat. Frozen meat, but Shayla didn't mind." Maeve brought the cloth to her face again but this time wiped tears from her eyes. "They were just lying there, stacked in the hut near the south wall, near the gate. The ground was too frozen to bury the dead, so they just packed them in the snow to wait for the thaw. When spring came, everyone thought animals had stolen the missing bodies." Maeve's voice cracked and hitched. She held the cloth to her lips. "Padera's children kept my Shayla alive."

"As the morvyn's strength grew, she craved more human flesh," Suri said.

Maeve nodded, "I didn't know. I didn't . . ." She was crying too hard then to speak anymore.

"Let's just hope Shayla still remembers the sound of her mother's voice." Suri held out Tura's staff for Maeve again, and without another word the old woman got to her feet and began to climb once more.

That morning when Persephone entered the Great Hall to take her shift watching Arion, she was surprised to find Konniger. She hadn't seen him in the lodge since

Arion had moved in, and so it was odd seeing him in the First Chair, leaning slightly forward, staring out the door. He wore the chieftain's fur over his shoulders but his leigh mor was wrapped in the summer style, pinned and belted at the waist, forming a skirt that revealed pale, hairy legs. The fire burned low; the room was quiet; Konniger was alone. This concerned Persephone. Konniger was never alone.

Since becoming chieftain, he traveled with an entourage. His drinking friends, cronies, and the growing number of men from Nadak were always around.

"Konniger," she said, trying not to sound like a guilty kid caught coming home too late.

"Persephone," he replied, slouching a bit to one side and resting his chin on a hand.

He knew she came there every morning to take over the next shift from Suri. No other reason for him to be sitting in that chair all alone. This was to be a showdown of sorts. He would chastise her for causing trouble, seek to bring her in line. She decided to get her words in first, state her case before the conversation got ugly.

"We've never really had a chance to talk since Reglan died," she began in a gentle, empathetic tone. Although not exactly friends, they'd known each other for years, and she knew this was her best chance to reason with him. "I, well, I'm sorry if I've made things harder for you. I was only trying to help. It's just that after twenty years of sitting up there, I guess it's hard to let someone else take over—hard to stand by and *watch* rather than *do*. I want you to know I'm going to try to be better. You're chieftain now. I respect that. I just hope you'll let me contribute—that we can work together in some way. I mean, I have done this job for a long time, and I think I have some knowledge you could benefit from. It seems stupid to be at odds the way we've been."

Konniger cleared his throat and took a breath. "You know, Tressa had been so excited to move in here." Konniger pointed at the rafters with a lazy finger. "She'd dreamed of it all her life. That woman knew I'd be chieftain one day, believed it even when I didn't. That's what a good wife does, keeps your dreams alive even when you don't believe anymore." He pulled himself up a bit in the chair, a seat in which he didn't look comfortable.

"All this heavy timber, solid roof, and this fine fire was so much nicer than the dumpy roundhouse we shared with my mother, my sister, and her husband, Fig. Can't forget old Fig. Bastard snores as loud as a thunderstorm. I swear he was the cause of the thatch coming off the roof each spring. And, of course, their brood of kids: four god-awful brats who are always crying or shouting. All of us crammed in on top of one another, which wasn't so bad in winter. Cold blew right through that thatch, you know? But in the heat of summer—brutal." He shook his head with a you-have-no-idea expression.

"I slept outside most nights starting around this time of year. Sometimes Tressa joined me." He smiled then and looked into the glowing coals before his feet. "We rarely slept *those* nights. She likes it outside. Enjoys the freedom that lying on grass gives. I couldn't wait to see what it'd be like here in the lodge surrounded by thick log walls, the comfort of fur, and the warmth of our own private fire."

Persephone nodded. "It's a grand house, this is. I remember being shocked when Reglan first showed me the bedroom. I thought so much luxury was obscene. I figured no one could ever be unhappy living in such a place, sleeping on a fancy bed all to ourselves, but I cried rivers within these walls."

A breeze blew in through the open door, stirring the flames between them. Konniger sat up fully and pulled the black bear fur tighter over his shoulders. From overhead came the faint sound of intermittent scratching accompanied by an occasional doglike whimper.

Minna, Persephone thought. *Why is she scratching?*

"I always thought I was destined for greatness," the chieftain said. "Out of eight kids I was the only one to survive to adulthood."

"Your sister Autumn is—"

"My sister Autumn isn't worth mentioning. I'm talking about *men*. She's only good for churning out—well, I mentioned the screaming brats already, didn't I?" He sighed and shook his head. "Eight kids. It was easy to believe that the gods had chosen me for some greatness. Why else did they send sickness, famine, and in the case of my brother Kerannon a gust of wind to kill them while sparing me? As I got older, I realized I was wrong. It wasn't that I was being spared; they just did a piss-poor job of slaughtering us. Gods can be just as lazy and sloppy as anyone else, I suppose. When Wogan dropped that tree on my father, I knew the gods didn't care for us. The man was a warrior—Shield to the chieftain—and he died crushed by a lousy tree. No, the gods don't like me and mine. Honestly, I don't think they like any of us. But look who I'm talking to." He laughed.

Persephone nodded. "It can seem that way at times."

"Yep. The gods are jealous of even the few fleeting instances of joy we manage to sneak in. Laughter rankles them, makes them think we have it better than we should, and they can't stand that." He lowered his voice a bit, as if imparting a secret or trying to prevent the gods from hearing. "You can tell because terrible things always follow fortune. If there's a birth, someone will die. If there's a good harvest, the next year there's a blight. Maybe the gods just love to see us suffer. That would explain why we still exist. We're toys—toys that the gods break and reassemble so they can experience the pleasure of breaking us again. The trick is to avoid being the toy that's smashed by being the toy that does the smashing."

He stared at her then, a long hard study, then nodded with some approved decision. "You're smarter than I expected. I admit I underestimated you. I bought the illusion that Reglan was brilliant; now I see it was all you. He tried to tell me once. Right after my father died, the day he asked me to be his Shield, Reglan told me *you* were the one that made everything work. I never thought he was serious. He was drunk at the time. We both were. People say stupid things when they're toasting the dead. He said you were the heart of this dahl, the *real* chieftain. You were the one with all the ideas, the one with the courage, the one with the passion." He paused, watching her.

Persephone felt he was giving her a chance to speak, but she had no words.

What can I say to that? Yes, I'm great, or no, the love of my life was a fool?

A moment later, Konniger went on. "After I became chieftain, I thought you'd be a good girl and quietly step aside, disappear into widowhood, and everything would work out. Tressa would have her fine house, and I would rule the way my father never got a chance to because the gods thought it was funny to drop an oak on him. Only it didn't work out that way, did it?"

"You're the chieftain, Konniger. I've never disputed that."

He smiled at her then, a disbelieving smirk. "All these years with Reglan, I knew you had friends in the other clans, but damn, woman." He laughed. "A Dureyan mercenary, seven Fhrey, a goblin, and a giant. You really called in some favors, didn't you? Don't know why you went to all the trouble. The God Killer would have been enough. He's a foot taller than I am and has a sword, for Mari's sake. Probably been fighting since he could walk. I think we all know he can beat me."

"I didn't bring him here to challenge you."

"I'm not an idiot, Seph. Of course you didn't. No one brings that much muscle just to oust someone like me from a chair. You have bigger plans, don't you?" He smiled. "You gave it away at the meeting, you know? That comment about uniting the clans. That's it, isn't it? Reglan was right. You're smart, but he never mentioned the ambition."

"Listen, Konniger. I don't know where you're getting all—"

"Easy, Seph. Relax. I'm not ambushing you, and I'm not here to scold you for disobedience."

"You don't sound like you're here to make peace, either."

"Not really."

"What, then?"

Above them, Persephone heard Minna's scratching and whining again, louder this time.

The noise made Konniger look up. "Your mystic left, and her wolf is still up there. I thought you might be confused when you found her gone. You came to me the day the Fhrey arrived to explain what was going on. That was big of you, so I figured I'd return the favor."

"And what is going on? Where's Suri?"

"She and Maeve went hunting the big brown bear together."

"Suri and Maeve went—? What are you talking about?"

"The two left a few hours ago to save Maeve's daughter."

"Daughter?"

"Ha!" he exclaimed, withdrawing into the chair, pulling himself tighter. "You didn't know Maeve had a daughter, did you?"

"Maeve *doesn't* have a daughter."

"She did. The old woman gave birth some fourteen years ago."

Persephone shook her head. "You're not making any sense. Have you been drinking?"

"Not a drop, but I assure you Maeve *did* have a child."

"It's not possible; everyone on the dahl would have known."

He shook his head. "Reglan kept it a secret. Hid Maeve somewhere—I don't know where—told everyone she had to go on a long trip to visit each of the other dahls and collect stories from the other clans or some such nonsense. Took her over a year. You remember that, don't you?"

Persephone did remember when Maeve had disappeared. She recalled how frustrating it was to be missing their Keeper. There were always things coming up, things Persephone didn't know the answers to, things that needed to be verified, and all of it had to be delayed until Maeve got back.

"But why would Reglan—"

"Reglan wouldn't let her keep it, of course. He couldn't. People would ask who the father was, and the answer would be awkward seeing as how he was married to you. What if the child bore a resemblance? Had her father's eyes?"

Persephone stumbled backward as if Konniger had shoved her. She laid a hand on the nearby autumn pillar for support.

"That's why you didn't know. You weren't allowed to. Wives never understand such things. He figured a lot of people might not, so Reglan kept things quiet. Sent Maeve away, and when she came back, she was supposed to come alone. Only problem was Maeve couldn't give up the child. She should have run off and not returned, but she's not smart like you. She came back to the dahl with the infant in tow. Maybe she thought if Reglan saw it, he'd change his mind. That's not what happened."

Konniger looked away at the fire, his hands squeezing tightly.

"When she showed up, Reglan called for me and my dad. The child had to be abandoned in the forest. Maeve put up a fight. What mother wouldn't? The task fell to me. I was the son of the Shield, invisible, trustworthy, and eager to prove my worth. They told me it was an easy task. *Just take the infant to the forest and dump it,* they said. *Someplace deep,* they said, *so she can't find it.* That part was easy. The hard part was taking the baby from Maeve, taking it and . . ." Konniger's face turned into a distasteful grimace. "And seeing her when I got back."

Konniger paused a moment and swallowed. "Maeve

screamed." He made a sound like a laugh, but there was no mirth in it. "I never heard a grown woman sound like that before. You'd have thought I was killing her. I can still hear it, still hear that high-pitched shriek. The baby cried, too, a chugging kind of wail. You know the sort they do? Did it all the way out there. Louder even than Autumn's brats when they're really worked up. I was glad to be rid of the thing."

Persephone leaned on the pillar. *He's lying. Reglan would never—*

"Kept crying, though. Amazing how far sound carries. I dumped her next to that cascade—same one where you killed Sackett and Adler—but even the sound of the falling water couldn't drown out the cries. Reglan and my father were so proud; I'd become a man in their eyes. But I didn't feel like a man. I swore I could still hear that baby crying—still do sometimes. That's why I hate Autumn's kids. They all sound the same."

Persephone didn't want to hear any more, but the words continued to flow over her. "When Maeve found me, I could tell she'd been weeping since I left. Old Maeve looked at me like she was dangling off a cliff and I was holding the other end of the rope. She wanted me to tell her where I left the baby. She was going to go get it and run away, I think. Too late, of course. I couldn't risk losing the respect of Reglan and my father. Still, I had to tell her something."

It can't be true. Reglan would never have had a child with Maeve, and if he had, he certainly wouldn't have ordered it killed just to save himself embarrassment. That wasn't the man I knew. That wasn't the man I loved.

And yet, she was certain Konniger wasn't lying. She could see it in his eyes, in the way he refused to look at her, in the way he was wringing his hands, and in the confessional tone of his voice, which sounded heavy and ashamed. Besides, Konniger wasn't smart enough to come up with all those details—he wasn't making it up.

He was telling the truth. "What did you say to her? What did you tell Maeve?"

"I told her a story about her prayers being answered— and they were—in a way. I told her that the gods had taken her little girl and changed her into a bear, a beautiful little cub. She believed me because she had to, because the truth would've killed her."

"You said she and Suri went to save her daughter? What did you mean?"

Konniger took a long inhalation, made a peak with the fingers of both hands, and gestured resignation by spreading his thumbs. "Maeve—she wasn't content to accept that her daughter was safe with the gods. I should've said that the infant turned into a raven and flew away. Instead, Maeve pictured this poor abandoned bear cub starving without a mother to provide for it, and she went looking. Every day she went to the forest, and I was terrified she might find her baby's remains, probably eaten by wolves. Wouldn't have taken them long to find her, not with all the wailing. I figured Maeve would eventually give up, but damned if she didn't find an abandoned cub. She took to feeding the animal, bringing food to the forest. I forgot all about it until the bad winter when the bodies disappeared."

Persephone and Reglan never learned what had happened to the bodies, just those terrible footprints in the snow. They didn't want to investigate too much for fear of what they'd find. In an attempt to stave off rumors that would devastate a community already desperate, she and Reglan spread a story. They stomped out the prints and said wild animals had dragged off the bodies, but Persephone knew that wasn't true. She could still see those footprints in the snow beside the drag marks. Small feet had made them, a woman's feet.

"Maeve was feeding her *daughter* our dead. I didn't say anything. Maybe I felt too guilty. Maybe I was scared Reglan would blame me. I'd just become the new Shield, remember? Didn't want to mess that up, and I didn't think anything would come of it. Never crossed my mind to wonder what would happen once a bear got used to the taste of human meat. You see, that winter, while all the other animals were starving, Maeve's daughter grew big. She grew strong and lost her fear of people. After having a taste of us, we became her preferred food. That's what the bear thought when she came across your son—food."

"The Brown? Maeve thinks The Brown is her daughter?" Persephone squeezed the pillar hard. "What are they going to do?"

"I don't know. Maeve woke me up before dawn, saying she was going with that loony mystic who knows how to drive the demon out of The Brown. I guess they think they can turn her back into a human or something. Maeve was so happy. Crazy is what she is—has been since Reglan made me take her daughter. She and the mystic left a couple hours ago."

"And you let her go? Why didn't you tell the truth?"

"See, that's the thing." Konniger looked into the flames of the fire with a haunted grimace. "Maybe it is the truth. I mean, Maeve searched the forest every day after I left the baby. She never found it, but she did find an abandoned bear cub. Maybe the gods were listening when I told her that. Maybe they heard and made it true."

"You have to do something!" she shouted. "Get the men together."

"And do what? Go where?"

Overhead the scratching continued.

"The wolf," Persephone said more to herself than to Konniger. "Follow the wolf!"

Persephone ran across the room, rounded the banister, and raced up the steps. *"Arion?"*

"Persephone, don't come in. The wolf wants out!" Arion called through the door. Persephone didn't need the warning as the door shuddered violently. *"Suri isn't here. She left her wolf with me. She's going after a bear and said Minna would get in the way."*

Claws attacked the door, rumbling the wood against

the frame. The ferocity of the assault halted Persephone and made her hesitate.

"*Are you all right in there?*"

"Yes," Arion replied. "*But I think you should send help for Suri. I'm worried she might get killed. She thinks a demon possessed a bear or something.*"

Even the Fhrey was worried!

"Minna?" Persephone said gently. "Can you hear me, Minna?"

The thrashing of the door stopped, and the wolf cried mournfully.

"*What is the wolf doing?*" Persephone asked.

"*Lying in front of the door, smelling you.*"

"Hey, Minna. Remember me? I need you to take me to find Suri. You'd like to see Suri, wouldn't you?"

"The moment you let that animal out, you'll never keep up with it," Konniger said as he climbed to the top of the stairs and stood behind her.

"I'll need a leash," Persephone said.

"That's a wolf, not a dog. It'll tear you to pieces."

"I don't think so." Persephone hoped that was true. It should be true. Minna had never showed any sign of aggression toward anyone on the dahl, not even the sheep or chickens, but then, Suri had always been with her.

It was what the tree said to do. And if you can't trust an ancient talking tree, what was the point of having one?

"Here." Konniger slipped off his belt and held it out. "For all the good it will do you."

"Don't give it to me," Persephone said. "You do it. I'll call the men together and tell them that you're organizing a hunting party, and that—"

"I'm not going anywhere. If you want to do this, you'll do it on your own."

"What? Are you serious? Your Keeper of Ways is going to get killed because of a lie you told!"

"I won't send men against that bear again. You of all people know the danger. The Brown isn't just a bear.

Who knows. Maybe your mystic is right. Maybe it is a demon."

"It's not a demon. But it will kill them!"

"I won't allow any men from this dahl to commit suicide going after that bear. I'm not as stupid as Reglan."

She glared at him, furious.

How can he just stand there? How could Mari have allowed such a man to become our chieftain?

Persephone found it hard to believe Konniger could be so cowardly, even when young. To take a baby from its mother and abandon it was despicable. But now he had a chance to make up for that mistake and he refused. Konniger would stand by while two women went to their deaths because he was too weak to own up to an embarrassing lie.

"You and Reglan were both wrong," she told him as she snatched the belt from his hand. "I've never wanted to be chieftain of this clan. Chieftains apparently kill babies and allow innocent women to die for their mistakes. But you've convinced me of one thing. The people of Rhen deserve better than what they've had, and they definitely need better than what they've got."

Roan was hovering over Malcolm, twisting a lock of hair and studying his collar, when Persephone burst into the roundhouse. Hanging on to a leather strap leashed to Minna, Persephone could barely restrain the wolf, who was intent on being somewhere else.

"Raithe!" Persephone shouted. "I need help. Suri and Maeve have gone looking for The Brown. They're going to get themselves killed if we don't catch them before they find her."

Raithe got up and reached for his swords. "Is this the same bear that killed your husband?"

"Yes."

Raithe looked toward the door. "Aren't we going to need more people, then?"

"We don't have time." Minna gave a stout tug and

began dragging Persephone back outside. "We—look, we aren't going to kill the bear; we're just stopping Suri and Maeve from getting near it. Maeve's an old woman. We should be able to catch them if we start now."

"Okay, fine," Raithe said.

"Thank you." Persephone let Minna pull her back out and toward the dahl's front gate.

"Malcolm!" Raithe shouted, grabbing his spear and the Dherg shield. "Run to the lodge and get another spear off the wall." He picked up a sheep's bladder fashioned into a waterskin and threw it toward the ex-slave. "And here, fill that at the well, then catch up to us." He looked at Roan. "It's okay if we borrow it, right?"

She nodded.

"I'm going?" Malcolm asked nervously.

"Yep."

"But I don't know anything about hunting bears."

"We aren't hunting a bear," Raithe said. "You just heard her."

"Then why am I terrified?"

"Because it will be dark by the time we get out there, because I'm going, and because the gods are infatuated with me this month."

"Tell me again why *I'm* going."

Raithe ran toward the gate. "It's your reward for hitting people with rocks."

CHAPTER TWENTY-THREE

The Cave

What length will a mother go to on behalf of her child?
How long is time? What is the depth of love?
— THE BOOK OF BRIN

Tall and narrow, the cave entrance was a jagged crack on the face of the mountain. Leafy plants grew on the ledges, but no trees dared approach. The dark void gaped with all the invitation of an open mouth spreading lichen-tarnished lips that dripped damp. Suri had explored many caves. Most were down by the Bern River, cut by the water along the cliffs. None were deep, and few were occupied by anything larger than swifts or foxes. Suri liked to think that she'd delved into every crevice in the Crescent Forest, but she hadn't been in this one. Tura had forbidden it.

When Suri was a child, few things were off limits. She played in the cascades of the forest streams, swam in the flumes of the Bern, climbed to the small branches of the tallest trees and to the peaks where eagles nested. She'd broken an arm, skinned her knees, returned with bee stings, and suffered through rashes from ivy and sumac. Tura patched her up and sent her on her way for more explorations and adventures. Such injuries were trivial, but Grin's cave was another matter. Real danger lay within, making it the single most interesting place in the forest.

Tura was right about everything. She knew when the

first snows would come, that the purple salifan berries weren't good to eat, and how to ease the pain of bee stings. She knew the language of the gods, the names of the stars, and the best way to skip a stone across a lake. Out of love and respect for Tura, Suri never went to the cave. Still, she paused in her travels whenever she spotted it and wondered what was inside. After so many years of speculation, Suri had created legends.

Grin wasn't at home, of that Suri was almost certain, and she waited among the muddy bear-print artwork of the "porch" for Maeve to climb the last leg of the journey. The old woman had cast aside most of her wool wraps, going so far as to remove the ever-present white cloth from her head, which she used to wipe the sweat from her face. The locks of white were silky and long, and for a moment Suri could see a younger woman's beauty.

"How did you manage to drag the—" Suri stopped herself. "The *meat* up here?"

"Oh—I didn't." Maeve puffed hard, steadying her quivering body on the rocks and wiping her red face. "I left the food at the bottom and whistled." She dabbed at her glistening neck and smiled as a breeze blew through her hair. Again, Suri saw the girl Maeve had once been. The hair helped, but it was the smile that made the biggest difference. Judging from the wrinkles on her face, Maeve didn't often do so.

"I don't think Shayla would have hurt me, but during that winter—that long, cold winter—I wasn't certain. Hunger can drive anyone crazy. I saw it on the dahl. Reglan executed people who had stolen from the granary. He told us it was necessary to maintain order, a deterrent and an example. But those killings also saved food, allowing others to live. When hungry enough, anyone is capable of doing terrible things. And Shayla wasn't the only bear. Without enough food, none of them could sleep through the winter, and it was too dangerous to climb up here with all the ice. I left the food down below, whistled, and moved away." Maeve looked into the darkness. "I've never been inside."

"Neither have I," Suri said.

Out of habit, Suri looked for Minna and felt a twinge of sadness. They'd done everything together. This would be the biggest adventure of all, and it hurt that Minna wouldn't be with her. She was certain the wolf was just as obsessed with the cave. Suri would have to remember everything that happened so she could tell Minna afterward, probably the only way to be forgiven.

Suri led the way in.

The cave was dry. Most of the ones near the river had ceilings that dripped and pools of water near the entrance. This was dusty and stony with the ends of roots and packed dirt. She spotted fur—brown fur caught on the wall and shed on the floor. There were claw marks as well. Places Grin sharpened her weapons. Despite its impressive reputation, the cave wasn't huge. The light from outside bounced in enough that once her eyes adjusted, she could see all the way to the back. The rear of the cave was a round alcove, a cozy den where Suri pictured the bear curling up for long winter naps. To the left was a pile, and Suri stopped when she realized what it was—a pile of bones. She saw the skulls of deer, foxes, squirrels, and sheep, but she also saw the unmistakable domes of human skulls. She counted eight, but the pile was deep. Strange how Grin had the same morbid decorating habits as the chieftains of Dahl Rhen.

As expected, Grin the Brown wasn't home. Suri looked over her shoulder, thinking that Maeve might be frozen with fear, especially if she saw the bones. To the mystic's surprise, the old woman pushed past with an eager look on her flushed face.

"What do we do?" she asked. Her loud, excited voice was magnified by the rock. Hearing her own echo, she grinned.

Suri walked to the nest that was covered in fur from a shed winter's coat and said, "This is where she sleeps." Opening a pouch that hung from her belt, she scooped up a handful of salt. "Elan, Grand Mother of All, and Eton, Lord of the Sky, help us free this poor girl from the demon spirit that holds her captive."

With that, Suri carefully sprinkled salt over the nest. "Demons can't abide salt," she told Maeve. "When Grin steps into her bed, the morvyn will recoil just as you or I would jump back after stepping on hot coals. Can't help it. The spirit and the body will separate, and when that happens, you need to call to your daughter. The demon won't cross the salt, but Shayla can. Once she's in your arms, the demon will lose its control and be forced to flee."

"Will she remain a bear?" Maeve asked.

Suri thought a moment. She honestly wasn't certain. This was her first exorcism. "I'm not sure, but since the child was changed into a bear by the morvyn, there's a good chance she'll return to her natural form when it leaves." Suri pointed toward the back of the cave. "We should wait back there."

Suri spread out more salt, creating a line that the bear would have to cross to reach them. When done, the two sat down side by side, and Maeve returned the staff to Suri. She took it and smiled. The trap was set.

The wolf was gone, the door was open, and the way was clear. No one made any attempt to stop Arion as she took her first tentative steps out of the room. The old woman with the missing teeth, Padera, had come up to watch her, but she didn't say a word. Not that Arion could have understood her if she'd tried. The old woman spoke only the Rhune language, and Arion had picked up too few words to make meaningful conversation. Apparently, Padera had no instructions to stop Arion from leaving.

Arion used the wall, running her palm along the rough wood. Even after so many days, she was still dizzy.

Might not be from the injury. Could be from being in bed for so long.

The dizziness would likely pass, but she still couldn't feel the world. After so long, she began to consider the possibility that the injury had crippled her permanently. The lack of feeling, the total numbness of spirit, and her inability to sense the passage of time or the life force of existence frightened Arion. She felt exposed, helpless, and ordinary.

She thought again of Celeste, thankful she had broken things off. She couldn't face her, not like this. Much, maybe all, of what had attracted her ex-lover was the power, stature, and position Arion held within the Miralyith.

Will I still have any of that? I should have died. Better if I had. It's not like I'm still in my first millennium. I've had a good long life.

Then she realized something else. Maybe she was grasping at figments, but perhaps she could teach— continue to pass down lessons exactly as Fenelyus had hoped.

Arion gripped the banister and descended the stairs.

This was the first she'd seen of the Great Hall with its soot-stained pillars and ceiling. Ash was everywhere. Dirt and grass had been tracked in across the threshold. The floor was so stained with grime and melted wax that she imagined the dark spots to be blood. Luckily, she wasn't nauseous, or her journey might have ended there. She walked through an empty room, focusing on the light entering the double doors.

The fresh air that greeted her at the exit was wonderful and helped level the world. She wasn't sure what she'd find outside. Arion only vaguely remembered her arrival and didn't recall looking around much. She'd been focused entirely on the Galantians—a nearly fatal mistake.

How many Rhunes live here? What do Rhunes do? Is Nyphron still in the village?

Arion realized she had no idea how long she'd been in that room. Days certainly, but how long she'd been unconscious and how many days had passed after that remained mysteries. It could be autumn for all she knew. Looking outside, Arion was relieved to discover spring flowers and new grass. Unless a whole year had slipped by, she couldn't have been recovering for more than a week or two.

The morning sun was high, smoke rose from cook fires scattered everywhere, and Rhunes of all ages scurried about. Many of them looked old, and she was reminded how short their lives were. As incredible as it seemed, she'd heard none of them lived beyond a single millennium. One rumor held that they didn't even live a full century, but she couldn't believe that. *What's the point of bestowing sentience on a creature with a life span hardly longer than dew on a summer's day?*

"And then I swear, with Ferrol as my witness, that . . ." a boisterous voice said in Fhrey, only to continue in the Rhune language, which Arion couldn't understand.

Hearing the sound of Fhrey voices, Arion was relieved. Gingerly stepping out of the lodge and onto the porch, she saw her kinsmen just down the steps. The Galantians lounged around a fire, drinking from large wooden cups and speaking a mix of the two languages, drifting from one to the other as if they couldn't tell the difference. The giant began singing an unflattering song about a goblin king named Balod. He abruptly stopped after spotting her. They all looked over, then scrambled to their feet, reaching for weapons.

Arion didn't move, didn't want to provoke them. She glanced at the creature that had sent the column of fire her way. Arion had no idea what it was but knew if it cast that spell again she'd burn. She watched the thing's yellow eyes as they watched her.

Can it tell? Can it sense I'm defenseless?

Nyphron set his cup down and approached her slowly. He was wearing his sword, and this time his hand *did* rest on the pommel. The other Fhrey who had visited her room, the one with the pair of swords, leapt to his side. No one else moved or spoke. They probably were waiting for her.

"Good morning," she finally said.

Nyphron took another tentative step toward her. "You're well, then?"

She didn't dare shake her head for fear of losing balance. "Yes, I'm better."

"I appreciate you speaking to me. Thank you for that. Have you considered what I've said?" he asked.

"I have."

"And?"

Arion considered her words carefully, and in her hesitation the Galantians grew nervous. "I'm willing to take your proposal back to Fane Lothian. I'm also going to forgive the assault upon me that I'd otherwise hold you responsible for. I should mention that such an act carries a death sentence. Instead, I'll tell the fane I fell off a horse."

She could see the surprise and hope in their eyes. This was more than they had expected.

"But there is a condition," she added.

Suspicion filled their faces. At the same moment, Arion saw that a number of Rhunes had stopped what they were doing and were staring at her. She no longer had access to the Art, but she still had the power to halt people where they stood.

"I require a service from you. One of the Rhunes who cared for me, a young tattooed girl named Suri—the one who has the pet wolf—has gone into the forest to confront a bear. Do you know the one of which I speak?"

Nyphron nodded.

"Good. I want you to find this girl and return her here."

"And why would I do that?" Nyphron said.

"Because I fear she is in great danger."

"So?"

"I was charged by the fane with the task of returning you to Estramnadon, but despite what you might think, I didn't come here to fight. I came to bring you back as gently and as kindly as possible. Like many back home, I feel your tribe has been treated unfairly. So I'm willing to risk the fane's displeasure and see that your grievances are heard. That is what I'm willing to do for you, but only if you do what I ask. Her fate and your own are now bound. Should Suri die, if she is fatally injured or otherwise lost, I won't help you. Instead, I'll become your most bitter enemy. All the stories you've heard about Miralyith are true, so believe me when I say you don't want that to happen."

"You want us to save a Rhune?" Nyphron asked.

"I do."

"Why?"

"Given that Suri left several hours ago and is intent on fighting a bear that will most assuredly kill her, are you certain you want to waste time asking unnecessary questions?"

Nyphron spun. "Galantians—to arms!"

CHAPTER TWENTY-FOUR

Demons in the Forest

She is always there. I see the Great Bear every night in the star-filled sky. To most people, it is just a group of stars. But to those who lived during that terrible time, they will always represent Grin the Brown. Even though I never personally saw her, stories of that beast scared me to death.

—THE BOOK OF BRIN

The sun had set, and Persephone clung to the light of the full moon as she plunged through the wood. She had no time to think, no time to dread. The wolf was pulling her hard, and all of them struggled to keep up. They followed a path of sorts, a division through the trees that at times felt familiar. Traveling so quickly and by moonlight, Persephone wouldn't have thought it possible, but she recognized things. Before long, she was certain they were on the same trail they had followed the day the wolf pack attacked.

You were going exactly *the wrong way . . . I figured you were hunting Grin. I followed your trail, and you were heading straight for her cave.*

Persephone had shivered at the idea back then, and now she was intentionally rushing in that direction.

We don't have to fight it, she reminded herself.

If they were lucky, they wouldn't see the bear at all. The goal was to save Suri and Maeve, not slay the beast. Still, for whatever reason she felt a weight upon her. First her son, then her husband, and now it was Persephone's turn. The gods had sent the bear as a curse on her family, and she was all that remained.

Is there any chance I will survive this night?

Even with that sobering thought, she had to go. She couldn't turn her back on Suri and Maeve. And she had to keep her feet following the old oak's path. How this was going to save her people from extinction she didn't know, but she had put herself into the hands of the gods and ancient spirits. Her fate was theirs to twist.

Reglan had a child with Maeve. The thought lingered like a bad aftertaste. It hovered, unapproachable, impossible to believe—but it was the truth.

Was it a single night of passion or a lifelong love affair?

If she thought hard enough, perhaps Persephone could recall knowing glances, awkward or halted conversations, moments that seemed insignificant at the time. But Persephone didn't want to remember. In her heart, she wanted to preserve the memory of Reglan: honest, courageous, and a leader who acted in the best interests of others. He was faithful. He defended the weak. He protected the innocent. Already that image was losing color, the impression eroding as Persephone struggled through the woods, imagining an infant abandoned in the dark and a mother's cries.

I never heard a grown woman sound like that before. You'd have thought I was killing her.

She shook her head in disbelief. *What an awful judge of people I am, first Iver the Carver and now my own husband. Men I've known my whole life yet never really knew at all. How could I have missed what Reglan and Konniger were capable of?*

Minna had endless stamina, but Persephone didn't. They were moving steadily uphill, and she was soaked with sweat and desperate for a break. With all her might, she pulled on Konniger's belt to rein the wolf in. They came to a stop in a world of trees, moonlight, and fireflies.

"Water," Persephone said to Malcolm between breaths. She wiped her face with the back of her hand, which was equally sweat-covered and provided no help.

Malcolm, who had caught up with them while they

were still in the open field, had arrived with a waterskin and weapons. In addition to helping himself to a spear and Reglan's shield from the lodge, he'd fetched an extra shield and spear for Persephone—and not just any spear. Malcolm had pulled down the great Black Spear of Math, the founder of Dahl Rhen and the grandson of Gath, that had been mounted above the First Chair.

"Weren't we here before?" Malcolm asked, puffing for air and looking around at the trees.

"Thinking the same thing," Raithe replied. He carried Persephone's spear for her since she couldn't manage it and the wolf at the same time, but he had showed her how to fix the shield to her back.

Minna sat, looking anxious, and started to whimper again.

"I have to say I'm a little disappointed we haven't caught them yet," Persephone said. "I mean, how fast can that old woman walk? She's more than fifty years old. I had no idea she was so spry."

"How much farther do you think until the bear's cave?" Malcolm asked. He leaned against a tree trunk and took a swallow after Persephone had returned the waterskin.

"I have no idea, but we're going to be too late, aren't we?" Persephone was peering up through the leaves at what little of the dark sky she could see. "At least there's a full moon tonight. That will help with whatever we find up there, right?"

"What if we find the bear?" Malcolm asked. "What do we do then?"

"Well," Raithe said, "we don't want to fight it. Just need to drive it off. So don't surround the thing. Give it a clear escape route. Then jab at it and make noise. If it comes at one of us, that person should fall back and the others should advance, jabbing to drive it away. It shouldn't stay around."

"Just point and stick, right?" Malcolm said.

"Yep."

When Persephone remembered how The Brown had

slaughtered a pack of wolves and then lingered to beat
on a stone door because it smelled humans inside, she
wondered about the likelihood of the bear *not sticking
around.* The Brown preferred human flesh.

*Dammit, Konniger, why didn't you tell them? Why
did you let them go?*

Minna stood up. Instead of pulling forward, she
turned back and began to growl at noises. Behind them,
they heard snaps and rustling; then faces emerged from
the darkness.

At that moment Minna bolted. Distracted and unpre-
pared, Persephone lost her grip on the belt. The leather
strap ripped through her hands, and the wolf raced
away. Darting into the shadows, Minna vanished.

"By Mari, Persephone!" Konniger exclaimed, out of
breath. "You set a cruel pace."

"Konniger?" she said, seeing him among the men
coming at them.

"Surprised to see me?" the chieftain asked, trotting
into the clearing surrounded by Devon, Riggles, and
several of the Nadak men. Konniger's long hair, usually
tied back, was left to fly free. Persephone had known
him for years, but in the dark of the forest he looked like
someone else. Konniger held his spear, and on his arm
he wore his big wooden shield, the one with the dented
copper-boss star reinforcing the center.

"I thought you said you weren't going to help."

"He's not," Hegner said, stepping into the moonlight.
He was wrapped in his leigh mor, a spear in his left
hand. The group must have run most of the way to catch
up to them, and there was a sheen of sweat on his face.
All of them were breathing hard. Hegner shifted away
from Konniger and the others, holding his spear tightly.
"He's here to kill you."

"What?"

"Oh, Stump, this is a bad time to change sides," Konniger said, looking at Hegner with a disgusted, pitying
shake of his head.

"What's going on?" Persephone asked.

"Konniger has been telling everyone you're in league with the Fhrey," Hegner explained between deep inhalations. "He said you ordered the burning of Nadak and Dureya to create a crisis that would justify the election of a keenig and would steal power from him and the other clan chieftains."

"That's insane!"

"He's also claimed you arranged the death of your husband—ordered the men in the hunting party to kill Reglan and blame it on the bear."

"That doesn't even make sense. You were there, Hegner. You fought the bear. It took your hand!"

Hegner shook his head. "No. It didn't."

Persephone blinked. Maybe she hadn't heard right. "What?"

"Your husband fought well, Persephone." Hegner raised his stump. "But he couldn't win against all of us."

She stared at Hegner as overhead the breeze tossed the leaves about and patches of moonlight shifted.

In the hanging silence, Hegner continued, "Konniger was also the one who sent me, Sackett, and Adler to kill you. Been waiting for a second chance for you to have an *accident,* but you haven't left the dahl, and it's too risky killing you inside the walls. That's why he told you about Suri and Maeve. He hoped you would follow them so you, too, could be killed by the bear."

"What's with the moonlight confession?" Raithe asked, slowly passing Persephone her spear, which she took with unsure hands.

"Adler, Sackett, Krier, Holliman . . . they're all dead."

"So?"

"They're also the ones who helped kill Reglan." Hegner spat at Konniger. "Krier wasn't killed by no bear. Did you really think I'd believe that? It's only a matter of time until I have my own run-in with The Brown."

"So you're not as stupid as you look," Konniger said. He took a long drink, lowered the skin, and wiped his mouth. Then he shook his head. "Well, no. I take that back. Would have been smarter to just run off. You would have lived."

"I'll help you fight," Hegner told Persephone. "And when we get back to the dahl, I can testify for you and explain what happened. I'll tell everyone how Konniger betrayed Reglan. That it wasn't you who ordered his death. In return, you just need to pardon me for my role in all of this."

Help you fight. Persephone squeezed Math's spear in both hands. *We have to fight? There are so many of them. I'm going to die here, right here, right now—Raithe and Malcolm, too.*

She considered pleading. She knew most of these men, some of them since they were children. *Maybe if I explained Konniger was lying . . .* but that wouldn't work. Konniger probably promised them the best lands, the best homes, and the women of their choice. That had to be why Moya was betrothed to Hegner. She was a reward.

"So that's your grand plan, is it, Stump?" Konniger laughed. "Not a very good one." He tossed the waterskin back to Riggles then without warning lunged at Hegner with the edge of his shield.

Hegner blocked with his spear, creating a hollow thud when the haft met the board. He also created a wide opening. The chieftain of Dahl Rhen took advantage of it and thrust the stone point of his spear up under Hegner's rib cage.

Persephone watched in horror as Konniger jerked and twisted. Blood ran down the spear's shaft, soaking Hegner's leigh mor. The Stump managed to remain standing for several seconds as if his body were too confused to realize he was dead. It caught on soon enough, and he fell among the ferns. With desperate, watering eyes, he looked first at Persephone and then at Konniger. He gasped, convulsed, spit blood, and then lay still.

Konniger looked down at him. "You've always been a disappointment, Stump. But you were right about one thing. That bear was bound to kill you, too."

* * *

Suri and Maeve sat in the rear of the cave, their backs against the wall. The sun had set hours earlier, but the full moon managed to illuminate the cavern with a patch of pale light that moved from right to left.

"I want to thank you for this, Suri." Maeve sat on her knees, leaning forward, watching the entrance with wide eyes. "You can't know what this means to me. I've been cursed for so long. I believed the gods hated me, that I was being punished. I didn't care. I deserved it, but for them to punish my daughter, my little girl, who was innocent . . ."

Maeve wiped her eyes and blew her nose. "How could they do this to her? I blame myself, of course. I shouldn't have come back. I should have stayed away. Most important of all, when I found out what Konniger was planning to do, I should have grabbed a sack of food and run away to Menahan. Maybe that's what Mari wanted. Maybe it's why she cursed us, because I was a coward. I let them take my child and leave her in the forest. I'm not a coward anymore. You've given me hope for the first time in years." She reached out, took Suri's hand, and squeezed. "Thank you so much for this. I know I can die now. I know I'll be forgiven if I can just see her face again. All I want is to know she's all right, that she's free and safe."

Suri didn't feel this was the best time to mention that she hadn't cast out a morvyn before. Not that it should matter. Tura had trained her well. Her mentor had explained about good-luck charms, crimbal rings, and the effect of salt on the unnatural. Loud noises scared demons, as did metal. The knowledge about metal was neither here nor there since she didn't have any. But still, it was a good thing to know.

Tura had explained how sleeping near a spider's web could catch nightmares and that knots prevented people from finding common ground. *If you see people having an argument over nothing, look for a knot in their hair or clothes,* Tura had said. *Untie it and the disagreements will vanish.*

The old mystic had taught Suri how mistletoe bracelets helped in healing and the importance of smoothing away an impression left in a bed after sleeping. If you didn't, a witch could use it to cast a curse on you. Tura had known everything, but Suri lacked firsthand experience. As she and Maeve waited, she wondered if she might be a little overconfident.

When they had set out, Suri had been certain it would work . . . practically certain . . . mostly certain. The longer she sat, the less certain she became. Tura had trained her, but Tura also said never enter Grin's cave. Perhaps the old mystic knew that Grin was a morvyn and that Suri wasn't strong enough to fight it.

Maeve interrupted her thoughts. "I feel like such a fool for taking so long, but I'd like to offer my condolences for the passing of Tura. So much has happened in the last few weeks that, well . . . I should have said something before now. Your mother was a wise woman."

"Tura wasn't my mother."

"Oh? But I thought . . ." Maeve looked puzzled.

Suri shrugged. "Our best guess is that I was stolen out of my cradle by crimbals who wanted to take me to Nog. But something happened on the way, and either they dropped me in the forest where Tura found me or I somehow escaped. Tura thought I was a little strange, so she figured the latter was more likely."

"How horrible," Maeve said with genuine sympathy. "How old were you when Tura took you in?"

"Don't know; young, though. Tura said I was tiny. Said I was so small that she would've missed me in that pile of leaves if I hadn't been crying. Apparently, I had nearly buried myself in them. Anyway, I cried so loud she said she could hear me over the roar of the cascades. We figure maybe that was why the crimbals dropped me; I could wail like the North Wind."

"Tura . . ." Maeve narrowed her eyes. "Tura found you in a pile of leaves . . . near a cascading stream?"

Suri nodded. "She showed me the place. I used to go there and sit, sit and think. Wondering, you know? I thought maybe I'd catch one of the crimbals and they might tell me how I came to be there. They might know who my parents were and why they didn't come looking for me. But crimbals are impossible to catch, hard to see even. You only get a glimpse of them out of the corner of your eye. When I was young, I imagined the crimbals hadn't stolen me at all, that maybe they had saved me. My parents could have been monsters, or maybe they'd been killed. Maybe I was carried away for my own good. It's possible my dying mother called to Wogan for help, and he sent the crimbals. I can still picture her handing me over to their keeping. Wogan might have told them to bring me to Tura rather than Nog, knowing she would take care of me."

"And now? Now that you're older? What do you believe?"

Maeve was looking at her intently. Normally, the old woman struck Suri as flighty. She was the sort who didn't listen when a person talked, or at least she didn't look at people. At that moment, Maeve focused on Suri to the exclusion of all else, and she found the intensity of that attention disturbing.

"I recently learned that parents of unwanted children leave their babies in the forest. I hope I wasn't one of those." Suri disliked the way Maeve was peering. That sort of thing would cause a moose to charge, but she guessed the old woman didn't know any better. "I've been thinking . . . that . . . well . . . if Tura hadn't found me, I could have suffered the same fate as your daughter. I suppose that's part of why I'm here. Aside from the whole stopping-the-demon-from-killing-everyone thing, of course."

"How old are you, Suri?" Maeve asked, her voice trembling, her eyes tearing.

"Not certain about that, either. Depends on how old I was when Tura found me. Fourteen, maybe?"

Maeve reached out and took hold of Suri's hands. The old woman was shaking.

"Are you cold?" Suri asked.

Maeve pulled Suri up. "We have to get out of this cave. We have to get out, right now!"

As Maeve grabbed hold of Suri's hand and started to pull, the light changed.

The moonlight coming in the cave's mouth was blotted out, leaving them in darkness. A heartbeat later the great bear's outline was obvious and nearly filled the entire opening. It took one step inside, hesitated, and then roared. The sound was deafening.

Grin knew they were there. Knew before she entered, most likely, and Suri was certain the bear didn't like unexpected guests. The great padded paws thumped on the dirt, her nails clicking on the rock. She advanced slowly, then roared again. Maeve screamed and threw her arms around Suri, squeezing her and crying, "No!"

"Remember to call your daughter's name when Grin reaches the salt," Suri whispered. She'd already told Maeve this twice but felt it was important to remind the old woman, since her former courage seemed to have fled at the sight of the bear. Such a thing was easy to excuse. Even Suri was having second thoughts.

Grin bounded forward in a charge and stopped right on the nest—directly on the spray of salt Suri had laid down.

"Now!" Suri told her. "Do it now."

"Suri!" Maeve cried.

"No, not me! Call your daughter's name. Call for Shayla."

Grin roared and reared up. The beast's head brushed the cave's ceiling, and its body blocked the exit.

Maeve ripped Tura's staff from Suri's grasp and shouted at the mystic, "Run!" Then the old woman raised the stick high above her head. "Back! Back, you vile beast! You can't have my daughter!"

Suri was both bewildered and amazed as the old woman advanced on the bear that towered over her, rolling its head as it growled. Maeve got in one good swing. Tura's staff struck Grin on the side. Then the bear brought a forepaw around and caught the old woman. Maeve shattered like an egg struck by a hammer. Long white hair and a dress fell to the stone.

The bear rose up again and roared at Suri—the last intruder.

It didn't work. The salt failed. Maeve went crazy and forgot her daughter's name. What a disaster.

The mystic retreated as far as she could, pressing against the rear wall. No escape, no place to go, no shelter, nowhere to hide.

You're always right, Tura.

The bear sniffed at the silent, still body of Maeve, then began its charge. The lumbering force of rippling fur and muscle drove forward, propelled by rock-gouging claws. Suri held her breath, bumping the back of her head against the rear wall as she tried to flee through stone.

CHAPTER TWENTY-FIVE

Trapped

*I looked often for that famous place. I wanted to see it
for myself, to peer into the brink and test myself. I never
found it. That forest has a way of keeping secrets, the
good and the bad.*

—THE BOOK OF BRIN

"Malcolm, Persephone," Raithe called. "Like before,
with the wolves."

They both knew what he meant and put their backs
together. Persephone pulled the shield off her back and
hooked her left arm through the straps. The enarmes
were made for bigger men, and she couldn't properly
reach the leather grip, catching it with only the tips of
her fingers. In her other hand, she held the legendary
spear, which also felt too big, too heavy.

"I don't know how to fight," she whispered over her
shoulder.

"Neither do I," Malcolm admitted.

"Doesn't matter," Raithe replied. "There's too many
of them. We're going to die."

Some of the men heard, and smiled. In the moonlight,
they looked like grinning ghouls. Persephone hoped
Raithe had said it to make them overconfident, a ploy
of some sort, but they didn't look like they needed any
reassurance. The brutes were in no hurry. They took
more swigs from their waterskins, then slowly began
spreading out, circling them, putting shields on, laughing with one another as they did. Most of the faces she
didn't know, and she didn't want to. They were men

from Nadak, and madness was in their eyes, the same sort of madness she'd seen in people during the famine. The Nadak men were starving, but what they hungered for was revenge—against her, against anyone.

She looked at Devon, the son of Derick, a gifted woodsman. She'd awarded the lad first prize for his calf in the autumn fair eight years earlier. He had been about twelve then. She still remembered placing the token over his head and how he'd smiled. He hardly showed his teeth because they weren't straight and had a terrible gap, but that day he couldn't help himself. Rosy cheeks, unabashed teeth, and one arm around his cow's neck— that was how she remembered him. Devon was grinning at her again, showing the same crooked whites, but there was no happiness in his eyes—just anger.

"This is close to where the wolves attacked," Raithe said. "The waterfall is to your left, Seph. Remember?"

"Yes."

Konniger circled them, shifting until he was in front of Persephone. Hegner's blood dripped down the length of his spear.

Going for the easy kill? she thought. *Such a brave chieftain!*

"This isn't personal, Persephone," he told her. "I considered marrying you, but I already have a wife, and Tressa . . . well, you know Tressa."

Off to the southeast, they heard a bear's distant roar. The sound was chilling in the dark wood. Three times it thundered.

Konniger glanced in the direction of the sound and chuckled. "I think you're too late." Then he stopped and focused on Raithe. "Thurgin, get on his left; Devon, on his right. These other two can wait; he's the problem. Remember, he's fast. We all need to attack at the same time. Just as if he were a bear."

"Not exactly fair of you," Malcolm said, holding Reglan's shield up and clutching his spear awkwardly.

Persephone didn't know where he found the courage to speak. She was terrified. Glancing at the dead body of

Hegner, she wondered what it would feel like when Konniger pushed the sharpened stone point into her.

"Fair?" Konniger replied, and pointed to the collar around Malcolm's neck. "Being a slave, I would've thought you'd be past such stupid notions as *fair*. Would you consider it fair for the bear when the three of you surround it? That's all this is, killing a dangerous bear, a bear and her two cubs."

"Don't hesitate, Seph," Raithe said as the men spread out. Remember to *whoop* like Suri would."

She knew what he meant and also what the attempt would cost. "I won't do it."

"They want you, not us," Raithe said.

"He's right," Malcolm told her.

Konniger closed in, clutching his spear tightly. The others took their lead from him and closed the circle around Raithe.

"Now!" Raithe shouted.

His outburst made everyone flinch except Malcolm, who despite his admission of martial ignorance stabbed with what Persephone thought was a skillful thrust. Malcolm's spear tip cut the exposed shoulder of a man who screamed and dropped back. Malcolm followed this by running full tilt into Konniger, bowling him over with Reglan's big shield.

The hole was opened before her. Dropping both shield and spear, she ran. The weapons would only slow her down. Maybe if she got away, they would leave Raithe and Malcolm alone. It was a hope, anyway.

Behind her, men cried out in effort and pain. She heard the crack of wood and another scream. It might have been Raithe, possibly Malcolm, but she couldn't tell and didn't dare look back, didn't dare slow down. Following the moonlit trail, it led to the familiar hollow of fiddlehead ferns and the babbling stream. She splashed through it, praying she wouldn't slip in the muck or catch a loose rock. Water sprayed, splashing her face and blurring her sight. She made it across, found firm footing again, and ran hard.

Only a few strides beyond the stream she heard someone crash through the water. "Can't get away from *me,* bitch!" Konniger shouted.

Feet slapped the dirt just behind her.

She ran as fast as she could, but even with a shield and spear, Konniger was faster. The rapid beat of his strides closed on her. She could hear his breathing, great puffs of air. She expected to feel the tip of his spear in her back. Instead, she heard him curse and his feet slide.

Perhaps he fell.

He hadn't fallen, but Konniger had stopped. They had reached the waterfall.

Persephone completely forgot to whoop as she ran off the edge.

Trapped against the wall of the cave, Suri panicked. She couldn't think; she couldn't move. The only thing in her head was the apology running over and over, *I'm sorry, Tura. You were right.* With her brain locked up, she watched as the huge brown bear lumbered forward. She saw it in perfect detail. Grin ran at her, lunging up and down, forepaws followed by rear. Thick fur undulated. Muscles on her shoulders rolled in waves as her claws reached out and scratched grooves into the dirt floor. Her head, which appeared small for her body, was nevertheless massive with its long snout. The bear roared, displaying four fangs, two long ones on top and two smaller ones on the bottom. All four resided in a mouth wide enough to envelop Suri's entire head.

She held her breath and pressed against the stone of the cave's rear wall, wondering if the bear would claw, bite, or crush her. Grin must have decided she had no desire to slam into the rocky wall and slowed.

That was when a flash of white slammed into the bear.

"Minna!" Suri shouted in shock.

The wolf launched herself onto the hindquarters of Grin and managed to hang on with a mouthful of fur.

The bear pivoted sharply, and the wolf lost her tenuous hold. Minna flew across the cave, landed on her side with a cry, but scrambled up again. She lowered her head, raised her fur, planted her paws, and growled at the giant.

Grin roared back.

Suri came off the wall. "Run, Minna! Run!"

She knew Minna wouldn't. If the wolf had broken down the door in the lodge and busted through the front gate of the dahl to get there, Minna was definitely going to die before abandoning her.

At that moment, as the wolf hunched and snarled, Suri knew that her only friend in the world would die. What hadn't occurred to her in the prelude to her own bloody end revealed itself in her desperation to save Minna.

"How'd you do that?" Tura had asked. *The old woman stared as the firelight bathed her features, flickering and dancing with the shadows that played all around their little home.*

Suri had shrugged. "I asked the fire spirit to come; isn't that right?"

Tura had nodded, but the old woman who knew everything had looked confused, apprehensive, even frightened. She hadn't been scared of the fire. The mystic was frightened of Suri. The truth was in the old woman's eyes as they shifted back and forth between Suri and the fire.

Why?

That singular question had lingered with Suri for many years.

If Tura couldn't call the fire spirit without the use of sticks and string, what difference did that make? What was so frightening about making a campfire or lighting a lamp?

It had taken years; it had taken seeing Arion attacked by a goblin; it had taken the look of death in the eyes of Grin as she advanced on Minna, but Suri finally understood.

She focused on the bear, briskly rubbed her hands together, and spoke the words of the gods. She clapped as hard as she could. The impact of one palm slapping the other caused Suri to wince. The effect on Grin was far more dramatic.

The bear burst into flames.

The fire started at her feet, orange and yellow tongues rapidly licking their way up the bear's thick furry body. Suri heard it, a sound like the single downstroke of a giant bird's wings. She felt it, too. Air sucked from the back of the cave brushed by her as the fire took a breath, grew, and enveloped the beast in a massive plume of brilliant light and blazing heat.

Minna jerked away as Grin became a torch.

"Minna!" Suri cried. "Over here!"

The wolf darted around the flaming bear, which rolled around on the dirt floor. Minna barely cleared the distance. With most of the flames extinguished, Grin let loose a horrible wail. She jerked and raced out of the cave in desperation.

Suri caught Minna and hugged the wolf around her furry neck. "Thank you, Minna! Thank you for saving me!"

Minna pressed her weight against Suri and looked up at her with an I-am-so-glad-you-are-all-right-but-we-are-definitely-going-to-talk-about-this-later expression. The wolf wore a belt around its neck, the rest of which trailed on the ground. "Since when do you wear leather?"

Then Suri remembered Maeve.

All Raithe knew was that Persephone had gotten past the men and into the trees. He and Malcolm had given her the best chance they could. He felt good about that—surprisingly good—as if the accomplishment was the first truly worthwhile thing he'd done in his life. His father would have scowled at his stupidity, but he imagined his mother and sister would have been proud.

Having recovered from his bash with Konniger, Malcolm had miraculously returned and pressed his back against Raithe's once more. The former slave and current storyteller extraordinaire was doing well.

Raithe had picked up Persephone's dropped spear and thrown it, dropping one man. Then he severed the points off three spears with Shegon's sword and split a shield, scaring the man holding it so badly that he fell and tripped the person behind him. Two spears were thrown. One went over his and Malcolm's heads; the other glanced off his fancy shield from the Dherg rol.

Raithe howled as loudly as he could and scared the lot of them into jumping back. He counted six remaining men. And even though he and Malcolm were just two, the group of men was terrified—terrified of the God Killer and his strange friend who dressed like a god.

"Where's Konniger?" one of them called out. "Is he dead?"

The ring of men paused and regrouped. Two went in search of the spears they'd thrown, leaving only four to watch them, none of whom looked happy.

"How you doing?" Raithe asked Malcolm.

"Splendid!" the man gasped. "Is bear hunting always this much fun? If so, let's never do it again."

"They'll probably gang up on you this time."

"Lovely! Any advice?"

"Pray."

"Which god?"

"All of them."

Raithe tightened his grip on the Dherg shield and Shegon's sword, then looked around for Konniger, but he couldn't see him. "Did you kill Konniger?"

"Just knocked him down," Malcolm replied. "I think he ran away."

The men surrounding them were hesitating longer than Raithe had expected. Several were looking over their shoulders into the trees, probably wondering why Konniger had abandoned them to fight the God Killer alone.

"Giving us a good long rest," Malcolm whispered. "I like that, but is this normal?"

Off in the darkness, near where one who'd overthrown his spear had gone, someone screamed.

"Palton?" another man called out, and ran in the direction of the noise. A moment later the snapping of tree branches erupted as the same man came back—sailing through the air as if thrown. He struck a tree to Raithe's left, bounced, and fell to the ground.

The thinning circle imprisoning Raithe and Malcolm broke apart as the men lost all interest in them. One man, only a pace away from Raithe, screamed and fell. After that, the rest scattered. In the darkness of the trees around them, Raithe saw nothing. He and Malcolm waited, listening. Snapping branches were followed by screams.

"It's like the forest is eating them," Raithe whispered over his shoulder, pushing harder against Malcolm. He peered out into the moon-dappled darkness, unsure what he'd see next.

Monstrous trees with gaping mouths? Ravenous beasts?

They waited, eyes darting with every crack or snap. Within minutes the sounds faded and then vanished. Only the breeze rustling leaves remained. Even the crickets were silent.

Raithe and Malcolm remained back-to-back, holding their weapons up, waiting. Raithe could feel Malcolm breathing and felt him shifting his head left and right.

"You scared?" Malcolm whispered.

"Little bit."

"Me, too—little bit."

Without sound, ghostly figures emerged from the black. The first thing that came to Raithe's mind was ghosts—ghosts, ghouls, wraiths, or—

"I hope those weren't friends of yours, God Killer," Nyphron said.

As he approached, beams of moonlight splashed

across his features, turning Nyphron's hair silver. Raithe saw that his sword was out, the metal stained dark. At his side walked Sebek, with Tibor and Nagon gleaming in the moonlight.

"Not friends of ours, no." Although Raithe was happy not to see carnivorous pines, he wasn't certain if the Fhrey were a better alternative. Seeing them with blades drawn was as disturbing as seeing even a familiar dog with its teeth bared.

"Good." Nyphron smiled. After wiping his blade, he sheathed it. "We're in search of the little tattooed one. Do you know where she is?"

"Suri? Why? What did she do?"

Nyphron shrugged. "I have no idea, but for some reason, Arion—the one your slave friend leveled with that rock—insists that we find and protect her. Anwir tracked the girl this far. I thought she was part of this mess." He gestured at the dead man who had been thrown.

The Fhrey weren't there to kill anyone. Konniger's men had just gotten in the way. Raithe allowed himself to relax a bit, lowering sword and shield.

"We were looking for her, too," Raithe said. "We think she's in a cave up there." He pointed with Shegon's sword at the moonlit path.

Nyphron looked and nodded. "Best be moving, then."

The whole group of Fhrey shifted like a school of fish, and in an instant they were gone.

"Wait!" Raithe shouted. "Did you see Persephone?"

No answer.

"What about Konniger?"

Only silence.

Raithe and Malcolm stood alone in the trampled circle in the moonlit glade. They looked at each other, then at the bodies at their feet.

"We're alive," Malcolm mentioned in disbelief.

"What about Persephone?" Raithe began walking around, terrified he would stumble over her body.

"She got away." Malcolm pointed into the trees. "I

saw her racing into the forest. I think she's fine. If she got to the rol, she's safe."

Raithe shook his head. "She didn't go to the rol."

"What are you talking about? That's what you told her to do."

"If I've learned anything about that woman, it's that she's unlikely to do what she's told."

"You think she went after Suri?"

"That's why we came out here, isn't it?" Raithe started to follow the Fhrey.

"But what if she didn't? What if she did go to the rol?"

"Then she's safe, and we can go look for her with Suri as our guide, right?"

Malcolm looked less convinced but nodded and followed Raithe into the trees.

The water felt as cold as it had the last time.

In the dark, Persephone was worried that she wouldn't know which way to swim, but breaching the surface, she kicked toward the sound of the waterfall behind her. Swimming as fast as she could, it didn't take long to reach the edge of the pool. Just when she thought she'd made it to safety, Konniger splashed down.

The chieftain was smarter, or more determined, than Char and his pack of wolves.

She dragged herself up on the ledge. Her skirt clung to her legs and water drizzled a trail as she moved toward the crack behind the falls. Konniger was swimming toward her, and she fought against a panicked urge to run. She knew all too well the dangers of running on slippery stone.

Konniger reached the ledge.

How is he so fast?

He didn't know where he was going, yet he still closed the ground between them.

No moonlight fell behind the falls and none penetrated the inky crevice. She felt with ice-cold fingers along the smooth stone, searching. Her hands became her eyes, and with outstretched arms, she made her way down the corridor.

The door will open if you press the diamond shape in the design at the top. On the outside there's no design, just a little rock sticking out a bit. You have to feel around to find it . . .

Persephone had both hands on the left wall, sliding all over. She hammered frantically on any imperfection that stuck out.

"You in here, Persephone?" The sound of Konniger's voice nearly made her scream.

She tried to be quiet, tried to hide in the dark, but she couldn't stop breathing.

"I can hear you," he said. "I can hear your heart pounding. It is pounding, isn't it, Seph? You don't mind if I call you Seph, do you? I noticed the Dureyan called you that. Are the two of you lovers? We made up that story about you and him, but maybe we weren't wrong after all. He's dead now. So is the other one."

Where is it? Where is it?

Persephone was sliding her hands everywhere, skidding across the surface.

Where are you, you culling rock!

"There's no way out of here, is there, Seph? You might as well give up. I'll make it quick. It's not personal. Honestly, I respect you. I wasn't lying earlier in the lodge. You're sharp as an ax. That's just the problem. I knew you didn't buy the story about a bear killing Reglan. I could see you moving all your men into place. It was only a matter of time before you ordered my death. You just waited a little too long, that's all. Given a few more hours, I'd have been the one hiding in the dark, trying to get away from Raithe, Nyphron, or maybe that ugly goblin thing. If the situations were reversed, I'm sure you'd kill me quick, right? No sense dragging this out. I swear to Elan and Eton that I'll cut your throat clean and quick. I feel I owe that to Reglan, you know?"

Shivering in the dark, she could hear Konniger, feet sliding on stone as he inched in. He was so close that she heard the water dripping off his clothes. When her toe touched the end of the corridor, she felt her heart sink. She was at the end in every way a person could be.

CHAPTER TWENTY-SIX

Beneath the Falls

*That night there was more than one killer in the forest,
the next day a lot more ghosts.*

— THE BOOK OF BRIN

Maeve hadn't moved.

Suri held Minna as she looked at the rumpled pile of
cloth that had been the old woman, her white hair
sprayed out in a fan. Suri spotted the finger of a hand,
palm up, and a leg's pale skin sticking out from under
her dress. She needed to check on her but was afraid to,
afraid to let go of Minna, afraid to see what the bear
had done. In truth, Suri was just afraid. Her hands were
trembling where they clutched Minna's fur. The last time
she'd been this scared was after finding Tura facedown
in the garden. This time was worse. Suri hadn't simply
arrived home to a woman who looked as if she'd picked
a stupid place to sleep.

Suri felt safe holding Minna, or as safe as she could
feel. Nothing was as reassuring as hugging a wolf, but
she had to check on Maeve. She might still be alive, not
that it would matter. Better if she was dead. Suri couldn't
do much for her if she wasn't.

"Wait here," she told the wolf as she rose on uncertain
legs.

Suri staggered toward Maeve. Along the way, she
picked up Tura's staff, which helped. Then she knelt be-

side the old woman. All that white hair obscured her face. Reaching out, Suri brushed it back.

Maeve opened her eyes.

Suri jerked her hand back. "I thought you were dead!"

The old woman managed a smile, not just with her lips but with her eyes. Looking up at Suri, she beamed.

"I'm so sorry," Suri said. "It didn't work. I don't know why. I did it right—I know I did. Tura said I was good at such things, and I am . . . usually. I've always been able to stop the goulgans from getting in the mushrooms. My wards worked even better than hers."

Maeve struggled to raise a hand. She only got it a few inches off the ground, where it hovered, shaking. Suri reached out and took hold of it.

"It's all right. It's all right," Maeve whispered in a thread-thin voice. "It did work."

Suri didn't understand. "It did?"

Looking around the cave, she searched for Maeve's daughter. She expected to see a naked baby or maybe a young girl, but only Minna was there. Having never exorcised an evil spirit, Suri had no idea what to expect, what to look for. It was possible she'd missed the moment when Maeve's daughter freed herself. A lot was happening, after all. Maybe the fire did it. That made a lot of sense. The fire could have distracted the demon and forced the girl's soul out the way the salt should have. The fire's brightness would have made it impossible for Suri to notice the transformation.

But then where is the child?

Suri looked around the cave once more and found nothing.

"I don't see her," Suri said. "Are you sure it worked?"

Suri felt Maeve's quivering fingers squeezing hers. "I can see her. She's safe and . . . and she is beautiful . . . she is so . . ."

Maeve's fingers stopped quivering. The sight went out of her eyes, but the smile, that giant grin, remained.

* * *

Persephone could hear Konniger breathing. He was panting.

With nowhere to go, she bent her knees, lowering herself and crouching down. She cowered into a ball, trying to become as small as possible. A child's plan, and as feeble as it was, this one hope was all she had.

Maybe he'll reach out, touch the end of the crack, and think I got away. He might doubt whether I came in here at all.

She didn't even dare to pray, not out loud. In her head, she begged Mari to save her, to hide her, to—

"It's really narrow in here, isn't it? How did you find this place?"

Persephone covered her face with her hands to muffle her breathing, which was far too rapid and loud. She cursed her body for needing air. And wondered if Konniger could really hear her heart beating. To her own ears it pounded at an alarming volume.

"Did you know there was a pool down here, or did you just jump and pray? I'll bet you didn't even see the cliff. I'm impressed you didn't scream."

She heard the scrape of his feet as he pressed closer and probably could have touched him if she extended her arm.

"You don't have that spear with you, do you, Seph? No, you dropped that. Lucky for me. Otherwise this—"

Splash!

The sound came from outside.

It's Raithe!

Somehow he had managed to escape and had come for her. Only one splash meant Malcolm was injured or dead, or maybe they had split up and he had gone to save Suri. What mattered was that Raithe was there, and he was going to save her.

Konniger stopped moving.

"Thurgin? Devon?" Konniger shouted. He was right next to her, and his voice was so loud that she jerked in terror. "That you?"

It has to be Raithe! It has to be! It has to be!

Persephone wanted to cry out, wanted to scream his name, but Konniger was so close. She had to wait, had to squeeze herself into the floor, to hide, to give Raithe time.

More splashing, and it was getting closer.

"Who is it?" Konniger asked, his voice less confident. "Who's out there?"

Still no answer came.

If it's Raithe, why doesn't he say so?

She heard Konniger shift, heard him take a step away and then another. "Who are you?"

The small patch of light that marked the opening of the crack vanished as something big blocked it out.

"Who in Elan's name are you?" Konniger cried.

The answering roar shook the stone.

Raithe and Malcolm moved as fast as they could but had no hope of keeping up with the Fhrey as they darted like deer through the trees. Their speed and silence, especially in the dark, was amazing and more than a little frightening. Raithe and Malcolm were left far behind and in awe.

Maybe they aren't gods, but they have to be magical— some form of crimbal, perhaps?

By the time Raithe and Malcolm reached the cave, Maeve was dead, and the Fhrey were building a litter to carry her body back to the dahl. There wasn't a bear— living or dead—and Raithe assumed it had been driven off.

Suri was alive. The young mystic crouched on her knees beside the Keeper of Ways with Minna curled beside her.

There was no sign of Persephone.

Raithe had been certain she would come there, forgoing the rol and trying to save Maeve and Suri on her own. A bloom of panic ignited as he began to doubt he would ever see her again.

No, he thought. *I'm being foolish.*

. He tried to convince himself that she had taken his hint and run for the rol. He wanted to believe she'd locked herself inside and was safe, waiting for them to find her. But as sensible as all that seemed, it was too good to be true. Nothing in his life had ever gone completely his way, and the gods still had their eyes on him. They always wanted blood. Maeve was dead, but one old woman wouldn't be enough to sate the appetite of gods.

"Suri," he said.

The girl turned her head and looked up slowly, her eyes taking time to focus.

"Can you show me how to find that waterfall?"

"The one with the Dherg rol hidden beneath it," Malcolm added.

Suri nodded. Then glanced back at Maeve, still with her baffled expression.

"Can you do it in the dark? Can you do it now?" Raithe asked.

Suri glanced back at Maeve once more, then stood up. "Not a good idea to go there now."

"Why?" Malcolm asked.

"Grin will probably go there."

"The bear?" Raithe said so loudly that the Fhrey looked over. "Why would Grin go there?"

"She likes caves to hide in when she's scared or hurt. We've taken hers, so she'll go there. I've seen her do it before."

"Scared? Hurt? Suri, did you do something to Grin?" Malcolm asked.

She nodded. "She was going to hurt Minna; I had to do something. That waterfall and pool is the nearest source of water, and she'll want to soothe the burns. If she lives, she's going to be in a really bad mood. Best to stay away."

In his head, Raithe heard laughter. The laughter of the gods. The sound made his skin crawl. He had chosen poorly and put Persephone right in the path of the bear, which, for reasons only Suri knew, was going to be in an enraged state. What made the situation so ironic was that the gods had known all along what Raithe had only just realized—how much he cared for Persephone. She might not be able to love him, but oddly enough, that didn't matter. Some things didn't make sense, some things were merely the whim of gods—gods who had a recent and irresistible infatuation with him. In his mind, a great brown bear's image flashed, rearing over Persephone, its massive claws spread and its jaws open wide.

"Persephone is there," Raithe shouted. "You need to take us, now!"

"We'll all go," Nyphron said, surprising Raithe. "Medak, Vorath, and Eres, pack up the old Rhune, and we'll meet you at the forest's edge when we get back. Everyone else . . ." He looked at Suri. "Follow the girl."

Suri glanced one last time at Maeve and then, together with Minna, trotted toward the cave exit.

As they headed out, Raithe heard Sebek speaking to Nyphron in Fhrey. *"Did he say what I think he said?"*

Nyphron nodded. *"They've found a Dherg rol."*

Persephone smelled the harsh odor of burnt hair as Konniger stepped on her hand in his frantic retreat. She couldn't help crying out in pain.

Konniger didn't notice. His priorities had changed. Finding Persephone no longer topped his list. Even when she pushed his foot away, he didn't seem to care.

Persephone lost her fear and got to her feet, shoving Konniger back.

Another roar sounded. The sound amplified by the stone walls was heart-stopping. The bear couldn't be more than one or two arm lengths away, but Persephone couldn't see anything in the darkness. She felt Konniger grabbing at her blindly with both hands.

He doesn't have his spear.

The chieftain grabbed hold of Persephone and tried pulling her around in front of him, but the crevice was too narrow. That far back, it was just a few feet wide, and she was determined to keep Konniger between her and the bear. She wrenched free of his grip and beat him with her fists and knees. In the blackness, she connected with some part of his face, something hard and bony. She heard a squish, his mouth or maybe his nose.

Konniger groaned in pain, and Persephone kept swinging, swinging in the dark. Then she pushed out with both hands and managed to raise one foot and kick. Konniger was hit hard. He staggered backward, stumbling away. Then he screamed. At the same time, she heard what sounded like the cracking of branches.

Persephone felt the movement of air and a wetness spray her face—a cool wave followed by a hot, moist puff. Konniger continued to scream, his voice rising higher in pitch and intensity with each crack and snap.

Persephone's hands were back on the wall where the door was supposed to be. She ran her fingers across the surface, clawing in desperation.

"Where are you!" she screamed aloud at the stone.

You have to feel around to find it, and it's too high for the pack to reach.

She stretched up, sliding her palms left and right, manically waving both arms. The stone was smooth, slick, and moist. *Blood. It's splattered with blood.*

"*Help!*" Konniger cried, not sounding at all like himself, not even sounding human. The high-pitched screech was something a small animal might make and was accompanied by a deep growl that she felt as much as heard.

Persephone's hand crossed a bump she'd missed before, and she slammed her fist against it, more in a physical expression of panic than any hope of success. She was rewarded with the green light's glow, a sliver that widened with the low grind of stone on stone. She fell into the rol, hitting her knees on the hard floor. The pain streaked up her body, making her cry out again. She sucked in a harsh breath, her eyes watering.

Behind her, the bear continued killing Konniger.

No, not killing, not anymore. She heard another snap but no cry, no screech. Konniger was dead. The bear was ripping what was left of him apart.

I'm next, she thought.

Gritting her teeth and opening her eyes, Persephone pushed off the floor. She was back in the little room with the glowing green stone, square columns, and ribbed archways.

I have to close the door!

Built by the diminutive Dherg, the doorway wasn't large; she had no trouble reaching the diamond at the top of the threshold. She pressed the stone plate. It moved easily enough, and the door obediently began to close, the stone slab sliding left to right with a steady grind.

Hadn't it slammed shut before? Watching the massive stone scrape its way shut, Persephone was certain it had closed faster the last time. *Close, damn you, close!*

Illuminated by the eerie green glow spilling out of the doorway, a vision of horror emerged. The bear had the better part of Konniger in its jaws and was shaking him, spraying his blood across the walls of the crevice. The animal's fur looked strange, not like fur at all but rather charred skin. It wasn't a bear. It couldn't be. She finally saw its true form. Suri and Konniger had been right. The Brown *was* a demon.

The bear's shining eyes saw her, and with remarkable speed the beast lunged. The door was almost shut, but the bear shoved its head through the opening and caught the stone with a paw. Whatever force was driving the stone stopped.

The bear roared again as it struggled to claw its way in, back legs scratching, struggling to catch on the opening, trying to pry it wider. Persephone had no idea what force caused the door to open and close along its track, but she prayed it had the power to crush the bear, to kill it.

Whether the bear wanted in or out no longer mattered. The stone was around its throat, and the beast was caught. It pressed forward and jerked back in frustration. With one paw still hooked, its claws gripped the edge of the door. Four dark claws as long and thick as fingers dripped blood—pieces of flesh trapped under each. The bear roared in anger and with an effort pushed its paw against the door.

Persephone watched in horror as the stone slab inched back. With another grunt, the bear pushed again. The stone gave another inch, the gap growing wider. Soon the bear would be able to catch the edge of the door with its back claws and heave it wide.

Inside the room and to the right of the door lay Raithe's old shield. The same one she'd used when fighting the wolves. Persephone picked it up and, just as before, used both hands to thrust the bottom edge at The Brown's snout. The animal wailed and growled. She hit the beast again and again, as hard as she could. The bear's face turned bloody.

The Brown jerked backward. In a panic to escape the blows, the bear withdrew the paw that had clutched the edge of the door. With its removal, the stone slab resumed its left-to-right march, closing once again. The gap remained too small for the bear to pull its head out. Trapped, The Brown twisted and jerked violently, but the door continued to close, pinching around its neck. Again Persephone bashed at the animal's face in the vain hope of somehow forcing it out. The bear wailed in desperation, fear, and anger.

As the door slid the bear's roar became a whimper.

Tighter and tighter the stone inched, squeezing the animal's throat. The Brown jerked harshly, still struggling to wrench its head free. Then the animal succumbed to panic. Ignoring all pain, it bucked and twitched, shrieking in such terror that Persephone took a step back.

Slowly, very slowly, the bear lost its strength. Persephone watched its face, its bloodied nostrils and eyes, as The Brown grew silent and still. Persephone continued to stand before it, holding the shield and rocking with the pounding of her heart.

After several minutes with no movement from the bear's head, she finally allowed herself to sit down. She sat right before the door, in front of the massive head of the bear, whose eyes remained open. Two small black globes like polished pebbles reflected the green light. Persephone felt her breathing hitch. She still held tight to the shield, and wrapping her arms around it, she began to cry.

At first, the tears came from the aftermath of fear— the sort of mortal terror she hadn't known before— which left her exhausted and stripped of dignity and pride. Yet that was only the beginning. In her weakened, exposed state, the dam burst. She relived the deaths of Mahn and Reglan, followed by her two younger children. She thought about Aria and her mangled son, Gifford, who somehow had survived against all odds. She imagined the deaths of Raithe and Malcolm, Maeve and Suri. She cried for all of them and for the innocents of Nadak and Dureya. Crouching on the floor in the eerie green light, she wept until she had no more tears. Then she lay down with her cheek against the stone. Closing her eyes, she tried to remember how to breathe, how to think, and how to live. Somewhere in that process, exhaustion overtook her, and she fell asleep.

They found her in the rol covered in blood, holding Raithe's old shield.

The dead bear was in the door, Konniger's remains just outside. They identified him by the copper boss of the shield floating in the pool. Konniger's spear was there, too, lost in the fall. He hadn't expected to fight a bear.

Raithe was the first one into the rol, with Malcolm, Suri, and Nyphron close behind.

He stood over Persephone, feeling his strength run out. He knew they would be too late the moment Suri told them about the bear's intentions. Dureyans weren't used to happy endings. That was one of the reasons he'd always enjoyed his sister's tales. They gave him hope— but they were just stories; reality always turned out differently. He stood over Persephone's crumpled body, vainly clutching the shield he'd left, and found himself wishing that *he'd* been her Shield. That he could have been there even if it meant dying alongside her.

Strange how I never appreciate anything until after it's gone: my family, my father, Dureya . . . her.

Slowly, gently, he bent down. "I'm sorry I wasn't here," he said, and kissed her on the forehead, surprised at how warm she still felt. Usually, the—

She woke with a jerk and pulled back, disoriented and frightened, until she saw them.

"Raithe?" Persephone said groggily.

Raithe sucked in a sharp, stunned breath. "Are you— are you all right?" he asked, shocked. An immense and uncontrollable grin stretched across his face.

Persephone hesitated and looked out at the bear still lying in the open doorway. Slowly she nodded. "Yes . . . yes, I think so. And you're all right, too." Her eyes brightened, then she hugged him. Arms tight around his neck, she squeezed, but only briefly. "Konniger said— but I guess he lied." Spotting Suri, she pulled back and exclaimed, "You're alive!"

"You have black hair," the mystic replied, then looked at the dead bear. "But I'm not in the mood for games just now."

"I wasn't playing. I—" Persephone stopped and looked around the rol. "What about Maeve? Where is she?"

Faces darkened, Suri's most of all. "Maeve died . . . Grin . . ." Suri continued to stare at the body of the bear lying outside the open door. "I don't think Grin was a demon; she was just a bear. Maeve fought The Brown— fought the bear for *me*, I think."

"Maeve fought The Brown?" Persephone asked, stunned.

"With Tura's staff." Suri held up the stick. "She was fierce." Suri petted the wolf. "So was Minna."

"How long have you known of this place?" Nyphron asked as the other Galantians filed into the rol and walked around the stone pillars, looking at the walls in fascination.

"We just learned of it," Persephone said. "Suri showed us."

The Galantian leader turned to eye the mystic. "The tattooed one?" he asked.

"Is this it?" Sebek asked him, pointing at the runes that circled the walls.

"Stryker," Nyphron called, and the goblin entered from where he had waited in the crevice. "*Vok on hess?*" Nyphron asked, in an unpleasant language that sounded as if he were coughing up something to spit.

Stryker drew back his hood, revealing a monstrous face and head. He gazed up at the writing. The creature, which was how Raithe thought of Stryker for he was too repulsive to be thought of as a person, shambled slowly around the room. The goblin raised a hand at the runes and pointed with its claws.

"*Et om ha,*" the goblin replied to Nyphron, and nodded. The Fhrey smiled.

Raithe extended his hand to Persephone. "It's nearly morning. I think it's time we took you home."

CHAPTER TWENTY-SEVEN

When Gods Collide

*I could not move, not my arms, my legs, or even my
head. I was forced to watch, and I was not even allowed
to scream.*

—THE BOOK OF BRIN

They exited the forest in a solemn procession by the first
light of dawn. Persephone, Raithe, Malcolm, and Suri
followed behind the Fhrey, who carried the shattered
bones of Maeve.

Hours before, Persephone had found the Black Spear
of Math right where she'd dropped it, within sight of the
glade battlefield. The weapon lay among the men's bodies. She was grateful Raithe and Malcolm were safe but
couldn't find any cheer in her heart for the victory. Many
of the dead had lived in Rhen all their lives. She knew
their parents, families, and friends, and not even her
own safety could lighten that weight.

Persephone's feet and skirt were soaked with morning
dew as she struggled to march through the tall grass. An
overwhelming exhaustion extended beyond muscle and
bone, even beyond the aftermath of the battle with a
giant bear. She felt empty, truly empty, to the point of
being erased. With the death of Konniger and the bear, a
portion of her life had reached a conclusion. Her memory of Reglan remained mortally wounded. Discovering
that he'd had a child with Maeve was a shock, but his
order to kill a baby and hide the affair for years was
beyond her ability to forgive. Persephone had drawn

strength from Reglan when he was alive and from his memory after his death. That morning she could no longer lean on him, and she wasn't certain where she found the strength to keep walking.

Suri matched her in expression as she stared out at the rising sun. She held something tightly in her hand and repeatedly looked at it with increasing concern.

"What's that you've got?" Persephone asked.

"A bone," Suri said.

A month ago such a reply might have surprised Persephone, but that morning Suri could have admitted to holding the beating heart of the Tetlin Witch and Persephone wouldn't have blinked.

"Grin was coming to kill everyone."

"That's why you went after the bear? Because you thought it was coming to attack the dahl?"

Suri nodded. "The bone told me Grin would attack this morning."

"Looks like Magda was right. We did what she said, and Grin has been killed."

Suri didn't look convinced.

"What?"

"The signs I saw indicated something that—something bigger. Grin was a bear with a hunger for human flesh but still just a bear."

"Maybe you just read them wrong. Saw more danger than there really was."

"What do you think, Minna?" Suri asked the wolf.

The wolf panted alongside her with saliva dripping off her tongue.

"Minna is not so sure," Suri said. "And Minna is a very smart wolf, maybe the wisest in the world."

The light rising from behind the jagged teeth of the forest turned the sky purple and orange and shone on the walls of Dahl Rhen. Persephone made out the banners flapping above the lodge roof. She slowed, then stopped altogether. She glanced at Suri, and her eyes narrowed.

What if Suri didn't read the signs wrong? What if the wolf is right?

"What's wrong?" Raithe asked after noticing she was several steps behind the rest.

"No horn," she replied.

"Is that unusual?" Malcolm asked. "It's just us, after all, and it's early."

"No men on the ramparts, either."

Circling, they found the gate open, both doors flung wide—too wide. Usually only Delwin and Gelston left early, and they had a habit of opening only the left side because the doors were heavy and the right one always stuck. Also, the gate doors had been thrown inward rather than pushed out. No one pulled the massive doors open from the inside; they were easier to push.

Nerves and exhaustion, that's all it is, she assured herself. *It would be strange if I didn't have a sense of dread creeping with me after what I've been through.*

Still, she couldn't shake the fear. She imagined walking through the roundhouses and finding everyone slain, just as she had found Konniger's men lying among the trees. What she actually saw when she stepped through the open gate was far less macabre, but far more disturbing.

Everyone on the dahl was awake and standing in perfect rows in front of the lodge, facing the gates. Persephone was startled at the size of the crowd. Even on meeting nights, when everyone was supposed to show up, not everyone did. The sick and injured didn't come, and there were always sick and injured. Usually, those caring for them stayed home, too. A dahl the size of Rhen required a lot of food, and there was always a hunting party or two that would be out, sometimes for weeks. And then there were those who didn't want to come. Padera had stopped bothering to show up years ago.

More disturbing than the number of people assembled

was the way in which they were grouped. Sarah was nowhere near Delwin or Brin. Roan was in the front row even though Gifford was in the back, and Moya was shoulder-to-shoulder with Tressa.

"Something is *very* wrong," Persephone whispered.

"Sarah? Moya?" Persephone called out. "What's going on? Why are you all out here?"

No one moved or spoke, and there wasn't a smile among them. But in their eyes Persephone saw screams. Raithe pointed toward the storage pit at a remarkable sight: two tethered horses.

The Fhrey laid Maeve on the grass. Nyphron drew his sword from its scabbard, and it made a gentle hiss against the metal sheath. The giant pulled free his massive sword. Sebek pulled both of his blades, and Tekchin drew forth a thin, delicate blade. Malcolm held his spear at the ready. Beside Persephone, Raithe put a hand on his sword but didn't draw it. Minna let out a low guttural growl, and Suri bent over to pat her neck.

They moved forward as a group but had taken only a few steps when a tall Fhrey, as hairless as Arion, emerged from the lodge and stopped them with his stare. Numerous rings pierced the skin of his ears, cheeks, and nose, and chains hung between them. On his hands, the fingernails were so long that they curled around themselves in yellowed swirls. His chest was bare, and he wore a skirt of gold. A mantle, also gold, draped across his shoulders and flowed to the ground. Beside him came a smaller, younger Fhrey wearing a shimmering robe of purple and white, the hood of the garment raised.

"*Nyphron, son of Zephyron.*" The god of chains spoke in Fhrey, and his voice boomed with unnatural volume. "*We've been waiting for you.*"

Surely that *is a god,* Persephone thought. Not a kind or benevolent one but the embodiment of great and terrifying power. His face lacked even a single hint of compassion.

Beside the god the younger Fhrey shifted his weight and fidgeted with nervous excitement like a boy on his first hunt. Behind them, eight more Fhrey strode through the lodge doorway. They carried swords and wore armor similar to that of the Galantians, but they had helms shaped like the heads of lions. They took up positions on either side of the younger Fhrey and stood in stiff lines, not dissimilar to the way everyone else was standing.

The god of chains walked forward, descending the steps of the lodge and moving through the ranks of villagers, who shifted in perfect unison to allow his passage. The other Fhrey remained on the elevated porch, watching.

"Gryndal, you cuckold cur and craven whore's son," Nyphron replied in Rhunic.

Persephone held her breath, her eyes wide, but the god of chains merely stared at Nyphron with suspicion.

"*It's a common Rhune welcome,*" Nyphron said, this time in Fhrey.

"*I'm certain.*" Gryndal advanced until he stood in the exact center of the dahl, with the villagers behind him and the Galantians in front. "*You know why I'm here.*"

"*Of course. You've finally found wisdom and decided to join the Instarya. Unfortunately, we don't—*"

Nyphron collapsed to his knees, fell forward, and gasped for air.

"*I'm not Petragar,*" Gryndal said, baring his teeth. "*And I'm not Arion. I won't be toyed with. I have full authority to act as the fane in these forsaken lands. You know what that means. All of you stand guilty of rebellion, rebellion against your fane, against your god, and against nature.*"

Gryndal walked around Nyphron, and as he did, Persephone felt a jolt, as if an invisible giant had grabbed hold of her neck and wrists and shoved her back a step. The unexpected lurch knocked Math's spear from her hand. The weapon fell to the grass, and she was unable to retrieve it. The unseen giant hands held her so tightly that she couldn't move. She couldn't speak and could barely breathe.

"*Fenelyus is dead. She, who ushered in the new order, was an anchor. It's time for the Miralyith to assume their proper place as gods and for ordinary Fhrey to realize they're just one more race that crawls upon the world.*" Gryndal bent slightly to look at Nyphron, who remained on his hands and knees, his face clenched in pain.

Stryker made a noise—something no one else had managed. The goblin also succeeded in sluggishly raising his clawed hands. This caught the god's attention.

"*You have a ghazel, I see. An oberdaza—an abomination. The Art is not for the likes of them.*"

Gryndal made a slight motion with his fingers, and the goblin flew backward. The sounds the goblin made weren't the cry of a man but the high-pitched shriek of an animal, not unlike the noises Konniger had made. But the goblin's screams didn't last as long; after some snapping he became still and silent.

Gryndal looked toward the young Fhrey standing on the lodge's porch. "*Have you met the prince, Nyphron? This is Mawyndulë, son of Lothian, come to see how gods conduct themselves—to witness justice. I'm his teacher, and you are today's lesson. The fane has granted me the power of execution to deal with the trouble you've caused. You have displeased us, and for that I'll take your life just as I crushed it out of your ghazel. But let it not be said that I'm an ungenerous god. Your life is over, but I'll allow the Galantians to live if they repent for their crimes—if they bow and worship as is proper.*"

He pointed to the gathered villagers. "*As your god, I demand a sacrifice. Demonstrate your remorse. The Rhunes are a plague upon the face of Elan, and you have wallowed with them for far too long. Destroy them. Cut them down as evidence that you are still worthy to be called Fhrey. In return, I'll grant you permission to live. Sacrifice their lives to your new gods, to the Miralyith, and I'll forgive your weaknesses. What is your answer?*"

"We don't take orders from a *culina brideeth*!" Sebek said.

Persephone didn't understand either word, but Gryndal certainly did. His eyes widened, and his lips drew back, revealing white teeth. Just then, the prince stepped forward, a puzzled look on his face. *"You care more for Rhune animals than your own people? Your own friends?"*

Nyphron looked up at the prince, helpless.

"Gryndal, let him speak," Mawyndulë requested.

"As you wish," the god of chains said, and the strain on Nyphron's face lessened.

"It is not that I care so much for the Rhunes," Nyphron said. *"But more that I hate you—you, your father, all the Miralyith, and, most of all, this miserable excuse for—"* Nyphron grunted in pain, his words choked off.

"Hate?" the prince asked incredulously. He uncovered his head, revealing that he, too, was as bald as Arion and the god of chains. He took a step forward as if to present himself more clearly, as if it was possible that Nyphron didn't recognize him. *"How can you hate me? I'm your prince."*

Gryndal twitched a finger, and Nyphron could speak again, though his voice was strained. *"You're not my prince. You're a worthless Miralyith."*

"Worthless?" The prince looked stunned. *"The Miralyith are your betters. I should think at a moment such as this you'd be painfully aware of that fact. How can you deny it?"*

"Because power doesn't equal worth," Arion said. She stepped through the lodge door, walking slowly and favoring her left side. *"Wisdom, the sort that your grandmother Fenelyus employed, is a far greater virtue."* She turned to Gryndal. *"I told you that I had agreed to take Nyphron's proposal to Fane Lothian. This madness can end in a sensible conclusion that doesn't require rivers of blood."*

"Acting as fane, I've heard and rejected that proposal," Gryndal replied.

"You can't." Arion descended the porch steps with some effort and approached the god of chains.

Gryndal fixed her with a withering stare. *"I'm empowered by Fane Lothian to do as I see fit."*

"As a member of the Miralyith, I demand that the fane personally hear what I have to say."

"As a member of the Miralyith?" Gryndal sneered. *"Not anymore. As you explained, your wound has ejected you from our order."*

"A Miralyith is not defined solely by the Art."

"Of course we are."

Arion faced him in the center of the dahl, in the open lawn beside the common well where the Galantians had camped, where the ladies of the dahl had led a well raid, and where Persephone had married Reglan. Now two godlike beings in shimmering clothes stood on that same grass, glaring at each other like a pair of contentious thunderclouds, and Persephone felt the same unease as if a storm were rising.

"The fane needs to know what I've discovered about the Rhune girl. About Suri. I won't let you kill them," Arion said in a low voice.

Gryndal laughed. *"How will you stop me?"* He faced the porch and looked to Mawyndulë. *"Power does equal worth. You are seeing the proof of that today. Fenelyus appointed Arion as your teacher because of her wisdom—I have to assume. Shall we see how well she fares against me?"*

He offered Arion a chilling smile. *"Go back to your bed, Arion. I'll grant leniency because I suspect that blow to your head has relieved you of your better sense, and because I'm certain the prince still harbors some misplaced appreciation of you."*

"But I told you, Suri is—"

"Quiet!" Gryndal shouted, and turned his attention back to the Galantians. *"Your leader is going to die. You can't save him, so save yourselves. I won't ask again. Destroy the villagers, or—"*

"Take off bandages."

As Suri took a step forward, everyone who could do so turned to look at the young mystic.

"Said it would come back," Suri said to Arion. *"Take off bandages."*

"How are you speaking?" Gryndal asked.

"With my mouth," she said. *"Does everyone play that game?"*

"I've silenced you."

Suri offered only a shrug. She looked back at Arion. *"The boar was only a bear, but . . ."* She pointed at Gryndal. *"His name is Grin—dal, yes?"*

Arion's eye's widened. *"Yes!"*

Suri nodded. *"The last part of the name was burned. Take off bandages I made for you, and it come back."*

"You sure?" Arion asked.

"Pretty sure."

"It's a Rhune. It can't be speaking," Gryndal insisted, continuing to stare at Suri in shock.

"That's Suri," Arion explained. *"The one you said couldn't exist—remember?"*

She began unwrapping the bandages from her head. A week's worth of fuzz and a horrible discolored bruise emerged.

Once the cloth was off, Arion's eyes went wide. She sucked in a startled breath and staggered back a step. The bandages fell from her hand, revealing a series of runes drawn on the underside, the same Dherg markings from the walls of the rol.

Gryndal scowled at Suri. *"Abomination! Worse than the goblin. A Rhune with the Art!"* He raised his hands toward her, but Arion raised hers as well. A warm wind blew past Persephone, billowing her hair.

Gryndal spun and glared at Arion.

"I'm feeling better," she said. *"And I won't let you hurt them, any of them."*

With those words, Persephone felt the pressure leave her throat, and she could move again. Nyphron got to his feet, and the villagers staggered. Mothers rushed to their children and husbands embraced and shielded their families. Some scurried off to their homes, but the vast majority stayed, eyes fixed to the center of the dahl where Gryndal and Arion faced off.

"*Suri has the Art,*" Arion declared. "*The Rhunes aren't animals, aren't worthless in the eyes of Ferrol. This changes everything.*"

"*It changes nothing!*" Gryndal said. "*Except to reveal that the Rhunes are a greater threat than previously realized.*" He turned and looked at Mawyndulë. "*Leave, my prince, and be quick. It is time I erased the Rhune menace. You would be wise to leave as well, Arion. I'm done playing games.*"

The ground began to tremble.

Persephone felt the vibration in her legs. Near the well, a rake fell. Along the side of the lodge, two splits fell off the woodpile. Dirt shook out from between the logs of the walls. Sheep bolted in panic. Minna retreated behind Suri, and overhead the clear sky grew dark with violently expanding clouds.

"Here it comes," Nyphron said, trying to steady himself. "I hate this part."

Arion clapped her hands. The ground stopped shaking. The sky cleared.

Gryndal glared at her again. He looked to the prince. "*Do you see that she is interfering with the fane's orders?*"

"*The fane doesn't have all the facts,*" Arion said. "*The fane's orders are outdated.*"

"*I want you to witness that she is defying your father's edict. Do you understand?*" he said directly to the boy.

Mawyndulë nodded.

"*It's important you do, because I must exercise the power granted to me by your father and not just with Nyphron, but Arion as well. This problem is too big, too deep for half measures. I was ordered to bring the thunder, and by the power vested in me, I shall!*"

"*Gryndal, don't!*" Arion shouted.

Gryndal said a single word and clapped his hands.

Arion grunted and cringed, glaring at Gryndal with a stiff, strained expression as if in great pain or suffering from heavy exertion. Then she folded her hands together and muttered softly. When she opened her hands, a gust of wind blew Gryndal onto his back.

"*Seriously, Gryndal?*" she asked with an incredulous look. "*I'm not one of your arena opponents, and I'm not a goblin witch doctor.*"

In an ominous jingle of rings and chains, Gryndal got to his feet. "*You're right. You're Cenzlyor, aren't you? Let's put that to the test, shall we?*"

"*Let's not. What you're doing is crazy,*" Arion said.

"*You shouldn't have interfered,*" Gryndal told her. "*It shows a lack of intelligence, a lack of foresight. Lothian granted me the Blessing of Ferrol. I'll kill you without consequence, but you can't attempt the same. Besides, on your best day I've always had more power, more skill—and Arion, this isn't your best day.*"

Gryndal whirled his arms as if opening invisible curtains and then made hooking gestures with all of his fingers, causing his nails to whip. A whirlwind curled around Arion, wrapping the asica around her and lifting her into the air. Arion was only a few feet off the ground when she shouted words Persephone didn't understand. The winds died, and Arion fell, collapsing to her knees. Even Persephone could tell the tornado had been a distraction: Before Arion hit the ground Gryndal had begun singing an incomprehensible tune and working an intricate pattern with his hands. As he did, the air above the dahl changed, losing transparency. Through it, the light of the sun narrowed and was aimed directly at Arion. Seeing it, she made her own gestures, rotating her hands as if winding a rope. Gryndal threw his arm forward as if throwing a ball, and a brilliant beam of blazing white light came from the sun and fired through the distortion.

Whatever Arion was doing, she completed it none too soon and deflected the blinding flash with her hands. The white-hot beam of light ricocheted off her palms, ripping across the ground between them. It left a scorched line as Arion struggled to redirect the light at

Gryndal. When the light got close, Gryndal dropped his arms and stopped singing, and the light vanished.

The two glared at each other across the zigzagging line of burnt grass. Nothing moved within the walls of the dahl. The remaining villagers watched with wide eyes and gaping mouths. No force held Persephone any longer, but she didn't dare move. Like everyone else, she held her breath in the face of powers beyond her comprehension.

Arion was breathing hard, perhaps hoping Gryndal might yield. He didn't. With a shout and a full-body spin that flared his golden mantle, he raised his palms to the sky, and with them rose the Killians' roundhouse. The whole building ascended: logs, daub, and thatch roof. A number of people scattered as the Killians' home hurtled skyward. Then, just as expected, it fell. Aimed at Arion, the house plummeted, and as it did, Gryndal clapped his hands and set the whole thing on fire.

With a punch to the air, Arion split the house in half. The divided dwelling crashed to the ground on either side of her. Both halves burst on impact, sending sparks and flaming debris in all directions.

Few things were more dangerous to a dahl than fire, and despite the obvious perils, Persephone finally found a purpose. "Bring gourds to the well!" she shouted, and ran forward as an unnatural wind blew, spreading the fire to Sarah and Delwin's home as well as Autumn and Fig's.

Tope Highland was ahead of her. Grabbing a jug already filled with water, he ran toward Sarah's roundhouse.

"No!" Arion shouted in Rhunic, but it was too late. Tope threw the jug's contents on the nearest flames, but the water never reached them. Instead, the spray of droplets froze into a hundred shards as sharp as daggers and flew toward Arion.

The flames Persephone had hoped to extinguish were snuffed out as Arion stole the heat and used it in a single bright burst that turned the ice into steam, leaving a hazy mist in its wake.

With growing anger, Gryndal darkened the sky. A swirling storm churned overhead, the likes of which Persephone had never seen. Morning turned to twilight as black sooty clouds boiled and spun. Arion moved her fingers feverishly but to no avail; instead, she staggered and cursed.

Soon lightning flashed behind the blanket of clouds. Pops of blue-white fingers flickered. Persephone felt her scalp tingle as one twisted bolt crashed to the ground right before her. Blinded, she staggered backward and fell with an undignified scream that went unheard amid the chorus of cries that erupted as bolt after bolt of lightning rained down.

Persephone cowered on the grass in terror as the world around her ripped apart in a nightmare of blinding flashes and sizzling cracks. She clutched at the grass and felt cloth strips beneath her fingers—Arion's bandages.

Piercing the roar of thunder, Arion sang a calming song. The lightning lessened and the thunder ceased. The clouds broke, letting sunlight beam through. In the aftermath, more fires burned and scorch marks blackened the area directly around Arion, who remained standing within a smoking circle.

"*Gryndal, you—*" Arion started to say, but the ring-adorned god stomped the ground and threw out his arms.

Persephone saw a worrisome puzzled look on Arion's face. A moment later, the ground beneath her began to bubble. Dirt turned to mud, and mud to tar, into which Arion sank. She started to speak and raised her hands, but Gryndal struck her with a stunning blow of wind that slammed her to the ground, where the bubbling tar gripped and dragged her down.

"No!" Suri cried.

Persephone watched as the young mystic focused on Gryndal and rubbed her hands together. Then she clapped. To Persephone's, and certainly the god's, amazement, Gryndal burst into flame.

Being close enough to feel the heat, Persephone retreated from the burning god. She'd taken only three strides when Gryndal put out the fire, but Suri had caught him off guard. When the flames were snuffed out, his cape and skirt were both blackened and his skin reddened.

With a horrific cry, Gryndal searched for Suri and spotted her where she had always been, just inside the wall between the gate and the storage pit. He raised his hands and began intoning a savage incantation. A blur of white streaked past Persephone as Minna launched herself at the god. Claws ripped at rings, and teeth at chains. Gryndal screamed in pain as several piercings were torn out.

He uttered a desperate syllable, and the wolf flew through the air. Minna yelped when she hit the grass.

"Halgavri!" Gryndal shouted, and shoved a palm toward the animal.

"Minna!" Suri cried as an unseen force tore up the sod, creating a deep furrow as it raced toward the stunned animal.

Raithe dove, catching Minna in his arms as he did. Together they rolled aside as the tearing force carried past, blowing open a hole through the dahl's wall that was large enough to put a road through. Logs, dirt, and grass exploded outward and down the side of the hill, leaving a cloud of dust and a new view of the forest.

"Kill them all!" Gryndal ordered his soldiers as he winced in pain and gingerly touched the wounds on his face and chest.

The Fhrey in the lion helms drew their weapons and climbed down from the porch.

"To arms!" Nyphron ordered, and the Galantians drew their weapons and fanned out to block the approaching lion-helmed soldiers.

Metal clashed as the opposing Fhrey turned the center of the dahl into a battlefield.

Still near the well, Nyphron blocked swings but didn't return blows. Sebek, the one with the twin swords, was less considerate. He gleefully disarmed his opponent, threw him to the grass, and then stepped on his knee, popping it. Grygor just picked up one of the Fhrey warriors and tossed him across the yard.

"Move!" Raithe ordered, grabbing Persephone's arm and pulling her back toward the gate where Suri had reunited with Minna. As they ran, the ground began to shake.

Persephone looked at Gryndal, expecting some new horror, but the god of considerably fewer chains was still focused on his wounds and appeared to be working at healing himself.

One of the braziers near the well toppled, all across the dahl thatch shook free of roofs, and the entire woodpile beside the lodge collapsed. Everyone staggered, several fell, and the fight between the opposing Fhrey paused. Both sides drew back in confusion. Everyone looked at Gryndal, but he appeared to be just as puzzled. The mystery was short-lived as the bubbling pool of tar erupted in a geyser of water. The force was enough to knock them all off their feet and spray the dahl with a fine mist of scalding water and hot mud.

When the mist cleared, Persephone saw Arion rising out of the hole, pushing to her feet. She was coughing, mud-covered, and slow to stand, but she managed it. Panting for air, she faced Gryndal once again.

Raithe had dragged Persephone to the gate and wasn't stopping. She realized he intended to get her out of there, and as wise as that was, she couldn't leave. Persephone hauled back on her arm and broke free of his grip.

"We have to fight!" she told him.

"How? With what?" he asked, shocked.

She didn't have an answer. She didn't even have Math's spear anymore. All she held was Arion's old bandages. She averted her eyes, unable to face his pleading expression when she had no reasonable answer. All she had was stubbornness and an overwhelming sense of obligation. She couldn't abandon her family. She would rather die with them than—

As she unconsciously wrung the bandages, charcoal rubbed off in her hands. Realization struck and she shot a look to Raithe and the Dherg shield he carried. "Oh, blessed Mari!"

An instant later her head filled with an incredible pain as a ringing erupted in her ears. Everyone on the dahl with the exception of Arion, whose fingers were intensely working patterns in the air, threw hands to their heads. Several, including Gryndal, fell to their knees. Where he sprawled, the grass grew at an astounding rate, grasping his wrists and fingers. The vegetation where he'd been standing attacked the ringed god with a fury, wrapping his legs and climbing along his body to enclose his face. Stronger, longer roots reached out of the soil and looped around the thrashing god, pinning him with a hundred tiny straps.

The ringing faded.

Persephone took the moment to speak to Raithe, and Nyphron whispered something to Grygor. The giant drew his massive sword and charged the Miralyith's prone form.

"*No!*" Arion shouted.

Taking her eyes off Gryndal, she cast a spell that knocked the giant off his feet and the sword from his hand. That was all it took. The grass appeared to have second thoughts about holding the ringed god any longer, and two fingers on Gryndal's left hand moved. Arion was thrown hard on her back, knocking the wind from her. The grass around Gryndal shriveled and died. He tore himself free just as Grygor retrieved his sword and started his swing. Then the giant simply stopped. He froze with the great blade partway through a horizontal swing aimed for Gryndal's neck.

Arion gasped for air but still managed to move her fingers. As she did, the giant was enclosed in what looked to be a soap bubble. Now it was her turn to suffer the imprisonment of grass as hundreds of blades began clutching at her fingers and ankles, wrapping around her head and across her mouth. Gryndal turned to face the giant, taking particular interest in the sword and how close it had come. *"You dare challenge me, Grenmorian?"*

Gryndal made a quick motion with his fingers. A burst of light ignited in a flash all around Grygor, but the attack broke harmlessly against the bubble.

"Medak! No!" Nyphron shouted as another Galantian, the small one with the knives, threw one and then chased it with another.

Both blades disappeared with a hiss and a cloud of vapor. Gryndal squeezed a fist, and Medak screamed until his head caved in.

Gryndal frowned at the Fhrey with a furious glare. He glanced back at the giant, but he was still protected by the bubble. Blood dripped down Gryndal's chest where rings had been torn out, and his skin was red and blotchy from the fire. With Arion trapped, no one else moved, and the dahl grew frighteningly quiet.

"Blasphemers!" Gryndal shouted in a voice so venomous that even his soldiers took a step back. *"How dare you challenge me! Me!"* Lightning flared once more overhead. *"And you,"* he said to the dead body of Medak. *"What a fool. The giant I can understand. He isn't a Fhrey. But you, you couldn't kill me without forfeiting your soul."*

"I can," Raithe said in Fhrey as he walked forward, making a point to step between Gryndal and Suri, who sat with Minna on the gravel path. His words were neither loud nor boastful. They were casual to the point of absurdity, as if he were challenging a drunk to an arm-wrestling match. He drew Shegon's sword and held it loosely in one hand, the little Dherg shield in the other, as he closed the distance between them. *"I am the God Killer."*

"So you're the one!" Gryndal laughed. *"You aren't a*

killer of gods, little Rhune. You only murdered a Fhrey. The Fhrey aren't gods—but I am."

"*Good,*" Raithe replied. "*Then this time when I kill you there won't be any confusion.*"

Gryndal smiled. "*Goodbye, would-be God Killer.*"

Gryndal raised one finger to hail the lightning. At the same time, Raithe raised the little shield, and Persephone prayed she was right. A jagged bolt flashed down from the overhead clouds and struck the shield in Raithe's hand. The jagged finger of blue-white light bounced back at Gryndal. The rest was lost to the blinding flash and the thunderous crack that followed. When Persephone could see again, Raithe was still standing. Across from him, Gryndal was on his knees, smoking.

Without pause or hesitation, Raithe stepped forward, eliminating the remaining distance between the two. Gryndal didn't move. Maybe he was already dead, but the Dureyan didn't stop. He swung for the exposed neck. With a single stroke of the blade and a follow-through that carried to his other foot, Raithe severed the ringed god's head.

For a moment, no one spoke or moved. The pause might have lasted only an instant, but to Persephone it stretched out for minutes. The prince, whom everyone had forgotten about, was still on the porch, staring at Gryndal's severed head, which lay on its left cheek in the grass. Mawyndulë's mouth was open, lips quivering as if trying to form words, but nothing came out. He blinked, and his brows furrowed in disbelief.

Overhead, the storm once more dispersed and the sun shone through.

The first to regain her senses was Suri, who ran to where Arion lay and began ripping away handfuls of grass. Looking down, Persephone was surprised to see Math's spear in the dirt not too far away. Walking over, she picked it up and thumped the butt of the shaft on the ground. "Clan Rhen!" she shouted, then raised the spear above her head. "Defend your homes!"

They all stared at her, wide-eyed, confused.

"You heard her!" Moya shouted, shoving those closest to her, including Tressa, whom she heaved the hardest. Tope picked up the rake that had fallen and raised it over his shoulder. Bergin the Brewer found an ax. The rest of the men and women of the dahl scurried off. They disappeared into roundhouses, and just as Persephone thought they might stay inside, they returned with shovels, knives, and spears. Moya herself pulled a torch from the post near the well. Roan emerged with her little ax. Tressa had a stone knife, and even Gifford raised his crutch menacingly as the crowd reconvened with stern, angry faces.

Nyphron looked toward the prince, then over to the lion helms, who still had their weapons drawn. "*It might be best if you escorted His Highness out of here. If there's a fight, he might die, and Lothian wouldn't like that.*"

"*Do as he says.*" Arion was back on her feet, wiping mud and grass from the sleeves of her asica.

The prince stared with tear-filled eyes at the corpse of Gryndal. He shouted, "*You're a traitor!*"

The words came out in a high-pitched rage, and with red-faced fury he began to gesture feverishly with his hands. His fingers moved as if he were manipulating some complicated and invisible thing. He spoke words Persephone didn't understand, singing them with an awful voice and a halting rhythm.

As he sang, a light formed before the young Fhrey. It whirled with a fiery streak and flew at Raithe, who raised the shield once more.

"*No,*" Arion said. There wasn't any force to her words, no effort, but the fiery ball snuffed itself out before it got anywhere near Raithe.

Mawyndulë chanted once more and waved his hands, but nothing happened. Mawyndulë looked livid. He tried again and again, and each time Arion blocked him with no real effort.

Once more the prince began to conjure. This time

Arion shoved out her palm and spoke a word. The prince was thrown off his feet.

Arion faced the lion-helmed soldiers with a granite glare. *"Take the prince out of here, now."*

"Don't listen to her!" Mawyndulë ordered in a shrill voice from where he lay on his back. *"Kill them all!"*

The Fhrey in lion helms hesitated.

"They can't," Nyphron said. *"Only your father can sanction the death of another Fhrey, and I'm guessing he didn't give anyone but Gryndal that lovely gift."*

Mawyndulë looked furious. He got to his feet and yelled, *"Kill all the Rhunes then!"*

The lion helms retreated from the Galantians and moved toward the mob of Dahl Rhen.

Raithe, Malcolm, and the rest of the dahl villagers moved to meet them.

"Stop!" Arion ordered, and the soldiers in the lion helms froze. *"You are Talwara Guards. You have one job. You must protect the prince. He's in danger here. Take him back to his father where he'll be safe. That's your only responsibility."*

"Fhrey can't kill Fhrey! I'm in no danger. And he killed Gryndal! He has to die!"

"Gryndal was going to kill me," Arion shouted back. *"He nearly did."*

"That doesn't change—"

A spear flew across the yard and pierced the wood frame of the lodge less than a hand's length from the prince's face. Mawyndulë gasped, staggered backward, and fell again. Malcolm stood in the courtyard without his spear. *"Fhrey can't kill Fhrey,"* Malcolm shouted. *"But if you stay—we'll kill you."*

The prince got back to his feet, his eyes filled with fear.

"Go home, Mawyndulë," Arion said.

"You're—you're defying the law. I'm your prince, and you must obey me."

"I don't care! Go home. Leave—all of you."

Mawyndulë looked fearfully at the mob gathered before him. He crossed the porch and descended the steps.

As he did, the lion soldiers rushed to create a barrier around the prince. As a group they marched toward the horses. *"I'll tell my father how you defied him. I'll tell him how you protected Gryndal's killer. He'll declare war. He'll send an army. An army of Miralyith!"*

"Out!" Arion shouted.

The prince climbed atop a horse. Then all eyes watched as he and his guards filed out of the dahl.

When they were gone, Arion waved her hand, and both gate doors slammed shut. She turned toward the lodge and staggered, falling to her knees once more.

"Take her back to the lodge," Nyphron said.

"Little help?" Grygor shouted from inside his bubble. *"Getting hard to breathe."*

"Oh, sorry." Arion looked embarrassed and the bubble burst.

Moya and Brin began escorting Arion up the steps when she stopped and looked at Nyphron. *"Are we friends now?"*

"I hate Miralyith," Nyphron replied. *"Today you've demonstrated precisely why. But . . . well . . . I also hate winter, mud, and biting flies, but I've learned to live with them."*

"Thank you for saving Minna," Suri told Raithe. She had an arm around the wolf's neck.

He was still in the center of the yard and had put his sword away but continued to hold the shield. At the sound of her voice, Raithe lifted his gaze from Gryndal's corpse and smiled at the girl and her wolf. He reached out and stroked Minna's head. "Can't let anything happen to the world's wisest wolf, can we?"

Suri stared at him for a moment, tears in her eyes. Then without warning Suri threw her arms around Raithe and hugged him.

CHAPTER TWENTY-EIGHT

The First Chair

I still remember when Persephone stood on those steps, when she faced us and said everything would be all right. I believed her. I think everyone did. Persephone was not a magician or a mystic, but she performed magic that day. She gave us hope.

— THE BOOK OF BRIN

Maeve was buried along with Jason the digger and Neft the builder, both of whom had been struck by lightning. Lyn the bead-maker was laid with them as well; she had been crushed by half of the Killians' flaming home. The Galantians took care of Stryker, Medak, and Gryndal's remains, the sight of which forever shattered the notion that the Fhrey couldn't be killed. They bled and died like any mortal. The display of power when Arion and Gryndal fought, however, demonstrated that some Fhrey did indeed possess godlike power.

Suitable to a day when so many had died and it appeared the world had slipped further toward an abyss, almost everyone on Dahl Rhen acted with quiet reserve. In addition to those killed in the battle, the villagers mourned the passing of their chieftain and the others, like Hegner, who had vanished overnight.

Surprised to learn that Tressa had no idea where her husband had gone, Persephone told her of Konniger's death. The woman faced the news with teary eyes but a straight back. Persephone told her that Konniger and the others had formed a rescue party after hearing about Maeve's and Suri's mission regarding Grin the Brown. Sadly, the bear had killed him and the others. She didn't feel it was necessary to explain all the details about how Konniger and The Brown had faced each other. As disagreeable as Tressa was, Persephone wanted to preserve the new widow's memory of her husband. No one should experience what she had with Reglan.

Suri surprised Persephone by showing no hurry to leave. After all that had happened, she had expected the mystic to depart immediately after the battle. Instead, she found the girl sitting beside Minna against the south wall.

"I don't suppose this—what just happened—will be the end of it? The end of the warning you originally brought me?"

Suri shook her head. "Still not big enough. This is the start, just the turning of leaves. Winter is still on its way."

Persephone frowned and nodded. "I suppose you'll be leaving us to return to the wood?"

Suri looked up as if roused from sleep.

"You know, this *could* be your home," Persephone said.

Suri looked skeptically at the massive hole in the ground that was still bubbling goo, then toward the shattered gap in the western wall. Her eyes scanned across dozens of scorch marks on the grass and through the roofs of homes.

"Okay." Persephone shrugged. "So Rhen has seen better days."

"When?"

Persephone smiled. "So maybe *I* should come live with *you*." She sat down beside the mystic and rested her back against the wall. "That was quite clever. What you did to Arion's bandages."

"The markings in the little Dherg caves block the spirits. I've never been able to start a fire in there and can't read bones. Nothing of the spirit world works when surrounded by those marks."

"You're very smart. You know that?"

Suri shrugged. Her gaze was focused beyond the opening in the wall. "Maeve—who was she?"

"Maeve? She was the Keeper of Ways for Rhen. The one who remembered all the old stories from our past. Luckily, she taught others, passing on what she knew. Brin, for example. She loves stories and has a great memory."

"What was she like? Who was she married to?"

"Maeve never married."

"She had a daughter."

Persephone nodded. "She wasn't married to the father."

"You know who he was?"

Persephone drew up her knees and straightened her filthy skirt over them. Her clothes were ruined, stained with blood. The blood was probably one of the reasons why Tressa hadn't questioned the explanation surrounding Konniger's death. That, and perhaps the widow already knew the truth. "I don't think it matters anymore. That's all over. All in the past."

"Not all of it," Suri said.

"What do you mean?"

"I think her daughter survived."

"Maeve's daughter? No, that was a story Konniger made up. Maeve's daughter died in the forest where she was abandoned fourteen years . . ." Persephone stopped and stared at Suri in sudden revelation. "Fourteen . . . might be more . . ."

"Might be less," Suri finished for her. "Is the father still alive?" she asked without turning. Her stare was still focused on the hole in the wall.

"No. He died a month ago. Konniger killed him and blamed it on The Brown."

Suri finally looked at her then. The tattoos around her eyes were bound up in thought.

"Twenty years ago I married Reglan," Persephone said. "Over the years, I bore my husband three sons. One died shortly after being born. Duncan barely made it to the age of three. Mahn grew to be a fine young man, but The Brown took him from me. I never had a daughter, but I always wished for one. My husband was blessed with a daughter, but he never had the chance to meet her. Nobody knew except Reglan, Konniger, and Maeve."

Tears filled Suri's eyes and drops spilled down Persephone's own cheeks.

Minna's head came up, and she looked at both of them as if they were insane.

Raithe sat outside Roan's roundhouse, one of the few near the center of the dahl that had suffered no damage at all. He was holding the broken hilt of his father's sword. Compared with Shegon's blade, it looked like it had been forged by a child.

"There you are." Malcolm walked toward him. The ex-slave had set down his bulky shield but continued to use the spear like a staff, walking in a most un-warrior-like fashion. He took a seat beside Raithe, his legs stretched out and sandaled feet crossed. Together the two stared at the breadth of the dahl and its people, who, having narrowly avoided a butchering or some magical cataclysm, were already back to their labors: fixing the hole in the wall and tending to gardens, sheep, and pots.

Just another day.

"What are you going to do with that?" Malcolm asked, pointing at the broken sword.

"I don't know. Seems stupid to carry it." Raithe drove the fractured blade that had started everything into the dirt beside him. He let go, and the sword handle quivered slightly. "Probably should have left it with my father. No one would have stolen it. Who'd want it?"

Malcolm nodded in solidarity, and Raithe realized that was what he liked most about the man. Malcolm was inclined to understand or at least to agree. Another holdover from years in slavery, perhaps, but Raithe found it a virtue nevertheless.

Across the dahl, Minna lay down beside Suri and Persephone as they talked near the wall.

Everyone should have such a loyal friend.

"What will you do now?" Malcolm asked.

"I don't know about that, either."

"Good to see you're on top of things."

"Everything's changed, you know?" He looked at the planted sword. "I'd grown up in my father's shadow. Fighting to survive, fighting to prove my worth to him. That was the stick I measured myself by. Miserable as he was, my father was all I had left."

Again Malcolm nodded. "We're both adrift without a rudder."

Raithe returned the nod and for the first time realized that both he and Malcolm had been freed that day on the bank of the Bern River. And just like Malcolm, he didn't have a clue what to do with that independence. Raithe was completely on his own for the first time in his life. He had dreamed of such freedom as if it were a faraway place, a made-up land that didn't really exist. But landing in Dahl Rhen by accident, he was lost. He had a hundred potential directions, a multitude of choices, and the enormity of the options left him paralyzed. Freedom, he discovered, had built a greater prison than his family or clan had.

In his imaginings, he fantasized about such grand things as a warm home made of wood, a granary with enough wheat to last a whole winter, a loyal woman he could talk to, a well that served up water that didn't taste of metal, and not one, but two thick blankets. Crazy thoughts, but dreams always were. No one held him back anymore, and if he made a plan, who knew what was possible. And yet he couldn't deny recent events and how his life had been changed. Maybe there was a plan, just not his.

"If you leave, I'll go with you," Malcolm said. "And if you stay, I'll stay."

Raithe sat up and leaned in. "Why?"

"The way I see it, each of us is all the other one has at

the moment. You don't have a clan or family, and neither do I. We're sort of our own clan, the two of us. And you've done well by me. I'm still alive after all, and I have this wonderful spear now." He thumped the butt against the dirt. "Do you think they'll let me keep it?"

"After that throw? They have to. Quite impressive, by the way. You nearly killed him."

Malcolm replied with an awkward smile. "Actually, I wasn't trying to hit him."

"Seriously?" Raithe said, even more impressed. "You meant to just miss him like that?"

"Yeah, except I was aiming five feet to his right."

"The spear hit inches to his left."

Malcolm smiled and nodded again. "Still impressed?"

"More than ever." Raithe grinned. "You know, once a man uses a weapon in battle, and if he survives, then the weapon bonds to him and becomes his."

Malcolm looked up at the spear towering over them and smiled. "Then maybe I should name it. People do that, right?"

"Some do."

"Okay, I'll call it Narsirabad."

"Excellent name, very fierce sounding. Is it a Fhrey word?"

Malcolm nodded.

"What does it mean?"

Malcolm smiled. "Pointy."

Raithe laughed, and Malcolm joined him. It felt good to laugh. It felt good to breathe the morning air and feel the heat of the sun on his face. And it felt good to sit beside Malcolm as if they didn't have a care in the world. Maybe they didn't. There wasn't any point in worrying about tomorrow. No one knew what it held—maybe nothing at all.

"What do you think I should do, Malcolm, my clansman? You probably understood everything they said, right? I only caught phrases here and there, but it sounded like this might not be over."

"No," Malcolm said. "Just beginning, I should think."

Cocking his head at Raithe and firming his mouth, he appeared to be giving the question his full thought and attention. He glanced at the sky, drew up his knees, and rubbed his chin. "When faced with certain death, running is sensible, but I think a man can make an unhealthy habit of it. Running can take on an importance of its own and become an excuse to avoid living a normal life."

"What's a *normal* life?"

"I was a slave; how should I know? I just don't think a person should give up trying to find out."

Raithe looked over at Persephone again. She was crying, wiping her cheeks with the palms of her hands. Their eyes met, and she sent him an embarrassed smile.

"We're going to stay, Malcolm."

Malcolm followed his stare. "I had a feeling we might. You like her, don't you?"

"She's different."

"Everyone is different."

"Then let's say I like the ways in which she's different. A wise man once told me no man can escape death, but it's *how* we run that defines us. And if I have to run, I think I'd like to go where she's going."

It began in the late afternoon.

The dead had been buried, and the worst parts of the mess cleaned up. Doing so had put the ground back under people's feet, and by early evening, as the sun dipped toward the tops of the Crescent Forest, it was clear to everyone that the world hadn't ended. As the news of Konniger's death circulated, it also became clear they were leaderless and in peril. Thoughts became whispers, which soon turned into questions.

Sarah, Brin, Delwin, and Moya approached Persephone as she stood looking at the murky crater in the middle of the dahl, wondering what could be done about it. They would need to fill it in if they were to reuse the land, but where would they haul the dirt from, and was filling it the best choice? Perhaps they could use the pit for additional storage.

"This is going to be a problem," Persephone told them as they came up to her.

Sarah, who led the group, didn't say a thing. She simply walked over and hugged her. Behind them, Roan watched from a distance.

"Seph, what are we going to do now?" Sarah whispered in her ear. "We don't have a chieftain or a Shield and no Keeper of Ways."

Delwin nodded. "We thought maybe you might have some idea. I mean, this hasn't happened before, has it? Reglan was chieftain for forty years, and his father ruled for nearly as long before him. We've always . . . I mean . . . we've usually just gone father to son, but Reglan's died and Konniger never had any—"

"Delwin!" Sarah snapped. "In the Grand Mother's name! Show a little compassion, would you?"

"I'm sorry, I—"

"It's fine," Persephone said, offering a forgiving smile.

"It's just that," Delwin said, lowering his voice as if the next part were a secret, "Brin tells us that in cases where there is no clear successor, like a son or a Shield, the Keeper of Ways is expected to administrate and oversee combat challenges for the First Chair. But Maeve is dead."

"We're afraid of what might happen," Sarah said. "Some of the younger men are already sizing each other up."

"She's right." Delwin nodded, agreeing with his wife. "Without a Keeper, fellas like Tope's sons and Wedon's sons are picking sides. We could have an intraclan war on our hands if something isn't done."

"We've had enough bloodshed," Sarah said with a pleading in her voice and eyes. "We don't need any more."

"And I sure don't want to see Tressa in charge," Moya said.

"Where is Tressa?" Persephone asked.

"Over at Bergin's," Moya said. "She's pretty drunk."

Persephone nodded.

"So do you know what we're supposed to do?" Delwin asked.

Persephone nodded. "Of course I do."

Her words and matter-of-fact tone took all of them by surprise, causing their smiles and looks of relief to be delayed.

"Come on, let me show you," Persephone said. Taking Sarah's hand and Math's spear, she led them to the steps of the lodge. Persephone let go of Sarah and climbed to the porch, then turned to face the dahl.

"You've all been hearing a lot of rumors about what happened last night, and you all saw what happened today." She spoke in a loud, clear voice.

It didn't take long for people to notice. The lodge steps had always been the altar of the chieftain, the pulpit where he addressed the dahl. Hearing her speak formally while holding that black spear, those who weren't already on their way rushed over.

"Konniger is dead," she said. "So is Maeve. They were both killed last night by the great brown bear that has been terrorizing this dahl. They, and many others, died. We mourn their passing, but let us be cheerful that the bear is at last dead."

With the growing quiet, her voice carried farther and people from outside the walls and inside their homes came crowding around, gathering before the steps.

"Some have asked, *Who will lead us?* The answer is simple. I will."

Moya began clapping, a great smile spreading across her face. No one else joined her.

"How can a woman be chieftain?" Cobb asked.

"How? Cobb, I've practically been chieftain for nearly twenty years. There wasn't a major decision Reglan made that we didn't discuss together before he ordered it. And who was it that brought the God Killer to us and welcomed the Fhrey when they arrived? Who took measures to save Arion's life—the Fhrey who just saved all of ours? And who was it that called everyone into battle this morning?" She raised the black spear over her head to remind them.

"What about the Ways?" Gelston asked.

"Brin, do the Ways of Succession, as taught to you by Maeve, prohibit a woman from sitting in the First Chair?"

Brin stepped forward. She looked back at her parents just briefly and then said, "No, ma'am."

Persephone smiled at the sudden honorific.

"But we'll need a warrior to lead us," Engleton said. "Not a woman."

"If there is anyone who doesn't want me as their leader, they have the right to challenge. That's also in the Ways, isn't it, Brin?"

She nodded and, with a poke from her mother, lifted her head and said, "Yes, yes it is."

"Of course, according to the Ways, I have a right to name a champion. Isn't that so, Brin?"

"Yes, ma'am."

"Raithe?" Persephone looked to where he stood beside Malcolm near Roan's house. "Would you please act as my champion?"

"Absolutely," he replied. "But in all honesty, you don't need me." Raithe turned so that everyone could hear him. "Persephone left out one important detail about what happened last night. That bear, the one that has terrorized this dahl and killed so many of your men, including the last two chieftains . . ." He nodded toward Persephone. "*She* killed it."

Eyes shifted between the two, clouded in disbelief and confusion.

"It's true," Raithe insisted. "She killed that big brown monster all by herself with no one's help. No one at all. And she didn't even need a spear or a sword."

"How, then?" Moya asked, astounded.

Raithe waited a second, then said, "She beat it to death with the edge of a shield."

Dahl Rhen filled with murmurs.

"With a shield?" Engleton asked.

"She killed The Brown with a shield?" Gelston asked.

The questions bounced among those gathered. Responses were words of doubt, statements of disbelief. With each comment Persephone saw faces looking over at her as if she were different.

Cobb, who spent a good deal of his time shouting from the top of the gate, was heard over everyone else. "Is that true?"

The crowd quieted.

"It's true," Malcolm said.

One by one all the Fhrey confirmed the truth of Raithe's words. No one thought to question their honesty or eyesight.

"Okay, then." Persephone looked out over the gathered crowd. "Anyone wanting to challenge my right to be chieftain, this is your chance."

She waited.

Faces turned, looking expectantly at one another.

"One of the Tope boys? One of Wedon's sons?" she asked. "No?"

The dahl was so quiet that they could hear the crickets in the field.

"Okay, then. As of this moment, I *am* the chieftain of Dahl Rhen."

The crowd began talking among themselves again, and Persephone held up her hands.

"Quiet!" Moya shouted. "Your chieftain isn't done."

"Thank you, Moya," Persephone said. "As chieftain, I have a few things to say. First, if I understood enough of what was said this morning, I fear the Fhrey among us will not be allowed to live peacefully in exile. As they risked themselves to defend us, I offer them Dahl Rhen not merely as a sanctuary but as their new home. Our fate and theirs are tied together from here on, for good or ill. And that goes for Arion as well. I plan to tell her this when she wakes. We lost many good men last night and two more this morning, both hard workers. I insist that as long as the Fhrey stay with us, they must contribute to the dahl and help provide meat for our tables."

She saw Nyphron's nod, and replied to him with a smile. Everyone else saw this as well and the murmurs quieted.

"As everyone knows, Maeve is dead. Dahl Rhen is without a Keeper of Ways. I therefore appoint Brin, daughter of Delwin and Sarah, to be the new chronicler of our people."

Moya clapped again, and this time a few others joined her. Padera and Roan were the loudest.

Persephone looked to Raithe then and took a deep breath. "I'm also appointing Raithe of Dureya, who has already saved my life more than once and stood faithfully by my side against certain death, to be my Shield, for I can think of no greater or more loyal warrior." She wondered if she should have asked first, but he didn't say no right away, and so she quickly moved on. "To Malcolm, who also stood his ground with me in battle and willingly offered to stand and die that I might live"—she extended a hand toward him—"I grant full citizenship in Dahl Rhen. We are short on men in general now, but even if that weren't so, we'd be eager for one with virtues such as yours."

Moya led the applause once more. This time the crowd was getting used to the idea, and Persephone could feel the shift from doubt to confidence. The people before her no longer saw an uncertain sunset but the coming dawn of possibilities.

Persephone pointed over everyone's heads. "For those of you who don't already know, that young woman sitting against the wall with the wolf is Suri. While all of you were asleep in your beds, she set out on a dangerous quest to save your lives—the same quest that took Maeve from this world."

Every head turned.

Suri lifted her face from between her knees and stared back. A moment later, Minna did likewise.

"To Suri I bestow the official title of the first Mystic of Rhen and also designate her as a personal adviser. I'm certain I'll consult with her frequently. Mostly because she's the only one I know who can understand the language and wisdom of trees."

This brought another murmur.

Persephone took another breath and brushed hair from her face. "I'm afraid what we've seen today isn't over. A storm is coming, I think—a war between the Fhrey and ourselves. What you witnessed this morning was only the beginning. Suri saw the signs a month ago, and I believe her. A terrible reckoning is still on its way. We as a people stand atop a precipice, backed up to the very edge. We have no choice. We must find the courage to fight for our lives even against those we once thought to be gods. Remember what you've seen today. Draw courage from the fact that even their most powerful die. You've seen that with your own eyes this day."

She pointed to the stone statue in the center of the courtyard. "We of Dahl Rhen worship the goddess Mari, who has saved us from destruction and is clearly more powerful than any Fhrey. She has delivered unto us the gifts of Raithe, Suri, Nyphron, and Arion. My hope is that she'll guide us through any storms in the future and deliver us to a new world where we don't need to live every day as if it's our last. A brighter tomorrow awaits us, for we'll live in a new age free of false gods where we can decide our own destiny."

The crowd applauded its approval, and Persephone took that moment to enter the lodge that was once again her home.

The eternal fire was out. Only a few coals still glowed. She grabbed some pieces of split wood from the pile and worked them in, then blew. Smoke rose. Persephone blew again, and a flame flickered. She tossed another log on. When she was satisfied the fire had caught, she walked over to the center of the hall and sat in the First Chair.

* * *

"That's a pathetic-looking spear," Nyphron said, approaching Malcolm where he stood on the wall near the gate.

Being an official member of Clan Rhen, Malcolm had volunteered to take the watch that night. After such a harrowing day, everyone else was asleep, the fires long out. Only the full moon looked down, revealing the walkway.

"I call it Narsirabad."

"Cute," Nyphron said, then, switching to Fhrey, he added, *"You've been avoiding me."*

"It's been a long day."

"And before? I've been here for more than a week. Why is this the first time we've spoken together? And why is it me coming to you and not the other way around?"

This time Malcolm replied in Fhrey. *"I didn't think it would be in either of our best interests to be seen together."*

"And I think you're growing a bit too fond of life outside the Rhist. Perhaps a taste of freedom has given you an appetite for more. Were you planning on running away?" Nyphron asked. *"Is that why you volunteered to watch the gate?"*

Nyphron didn't give Malcolm a chance to answer. He walked past him along the rampart, his eyes peering out into the darkness to the northwest. When he spoke, it was in Rhunic. "When I was young, that out there was my playground. Avrlyn was a grand gateway to high adventures. The snowcapped mountains of Hentlyn were home to the violent Grenmorians. The jagged teeth of the Adendal Durat hosted the hill goblins. The meadows were rich with game, and the Harwood filled with dark secrets. I bathed in the gold sunsets, wandered beneath the moon, and gleefully accepted every challenge. Even among the Instarya I'm a legend, a hero."

"Alon Rhist had been a hero," Malcolm reminded him. "So had Atella. The stories all end the same."

Nyphron took a step closer to Malcolm and leaned in, placing a hand on top of the one the ex-slave was using to hold Narsirabad. He whispered in Fhrey, *"I thought I told you to kill Shegon."*

Malcolm replied with a guilty, uncomfortable smile.

"I sent you with him for that specific reason. Did you forget? Imagine my surprise when I discovered Raithe, instead of my slave, is the God Killer."

"I'm not your slave. I belonged to your father."

"I'm sorry, didn't you hear the news? He's dead. That makes you my property."

"I'm not sure slavery is one of Ferrol's laws."

Nyphron laughed softly and licked his lips. *"You of all people know I'm not a stickler for rules."*

"But not even your father saw me as his slave."

"My father wasn't all that bright—as evidenced by his death. Now, do you want to explain your memory lapse? How is it that Raithe is the one who killed Shegon? Why wasn't it you?"

"Two reasons," Malcolm said. *"First, as you just pointed out, many would see me as your property and that would link you to Shegon's murder. You don't want that."*

"A risk I was willing to take."

"And second, I suspected that when Meryl and I returned, pointing fingers at each other, you'd have us both executed—and that wasn't a risk I was willing to take."

Nyphron pursed his lips and nodded. *"Very clever of you. And you're right, but I'm not sure how I feel about that. I don't think anyone has outwitted me before. Makes me nervous."*

"Given what you're planning, I think you ought to be nervous, don't you?"

Nyphron shook his head. *"No. All that I've done and will do was predestined, ordained by god."*

Malcolm raised a skeptical eyebrow. *"Really? Which one?"*

Nyphron offered a mischievous grin. *"I haven't decided."*

Glossary of Terms and Names

Airenthenon: Although the Forest Throne and the Door predate it, the Airenthenon is the oldest *building* in Estramnadon. The domed and pillared structure where the Aquila holds meetings.

Alon Rhist: Fourth fane of the Fhrey, who died during the Dherg War. He was replaced by Fenelyus. One of the outposts on the border between Rhulyn and Avrlyn bears his name.

Alysin: One of the three realms of the afterlife. A paradise where brave warriors go after death.

Aquila: Literally "the place of choosing." Originally created as a formalization and public recognition of the group of Fhrey who had been assisting Gylindora Fane for more than a century. Leaders of each of the tribes act as general counsels, making suggestions and assisting in the overall administration of the empire. Council members are elected by their tribes. The Aquila holds no direct power, as the fane's authority is as absolute as Ferrol Himself. However, the Aquila does wield great influence over the succession of power. It is the Curator and Conservator who determine who has access to the Horn of Gylindora.

Arion (Fhrey, Miralyith): Tutor to Prince Mawyndulë, daughter of Nyree and Era, former student of Fenelyus, who bestowed the nickname Cenzlyor.

Art, the: Magic that allows the caster to tap the forces of nature. In Fhrey society, it's practiced by members of the Miralyith tribe. Goblins who wield this power are known as oberdaza.

Artist: A practitioner of the Art.

Asendwayr: Fhrey tribe whose members specialize in hunting. A few are stationed on the frontier to provide meat for the Instarya.

Asica: A long Fhrey garment similar to a robe. Its numerous wraps and ties allow it to be worn in a number of configurations.

Avempartha: Fhrey tower created by Fenelyus atop a great waterfall on the Nidwalden River. It can tap the force of rushing water to amplify the use of the Art.

Avrlyn: "Land of Green," the Fhrey frontier bordered on the north by Hentlyn and Belgreig to the south. Avrlyn is separated from Rhulyn by the east and south branches of the Bern River.

Battle of Grandford: First battle in the war between Rhunes and Fhrey.

Belgric War: A war between the Fhrey and Dherg. Also referred to as the Dherg War.

Bendigo: Evil spirit capable of possessing people and animals.

Bern: A river that runs north–south and delineates the borders between Rhulyn and Avrlyn. Rhunes are forbidden from crossing to the west side of this river.

Book of Brin: First known written work chronicling the history of the Rhune people. Its origin dates back to the time of the first war between Rhunes and Fhrey.

Breckon mor: The female version of the leigh mor. A versatile piece of cloth that can be wrapped in a number of ways.

Brideeth: Fhrey profanity. A term of extreme insult.

Brin (Rhune, Rhen): Daughter of Sarah and Delwin, mentored by Maeve; creator of the famed Book of Brin.

Brown, The: A ferocious bear that lives in the Crescent Forest. She has been responsible for the deaths of many residents of Dahl Rhen. To Suri and Tura she is known as Grin or Grin the Brown.

Caratacus (Fhrey): Famed sage adviser to the first fane. A legendary figure who brought Ferrol's horn to Gylindora Fane. Creator of the Forest Throne.

Card or carding: The step that comes between shearing and spinning wool. Combs are used to detangle, clean, and intermix fibers to produce a continuous web of aligned fibers.

Carfreign Arena: A large open-air field where contests and spectacles are held. A building where sports and entertainments are performed.

Cenzlyor: In the Fhrey language it means "swift of mind." A title of endearment bestowed by Fane Fenelyus onto Arion, indicating her proficiency in the Art.

Clempton: A small village of Dureya, home of Raithe.

Cleve: A simple and practical type of short sword, favored by the Instarya tribe of the Fhrey.

Conservator of the Aquila: One of the two people responsible for administering the process of succession. Together with the Curator, the Conservator determines who has the right to blow the Horn of Gylindora.

Crescent Forest: A large forest that forms a half circle around Dahl Rhen.

Crimbal: A fairy creature that lives in the land of Nog. Crimbals travel to the world of Elan through doors in the trunks of trees. They are known to steal children.

Cul: Rhunic profanity often used for a despicable person.

Culina brideeth: Fhrey profanity that suggests an inappropriate relationship with one's mother.

Curator of the Aquila: Vice fane. Keeper of the horn. One of the six councilors of the Aquila, elected by a vote of senior councilors. Leads meetings of the Aquila in absence of the fane. Chairs the Challenge Council, which decides who gets the right to blow the Horn of Gylindora. Together the Conservator and the Curator determine the process of succession and judge the challenge process.

Dahl (hill or mound): A Rhune settlement that is the capital city of a given clan and is characterized by its position on top of a man-made hill. Dahls are usually surrounded by some form of wall or fortification. Each has a central lodge where the clan's chieftain lives, along with a series of roundhouses that house the other villagers.

Dherg: One of the five humanoid races of Elan. Long-lived, skilled craftsmen, they have been all but banned from most places aboveground. They are exceptional builders and weaponsmiths.

Didan (Rhune, Dureya): Raithe's brother.

Door, the: A portal in the Garden of Estramnadon that legend holds is the gateway to where The First Tree grows.

Drome: God of the Dherg.

Dureya: A barren highland region in the north of Rhulyn, home to the Rhune clan of the same name.

Dureyan: A member of the warrior clan of Rhunes.

Eilywin: Fhrey architects and craftsmen who design and create buildings.

Elan: The Grand Mother of All. God of the land.

Enarmes: Straps attached to the back of a shield. Used for gripping or to slide an arm through to attach to a person's forearm.

Era (Fhrey, Umalyn): Father of Arion, husband of Nyree.

Eres (Fhrey, Instarya): A member of the Galantians. His main prowess is with spears.

Erivan: Homeland of the Fhrey.

Ervanon: Northernmost outpost of the Fhrey.

Estramnadon: Capital city of the Fhrey in the forests of Erivan.

Eton: God of the sky.

Fane: Ruler of the Fhrey, whose term of office extends to death or to three thousand years after ascension, whichever comes first.

Fenelyus (Fhrey, Miralyith): Fifth fane of the Fhrey. First of the Miralyith, who saved the Fhrey from annihilation in the Belgric War.

Ferrol: God of the Fhrey.

Ferrol's Law: The irrefutable prohibition against Fhrey killing other Fhrey. Exceptions can be made by the fane (or a person the fane designates) in extreme situations. Breaking Ferrol's Law will eject a Fhrey from society and bar the perpetrator from the afterlife. Since it is the Fhrey's god that will pass judgment, no one can circumvent Ferrol's Law by committing murder in secret or without witnesses.

Fhrey: One of the five major races of Elan. Fhrey are long-lived, technically advanced, and organized into tribes based on profession.

First Chair: Honorific for the chieftain of a dahl.

Five Major Races of Elan: Rhunes, Fhrey, Dherg, ghazel, and Grenmorians.

Florella Plaza: A large public square with an elaborate fountain outside the Airenthenon in Estramnadon.

Forest Throne: Seat of the fane, located in the Talwara in the capital city of Estramnadon.

Galantians: The Instarya patrol led by Nyphron and famed for legendary exploits of valor and bravery.

Garden, the: One of the most sacred places in Fhrey society, which is used for meditation and reflection. The Garden is in the center of Estramnadon and surrounds the Door.

Gath (Rhune): The first keenig, who united all the clans during the Great Flood.

Ghazel: "Goblin" in the Dherg language.

Ghika (Fhrey): Third fane of the Fhrey, who refused to grant King Mideon (of the Dherg) access to The First Tree, thus starting the Belgric War in which Ghika was killed.

Gifford (Rhune, Rhen): Incredibly talented potter of Dahl Rhen. His mother died during his birth; due to his extensive deformities, he wasn't expected to live more than a few years.

Goblin: A grotesque race feared and shunned by all in Elan. Known to be fierce warriors, the most dangerous of their kind are oberdazas, who can harness the power of elements through magic. In the Dherg language, they are called ghazel.

Grandford: A stone bridge over the narrow river gorge of the Bern River that separates Dureya from Alon Rhist.

Grantheum Art Tournament: A yearly event held to determine the Miralyith who is the most skilled at using the Art.

Green Field Guides: Fhrey who travel into the wilds outside of Estramnadon.

Grenmorians: The race of giants who live in Elan.

Grin: The name Suri and Tura gave to "The Brown," a ferocious bear of the Crescent Forest.

Gryndal (Fhrey, Miralyith): First Minister to Fane Lothian. Respected as one of the most skilled practitioners of the Art.

Gula-Rhunes: A northern three-clan alliance of Rhunes who have a long-standing feud with the seven southern Rhune clans. Historically the Fhrey have pitted these sides against each other and fostered their mutual animosity.

Gwydry: One of the seven tribes of Fhrey. This one is for the farmers who are responsible for raising crops and livestock.

Gylindora Fane (Fhrey): The first leader of the Fhrey. Her name became synonymous with "ruler."

Hentlyn (land of mountains): Area to the north of Avrlyn, generally inhabited by Grenmorians.

Herkimer (Rhune, Dureya): Father of Raithe, killed by Shegon.

Hiemdal (Rhune, Dureya): Father of Herkimer and grandfather to Raithe.

High Spear Valley: Home of the three clans of the Gula-Rhunes.

Horn of Gylindora: A ceremonial horn kept by the Aquila that was originally bestowed to Gylindora Fane by the legendary Caratacus. The horn is used to challenge for leadership of the Fhrey. It can only be blown upon the death of a fane or every three thousand years during the Uli Vermar. When blown at the death of a fane, it's the fane's heir that is challenged. If the fane has no heir, then the horn can be blown twice, providing for two contestants.

Imaly (Fhrey, Nilyndd): Descendant of Gylindora Fane, leader of the Nilyndd tribe, and Curator of the Aquila.

Instarya: One of the seven tribes of the Fhrey. Instarya are the warrior class, stationed on the frontier in outposts along the Avrlyn border.

Jerydd (Fhrey, Miralyith): The kel of Avempartha.

Keeper of Ways: The person who learns the customs and traditions of a community and is the authority in such matters. Keepers pass down their knowledge through the oral tradition.

Kel: Administrator or governor of a prestigious institution.

Knots: Known to disrupt the natural flow of the Art, often creating difficulty in communication and preventing consensus building. Once a knot is unraveled, so, too, are arguments unknotted, leading to eventual agreement.

Konniger (Rhune, Rhen): Shield to Chieftain Reglan of Dahl Rhen; became chieftain after Reglan's death; married to Tressa.

Leigh mor: Great cloak. A versatile piece of fabric used by Rhune men that can be draped in a number of ways, usually belted. A leigh mor can also be used as a sling to carry items or as a blanket. Usually, they're woven with the pattern of a particular clan. The female version, known as a *breckon mor,* is longer, with an angled cut.

Leshie: One of a multitude of mischievous wood sprites that inhabit forests. Leshies delight in leading travelers astray.

Lothian, Fane (Fhrey, Miralyith): Supreme ruler of the Fhrey, father to Mawyndulë, son of Fenelyus.

Maccus (Rhune, Rhen): Dahl chieftain and the great-great-grandfather of Reglan. He ruled the dahl from about a hundred years before the reign of Reglan.

Maeve (Rhune, Rhen): Keeper of Ways for Dahl Rhen.

Magda: The oldest tree in the Crescent Forest; an ancient oak.

Mahn (Rhune, Rhen): Son of Persephone and Reglan. Killed by a ferocious bear known as The Brown.

Malcolm (Rhune, no clan affiliation): A slave living in Alon Rhist.

Malkin: A child taken by crimbals who later escapes Nog to return to the world of Elan. Malkins usually reappear at the age of fourteen, although they might have been gone for much longer, since time doesn't pass at the same rate in Nog as in the world of Elan.

Manes: Ghosts of the dead who live deep in the earth and emerge through a deep shaft, cave, or chasm. Manes seek out the living members of their family and torment them for any misdeeds (real or imagined) that the manes feel were perpetrated on them in life.

Math (Rhune, Rhen): Founder of Dahl Rhen and grandson of Gath.

Mawyndulë (Fhrey, Miralyith): Prince of the Fhrey realm. Son of Fane Lothian and grandson of Fane Fenelyus.

Medak (Fhrey, Instarya): A member of the Galantians, skilled at throwing knives.

Menahan: A Rhune dahl known for its wool.

Mideon, King (Dherg): A key player in the Belgric War between the Dherg and the Fhrey.

Minna: A wolf that travels with Suri.

Miralyith: Fhrey tribe of "Artists." People who use the Art to channel natural forces to work magic.

Morvyn: Evil spirit capable of possessing animals and humans. When taking over humans, it has the ability to transform into an animal while maintaining near-human intelligence.

Mynogan: Battle, Honor, and Death. The three gods of war worshipped by the Dureyans.

Mystic: Individuals capable of tapping into the essence of the natural world and understanding the will of gods and spirits.

Nadak: A region in the north of Rhulyn that is home to the Rhune clan of the same name.

Nagon: The name of one of Sebek's two swords. The word is Fhrey for "lightning."

Naraspur: Name of the horse that takes Arion to Alon Rhist.

Nidwalden: Mighty river that separates the land of the Fhrey (Ervanon) from Rhulyn.

Nifrel: Below Rel. The most dismal and unpleasant of the three regions of the afterlife.

Nilyndd: Fhrey tribe of craftsmen.

Nog: Home of the crimbals, where time moves at a different rate than in Elan.

Nyphron (Fhrey, Instarya): Son of Zephyron and leader of the famed Galantians.

Nyree (Fhrey, Umalyn): Mother of Arion and former wife of Era.

Padera (Rhune, Rhen): Farmer's wife and oldest resident of Dahl Rhen.

Parthaloren Falls: Largest waterfall in the known world, it drops the Nidwalden River thousands of feet. At the top of these falls stands the great Fhrey tower of Avempartha.

Persephone (Rhune, Rhen): Wife of Reglan and Second Chair of Dahl Rhen.

Pontifex: Name of Nyphron's sword. One of the Fhrey names for the wind.

Raithe (Rhune, Dureya): Son of Herkimer, also known as the God Killer.

Raow: A feared predator that eats its prey starting with the face. Raow sleep on a bed of bones and must add another set before going to sleep. A single raow can decimate an entire region.

Reglan (Rhune, Rhen): Chieftain of Dahl Rhen and husband to Persephone.

Rel: One of the three regions in the Rhune afterlife.

Rhen: A wooded region in the west of Rhulyn that is home to the Rhune clan of the same name.

Rhulyn: "Land of the Rhunes" bordered by the Fhrey's native lands of Erivan to the east and the Fhrey outposts in Avrlyn to the west.

Rhune: One of the five major races of Elan, the race of humans. The word is Fhrey for "primitive," and for some, it is seen as derogatory. This race is technologically challenged, superstitious, and polytheistic. They live in clusters of small villages, and each clan is governed by a chieftain. There are two major groups of Rhunes, the Gula-Rhunes from the north and the southern Rhulyn-Rhunes. The two factions have warred for centuries.

Rhunic: The language spoken by the humans who live in Rhulyn.

Roan (Rhune, Rhen): Ex-slave of Iver the Carver.

Sackett (Rhune, Rhen): The new Shield of the chieftain of Dahl Rhen under the leadership of Konniger.

Salifan: Fragrant wild plant with multiple uses.

Season pillars: Twelve pillars inside a lodge that surround the dais of the First and Second Chairs. They are arranged in sets of three, the groups representing spring (west), summer (south), fall (east), and winter (north).

Sebek (Fhrey, Instarya): Best warrior of the Galantians.

Second Chair: Honorific position held by the wife of the chieftain.

Shegon (Fhrey, Asendwayr): A hunter of Alon Rhist who provides the warrior tribe with fresh meat; killed by Raithe.

Shield: Also known as "Shield to the chieftain" or "chieftain's Shield," the chieftain's personal bodyguard, and generally the finest warrior on the dahl.

Standing stone: A monolith or part of a group of similar stones. Their size can vary considerably, but their shape is generally uneven and squared, often tapering toward the top.

Suri (Rhune, no clan affiliation): Young mystic raised by Tura. She's always accompanied by a white wolf named Minna.

Tabor: A woodland spirit that pushes people off cliffs or drowns them in rivers or lakes.

Talwara: The official name of the Fhrey's palace where the fane resides and rules.

Tet: A swear word derived from *Tetlin Witch*. Over the years it's been perverted to mean "excrement," as in, "You don't know tet."

Tetlin Witch: An immortal being thought to be the source of all disease, pestilence, and evil in the world.

Thym (Fhrey, Umalyn): Priest of Ferrol who ministers to the Instarya each summer.

Tibor: The name of one of Sebek's two swords; the word is Fhrey for "thunder."

Tirre: A region in the south of Rhulyn that is home to the Rhune clan of the same name.

Torc: A rigid circular necklace that is open at the front.

Tressa (Rhune, Rhen): Wife of Chieftain Konniger of Dahl Rhen.

Trilos (Fhrey, unknown tribal affiliation): A person obsessed with the Door in the Garden.

Tura (Rhune, no clan affiliation): An ancient mystic who lived in the Crescent Forest near Dahl Rhen; mentor to Suri. She predicted the coming of the Great Famine.

Uli Vermar: An event that occurs three thousand years after the crowning of a fane, when other Fhrey can challenge the sitting ruler. This is done by petitioning the Aquila and being presented with the Horn of Gylindora.

Umalyn: The Fhrey tribe of priests and priestesses who concern themselves with spiritual matters and the worship of Ferrol.

Urum River: A north-south Avrlyn river west of the Bern.

Vellor: A stringed musical instrument created by the Fhrey.

Wogan: Chief woodland spirit, who serves as guardian of forests.

Yakkus: A demon of disease that can assume the form of any animal, including humans.

Zephyron (Fhrey, Instarya): Father of Nyphron, killed by Lothian during the leadership challenge after the death of Fane Fenelyus.

Acknowledgments

It's been said that you don't want to know how two things are made: legislation and sausage. I feel exactly the opposite about how a manuscript becomes a finished book. I wish readers had a better understanding of the publishing process, as it would elucidate the enormity of this monumental task. Generally, you only see one name—the author's—gracing the cover. But my contributions are just the tip of the proverbial iceberg, and it's a shame that the hardworking people who made this book possible aren't likewise recognized. I'd like to take a minute to rectify that by mentioning some of them.

First and always, I want to thank Robin, the love of my life, my best friend, and the most capable person I've ever met. Why she's chosen to spend the last thirty-six years with me is a mystery, but I'm forever grateful for her hard work on this book and all my novels. For those who don't know, Robin fills several essential roles: alpha reader, line editor, beta test administrator, project manager, business manager, marketing guru, and liaison to my agents, editors, publicists, and various sales and marketing people. She is the best structural editor I've ever seen—and I've worked with some of the most respected professionals in the genre. The acquisition editors at Del Rey and Orbit have mentioned how clean my novels are. If that's true, it's because of Robin sweeping up behind me before others have a chance to see my mess.

Next up are my beta readers, an amazing group—or in the case of this book, two amazing groups. You see, Robin actually ran two separate beta reads for *Age of Myth*. The first resulted in substantial changes based on their incredible feedback. Then the revised draft went through another round. Beta reading my books isn't for the faint of heart, as Robin really puts the groups through their paces. They must rate each chapter (or reading session) on a scale from one to five on several matters: characters, plot, pacing, and overall impression. Beta readers also have to answer questions about what they liked, didn't like, felt confused by, or were surprised by. Finally, they are asked whether there was anything they wanted to see but didn't. She even asks for predictions on what will happen to determine if they've nibbled at any dangled bait. As you can see, being a beta reader is not a trivial task, and this book is significantly better due to the efforts of several dozen people. With the final manuscript in their hands, they'll be able to see their contributions. I'm deeply indebted to them for helping to make a better book.

Of course, I want to thank the people at Del Rey, starting with Tricia Narwani, my editor. Tricia was a huge fan of my work even before seeing the manuscript for *Age of Myth*, and made the process of integrating with all the departments within Del Rey effortless for Robin and myself. She went the extra mile on more than one occasion and paired us with our top choices of collaborators (whom I'll discuss in just a minute). Tricia has always made me feel that she values my work, and I've felt an obligation to validate her faith. Since we creative types tend to be insecure, I can't overstate the importance of having an editor who loves your work. I hope I've held up my end of the bargain and provided a book she's equally proud of.

But Tricia is just one member of Del Rey, and I also

want to give a tip of my hat and a hearty thank-you to some other fine people. To Scott Shannon, Del Rey's SVP, I want to express my appreciation for your ability to assemble such talented individuals. Also, like Tricia, your love for my work—and the enthusiasm for getting your hands on the second book—is greatly appreciated. A few other people at Del Rey whom I'd like to thank include: Keith Clayton (associate publisher), Joe Scalora (marketing director), David Moench (publicity director), and Tom Hoeler (assistant extraordinaire).

There are plenty of others I'm not thanking—for instance, all the hardworking people in the areas of production, marketing, and sales—but that's only because I don't know your names. I've learned a lot about publishing in the last five years, and I know how instrumental your efforts are in my success. I want you to know, I'm appreciative for all your hard work. I'm not sure if it takes a village to raise a child, but it certainly takes a large number of people to successfully launch a book, and I hope you are proud of what we've produced together.

Just a few more people, I promise. My love for the artwork of Marc Simonetti is well known, and I'm thrilled that his stunning illustration is once again gracing the cover of my book. When it came time to choose a cover artist, Tricia and Del Rey's art director Dave Stevenson asked me to propose some of my favorite artists, and, of course, Marc was at the top of my list. Not only did Dave select an exceptional illustrator, but he and Tricia worked closely with Robin and myself for developing the brand of the series. Dave, I hope we didn't give you too many gray hairs, and we're thrilled with the final result. Thank you for your talent and for including us in the process.

Like my feelings toward Marc, my devotion to Tim Gerard Reynolds is also well known, and once more he lends his exceptional narration to this and all the books of the series. If you've not listened to his audiobooks before, give him a try. I have a number of free shorts on audible.com ("Professional Integrity" and "The Jester"), so you can try him out without cost. He's making quite a name for himself—something I'm proud to have played a small part in. Thanks, Tim, you'll always be the voice of Riyria and The Legends of the First Empire, and I'm hoping to have many more books for you to narrate in the future.

I also want to thank three talented copy editors: Eric Lowenkron, Linda Branam, and Laura Jorstad. This was my first time working with Eric, but I've had the pleasure of collaborating with Laura and Linda before (both were editors on *The Death of Dulgath,* and Laura was one of the editors for *Hollow World*). Anyone who has seen my advice on self-publishing will know the importance I place on professional editing, and these three individuals epitomize the highest level of skill; their contributions can't be overemphasized. I must say I'm in awe of the things these three have caught and overjoyed with the improvements they've made. Because they have done their jobs so well, I look good. I assure my readers, these are the unsung heroes of this book, as only I, and Tricia, know their full contributions, but trust me, they're nothing short of monumental. So thank you all.

And last, but certainly not least, I want to thank my readers for your enthusiastic love of my work. It is you who pay the salaries of myself and all these incredibly talented people. We are forever grateful for your support, and pleasing you is what pushes each of us to produce our very best work. I hope you'll conclude that we cleared the high bar we've set for ourselves.

Before I go, I'd like to mention just how much I enjoy hearing from you. So if you like this book (and even if you don't), feel free to drop me a line at michael .sullivan.dc@gmail.com. I'm always interested in hearing what you have to say.

Well, that's all, folks, until next time. I plan to keep writing, and I hope you'll keep reading.

READ ON FOR A SNEAK PEEK AT

Age
OF
Swords

BOOK TWO OF

The Legends of the First Empire

We hope you have enjoyed *Age of Myth*, the first book in the Legends of the First Empire series. We're pleased to present you with a sneak peek of the second book, *Age of Swords*, available now. Enjoy!

CHAPTER ONE

Broken

Most people believe the first battle of the Great War occurred at Grandford in the autumn, but the truth is it started three months before on a beautiful summer's day in Dahl Rhen.

— THE BOOK OF BRIN

Gifford knew he would never win a footrace. He was late coming to this realization; everyone else knew it the day he was born. His left leg didn't have much feeling, couldn't support his weight, and dragged. His back wasn't much better: Badly twisted, it forced his hips one direction and his shoulders another. For years he held out hope he'd get better. He'd believed that if he tried hard enough, long enough, he could straighten up and stand on two feet. It never happened.

But his leg and back weren't the worst of it.

Gifford was cursed with only half a face. He had the other half, exactly where it ought to be, but like his leg, it, too, was useless. The left side didn't move at all, making it difficult to see and torturous to talk.

But his face wasn't the worst of it.

When he was eight, Gavin Killian had dubbed him the goblin, and Myrtis, the brewmaster's daughter, said he was broken. Of the two he preferred goblin—at the time he'd had a crush on Myrtis. When growing up it seemed everyone had called him something, none complimentary. Over the years the names faded. No one called him the goblin anymore, and although people probably still thought he was broken, no one said it—at least not to his face.

But the name-calling wasn't the worst of it.

He had trouble controlling his bladder. The accidents occurred mostly at night, and he frequently woke in a soaked bed. For most of his life his "morning baths" had been the worst of it. Yet as with all his other adversities, he'd found a way to cope, a way to persevere. He drank sparingly and never at night. Even on the coldest winter nights when the villagers of Dahl Rhen huddled together in the main lodge for warmth, he always slept alone, which was easier than he would have liked.

Although Gifford's roads appeared narrower, rockier, and strewn with more thorns than others, he always found a way to deal with life's setbacks. Nothing came easy, but Gifford refused to see himself as a victim. He was alive, generally happy, and people loved and praised the pottery he created. That was more than many people had, and more than enough to satisfy Gifford.

And yet whenever he looked at Roan, he knew the worst of it—the worst part of being him—was that the only thing he truly wanted was forever beyond the reach of his feeble body, and no amount of positive thinking would change that.

Roan lashed the wood-and-tin contraption to his left leg, tightening the leather straps. She knelt before him wearing her work apron, a smudge of charcoal on the side of her nose. Her hair was pulled back in a short ponytail, which was so high on her head that it looked like a rooster's crest.

Her clever little hands were marred by dozens of cuts from working with sharp metal. He wanted to hold them, kiss the wounds, and take the pain away. He'd tried once, and it hadn't gone well. She'd pulled away, her eyes wide with fear and a look of horror on her face. Roan had an aversion to being touched, and not just by him, thank Mari. Mountains of praise for his beautiful cups and amphorae wouldn't have been able to offset the anguish if her reaction had been limited to him.

Roan yanked hard on the ankle strap and nodded with a firm, determined expression. "That should do it." She stood up and dusted her clean hands symbolically. Roan's voice was eager but serious. "Ready?"

Gifford answered by pulling himself up with the aid of his crafting table. The device on his leg, comprised of wooden planks and metal hinges, squeaked as he rose, making a sound like the opening of a tiny door.

"Do you have your weight on it?" she asked. "Put your weight on it. See if it holds."

For Gifford, putting weight on his left leg was akin to leaning on water. But for Roan he'd willingly fall on his face. Perhaps he could manage a roll and make her smile. She rarely smiled and never laughed. If only he'd been born with two stout legs, strong and agile, he'd dance and twirl like a fool and make her smile, make her laugh. Gifford would show Roan what he saw when he looked at her, but broken as he was, the twisted potter made a poor mirror and could only cast back a shattered reflection.

Gifford tilted his hips and out of faith and love, shifted some weight to his left leg.

He didn't fall. A strain tugged on the straps wrapped around his thigh and calf, but his leg held. His mouth dropped open, his eyes widened, and he saw Roan grin.

By Mari, what an amazing sight.

He couldn't help smiling back. He was standing straight—or as straight as his gnarled back allowed—he was winning an impossible battle using magic armor Roan had fashioned.

"Take a step," she coaxed. Both hands were clenched in fists as if she were hanging on to something invisible in front of her.

Gifford shifted his weight back to his right side and lifted his left leg. Swinging forward, it squeaked again. He leaned and took a step the way normal people had done a million times. The moment he did, the brace collapsed.

"Oh, no!" Roan gasped as Gifford fell face-first,

barely missing the set of newly glazed cups drying in the morning sun.

His cheek and ear slapped the dirt, jarring his head. His elbow, hand, and hip took most of the punishment. To Roan, it must have looked painful, but Gifford was used to falling. He'd been doing it all his life.

"I'm so, so, so sorry." Roan was back on her knees bent over him as he rolled to his side. Her grin was gone, and the world less bright.

He couldn't help feeling it was his fault. "I'm okay, no pwoblem," he said. "I missed the cups."

"The hinge failed." She struggled to hold back the tears as her injured hand ran over the brace.

How many cuts came from building that brace for me?

"The strut bent," she said. "The copper just isn't strong enough. I'm so sorry."

"It held fo' a while," he said to cheer her up. "Keep at it. You'll make it wuk. I know you will."

"There's an additional force when you walk. I need to account for the forward motion and the additional weight when your other leg is raised." She slapped the side of her head several times, eyes flinching with each blow. "I should have realized that. I should have. How could I not?"

He instinctively grabbed her wrist to prevent additional blows. "Don't do—"

Roan screamed and jerked away, drawing back in terror. When she'd recovered, they exchanged embarrassed looks, mirroring each other. The moment dragged unpleasantly until Gifford forced a smile. He didn't feel like smiling. He wanted to crawl into a hole and weep. But he donned the expression the same way he forced himself to get up each morning and greet a world that wasn't meant for him.

The smile wasn't one of his best, but it was the best he could manage and, whether Roan knew it or not, he offered it out of love.

To ease past the uncomfortable pause, he picked up their conversation where it had left off. Pretending that nothing had happened. "How could you know something that's not been done befoe, Woan?"

She blinked at him twice, then shifted her focus. She wasn't looking at anything in particular; she was thinking. Sometimes Roan thought so intensely that he could almost hear it. She blinked again and emerged from the stupor. Roan walked over to Gifford's craft table and picked up one of his cups. The awkward moment had vanished as if it had never existed.

"This design is new, isn't it?" she asked. "Do you think it could hold its shape at a much larger size? If we could find a way to—"

Gifford's smile turned genuine. "Has anyone told you yew a genius, Woan?"

She nodded, her little rooster crest whipping "You have."

"Because it's twue," he said.

She looked embarrassed again, the way she always did when he complimented her, the way she looked when anyone said something nice, but it was a familiar uncase. Her eyes shifted back to the brace and she sighed. "I need something stronger. Can't make it out of stone; can't make it out of wood."

"I wouldn't suggest clay," he said, pushing his luck by trying to be funny. "Though I would have made you a beautiful hinge."

"I know you would," she said in complete seriousness.

Roan wasn't one for jokes. Much of humor arose from the unexpected or absurd—like making a hinge out of clay. But Roan's mind didn't work that way. To Roan nothing was too absurd, and no idea was too crazy.

"I'll just have to think of something," she said, and started unbuckling the brace. "Some way to strengthen the metal. There's always a better way. That's what Padera said, and she's always right."

The wind gusted and blew Gifford's cloths from the crafting table. Two cups fell over with a delicate clink.

Thick voluminous clouds rolled in, blotting out the blue and blanketing the sun. Around the dahl people urgently trotted toward their homes.

"Get the wash in! Get the wash in!" Viv Baker yelled at her daughter.

The Killian boys raced after chickens, and Bergin rushed to shut down his new batch of beer, cursing as he did. "Perfect blessed day a minute ago," he grumbled, peering up at the sky as if it could hear him.

Roan glanced at the cups and bowls scattered around the craft table. Gifford had been having a productive day before Roan stopped by, but he was grateful for the distraction.

"You need to get your work inside." She redoubled her efforts to remove the brace, but was having trouble with one of the buckles. "Made this one too tight."

The wind grew stronger. The banners on the lodge were cracking with sharp reports. The fire braziers near the well struggled to stay lit, but lost their battle. Both were snuffed out.

"That's not good," Gifford said. "I've only seen them blown out once. That was when the top came off the lodge."

Another gust made his whole set of cups ring together. Two more toppled, rolling on their sides and making half circles on the tabletop. The thatch on his little house rustled. Still on the ground, Gifford felt dirt and grass hitting his face and arms.

Roan, frustrated with the buckle, reached into one of her two new pockets. She pulled out her snips and cut the leather straps, freeing him. "There, now we can—"

Lightning struck the lodge.

Splinters, sparks, and a plume of white smoke were followed by a clap so loud that Gifford felt it pass through him. Thunder rolled like an angry growl. One section of the lodge's roof had sheered off, giant logs split, and the thatch had caught fire.

"Did you see—" Gifford started to say when another

bolt of lightning struck the other side of the lodge. "Whoa!"

He and Roan stared in shock as a third and then a fourth bolt pelted the log building. Cobb and Bergin were the first to react, and the two ran for the well, picking up water gourds on their way. Then another clap of lightning hit the well's windlass, bursting the pole in a cloud of splinters. Both men hit the ground.

More bolts of lightning rained down, both inside and outside the dahl. With each blast came screams, fire, and smoke. All around them people ran to their homes. The Galantians, Fhrey warriors who had been welcomed to the dahl when exiled, came out of their tents and stared up at the sky. They looked just as scared as everyone else, which was as disturbing as the cataclysmic storm. Until recently, Rhunes had thought Fhrey were indestructible gods.

Gelston the shepherd ran past. While making his way between the new woodpile and the patch of near-ripe beans in the Killians' garden, he became struck. Gifford didn't see much, just a snaking, blinding brilliance. When his sight returned, Gelston was on the ground, his hair on fire.

Gifford shouted to Roan, "We need to get to the sto'age pits. Wight now!"

He pushed himself up with his crutch and started hopping toward the storehouses.

"Roan! Gifford!" Raithe and Malcolm ran up. Raithe still carried his two swords, the broken copper slung on his back and the Fhrey blade hanging naked from his belt. Malcolm held his spear with both hands. "Do you know where Persephone is?"

Gifford shook his head. "But we need to get to the pits!"

Raithe nodded. "I'll spread the word. Malcolm, help them."

Malcolm moved to Gifford's side and put his shoulder under the potter's arm. He mostly carried Gifford to the big storage pit, while Roan followed close behind. With the first harvest still more than a month away, the pits were nearly empty. Lined in mud brick, the hole retained the smell of musty vegetables, grain, and straw. Other members of the dahl were already there. The Bakers and their two boys and one daughter huddled against the back wall, eyes wide. Engleton and Farmer Wedon peered out the open door at the violence of the storm. Brin, the dahl's newly appointed Keeper of Ways, was there as well, but she seemed to be on her way out.

"Have you seen my parents?" Brin shouted the moment she saw them.

"No," Roan replied.

Outside the thunder cracked and rolled continually. Gifford could only imagine the lightning strikes that accompanied them. Being down in the pit, he couldn't see the yard, just a small square of sky.

Brin started to bolt from the pit. The young girl sprang like a fawn, but Gifford had anticipated her dash. Unlike the crippled potter, Brin *could* win a footrace and was easily the fastest person on the dahl. The fifteen-year-old girl regularly won all the sprints during the Summerule's festival, but Gifford caught her by the arm.

"Let me go!" She pulled and jerked. "I need to find my parents."

"It's too dangewous."

"I don't care!" Brin jerked hard, so hard she fell, but Gifford still hung on. "Let me go!"

Gifford's legs, even his good one, were mostly useless, and his lips slid down the side of his face because he didn't have enough muscle to support them. But he relied on his arms and hands for everything. Thurgin and Krier, who had always picked on him, once made the mistake of challenging Gifford to a hand-squeezing contest. He had humiliated Krier, making him cry—his name only made the embarrassment worse. Thurgin was determined not to suffer a similar fate and cheated by using both hands. Gifford had held back with Krier but didn't see the need with a cheater. He broke Thurgin's little finger and the tiny bone that ran from his fourth knuckle to his wrist.

There was no possibility that Brin would break free.

Autumn, Fig, and Tressa stumbled through the door, all of them exhausted and out of breath. Heath Coswall, the Killians, and Filson the lamp-maker came through just after. They dragged Gelston, who remained unconscious, his hair mostly gone but no longer on fire. Bergin followed them. Covered in dirt and grass, he reported that the lodge was burning like a harvest-moon bonfire.

"Has anyone seen my parents?" Brin shouted. No one had.

As if the wind and lightning weren't enough, hail began to fall. Apple-sized chunks of ice clattered, leaving craters in the turf where they impacted.

More people raced into the shelter of the granary, running with arms, pots, and boards over their heads. They filed to the back, crying and hugging each other. Brin watched them come in, always looking but not finding the faces she sought. Finally, the Fhrey, with shields protecting their heads, charged in along with Moya, Cobb, and Habet.

"Where's my mother!" Brin pleaded. Once again the girl charged for the door. This time Moya assisted Gifford by catching her as well.

"You can't," Moya said, her hair a wild mess. "Your house is burning, there's nothing—"

Outside a roar grew like the angry growl of a colossal beast. Everyone stared out the doorway as the sky grew darker still, and the wind blew with even more force. Then, as everyone watched, the Bakers' roundhouse was ripped apart. First the thatch was blown away, then the wood beams were ripped free, and finally the walls succumbed. They didn't fall. The logs were sucked into the air. Then the foundation of mud bricks was sheered and scattered. After that, the entire world outside the storage pit was lost to a whirlwind cloud of dirt and debris.

"Close the door," Nyphron ordered. Grygor, the giant, started to haul it shut just as Raithe arrived.

"Has anyone seen Persephone?"

"She's gone. Went to the forest," Moya shouted as she grabbed and pulled him in.

Grygor slammed the door closed.

"No!" Brin screamed. "My parents are still out there!"

Gifford let go of her then, and the girl fell to her knees, weeping.

Raithe drew close to Moya. "Did Seph really go into the forest?"

Moya nodded. "Her, Suri, and Arion. They went to that oak tree again, to ask it more questions."

"That's on top of a big hill, up in the open glade," he said to nobody in particular. Raithe looked like he might be sick. There had been rumors that the Dureyan was in love with their chieftain, but then a lot of recent rumors had turned out to be untrue. Seeing Raithe's face, Gifford lacked any doubt. If Roan was still outside, he would have looked the same way.

They all sat or knelt in tearful silence as the roaring grew louder. All around Gifford, people quivered, whimpered, and stared at the dark ceiling, no doubt wondering if it would rip away or cave in and bury them.

He stood beside Roan, the weight of the crowd pressing them together. It was the closest he'd ever been to her. Gifford could feel her warmth, and smell the scents of charcoal, oil, and smoke—the smells he'd come to associate with Roan and all things good. If the roof collapsed and killed everyone, Gifford would have thanked Mari for that final kindness.

The granary was little more than a hole in the ground, but given that it protected the dahl's food supply, the pit was solidly built to withstand just about anything. The best wood and rock went into its construction. The walls were dirt and stone, the ceiling braced by logs driven into the ground. This was the place where most of Gifford's work ended up. Harvests of barley, wheat, and rye were poured into huge clay urns he had made. Their tops were sealed with wax to keep out the mice and moisture. The granary also shielded wine, honey, oil, vegetables, and a cache of smoked meats. After the long winter most of the stores were gone, and the pit was little more than a hole, but it was a sturdy one. Still, the ceiling shook, and the door rattled.

The only bit of light that continued to enter the bin was through the narrow slit where the door didn't precisely meet its frame. This sliver of white flickered violently.

"It'll be okay," Gifford told Roan. He said it in a whisper as if it were a secret he'd chosen to share with her alone.

Brin, Viv Baker, and her daughter Hest were crying loudly. And it wasn't just the women. Cobb, Heath Coswall, Habet, and Filson wept openly as well. But Roan wasn't like them. She wasn't like anyone, and that was why he liked her. When she turned to look at him, the light from the door highlighted the contour of her face. She wasn't crying and didn't look scared. There was just an intensity in her eyes. If there weren't a dozen people between Roan and the door, if she were alone in the dark, he had no doubt she would have gone outside. She wanted to see. Roan wanted to see everything.

The clatter of hail stopped, but rain fell in bands, hard at times then lighter, only to pound once more. The howl of the wind faded. Even the cracks of lightning fell silent. Finally, the light from the door became bright and unwavering.

Nyphron shoved the door open and crept out. A moment later, he waved for them to follow.

Everyone squinted against the brightness of the sun, struggling to see. Thatch and logs were scattered everywhere. Branches, leaves, and broken planks of wood littered the yard. One of the lodge's banners lay on the ground, its ends frayed. Not a single roundhouse had survived. The breadth of the dahl was a vacant field of mangled dirt and debris surrounded by the still-intact wall. All that remained were bare spots where grass hadn't grown and a score of fire pits that continued to smolder. Overhead, clouds were breaking up, and Gifford already spotted patches of blue.

"Is it over?" Heath Coswall asked from the back.

As if in answer, a loud boom sounded and the dahl's front gate trembled.

"What is that?" Moya asked, speaking for everyone.

Another bang hit and the gate began to buckle.